The Best
AMERICAN
SHORT
STORIES
2022

GUEST EDITORS OF THE BEST AMERICAN SHORT STORIES

1978 TED SOLOTAROFF
1979 JOYCE CAROL OATES
1980 STANLEY ELKIN
1981 HORTENSE CALISHER
1982 JOHN GARDNER
1983 ANNE TYLER
1984 JOHN UPDIKE
1985 GAIL GODWIN
1986 RAYMOND CARVER
1987 ANN BEATTIE
1988 MARK HELPRIN
1989 MARGARET ATWOOD
1990 RICHARD FORD
1991 ALICE ADAMS
1992 ROBERT STONE
1993 LOUISE ERDRICH
1994 TOBIAS WOLFF
1995 JANE SMILEY
1996 JOHN EDGAR WIDEMAN
1997 E. ANNIE PROULX
1998 GARRISON KEILLOR
1999 AMY TAN
2000 E. L. DOCTOROW
2001 BARBARA KINGSOLVER
2002 SUE MILLER
2003 WALTER MOSLEY
2004 LORRIE MOORE
2005 MICHAEL CHABON
2006 ANN PATCHETT
2007 STEPHEN KING
2008 SALMAN RUSHDIE
2009 ALICE SEBOLD
2010 RICHARD RUSSO

2011 GERALDINE BROOKS
2012 TOM PERROTTA
2013 ELIZABETH STROUT
2014 JENNIFER EGAN
2015 T. C. BOYLE
2016 JUNOT DÍAZ
2017 MEG WOLITZER
2018 ROXANE GAY
2019 ANTHONY DOERR
2020 CURTIS SITTENFELD
2021 JESMYN WARD
2022 ANDREW SEAN GREER

The Best AMERICAN SHORT STORIES® 2022

Selected from U.S. and Canadian Magazines
by ANDREW SEAN GREER
with HEIDI PITLOR

With an Introduction
by ANDREW SEAN GREER

MARINER BOOKS
New York   Boston

HarperCollins books may be purchased for educational, business, or sales promotional use. For information, please email the Special Markets Department at SPsales@harpercollins.com.

FIRST EDITION

ISSN 0067-6233
ISBN 978-0-358-66471-0
ISBN 978-0-358-72440-7 (LIBRARY EDITION)

22 23 24 25 26   LSC   10 9 8 7 6 5 4 3 2 1

"A Ravishing Sun" by Leslie Blanco. First published in *New Letters*, May 2021. Copyright © 2021 by Leslie Blanco. Reprinted by permission of Leslie Blanco.

"The Little Widow from the Capital" by Yohanca Delgado. First published in *The Paris Review*, issue 236, March 2021. Copyright © 2021 by Yohanca Delgado. Reprinted by permission of Yohanca Delgado.

"Man of the House" by Kim Coleman Foote. First published in *Ecotone*, vol. 16, no. 2, November 2, 2020. Copyright © 2021 by Kim Coleman Foote. Reprinted by permission of Kim Coleman Foote.

"The Wind" by Lauren Groff. First published in *The New Yorker*, February 1, 2021. Copyright © 2021 by Lauren Groff. Reprinted by permission of Lauren Groff.

"The Hollow" by Greg Jackson. First published in *The New Yorker*, November 29, 2021. Copyright © 2021 by Greg Jackson. Reprinted by permission of Georges Borchardt, on behalf of the author.

"Detective Dog" by Gish Jen. First published in *The New Yorker*, November 22, 2021. From *Thank You, Mr. Nixon: Stories* by Gish Jen, copyright © 2022 by Gish Jen. Used by permission of Alfred A. Knopf, an imprint of the Knopf Doubleday Publishing Group, a division of Penguin Random House LLC. All rights reserved.

"Sugar Island" by Claire Luchette. First published in *Ploughshares*, vol. 47, no. 1, Spring 2021. Copyright © 2021 by Claire Luchette. Reprinted by permission of Claire Luchette.

"The Souvenir Museum" by Elizabeth McCracken. First published in *Harper's Magazine*, January 2021. From *The Souvenir Museum* by Elizabeth McCracken. Copyright © 2022 by Elizabeth McCracken. Reprinted by permission of HarperCollins Publishers.

Contents

Foreword

I GET A lot of credit for discovering new writers, but I must share it with the hundreds of editors and staff of literary magazines who each year read thousands of submissions. These people are the true vanguard of publishing. At the very least, this series would not exist without them. And without them, countless great writers would never have been able to launch their careers. *Stylus* was the first to publish Zora Neale Hurston. In 1936, *Manuscript* brought out the debut story of Eudora Welty. *Story* was the first home to J. D. Salinger and Carson McCullers. In 1950, *Folio* published an unknown writer named Alice Munro. *The Northwest Review* (closed in 2019) debuted George Saunders in 1986. Kelly Link first published in *Century* in 1995, and 2008 saw the first fiction by Jesmyn Ward in *A Public Space*. *The Threepenny Review* can take credit for first printing a story by Imbolo Mbue in 2015. Imagine the world of fiction without James Baldwin, whose first story was published in *Commentary,* or William Faulkner (thank you, *Mississippian*).

To submit a story to a journal, a writer need not live in New York City or have connections to the publishing world. A wealth of literary magazines signals a democratically healthy literary culture. Unfortunately, partly due to economic pressures in the face of the pandemic, certain American magazines have been or are in danger of being defunded and shuttered. In the best of times, running a literary journal is not considered a profitable venture. The University of Alaska closed a number of liberal arts programs, including the *Alaska Quarterly Review,* which is now being kept alive on a volunteer basis. Purdue placed a moratorium on admissions to their graduate English department. Its literary journal, *The Sycamore Review,* will no longer have graduate students to continue to manage and publish it. Bard College announced that it would close *Conjunctions* (the publisher of Sanjena Sathian's story in these pages), but after a swell of support for the magazine, the school changed course.

Consider doing this series and literature as a whole a favor. If you read a story in these pages that you love and if you can afford it, subscribe to the magazine that initially published this story. Chances are you'll like their other stories (and essays and poems and art). Writers and students of writing: I am talking to you first and foremost. The threat to magazines of defunding is real right now. These journals cannot exist on grants and emergency funds alone. If you want someone to publish *you* someday, please do what you can to help keep these journals running.

On display in this volume of *The Best American Short Stories* are twenty emotionally and intellectually engaged writers. I found myself drawn to the basics this year: ease of language, innovation, humor, truth, the ability to tell an interesting and important story. Often new writers are taught to explore what is at stake for their characters. This can be love or even life, a sense of self, anything really. As a reader, I want to feel that what I am reading matters, that the story knows something profound, goes somewhere worthwhile, tries something difficult or risky, something significant. Thankfully, there was no lack of good candidates. Andrew Sean Greer was a terrific and open-minded guest editor, amiable in the face of several scanning errors. I was not surprised that he assembled a list of charming and imaginative stories, tales that transport and deeply move the reader just as his own books do.

This is my sixteenth volume of *The Best American Short Stories.* On my lesser days, I fall prey to thinking that I've read every sort of writing under the sun. But then I read a searingly original story about family, one like Kim Coleman Foote's "Man of the House." Think you've read enough friendship? Check out Greg Jackson's brilliant story "The Hollow." Great writing obliterates cynicism. In the hands of a writer comfortable with their own vulnerability, voice, and humanity, lassitude tends to fall away. If you want to read a story that does not waste a single word, check out Leslie Blanco's electric "A Ravishing Sun." (And do not miss Blanco's stunning contributor's note.) If you prefer humor and deep char-acterization within the first page, read Claire Luchette's "Sugar Island." The masterly Alice McDermott brings forth the strange profundities of life during quarantine in her story "Post." In "The Little Widow from the Capital," Yohanca Delgado delivers an un-forgettable collective narrative about Dominican immigrants. Héctor Tobar's Kafkaesque story, "The Sins of Others," holds a fun-house mirror to the American immigration system.

As we lurch our way through and hopefully out of a pandemic that is more persistent than any of us would like; as we witness an autocracy attempt to violently overtake a democracy in Ukraine and the threat of another world war; as the news of climate change alarms almost daily, the power of good art, of excellent fiction to reorient the reader toward what truly matters never fails to in-spire me. A character in Kevin Moffett's story says, "Laughter's supposed to be shared. . . . Even before humans could talk, we laughed; I can't remember why. Something to do with showing we mean one another no harm, or surviving danger, the over-whelming relief of it." In Bryan Washington's gorgeous, sad story, the narrator's brother says, "You're not just who you think you are, but you're who everyone else sees, too. You're all of those things. . . . At the same time. Forever." Reading these stories, I was reminded of the value of societal cohesion and kindness. We must take better care of each other.

Many thanks to Kaitlyn Choe, April Eberhardt, Yael Goldstein Love, Sara Komatsu, Susan Shepherd, Marie Unger, and Christine Utz for their help reading.

The stories chosen for this anthology were originally published between January 2021 and January 2022. The qualifications for selection are: (1) original publication in nationally distributed American or Canadian periodicals; (2) publication in English by writers who have made the United States or Canada their home; (3) original publication as short stories (excerpts of novels are not considered). A list of magazines consulted for this volume appears at the back of the book. Editors who wish their short fiction to be considered for next year's edition should send their publications to Heidi Pitlor, c/o The Best American Short Stories, P.O. Box 60, Natick, MA 01760, or links or files as attachments to thebestamericanshortstories@gmail.com.

HEIDI PITLOR

Introduction

READERS, I BRING good news: the American short story is thriving. I sound like a president giving a State of the Union, but in a way that is what these annual publications are: celebrations of an art form whose death, in online forums, has been greatly exaggerated. For here we are: in a time when, more than ever, we realize the great necessity of art. Even the hardest working pandemic parent has found themselves desperately turning to a book, a show, a film, a song for comfort. Sometimes for escape, sometimes for insight; a short story can be either or both. Or neither, in fact. Ignore those online forums. Who says a nineteenth-century art form can't flourish in the twenty-first? This is my introduction, so I say it can!

Nobody, not even my mother, will agree with my choices, and that's what makes family dinners fun. These stories are absolutely my taste. But what a feast it has been! Reading excellent stories of joy and heartache, experiencing innovations of language and form, discovering great new writers and rediscovering beloved masters. It has been a feast of fairies, where I ate as much as I could and still wanted more. I wanted them all! Alas, the game is I can pick only twenty. Complaints may be sent to my mother.

Let me tempt you with some of the offerings. . . .

Who could resist, for example, a story from the imagination? In the grand American tradition of Hawthorne, Irving, and Poe? Consider one echoing our current anxieties, such as Sanjena Sathian's "Mr. Ashok's Monument," in which the magical and sublime, in modern-day India, become the property of bureau-crats, for whom humanity is hardly as important as their petty concerns. Or, if you are intrigued by an America where citizens accused of a crime pick immigrants to serve as proxies, I urgently suggest Héctor Tobar's wonderful "The Sins of Others." Might I also interest you in Karen Russell's extraordinary "The Ghost Birds," set in a horrifying future landscape, in which a father takes his daughter on a bird-watching expedition—for the ghosts of extinct birds? Or perhaps you would prefer "The Little Widow from the Capital" by Yohanca Delgado, the story of a Domini-can woman who arrives in a contemporary apartment building, astonishing the neighbors with her sewing, her suitors, and her spells. And I must recommend the tale of Finnish siblings, labor-ing in the Northwest, who come across a boy (merboy? selkie?) who brings their lives to a terrible choice, the tale of "Soon the Light" by Gina Ochsner. I must admit I have a weakness for a ghost, a spell, a selkie—but, really, don't we all?

You may have guessed I am a writer myself, and so, like a cat burglar invited to a country manor, my taste runs to what I can steal; imitation, as they say, is for amateurs. I am a kleptograph. What catches my magpie eye is anything I haven't seen before. Anything new, surprising, shiny. And it may surprise non-writers (who is everybody I ever met on a plane) that, just as painters go on about paint, photographers about light, and actors about themselves, writers obsess about words. For those among you ea-ger for a taste of something new, I want you to try Okwiri Oduor's "Mbiu Dash." Listen to the rhythm of this opening sentence, some-thing every writer should listen to carefully: "We were all there the day Mr. Man came to town." The meter makes it scan beautifully: "We were *all* there the *day* Mr. *Man* came to *town.*" It is a skillful choice of words. Creating the magic necessary to get a story going is hard, but look how effortlessly Oduor does it: "We thought to ourselves, 'A man like this must have a good story lodged beneath his tongue.' We knew that we wanted him to stay for as long as it took to get that story out." Lodged beneath his tongue. Isn't that something? Or take a look at a piece by Leslie Blanco, whose "A Ravishing Sun" so startlingly captures grief and mental illness not just by its story, but by *the language in which it is told.* Watch this paragraph (about a motorcycle accident) rolling around in time: "When I look up, Xavier has blood pooling in the wells of his eyes. Xavier has blood flowing in rivulets down his face. Xavier. A name a little too much like a savior. A name I like to roll happily in my mouth. *Get married,* the bride's grandmother said. *Put me out of my misery. You two make me want to be eighteen again.*" It makes me catch my breath. Finally, at the risk of becoming that old man who wants to play you every cast album in his collection, let me show you Greg Jackson's "The Hollow," a beautiful story of an old friend who has wandered into another plane of being: that of an artist. I just want to show the technique; Jackson begins the story with long, complex sentences ("Jonah Valente had been an object of amusement to Jack and his college classmates, and presumably he had gone on being one to other people ever since." Beautiful, flowing, and a little funny. The author, however, ends the story (no spoilers) in a series of stark simple phrases: ("Cool. A light breeze. The market hummed. A burble of chatter. Dogs' barks." And so on.) That is a master class, as they say, in technique: changing the shape of sentences to affect the reader's emotions. I have my eye on stealing that last one, by the way. Don't tell a soul.

The language in which it is told. I want to repeat that because it's something so easily lost in our conversations about storytelling. We are rightfully interested in what the story is *about,* but equally important (and mostly unexamined) is *the language in which it is told.* Because being a good storyteller is more than having a good story; we all know this. It is knowing how to tell it. The right words for *this story.* That is what I want to celebrate in the authors of this collection. These are fantastic stories, but these are also fantastic storytellers. Fantastic writers. I stress that because I know they worked hard on their choices, often so hidden from readers, choices that affect our experiences as readers. Part of the joy of storytelling is the variety of storytelling. I want to point out and celebrate that variety.

Which leads me to innovations in storytelling beyond language: *how* the story is told. This all seems effortless to readers—and it is meant to be so. But imagine sitting before a blank piece of paper with the universe of possibilities before you—shall I tell it in first person? From the future? Looking into the future? The point of view of a bystander? A dog? In reverse?—and you almost want to give up. In fact, I suspect, many of these writers did give up. And then, one day (perhaps reading a beloved author or, secret of the trade, a poet) they found the way into the story. The way into the story; I mean those myriad choices writers make, sometimes without thinking, sometimes finding the right way by chance or experience but more often finding by trial and error. Consider, for instance, Meghan Louise Wagner's "Elephant Seals," in which the initial story is rewritten over and over, variations on a theme, until every possible branch is laid out for us. Or Kevin Moffett's "Bears Among the Living," which is given to us in shards of prose, some humorous, some poignant, some philosophical, so that we piece together the story in our minds rather than having it laid out linearly for us. Or Erin Somers's "Ten Year Affair": a story with two timelines of a love story, one of which takes place entirely in the protagonist's mind, with an ending that wraps the form and content together perfectly. And let me point out the brilliance of Lauren Groff's "The Wind": it is a story of a woman escaping her abuser with her children. But Groff has not chosen to tell it in third person, or from the point of view of the woman, or even the point of view of her child. The narrator is the *daughter* of the child. The granddaughter. Someone who was not there. It makes the story somehow grander and more terrifying, because it is a story passed down through generations, a story told to make sense of who these women are. A myth, in the sense of story crucial to these women. That simple choice—and an unusual one—puts enough emotional distance between the narrator and the characters to remove any cliché or sentimentality. Instead: there is dignity, sorrow, and rage. In the end, I was in tears. This choice is impossible for me to steal. I think it belongs to Groff alone.

How do you write about hard things? That is the question many writers ask before sitting down. They know their terrors and fears, but worry they will not get them across properly, and to fail to do that would be to betray what is most important. Many give up and tackle smaller, easier subjects. But we all know that unless you are touching on your own private fears and heartaches, your own hardest stories, then you are not (as my Montana professor William Kitteredge used to say) "even in the ballpark." I am not much for sports metaphors, and have spent most of my life avoiding ballparks, but he's right. Clever is impressive; clever gets attention; clever is satisfying. But telling a hard story is the actual job.

Take a look at two very different stories. One is "Sugar Island," by Claire Luchette. It is the simplest kind of story—two lovers picking up a couch for an apartment—but there is a telescoping of time within the story, and especially at the end, that allows it to be told both in the moment of romantic doubt and pleasure and in a future memory of pain. And isn't this how we really look on the past? Both with the purity of how we felt colored by how we feel now? The other story is Bryan Washington's "Foster." In it, two stories are overlaid. One is of a man who is fostering his brother's cat while his brother is in prison. The other is of the protagonist and his boyfriend, living together with the cat. The dialogue is told without quotation marks, a choice that creates a distance for the reader (quotation marks make reading dialogue "easy," which is why you always see them in juicy airport novels). That distance cools down a story with powerful emotions running under it. At first, we think we are reading a simply cat-couple story. But the story has secrets; the narrator has secrets. We learn the stories behind this story. And by putting them in the shadows—the hard stories—instead of in the foreground (with the cat), Washington breaks our hearts. It is a difficult thing to pull off. My hat goes off to him. (I am also personally gratified that these two queer stories have so completely broken out of what the mainstream expects of them; there is no identity crisis, no family drama, no bleak hedonism or mordant wisdom or fabulousness; queer people, like all people, have many stories to tell.) My hat also goes off to Kim Coleman Foote. In "Man of the House," the "story" is of Jeb, a New Jersey man who decides to go down South to visit his uncle Abe. Jeb's predecessors moved from the South to New Jersey to flee racism, and Jeb wants to find his uncle Abe to understand that story (we are, I presume, in the 1970s). But we don't begin there—we begin with the death of Jeb's mother, the insistence of his sister Verna on clearing out his hoarded items. We are given the family first. And then his journey. Jeb is not himself aware of the history of the Great Migration; he is not even fully aware why he awakens one morning and drives south. But this choice of how to tell the story places him in the history of his family, and places the simple story against the complex and grief-stricken story of Black migration at the beginning of the twentieth century. Foote paints this history in the background, which makes Jeb's actions and struggles both his own and part of a legacy of hope and pain. It is a profound choice by Foote, one that makes for a powerful story.

The subject of hard stories brings a question: How can a short story address what is happening now? Many teachers caution against writing about the present; it is painting on a curtain in the wind. I myself have never tried. My writing is too slow a response to something in need of urgent action; I am that person who knows the right thing to say only while walking down the stairs after the party (*l'esprit d'escalier*). So I have all the more admiration for the writers who have captured this moment—the moment of 2022—and without them this edition of *Best American Short Stories* might seem like that of any other year. Alex Ohlin's "The Meeting" describes the slow self-destruction of the technology industry—still ongoing as I write—with all the gobbledygook biz-talk and half-witted confidence of Silicon Valley, the Californian exuberance and arrogance that I suppose I myself possess, the blindness to the human condition, to the actual threats in our lives. What seemed so important in 2019 . . . how could we have cared so much? How could any boss have made us think to care? How could we have forgotten we're people? How can we prevent ourselves from forgetting again?

In the same vein, Gish Jen's "Detective Dog" is a miracle of both timely and enduring storytelling. In it, our present situation provides the tension that forces the characters to action. That tension is of a Chinese émigré family living in New York City in the era of COVID and anti-Asian bigotry. Their locked-in life brings a teenaged son's rage to a boil, accusing them of not caring about protests in Hong Kong; he takes up and leaves them in disgust. Jen writes of his mother, Betty, our protagonist: "What is a mother but someone who cannot stop anyone?" That helplessness surfaces when their boy Robert asks for help with his homework: explaining a family mystery to a pet. The kind of Zoom homework so many parents have helped with. Robert calls himself Detective Dog. Quietly, lovingly, Betty answers his questions. And, in answering them, a moment in time is captured perfectly: the past that precedes it, the anxiety that shapes it, and the unknown future that undoes every effort to keep it safe. I wept and wept to read Jen's words. So, too, Alice McDermott, whose story "Post" is the careful delineation of the particular terror, humor, and grief of the first years of COVID, told in the story of couple who are thrown together by the virus and its consequences; all of us will recognize ourselves there. It is the story for the record of what we have all gone through.

Another way to tell a hard story—sometimes the only way, the only liberating way, and my favorite way—is with humor. Those who don't understand humor think it is an easy way out; friends, it is hard way out. It is going through pain into something else, something that will release the writer and the reader. It is difficult and it is rare. There is humor in so many of these pieces (Oduor, Jackson, Sathian, Delgado, and others), as there was in Shakespeare—not just to lighten the mood, but to illuminate the story from another side. To show our weaknesses and follies, not just our strengths. I relished being with the characters in Elizabeth McCracken's story "The Souvenir Museum" precisely because a story of heartache was told with such suppressed hope and love; how else could you tell the story of an old boyfriend discovered at a Viking reenactment park except with laughter? Life is serious, serious precisely because it is absurd. In Kenan Orhan's masterly "The Beyoğlu Municipality Waste Management Orchestra," the title itself reveals the absurdity we are about to encounter, the absurdity of authoritarian regimes, of arbitrary violence, of cultural repression. In it, a trash collector in Istanbul secretly keeps the "forbidden" items she finds in a composer's trash: first a banned instrument (a violin) and then another, for any music not traditionally Turkish has been banned, as are books, and then, one day, in the trash bin, she finds the composer himself. Gradually she gathers the items, and people, discarded by the regime and keeps them in an attic. An orchestra forms. I could go on . . . but then that would be the story. It is a masterpiece, both roaringly funny and deadly serious. We know these horrors are happening right now. We live in a time of death and repression, of war and bigotry. Orhan's story captures it all with intelligence and, magnificently, laughter.

Art is how we're going to survive this—and by "this," I mean anything you might have in mind. A virus, a partner, a family, a country, a world in trouble and grief. That is how I felt reading these stories, and many others, this year. That is what I found so heartening—the future is unknown, and of course terrifying, and, in hard times, some rage, some cower, some bellow nonsense, and others get down to work. But writers: we take notes. From these notes we make something new. Something we don't even understand ourselves; we only know it is vital when we make it. For whatever happens, we know this: art is also what will survive us.

And Mom: I hope you approve.

ANDREW SEAN GREER

LESLIE BLANCO

A Ravishing Sun

FROM *New Letters*

LIGHT, IS WHAT I remember.

Joy.

Honeysuckle vines wild against fences, dresses with tiny, in-laid pearls, a vineyard, Xavier and I new as baby's skin. A Long Island wedding. We are so radiant the bride's grandmother says we should get married on the spot.

And on the winding road the next morning: a motorcycle appears out of a blind curve.

Inside me, as palpable as a feather along the skin, a shifting. Of perception. Of the lens. And a moment of knowing—long as a lifetime—that nothing will ever be the same.

Head-on.

The motorcycle taps the front fender, taps it, nothing more, and then suspends itself in the air like a scorpion preserved in glass. That bright ball of neon shoots up like a joy ride, like a stunt. Tap, and up like a rocket, like a special effect. I don't want to understand. Rider separates from machine. A missile—a person— flies toward us. The roof collapses. The windshield explodes.

The slow motion part?

The sensation of seeping.

The spinning.

The shower of glass.

My mind goes still. An ocean of silence fills it. It's peaceful. I know it's crazy to say. But it's peaceful.

Breath.

My breath.

Shards of glass around my painted toes.

When I look up, Xavier has blood pooling in the wells of his eyes. Xavier has blood flowing in rivulets down his face. Xavier. A name a little too much like savior. A name I like to roll happily in my mouth. *Get married,* the bride's grandmother said. *Put me out of my misery. You two make me want to be eighteen again.*

But Xavier and I aren't eighteen. Ours is the love of try, try again. And something flesh-colored and lumpy is splattered on the front of his shirt.

We should not know how to recognize a fragment of human brain, not one of us.

Xavi?

He isn't dead. His lips are moving. He is saying words I can't hear, can't understand. And I know then that the splatter on his shirt isn't his own.

A delayed panic. A fear of the car catching fire. In the dappled sunlight. Under the picturesque trees. A sudden impulse to do something.

I open the door.

Sunshine. Flower petals in the air.

I look for the motorcycle, for the body. I look everywhere except at my feet.

At my feet.

By then, people are milling, afraid to go near him.

Not me.

I touch him.

I speak to him.

I see his spirit leave. I *see* it. Like an *S* rising up, swishing its tail like a fish, wishing, longing. Then a whoosh—not a sound, a feeling in the silence—so fast in every direction, touching every tree, every molecule, every drop of sky.

Exhilarating.

Until I understand what I am seeing. And then the swarm of dark flies, the stink of carrion, the weight—a boulder—that falls and pins me to that asphalt, to that story. For years.

Lunacy begins at the periphery with small, slipped details that at first appear to mean nothing. I know it even as it happens. Already at the emergency room, objects are not as they used to be. The vending machine has an air of unreality about it. The fluorescent lights feel theatrical, and the world feels frozen, brittle, as if any moment I might fall through the floor. Already, staring at the potato chips, at the stale nuts, I am thinking of Philip in a way I haven't for months. Philip and despair. Philip and prognosis. Dark, glossy curls. Guarded, dutiful face. The wedding tuxedo in the back of our closet that he insisted on buying, not renting.

I get nothing from the vending machine. I only needed to look at it. I risk the brittle floor and then, behind a faded seafoam curtain, I watch the PA vacuum glass off Xavier's body with a Dirt Devil, administer four stitches to the cut on his forehead, eight more to his forearm. Twelve stitches. Impossibly, only twelve. I watch as if I've never administered stitches myself. I don't say I'm a doctor, that I've completed every requirement, have my diploma, my license, but will never voluntarily sit in a hospital break room again. That six months ago, when I met Xavier, I left everything behind. That in two weeks we're moving in together. That I've enrolled for six more years of school. To do what I wanted to do in the first place.

Instead, I imagine the moment just before the motorcycle. Laughing. *Maybe we should pull off behind the dam for a quickie. At my parents' place we'll have to sleep in different bedrooms. Cubans,* I say and shrug. *Catholics,* he says and shrugs. The blind curve. The moment of knowing with its catalogue of potential morbidity: fatality, internal hemorrhage, brain injury, peripheral neuropathy, opportunistic infection, amputation, paralysis. Philip, right there, invisible. A sinking feeling, not even a thought. I push him away. I think of the dead man's helmet obscuring all visible damage, the visor up, his head resting on the pavement as if he has only lain down for a nap. I think of the two parallel streams running downhill, fluorescent green, deepest red. I think of his open eyes, his tanned skin, of whispering to him. *Everything's okay. The ambulance is coming. Those people have excellent training. I know that for a fact.*

It's so absurd. I've dissected a corpse. In the hospitals where I did my rotations, people died left and right, but I've never actually seen it. The *S* reaching up. The last exhalation filling the world like omniscience.

My mother arrives to the emergency room in a flurry of helpless panic.

My father does not come at all. I take his phone call in the

parking lot, outside the automatic double door. He doesn't ask me
if I'm all right. The series of questions he does ask me amounts to
an interrogation.

Who was driving?

Why did you let him drive your car?

Were you speeding?

Even when I have absolved us of all possibility of blame, even
when I tell him the police estimated the motorcycle was going 70
in a 25, that our skid marks show us on our side of the road, that
the motorcycle left no skid marks at all, he isn't satisfied. He falls
silent, but he does not show concern, he does not give me anything that might pass for support.

Keep me posted, he says and hangs up.

That night, I sneak into Xavier's room and stare at him as he
sleeps in the guest room of my parents' house. All limbs accounted
for. No disfigurement. Alive.

I take off my clothes. I wake him by climbing on top of him
and putting my hand gently over his mouth. His eyes are surprised
when they open, unsure, then grateful. It isn't desire that drives it.
I want to wake up. From that blank mind—the roof collapsing, the
windshield exploding—from that consuming ocean that no longer
feels peaceful. I don't have any other way to say it. I am not in my
body, and I want to come back.

But it doesn't work.

I don't want to get into any cars, even parked ones. A fear. A resistance. Like a radioactive glow emanating from the metal and the
spark plugs and the reclining seats.

Our leases are up on the Lower East Side, and our new lease
doesn't start for another week, so we have to stay at my parents'
house, and on the road we have to drive if we leave, there is a
bloody splotch like badly cleaned-up roadkill. That was his head.
That was my hand, reaching, and two parallel streams running
downhill: the car, the motorcyclist, bleeding out.

In my own skin, I am only comfortable in bed, swaddled in silence.

My mother comes in squeaky slippers. She wants me to go to
Mass with her. Pray. Get out the rosewood rosary she got me for
my First Holy Communion. She doesn't understand why I can't
get out from under the covers, why I get up and then get back in.

Xavier goes into the city to talk to a pastor he's never met. When he returns, the clouds are gone from his eyes. It seems wrong to me. Flip. But then I turn it on myself, put blame into it. Xavier never saw the *S,* the sheet drawn over the motorcyclist's face. He had to be told. Strapped to a gurney in the ambulance, he started sobbing and couldn't stop. I can't shed a single tear. So which one of us is abnormal?

All practicality, full of hope for the future, Xavier makes coffee, buys packing tape, rents a U-Haul. He sits on my bed. He tells me he dreamed of a drop of water bouncing up from the surface of the ocean and then falling back in. *The motorcyclist is home, Lucy, that's all, it's how we all go.* For a moment I hate him for this wisdom, this reductionism. I don't tell him about the *S* reaching for the sky. Again. Again. The *S.* The sky a vault of breath. Or that I tried to tether his spirit, after I understood, holding his hand on sun-hot asphalt, whispering lies.

Five days after the accident, when I wake and begin weeping before I can even muster the energy to sit up, my mother runs in, takes one look at me and yells to my father—"She's crying!"—as if she is wholly unqualified to handle such an eventuality.

My father comes. He takes my hand nervously and tells me it's shock, that it will pass, and finally, when I cannot gather myself even for three full seconds, he does what he always does: he loses his temper. *Consider this your wake-up call, Lucy,* he says, *the universe is telling you to get your life in order.*

What the hell are you saying? I ask him.

But I know what he's saying. He wants me to regress. To my husband. To my career. To socially condoned misery.

Scholar? my father's said. *What does that mean, scholar? Are you changing it to historian now? What does historian mean? What will they pay you for, exactly?* He acts like he's never heard of a university. Like he's never read a history book. Seen a documentary. *Do you have any idea how much I paid for your medical school? You're a doctor. Do you hear me? A doctor.* And every time he's greeted Xavier—not a doctor—he's looked him up and down with a scowl, as if Xavier was an intruder, a hitchhiking vagrant I picked up at the side of the road.

This is your wake-up call.

Wearily, with no anger or amusement, my sister's words echo in my head. *If you're going to rebel, couldn't you have picked something more exciting than Cuban history, for God's sake? Couldn't you have become a fucking stripper?* My sister. Also a doctor. Married to—what else?—a doctor.

On the messy bureau across from my bed, in the room in my parents' house with all my high school preoccupations—black-and-white sketches of Snow White and the Wicked Witch, poster-sized photos of ballerinas en pointe, a panorama of Cuba's Valley of Viñales—still framed on the walls, I can see the stack of textbooks I bought prematurely, out of excitement. *Cuba: Between Reform and Revolution. The Cuban Revolution: Origins, Course and Legacy. The Lost Apple: Operation Pedro Pan, Cuban Children in the U.S. and the Promise of a Better Future.* By the time my father leaves my room, despite the trace feelings of defiance beginning to stir in me, the books look like traitors, like the impulse buys of an impetuous little girl. Or maybe the impulse buys of a little girl unduly influenced by a personage named Xavier.

Maybe the third week I knew Xavier, I showed up for dinner at his apartment and he met me at the door wearing a Balinese sarong and nothing else. The lights were off. Candles were lit on every surface, like torches. He was blasting opera and the whole place smelled of the curry he was cooking. Maybe this would have made no impression on someone else, on hipper, more bohemian New Yorkers, but never in my conformist, immigrant life had I experienced anything approaching his level of uncontained self-expression.

He scared me. He drew me the way light draws winged insects. The unexpected infinity of passions, of joyfully seizing whatever life makes available. He was exuberant, recklessly optimistic, interested in everything, best friends in five minutes with the man at the next table at a restaurant, or the traveler at the bar, liable to offer his couch to any nomad passing with a camel. Four times he broke up with me amiably, once on Valentine's Day, convinced it was too soon after my separation, or his broken-off engagement, or that I meant what I said: I wasn't going to get legally married ever again. Each time he came back sheepishly the next day.

I broke up with him too, once. For the same reasons.

It was maddening. Pushing and pulling, a friend of mine called it, the Great Honesty Experiment. She and I used to do an interpretive dance around her living room: sea anemone—so beautiful and exposed, trying to tempt a little fish—closing quickly at the first sign of a serious customer, closing quickly and counter-productively, closing anxiously, closing even before the certainty of a next meal.

So when Xavier and I decided to give this a shot in earnest, I couldn't really blame my father. Though I did.

We've been two black sheep since the beginning, Xavier and me, the crows above us laughing, like wiser older brothers, and kicking down snow.

I try to channel Xavier's energy. Downstairs and in the front yard of the house, he is airing out hand-woven rugs and determining what comes with us and what goes into storage. Savior. My second chance. I think of the *S* reaching up. I think of the stream of blood flowing downhill like water. But not my *S*, not my blood. My father has already thought to point that out. *You didn't die, Lucy. You're fine. Snap out of it.*

I don't remember telling my father about the *S*. Where? In the parking lot outside the sliding doors of the ER? Or that night, when we came home to his face—stern, worried—in the rectangular frame of the open front door? I only remember what he said. *That didn't happen. That's just something your brain does.*

Seeping, like my soul leaving my body.

Breath.

My breath.

I don't believe in karma, or fate, or any of the rest of it, but there's something I haven't told anyone about the motorcyclist who jumped headfirst through my windshield. He looked like the husband I have not yet fully left. Philip, yes. The doctor. The saint. Same coloring and slight build, the same indifference to fashion. By that I mean brand-less jeans and the kind of sneakers his mother bought him in junior high because they were cheap-est. Philip. Who doesn't want the divorce. Who's cried, begged, pleaded. Whose dark, curly hair was long and carefree when we met, cut closer and closer to his scalp each passing year. Who was loyal, dutiful. And eventually, deadened, plodding, one foot in front of the other, like a man made to march. Somehow his has be-come the last word, Philip's, and the motorcyclist's, wedded. The motorcyclist's tattooed wrist, frail side up on the pavement—not

Philip's, not Philip's, I keep telling myself that—pierces my chest, is a catalyst, a combustible that makes a volcano of my guilt.

I let Xavier pack all my things into the U-Haul. I get in it and ride it upstate, rigid and terrified, as if I am riding in a rolling coffin. I unpack. I go to my orientation. I meet the other students, the professors, have drinks on the grass in the quad. I start classes.

Everywhere I go, I'm only half there. It's as if I'm standing a foot behind myself, watching. As if everything is happening to someone else. When I finally open the books, my stomach churns as if I've taken poison. My head begins to throb. My vision blurs.

Get your life in order.

But I gave Philip time, like he asked. Too much time. And words. And quiet therapists' offices with beige armchairs.

There are so many things I can blame for the failure of our marriage, but I blame medical school. The crushing pressure, doubling down on both of us, the hours of sleep lost to studying, the sheer volume of information obliterating all natural curiosity. The fear—terror—of making one fatal mistake. Daily, all impulses of optimism receded into the past. The world drained slowly of wonder, of beauty, until all that was left was illness. And then: adulthood. No more mischief. No more skinny dipping, our olive skins glistening, in a darkened indoor pool after closing time. No lazy afternoons in the sun. No beaches. No jokes. The smile on his Mediterranean face turned slowly into an insomniac's scowl, his lean, tan arms faded almost to ash. I know all that doesn't necessarily follow, it doesn't have to, but it did, with us.

And now in hospitals, outpatient clinics, private practices, the walls close in on me, the air feels as if it has been replaced with hydrogen cyanide. I want to be outside, with the living. With the scavengers and the sinners. With Xavier.

Xavier is a freelance journalist. He works as little or as much as he wants, picking his stories according to the exotic location he wants to visit. Dubai, Tibet, Kazakhstan, the Takla Makan desert, one of the driest places on earth, with a name that means He Who Goes In Does Not Come Out.

He has no office to go to. No patients who will die without him. Hardly any obligations at all. That's what drew me.

But suddenly Xavier—what he does, what he doesn't do—seems irresponsible, frivolous, perilously lacking in moral fiber or financial prudence.

At night in our newly rented house, Xavier pours me a glass of wine and examines me with bright eyes. He wants to know everything. What I'm reading. If I like the professors. If I think I can be friends with any of the other students. I put on a show, but after a while he has to ask. *Are you all right?*

Yeah. Bit of a headache.

Another one?

Yeah. I try to smile. *I think I'll get to bed early.* And I stand up.

It's not just the car accident. The *S.* It's the divorce. It's the career change. It's moving in. My parents aren't speaking to me, because I yelled at my father for what he said—*get your life in order*—or I am not speaking to them—because he said it, because he always says it—and I haven't actually done any of the reading.

Every motorcycle I see accelerates my breath, the real ones as well as the ones I only imagine rushing at me out of the corner of my eye. My life begins to feel like a horror movie, my body braced— always braced—for the bad about to happen. It cannot relax. It cannot drop vigilance.

I go to the campus mental health service. I take up meditation at their suggestion. For a week, sometimes two, it's like the sky clears. I do my reading, I feel the pull of excitement and curiosity. And then I cannot convince myself that someone's spilled green slushy on the sidewalk isn't a spill of bodily fluids. And at the dark wine bar full of Spanish leather, everything romance and beguiling mystery, I cannot convince myself the bartender is not pouring me a goblet of blood.

Everything all right? Xavier's hand on my forearm.

I have to go outside to breathe the cold air, sobering, almost aggressive as it pushes into my lungs.

A car pulls out of a parking spot and accelerates, and a boy out too late shoots out on a skateboard and grabs the bumper for a free ride. I visualize him against the pavement, two parallel streams running out from under his head, and I have to sit down on the frigid concrete and put my head between my knees. I have to focus on my breath. Until my mind succeeds at putting us in boxes: a boy who has never been touched by death, a woman who cannot un-touch it.

It turns into this:

I don't sleep anymore. Not in any kind of normal way.

The nausea never leaves me. The grief. The fear.

The *S*. The tattooed wrist.

My scalp constricts around my skull like a vise. But it isn't only my head, a searing throb behind the eyes, my vision a blur with no depth, no perception. The pain coils around my spine, reaches into my stomach, and ends . . . nowhere.

CAT scans, blood tests, cocktails for anxiety. It is humiliating to be on the other side of these investigations.

I take my medicine begrudgingly—an admission of failure—and none of it goes well. Neurontin keeps me in such a fog it's impossible to select eggplants from the stack at the grocery. Flexeril, Soma, Skelaxin, Baclofen—muscle relaxants—keep me practically, but not actually, asleep. And epilepsy drugs, off-label for migraines, for cluster headaches, for unexplained vision changes. I can't sleep, and then I sleep for eighteen hours a pop. The cure is worse than the illness and is in fact no cure at all. Psychiatric buzz words characterize my appointments. Somatizing disorder. Adrenal time. Memories that exist with an altered time signature. Memories stored in isolation from reality. Memories rehearsed as if for a guarantee against the future. Theories—circular, endlessly spinning theories—that help not at all.

Meanwhile, everything is loud, I'm dizzy, vomiting, head pounding, I can't get out of bed for five days, ten days, then a little better for a week, and then it starts over.

There is no injury they could have seen at the emergency room after the car accident. There is no injury—none—that they can see.

The world becomes confusing. When I wake up in the morning, I can't remember if Xavier is home or if he's gone on assignment. Some days I cannot remember my phone number, or the names of the professors I am asking for extensions. I can't remember expressions. The turns of phrase. Or the word. The word for when you sense but can't remember that whatever just happened has happened before, in exactly the same way.

Some days, Xavier sits by the bed and strokes my hair, and I

think of that grandmother from the wedding. Not her encouragement, her validation, but her toast, her advice. *Treat each other gently.
Not all days will be as joyful as this one.*

Winter comes like a mirror. A vast gray cloud pressing down.
Snow that never stops. Gusts of wind that force me back into the
house as into a cave.

One day, Xavier bundles me up and drives me to Lake On-
tario. Hand warmers in my boots and my gloves, only my Carib-
bean face exposed. He walks me down a wooded path and out
onto the sand. He runs to the water and walks on it. He stands
on the crest of a wave. *Isn't it beautiful?* he says, beaming. *It's frozen
all the way across!*

Frozen all the way across.

I cannot cry. I cannot even breathe.

539 Suicide Lane, that's what someone in the support group calls it.

It's more common than you think. Ask anyone walking the
streets outside if they've ever had an hour like this, or a year. Yes.
A whole year of wondering—idly—how to do it. Of hoping, with
nothing like intent, for a bus in the middle of the street.

Xavier worries about money, but I don't notice. Xavier feels
sad—the motorcyclist, his called-off wedding, the way his own family has rejected him—but I don't notice. Xavier feels panic, covers
it with optimism and denial, he feels insufficient, trapped. I don't
notice. And every cheerful thing he says repels me like the wrong
end of a magnet.

He introduces me to the Tarot, and I pull the card from the
deck again and again: the Tower, the archetypal tower, crumbling,
in flames, and a person jumping, falling through thin air.

I don't know who I am.

In India, they call this condition the day before Enlightenment.
Upstate—you can imagine—they give me more minuscule, inef-
fectual doses of distraction.

But it isn't 539 Suicide Lane. Not really. It's just 1, just looking down the road of what could be. And the comforting—so
comforting—notion: Plan C.

Xavier, domestic by then, fetching in no shirt and his sky-blue
pajama pants, can sometimes console me, but I don't tell him, and
he does what Philip would never have done. He goes away. He
needs a break, he says, from the backwater we've moved to. A va-

cation. A month in a friend's garret apartment in the West Village.
He leaves. He leaves me.

And I hate him. I hate him in earnest.

When Xavier insists I visit him for the weekend, he throws a dinner party. White wine, a roast chicken, fingerling potatoes, sautéed
spinach, and his signature pan-fried risotto cakes. I left Philip for
Xavier ten days after I'd met him and Xavier called off his wedding nine days out, a story he celebrates loudly in front of every
audience. The very retelling feels to me like an indictable offense.
The subsequent laughter strikes me as excess, as disrespectful. The
world should be dressed in black. We should all of us be building
a city underground.

My head again. What's wrong with me?

I have no medical answers. This is happening because I'm a
Cuban, I begin to think. It's an immigrant thing. A refugee thing.

Because in all of this, Xavier is opposite to me. Hopeful. Nau-
seatingly positive. Blue-eyed, fair, so blond that when he sleeps, he
looks like a child, like a mischievous little cherub finally, finally
tired out. Obviously, Xavier is not a Cuban. Not that I would know
what to do with a Cuban. Locked horns all day and all night—
like my father and me—voting Democrat just to spite him, picking
fights about coffee brands, yelling, threatening divorce, compen-
sating with gifts I can't afford, sitting mute and holding hands
in front of Univision every time another dissident is executed in
Cuba.

Dance with me, Lucy, Xavier says, in the tiny garret apartment.
Someone has turned on the big band station and Xavier knows
how to swing. I try. I don't want to tell him about the headache.
Finally I feign a laugh, say the space is too small for dancing.

When everyone is gone and the only noise is the hum of the
city beyond the windows, I decline Xavier's invitation to join him
in the shower. I climb onto his friend's lofted bed. I crawl into the
little alcove, press my back against the wall, and I weep. For no
reason. For no good reason. Is this a life, with Xavier? Weeping at
a nonstop party? The one who lived, who wasn't even driving and
can't go on, doesn't know how, isn't capable?

My father never told me that during the Bay of Pigs invasion, he
and his parents were stuffed into a school auditorium in Havana

with hundreds of other suspected counterrevolutionaries and held at gunpoint by fifteen-year-olds. Or that his father was tortured in jail for refusing to put a Communist plaque on his desk at work. Or that his mother began to lose her mind when the secret police made a headquarters across the street. My mother told me, after I started reading the history books. But I knew it even before she told me. I knew it by the way my father holds his body, by the way his papers have to be arranged just so, by the way he cleaves so tightly to the notion of progress, of never looking back. *You can't slow down,* he's said to me so many times. *You've got to keep moving. You've got to go forward. You've got to succeed.* And at night, he surfs the news channels with a look on his face of intense vigilance. As if reading facial expressions for code. For deception. For apocalypse.

Childhood abuse predisposes you to this kind of thing, verbal or otherwise, that's what therapists say. A sensitive temperament. Trauma of any kind. Explosions, certainly. Or an early fright. Or a prolonged period of stress. A consistent feeling of unsafety.

Genetics are involved. Propensities. Sequencing.

But another kind of genetics too, that's my theory. For a child, from a parent, panic is heritable by touch, by proximity. Calamitous thinking, too. Threatening, traumatized, dysfunctional patterns. Threaded into the DNA.

All it takes, then, is a confluence of traumatic events in a short period of time—a divorce, a career change, a family feud, actual, physical violence—and your brain connects a zillion dots of personal and ancestral suffering.

The ramifications are predictable: mild or even extreme agoraphobia, a preference for the bare feet against the earth, hiding like an animal wherever you can see all means of egress.

Xavier is impulsive, I've always known that. Or he wouldn't have called off his wedding nine days out. After knowing me little more than a week. Not *for* me, exactly. But *because* of me, yes, that's almost a certainty.

Impulsive. Unreliable. Of limited and inconsistent means. Xavier.

But also kind.

When he comes back from his vacation in the city and finds

me in a ball in the bed, not having eaten for days, he's lost his resentment, his frustration, and he crawls in with me. He lets me cry against his shoulder. He strokes my hair and holds me against his broad chest. *The worst is over, Lucy-Lu,* he says softly. *You're finding your feet. Every day you're finding new ground. Look how brave you've been. Half the world is too afraid to take a risk and try something different. Half the world would rather live in misery. Or blow something up. Everything's okay now.*

Everything's okay now.

The ambulance is coming.

Those people have excellent training.

I go to the neurologist. Again. Again. He's condescending. He treats me like a psychosomatic. Like a head case.

I am a head case. I say I want to be with the living, but I spend my time studying the dead. I say I want to take risks—*carpe diem!*—but I won't even go to the library.

Secretly, without admitting, I believe all of this is Xavier's fault. If not for Xavier, I would never have left medicine, displeased my parents, abandoned Philip. I would never have dared to think this fucked-up world could be a safe place for me. That sane people—full-blown adults—have a right to be happy. I would never have touched ecstasy. Like a manic-depressive. Like an idiot.

So many classes of controlled substances, of numbing down. Relief filled with venom. A milder kind of impermanent death.

I lied before, all right? I believe in karma. And superstitiously, in Santería, in the lethal power of anger. I think you can hex someone as easily as you can spit on the ground. This knowledge arises, takes weeks to coalesce into form: in reliving that instant of knowing—the motorcycle suspended in air, the dappled sunlight—again, again, I'm making up a story for myself. A story that becomes a reality, goes back to story, reality, story. It's a fist of anger hurling through the air. It's the men—the father, the husband, the dictator—on their thrones. And there's no other option. I am the bad girl. Leaving my responsible career, my good, dutiful doctor, what everyone wants for me except me. For what? To call them out, to rabble-rouse, to make a shitload of trouble. So they punished me. And any time they want to—when I open those history books, when I slip into bed with a man who believes so recklessly in freedom—they can punish me again.

I think about it every day, but I don't walk away from Xavier.

One Friday in July, my *Cubaneo* flares up.

You left me, I say. *You were a coward. You thought I was contagious.*

You're right, he says. *I was a coward.*

His appeasement infuriates me. *Stop being such a fucking child,* I say. *This is serious. Life is serious.*

There. I've said it. I've admitted to myself I can't understand how he's made it to adulthood—filled in such a robust body, a chest with hair on it—with all his undimmable radiance intact. That there's something suspect about it. That it reeks of privilege. And exploitation. And imperialistic entitlement. And immaturity. Happy self-absorption that is culturally—and historically—sickening.

Okay, he says. He looks angry. Desperate. At the end of his rope. *Yes,* he says. *Fine. Absolutely. Life is serious, Lucy. And then what?*

This is the part of the story where there's supposed to be a big climax.

There's no big climax.

One day I do the simple thing. The hard thing. I get up.

I can't tell you why. Why that day. Why at all.

Except: the getting up is a form of revenge. Against Philip—his eye rolls, his interruptions, his disparagements—because that's what it came to, a slicing, belittling knife alternating with the subtlest, most calculated put-downs and not a drop of sainthood left. Revenge, too, against my father, that "little" Operation Peter Pan refugee. The unacknowledged truth that bursts like a giant bubble through lava? His lifelong actions toward me amount to exactly the same kind of cruelty, and his historically verified suffering offers not an ounce of justification for it.

It's not so easy for me to say it, but there's revenge against Xavier too. I mean, fuck this shit. *Learn to be gentle with each other,* yes, fine, but why should Xavier—and his class, his type, his ethnicity—have the only permanent lease on possibility?

And finally, revenge aside, what is history, really, but collective adrenal time? Memories that exist collectively with an altered time signature. Memories collectively stored in isolation from reality.

Memories rehearsed as if for a guarantee against the future which never, no matter what historians say, repeat, not really, not to the same people, not the same way.

I get up. I fall again. I get up.

There are Good Samaritans on that road. "Scholars." I never tell them any of this, but they must see it all over my face. The way they fuss and tell me how smart I am. The way they line up to feed me. And Xavier. Of course Xavier. He holds my hand as my soul tries to leave my body. He tethers me. He tells me lies. Beautiful, romantic, optimistic lies.

Youth is a perfect sphere—crystal, hollow—dropped by the moon at our birth. All our lives we think we're floating—flying—toward the earth. But we fall. Fragile. Eyes wide open, faces excited with anticipation, with something like pride. That's what I knew, in the days of upstate winters.

Xavier disagreed wholeheartedly. Forget the moon. The card he pulled from the Tarot deck again and again—do I even have to write it?—was the Sun. For him, all experience was fruitful. On a walk through snowy woods he told me about the tree he saw once. A shard of glass was wedged into its trunk.

Who would do a thing like that? I said.

It doesn't matter. Listen. The trunk grew around it, he said, *unimpeded but not unaffected.*

That's what he did with the dead motorcyclist. He mourned him, instantly, without hesitation, by eating him—like a handful of almonds, like a steak sandwich—then he grew around him, *unimpeded but not unaffected,* and he took it even one step further. He made him useful. He wrote about him. He honored him by carrying him around—by giving him a place in history—and then, by living.

So did I. Finally.

The analyst's couch, yes, the face carefully devoid of judgment. But mostly, I found solace in the bark of a sacred tree. In a stone Buddha. In a silent river. Outside, every spring: a resurgence like a betrayal, unstoppable, luminous, the unfair advantage the living have over the dead. I can't explain it, but maybe you can hear it: the indifferent exuberance—alive, alive!—of birds at dawn?

As a result, I can get into any car now. I prefer buses, admittedly, trains, rubber dinghies. I've stopped rehearsing the likely blow to the rear fender, the sideswipe, the coma.

I'm off the pills.

I'm out of the bed.

Most days.

But I was right to know it—the seeping soul, the shift of the lens—that my life would never be the same. Every day when Xavier kisses me goodbye to go to the grocery, or the airport, I think it will be the last. Accident, heart attack, melanoma, flu, schizophrenic stabbing. The mind spins so many webs. At the door, or my desk, or the cozy armchair I'm in right now, I entertain these thoughts. And I set them aside.

This morning, the house is quiet. It smells of coffee. I can still feel the kiss Xavier placed on my neck before he went downstairs, and for the first time in a long time, I don't remember waking to notice the razor thin scars next to his eye. I don't think of Philip, or the accident. In my morning meditation, I feel free of all of it, though I speak, as I sometimes do, to the dead motorcyclist. He comes to me with a sad face and holds my upturned wrists solemnly, as if holding my heart.

But there's something deceptive about all this domesticity, all this calm.

That nameless panic in my chest hasn't so much faded, as brought things into focus.

Everything is visceral now. Sharper. Closer.

My synapses crave as if for hallucinogens. Electricity—that's the only word for it—courses through me like crack, like meth, and my system of nerves is so easily overwhelmed. What I'm talking about—presence, living—holds no artifice now. No veil. No distance.

Pleasure is letting the tidal wave hurl me into rocks.

Pain is floating gently into the face of a ravishing sun.

YOHANCA DELGADO

The Little Widow
from the Capital

FROM *The Paris Review*

THE WIDOW ARRIVED at LaGuardia on a Sunday, but the rumors about the woman who had rented a big apartment, sight unseen, had taken an earlier flight. We had already reviewed, on many occasions and in hushed tones, in the quiet that comes after long hours of visiting, what little we knew about the widow and her dead husband.

About her life in the old country, we asked the obvious questions: Were there children? Cheryl heard from a friend who still lived in the Dominican Republic that they had only been married a year when he died. Had her husband been rich? No, our sources in the old country said, poor as a church mouse, with a big family to support out in el campo. Had the husband been handsome? Yes, in a rakish sort of way. And with what we knew we created him in our minds: medium height with a mop of curly hair and an easy laugh, walking down Saona Beach in a white linen guayabera, dropping suddenly to one knee. We ourselves felt a flutter in our hearts.

On the day the widow finally arrived in New York, the rain came in fast, heavy drops that sounded like tiny birds slamming into our windows. She emerged from the taxi with a single battered suitcase and, little-girl small, stared up at our building as the rain pelted her face. Behind us our men and children called out for their dinners, but we ignored them. We would wonder later if she had seen our faces pressed up against the windows, on all six floors, peering out over flowerpots full of barren dirt.

We watched her until she made her way out of the rain and

into the lobby. Those of us lucky enough to live on the fourth floor squinted through our peepholes or cracked open our doors as the super carried her suitcase to the three-bedroom apartment she was renting. How could she afford it?

The little widow walked behind the super, her gait slow and steady on the black-and-white tiles of the hallway. He was rambling about garbage pickup and the rent. She was younger than we expected her to be, thirty, maybe. The amber outfit was all wrong for the chilly autumn weather. She was from Santo Domingo, but she looked like a campesina visiting the city for the first time, everything hand-sewn and outdated by decades. She wore an old-fashioned skirt suit, tailored and nipped at her round waist, and a pair of low-heeled black leather pumps. Seeing them made us glance down at our own scuffed sneakers and leggings. On her head, she wore a pillbox hat, in matching yellow wool sculpted butter-smooth. She dressed her short, plump body as though she adored it.

Instantly, we took a dislike.

We ourselves had been raised on a diet of telenovelas and American magazines, and we knew what beauty was. We gathered after dinner to laugh at her peculiar clothes. We murmured with fake sympathy about her loneliness, and joked that she might turn our husbands' heads. When we ran into her, though, we smiled and asked her how she was finding New York.

We began to invent stories about the little widow's life: torrid affairs that had driven her husband to die of heartbreak, a refusal to give him children, a penchant for hoarding money—we repeated the tales until we half-believed them. The drama of the little widow's previous life became richer and denser, like a thicket of fast-growing ivy. Who did she think she was, anyway? Living alone in that big apartment?

The little widow seemed to understand what we expected of her: she muttered only quiet thank-yous when we held the door open as she struggled with her groceries, or when we helped her up after she slipped on a patch of ice in front of the building and landed flat on her back. As briskly as she could, she composed herself and disappeared, her head bowed low into the collar of her quaint amber coat.

When we heard that the little widow could sew, we started bringing her dresses and pants to hem, mostly because we wanted to know how she lived. The little widow's three-bedroom apartment was laid out like the others, but as she worked, our eyes darted hungrily between her and the contents of her sewing room.

Her hair was curly, dyed reddish brown, and cut short around a pointed chin. When we got to see her up close, we noted that though she did have deep creases at the corners of her eyes, she did not have a widow's peak. Her eyes were a dark hazel, and her pupils so small they looked like pinpricks.

The little widow had wallpapered her sewing room with a cheap burlap. When one of us slipped a fingernail underneath a panel and discovered that the rough cloth was glued on, we crossed ourselves and said a quick prayer for the little widow's security deposit.

On that burlap the little widow had embroidered massive, swaying palm trees, so finely detailed that we could almost feel a salty breeze warm our faces as we stood on her tailor's pedestal. Running our fingertips across the embroidered walls we could feel the braille of her labor; the grains of sand were individually stitched, as if the little widow knew each one. The ocean seemed to ripple and surge as the little widow worked around us in meditative silence, kneeling near our ankles with a pin between her lips. She was so gentle and fluid in her movements, her soft skin creasing like a plump baby's around the pincushion she wore on her wrist.

We liked her in those moments, but even so, we didn't invite her to our birthday parties or gatherings at Christmas, though we knew she was alone in that large apartment, watching the passing of the seasons, just as we did, through black-barred windows.

We imagined she would soon have to take in a subletter to make ends meet. We mentioned that a cousin was coming to work at a coffee-filter factory and needed a place to live. She didn't have a lot of money yet, we explained, but she would be able to pay back rent on a room once she started collecting paychecks. And that could be a good source of extra income!

The little widow tilted her head to one side and appeared to think about it. She said yes, and Lucy, a single girl from Higüey, moved into the little widow's spare bedroom.

The goodwill the little widow won among us was short-lived. On a visit to get a skirt hemmed, Sonia asked to use the restroom and snuck into the little widow's bedroom. Like the wall of her sewing room, the wall across from her bed was covered with burlap, and on that canvas the little widow had hand-stitched tidy rows of Limé dolls.

The faceless dolls looked just like the clay figurines tourists bought as souvenirs. They varied in hair and clothing—some wore their hair in a single thick plait, draped down the side of their necks, and some wore it down around their shoulders. Their dresses were every color of the rainbow and some wore Sunday hats and carried baskets of flowers. But rendered in the little widow's hand, these familiar dolls took on an eerie quality. Sonia studied the wall for a long time and became convinced that the dolls represented us.

She took a picture and texted it to the group. We looked at the faceless dolls, with their caramel skin and their ink-black hair styled into bouffants and braids and pigtails. Then we looked at each other, with our jeans and winter boots and blond highlights.

The resemblances are uncanny, we said. And so a rumor spread that the little widow was a witch come from Santo Domingo to ensorcell us and steal our husbands. We rummaged in our drawers for our old evil-eye bracelets. We started going to the dry cleaner's down on Broadway to get our clothes hemmed.

When we ran into the little widow in the halls, she smiled at us sadly, but said nothing.

To this day, we do not know how Andrés and the little widow met, but the rumor is that it happened through mutual relations from the capital.

Unlike the little widow, Andrés was a New Yorker, born and bred, and he spoke in a brambly, chaotic Spanish that she seemed to find charming. On their first date, the little widow wore a silk slip dress, hand-embroidered with small, delicate birds. He wore a blazer, jeans, and dress shoes. They stayed out until two in the morning, and when they came home, we heard her laugh ringing in the halls, a lovely, alien sound.

The next day he delivered to her a bouquet of radiant, limp-necked sunflowers. She arranged them in a giant vase by the window in her sewing room. Then in the weeks that followed, he could be heard in the small hours of the morning, serenading her on his guitar. He wrote her poetry, and according to Gladys—who took to pressing a glass against the wall she shared with the little widow—it wasn't half bad.

He was about thirty, like the little widow. But unlike her, he wore his age gaily. He was boyish and relaxed, and we often spied him leaning on doors and smoking cigarettes near the trash cans. He kept his hair cut in a neat fade that he refreshed every two weeks. He used the creaky metal ladder on the fire escape to do pull-ups until the super told him to stop. We decided that we liked him, tsk-tsked that he was too good for the little widow, with her opaque melancholy and insufferable pride.

It is said that he proposed to her right in her sewing room. Relieved that she was finally on the right track, heading toward a life we understood, we flocked in a squealing, air-kissing mob to her apartment to admire the ring: a small round diamond on a simple gold band. The way she wore it made it look like something Elizabeth Taylor would have been proud to own. There was a new lightness in the little widow that we liked to see, in spite of ourselves.

She smiled often, sometimes for no apparent reason, and it was a strange, unfamiliar smile that made us think of sunlight bursting through a cloud-choked sky. The wedding was set for the following month and the weeks flitted by. Lucy told us the little widow was hard at work on a wedding dress and that she mooned around the house, dreamy, distracted, and in love.

It all fell apart as quickly as it had come together. Five days before the wedding, Lucy woke up in the middle of the night to find Andrés standing at the foot of her bed. He had come in with the little widow's key, he said, and he had come in to see her.

Lucy leaped up and, assuming he was drunk, tried to walk him back to the door. But he refused to go and instead pinned her against the wall, which the little widow had recently embroidered with sunflowers. He attempted to unfasten his pants. Now scared in earnest, Lucy screamed and shoved him to the floor.

The little widow appeared quickly and without sound, like a ghost. She had been working; she had a needle pressed between her lips, and one lip was bleeding. She looked from Andrés to Lucy and understood everything.

Without a word, the little widow took Lucy by the hand and led her into her own bedroom until Andrés was gone, and then she dead-bolted them into the apartment for safety. The little widow kept vigil by Lucy's bed until she fell asleep, then locked herself in her own room.

For two days, the little widow didn't speak, or eat, or sleep. She subsisted on a nightly glass of morir soñando, which she drank to appease Lucy. The girl blamed herself for everything and thought it a small penance to squeeze the orange juice for the little widow's drink.

Because we didn't know yet that the little widow was rich, we assumed Andrés returned two nights later because he loved her.

Florencia spotted him from her window on the first floor and it only took a few minutes on the phone to spread the news. By the time he was at the little widow's door, we all hovered at ours, swatting away needy children and chatty husbands.

On every floor, we cracked our doors. His pleas reverberated through the tiled hallways, filling even the central stairwell. Our hungry ears consumed every sound: The wet, racking sobs. The thud of his knees dropping onto her welcome mat. The wailing against the hard wood of the little widow's door.

He was sorry, he insisted. It hadn't meant anything. Who was Lucy to him?

After nearly an hour, it seemed to us that he planned to spend the night there, performing this noisy contrition. Then the little widow flung open her door with a whip-sharp bang that sent an echo all the way down to the first floor.

"What," she said, her voice a small, cold blade, "do you think is going to happen next?"

All through the building, our ears pricked up.

"You're the love of my life," he moaned. Cheryl, watching from her apartment across the hall, could attest to the fact that he was still, at this point, on his knees.

"And are you mine?" The little widow crossed her arms over her chest. She wore a silk dressing gown, embroidered with human hearts the size of silver dollars.

"Yes, yes," he cried, pressing his face to her bare feet.

The little widow stepped back to free her feet, and then stepped around him, out into the hallway. "Let these busybodies witness," she said. And now we could see that her eyes were red and her curls ravaged by nights of insomnia.

Andrés hobbled after her, on his knees, making mournful sounds.

"Let these *chismosas* be my witnesses," she said again, waving her hand and locking eyes with Cheryl, who later told us that she had nearly died of shame. "If you bother me again, you will not live to tell about it."

Andrés clasped his hands together in a prayer motion and mutely held them up to her.

The little widow looked at him as if he were a turd on the sidewalk. She shoved him aside, walked back to her door. "You heard me," she said, one hand on her doorknob. "Not a single knock."

She closed the door and left Andrés to gather himself off the floor and wipe the snot from his face. We thought we'd never seen a man renounce his dignity quite so definitively and that realization seemed to hit him at the same time. Grimacing, he wiped his mouth, and cursed under his breath. He kicked the door as hard as he could. Once, twice.

"You think you can control me," he said. "I'll show you control. And Lucy, too." He slammed the heel of his hand on the door.

Only Cheryl—who slowly and silently slipped the chain lock into place, all while holding her door ajar and keeping one eye firmly on Andrés—can describe what happened next, and only you can decide if you believe it.

Andrés raised his arm again, and as he drew it back for another blow, it froze. The arm appeared to be stuck to his head, as if glued there. His back still to Cheryl, Andrés shook himself and tried to use his other hand to pry it loose, but that one became attached, too, and then it looked like he was holding his hands to his head, the way men do when their baseball team is losing. He began to make a frantic humming sound.

When he turned to Cheryl, with the purest, most desperate panic she had ever seen blazing in his eyes, she discovered that his lips had been sewn shut with large, sloppy stitches.

He dropped to his knees with a grunt, and then bent in half at the waist. He kept folding in on himself, over and over, becoming smaller and smaller, his moans of distress more and more distant, until he was just a small scrap of cream fabric that fluttered to the floor in front of apartment 4E.

No one knocked on the little widow's door after that. Three days passed in shallow breaths.

In our apartments, huddled together over coffee, we discussed what we knew and filled in what we didn't. We imagined the little widow, dead-eyed and small in her cavernous apartment, punching a threaded needle through cloth—until she folded the entire building in on itself, apartment after apartment, life after life, collapsing together—until she could tuck it all into her little silk coin purse and carry us away forever inside her handbag.

We pretended we were innocent. Weren't we like an old fan, just moving the air around? We tipped over our coffee cups and saw in our fortunes an angry darkness that threatened to swallow us. And hadn't we sensed it from the beginning?

For the first time, it occurred to us to call our families, the ones back in the old country, to find out the full story. We pooled our facts together. We knew the story people liked to tell, but now we were detectives. We dug deeper, asked our distant aunts to ask their cousins what they knew, and were stunned at how shallowly buried the truth was.

The little widow had married for love right out of high school, to a man who was primarily interested in her family's money but liked her well enough besides. When the new couple said they wanted to move from the capital to the beach, her parents bought them a big, sprawling house on the coast near Bávaro, and hired three live-in servants to work there. And the little widow was happy! She loved the beach; it was said that she went swimming twice a day, that she walked up and down the shore as if she wanted to memorize every gull, every seashell, every grain of sand. It was at this time that the little widow began to embroider seascapes and mermaids, her head bent low over her needle and hoop.

But middling affection does not a good man make. The husband began to throw his weight around the house, speaking cruelly to the servants, punching walls, breaking things. The little widow miscarried their first child under mysterious circumstances and mourned the loss in private. She focused more than ever on her work; sometimes the light in her sewing room burned through the night.

Less than a year later, a servant filed a police report against the husband, saying that he had forced himself on her and she had become pregnant. The husband's proximity to the little widow's influential family allowed him to avoid serious charges. But he did not live to see another year; the servant's husband shot him, point-blank, as he walked down the beach near the house.

The little widow's parents swiftly stepped in, at their daughter's request, to scatter the tragedies of the story in the wind. They paid the hefty bribes required to free the servant's husband and sold the beach house to American tourists. The little widow quietly went away.

Her wedding to Andrés had been scheduled to take place at Our Lady of Lourdes, the crumbling, majestic old church we attended, and on that day, we dressed for Sunday Mass.

Someone's mother-in-law in Queens said she spotted someone who looked like Andrés slinking out of a bodega, but who could be sure? The tiny scrap of cream fabric had long since disappeared in the building's hustle and bustle. We knew for certain that the wedding was canceled. But for reasons we still can't explain, we sent our husbands and kids ahead to Sunday school and lingered in the building. The wedding had been scheduled for four in the afternoon, and when the time came, we opened our doors and, like cuckoos from their clocks, stepped out of our apartments and crowded into the narrow fourth-floor hallway.

By then we knew her name, and we started slowly calling it, in unison. Lucy came out first, dressed in sweatpants and looking like a wrung-out dishcloth. When we asked her if the little widow had spoken to her, she shook her head sadly.

A thud inside, the sound of footsteps, and our murmurs dissipated into a tense silence. When the little widow opened her door, she wore an enormous white silk wedding dress.

On her head, she had crowned herself with a ring of white silk flowers, embroidered with red drops of blood, delicate as anything we'd ever seen. Her face seemed younger than we remembered, though her undereyes were bruise-blue from lack of sleep.

She maneuvered the seemingly boundless skirts of her dress through the tight doorframe and began making her way to the elevator. With a gasp, we parted like a sea to let her pass. At least six feet of heavy, layered skirts embroidered to the last inch with small, careful cursive letters trailed behind her.

Unfamiliar-yet-familiar names were scattered densely across the silk like polka dots. Women's names from the old country: the Dominican *y*'s, the florid, delirious layering of syllables. We knew our people.

We did not recognize these specific names and we did not dare ask anything of the little widow. Instead—and without thinking—we formed two lines and picked up the train of the dress to keep it from getting soiled as the little widow walked slowly down the long corridor with her head bowed and her hands clasped.

Mutely, we helped her enter the elevator and passed her the skirts, which foamed up around her, rising well past her shoulders. As the heavy door slid closed, she gave us the brokenhearted smile we had come to recognize.

"Up," we half whispered, half barked, after pressing our ears to the door. We ran toward the stairs, taking them two at a time to keep up with the old elevator, jostling one another at each landing—until we saw that the little widow was going up to the roof.

She walked out onto the silver-painted cement with us trailing behind. The air was cold but we hardly noticed. We elbowed each other and pushed to get close enough to see her without touching her, though when one of us shoved through and blurted, "Don't jump, *viudita*! Don't do it!"—she spoke for all of us.

The little widow turned to look at us, like a somnambulist shaken brutally awake.

Then, before anyone had a chance to stop her, she sprinted across the silver roof, clutching her frothing skirts to her sides. She climbed onto the ledge and we saw, or thought we saw, the cream soles of her naked feet.

She turned to face us. Behind her the sun had begun its plunge to earth, the sky ripe-mango orange behind needle-sharp skyscrapers. The little widow's dress lathered all around her, making her look ten feet tall. Why hadn't we seen before how beautiful she was?

The little widow's eyes shone. It was as if she were recognizing us, each of us, across a crowded room. Afraid to approach, we formed a semicircle around her, willing her to stay.

For a long moment we were mesmerized, frozen where we stood, in our regret.

When we came to our senses and reached for her, surging forward together—to grab hold of her dress, at least, to keep her from falling the seven stories to the street below, we didn't move fast enough. She took up her dress again, great big fistfuls of it, and with her back to the sky, let herself fall.

The whine of a car alarm below halted our hearts. We rushed to the edge and peered over. And what we saw—how to even describe it? The dress dissolved into a thousand pigeons, and they filled the space between our building and the next with brown and gray and white, with the sound of wings flapping. The air was thick with the feathery thrum of their wings as they flew away in different directions, toward downtown, toward the river, toward the Bronx, and skyward, toward heaven.

The little widow was gone. All we had left—as we huddled together for warmth on that silver roof and watched the sky deepen to the bruised plum of Manhattan night—was the story. And so we told it again, and again, until we had stitched the details into our memory.

We carried the story back to the patios of Santo Domingo, where we sat at dusk with the yellow light of our old family homes behind us, listening to the crickets and the slow creak of our wicker rocking chairs, and told the tale again, except this time it ended like this: in some far-flung town, maybe here in the old country, maybe back in the new, the little widow appeared with a small suitcase in hand.

Here, our eyes brightened and we leaned forward.

This time she arrived without fanfare, we said, and her neighbors liked her right away. The little widow wore an amber-colored dress, hand-sewn. Perhaps a little older than we remembered, but still recognizable, with her full cheeks and shiny curls. She signed a lease for a house by the beach. She was already picturing the magic she would create on these new walls, and we, too, thrilled to imagine it.

Man of the House

FROM *Ecotone*

HIS MUH WAS barely a week in the ground when his phone rang with Verna on the line.

"Jebby, how soon can you come by the house?" she said in her sugary telephone voice. "I need you to remove your things from the yard."

A sick feeling came to Jeb's stomach. For the first time since they had moved into their childhood house, it was inhabited by a single person and she thought she owned it. Verna had paid the property taxes, but Jeb had helped their mother with household expenses since he was a teenager. And the deed was technically still in their mother's name. That meant Jeb had a right to the place. He'd used the yard for storage for decades, so why should it bother Verna now? Not wanting to risk her winter mood, which could make her go off on you at the drop of a dime, he asked calmly if he could move some things to the basement.

"It's full already."

Lyin ass.

"What about the bedrooms, then?"

"I'm using them too."

"Come on, Verna. Ain't you sleepin in the parlor like Muh was? What you doin with both those rooms upstairs?"

"That's my business."

Hands starting to sweat, he scrambled for an alternative. Maybe build a fence? But it would take too long to collect wood. The pieces would be mismatched. That wouldn't suit her either.

"When are you coming, Jeb?" Her words had taken on that

ragged edge like their mother's at her exploding point. "My girl-friends are joining me for tea next week and I don't want them looking at all this junk."

Her friends had been by before and seen the yard, along with everybody else in Vauxhall. And their mother never called it junk. She didn't exactly offer compliments, but she once compared it to artwork in a museum she visited over in New York with the family she kept house for. But the man who created the work in the museum was white, and an artist at that. Jeb didn't consider his things art. They were simply what people no longer wanted—what they thought was worthless. When he started working as a trash man, he was shocked at what people threw away. The broken chairs and rusted doorknobs, patched tires and dented pots, scrap metal and auto parts, used cans and bottles. So much of it could be mended and resurrected, unlike people when they die.

"Muh didn't mind my stuff," he muttered.

"Mother didn't mind *nothin* her baby Jebby did."

There it was: the real reason she wanted his things gone. Jeb could acknowledge that their mother did beat and yell at him less, but he figured it was because their daddy had given him more than his fair share. Jeb had practically been the old man's whipping post. And it was natural for their mother to defer to Jeb about matters after their daddy died. After all, Jeb became the man of the house.

He tried to get Verna off the subject by proposing the fence, but when she hissed the word "junk" again, and "eyesore," their conversation dissolved into yelling and cussing, with Verna dropping more of her *g*'s. Before slamming the phone down, she said: "I'm gon get a dump truck over here tomorrow and I'm movin it *all* out, motherfucker."

This coming from the queen of lies, Jeb didn't believe it—who in God's name did she know with a dump truck? But he never knew when to call her bluff. That afternoon, he rounded up his closest friend Booker, his hunting buddies, and a former coworker. As they congregated in the yard on Waldorf Place, surveying his life's savings, Jeb noticed Verna peeking from the kitchen window at back. Glowering at her, he mumbled for the men to choose items as payment for helping him.

They made their selections and Jeb cringed, especially when his coworker, who also had an eye for the salvageable, indicated the brass bed frame, which had turned green. Jeb had found it last year before he retired and thought it would work well with his muh's cot. He felt bruised when she refused it. He decided to use it himself, but his woman Faye didn't like it either.

It distressed Jeb just as much to part with the porcelain sink with the roses on it, which Booker claimed. That sink marked the week his wife Bertha left him. It had been abandoned on the curb in front of a mansion in Maplewood, and he had imagined attaching it to the spigot in the basement. The spigot was still bare; Jeb had moved out of the house not long after Bertha to live with Faye and never got around to doing it. He comforted himself with the thought that there was no use installing the sink now. Verna didn't deserve his belongings.

Within hours, they had everything loaded into several pick-ups, including Jeb's. Jeb got in the lead, cussing Verna the three short blocks to the woods at Vauxhall's southern boundary. It was the one place he could think to store his things, at least for the meantime.

Faye had made it clear long ago he couldn't keep anything in their house. When they moved in together after Bertha split, he started stockpiling old newspapers and magazines, which vanished at wintertime. He confronted Faye, who told him she'd tossed them. Jeb raised his hand to smack the matter-of-factness off her face. She, half his size—the same height as his muh—put her hands on her hips and said, "You wanna hit me, Jebby Coleman? I ain't that wife of yours. You hit me and you can pack the rest of your shit and hit the road." She must have been drunk; she never cussed unless she was drunk. Jeb remained enraged but had to admire a woman who told him to leave the house he paid rent for. She was just like his muh in that way. Not at all like Bertha, who never put up a fight. Somehow that had always made him want to hit her harder.

When the caravan of pickups entered Bam's Woods, Jeb guided them along the footpath the high schoolers—including his own children at some point—had made crossing to the bus stop. From there, he veered into the thicket, his truck bringing down saplings and scraping past maples and birches as he forged his own road. The caravan reached a spot where there were no trees carved with initials and hearts of teenagers in love, and the men got to digging.

As they placed his things into the shallow pit and covered them

with tarps and branches and leaves, Jeb told himself it was temporary, but he felt discomfort in his chest. If he had to put a word
to it, he would call it empty. It was like when Bertha gave birth to
their first child. Booker and a few other buddies chipped in to buy
cigars, and Jeb grinned as they said he must be proud, but when
he looked into that fist-sized face that was already so much like his,
so much like his daddy's, he felt irrelevant.

A few days after clearing the yard, Verna phoned again. Jeb's pressure shot up hearing her voice. He waited for her to say he'd made
a mess, but she was in her summer mood. He preferred that mood,
even if it frightened him somewhat, she talking so fast at times he
could barely understand. Her lies also took on epic proportions.
    This time, Verna was calling wanting to know if Jeb had bottles.
The Maxwell House ones. Sure he did—now sitting in the woods.
He wanted to berate her but refrained, telling her he'd stopped
collecting (he hadn't; the camper on his pickup was already filling). Neither did he ask why she wanted them. She had two years
on him at sixty-three, and the older she got, the more she fixated
on the oddest things. Her memory was going too: the next time
she rang him, it was as if she'd forgotten their conversation, and
she was asking for bottles again. He started to let Faye answer the
phone, and she'd tell Verna that he was out, or on the john.
    When Verna popped into the Vauxhall Diner, Jeb choked on his
dinner. She knew where to find him—he'd eaten there every night
since their mother died—but Verna had never visited him at the
diner before. It was chilly outside, and all she had on was a short-
sleeved housedress and gym shoes with no socks. Her gray edges
peeped from beneath her kerchief. She scurried down the aisle,
drawing stares, and slid opposite Jeb in his booth. Disregarding his
frown, she rattled his arm with a surprisingly warm hand, grinning.
    "Jebby, I've been thinking: we should go down South—you, me,
Rosine, and Alma!" She rushed on about escaping the approaching winter, and seeing how Alabama and Florida had changed
since Segregation ended, and visiting all the towns their family
ever lived in, and finding their grandparents' graves to put markers on them like they'd done for their mother, so they could officially pay their respects.
    Jeb shook his head and cut into his smothered pork chop.
Sometimes he didn't know what planet she was living on. Nobody

would be interested in her family field trip, and she should know it. Firstly, he was still upset over the yard. Their sister Rosine was seething too, about Verna taking over the house, even though Rosine had left when she married and only returned on Friday nights to brawl with their mother. As for Alma, the youngest, whenever she heard Verna blathering about the past, she would grumble that it was a foolish thing to dig up.

None of them clung to the olden days like Verna did. Perhaps it was because she was the oldest and remembered the most, she being eight when they left the South. Up in New Jersey, their granpop was the sole adult who used to share stories about bygones. Verna would listen, but the tall white-haired man scared Jeb and their other sisters, with his eyes glazing as he confused them for ghosts.

Furthermore, Verna knew how mention of the South could send Jeb on a tirade. During that Civil Rights mess, he was infuriated to see on television and in the papers the vicious way white folks treated Colored people. The lynchings, the bombings, the marches, the water hoses, the dogs—it was like something from another country. And then there was the reason their family came to New Jersey, if it was true at least, since Jeb overheard it from Verna talking to her husband: the sheriff of Dothan, Alabama, put out a hunt for a "tall nigger" who'd stolen bloomers from a white lady's clothesline. Their daddy, uncle, granpop, and a cousin, all fitting that bare-boned description, caught a night train north to avoid getting killed.

Verna grabbed the ketchup bottle, pounding it against the tabletop with every word: "And we could search for Uncle Abe, see if he's still living."

Jeb shivered, finally feeling what she was radiating. His last encounter with their uncle was imprinted in his mind: that brick-cold day in December 1920 when their daddy's casket was lowered into the ground at Hollywood Cemetery, a few minutes' drive east, over in Union. No one had seen or heard from their uncle since. Jeb squirmed, remembering how he used to resent his uncle for abandoning him.

Verna twiddled the bottle cap, saying, "Mother and all the old folks are gone. Who do we have left up here, Jebby?"

Her eyes had lost their shine and were welling. Never knowing how to respond to tears or her mood shifts, Jeb stared into his plate, pushing around the last of his food. He wanted to tell her to stop looking backward all the damn time. She had her children and grandchildren, and more so than he. Her daughters lived a few blocks from Waldorf Place, whereas his children had left not only Vauxhall but the county, moving far away from him. He received visits from just two of the five. But then, he deserved it, didn't he, after how he treated their mother?

Unnerved, Jeb was about to ask for the check when Verna sat up straighter, cleared her throat, and started laying out travel plans. Peeling at the bottle's label, she suggested they stop in North Carolina to sleep overnight.

"Our first stop from there," she said, "should be Campbellton."

"Yeah, yeah," Jeb said between chews.

It was where their family lived for a spell in Florida, one of the towns she couldn't resist mentioning in her stories. Jeb almost choked again, though, when she said she'd found a letter from Uncle Abe. It was postmarked from Campbellton just a few years ago. She'd found it when sorting their mother's things.

Anger prickled at Jeb's temples. Why hadn't his muh told him? He used to ask every so often if she'd heard from his uncle, and it was always no. He'd started to believe his uncle must have died.

"Campbellton was no bigger than a minute," Verna said, rolling the ketchup bottle in her hands. "You remember, don't you, Jebby?"

He sighed and resumed chewing. She knew the answer.

"It could be an adventure trying to find him, and you know how you like to drive, Jebby."

He stared at the tattered bottle label, at Verna's eyes, which were glittering again. Even if their uncle was waiting for them alive, the idea of being sequestered in his truck with Verna didn't thrill him. At all. He dipped the last piece of meat into his applesauce and told her he'd think about it.

Indeed, it was all he could do the next week. At card games with his buddies, they had to yell his name to make him follow the conversation. He would be lost in thought, reminiscing about his uncle, the memories coming sharper than ever.

He remembered Uncle Abe as a tall and quiet man like his daddy, except that Abe was prone to smiling. His wife was a healthy woman who liked to show all her teeth when she laughed. They would visit Vauxhall once a month from Orange on a horse-driven cart piled with their two kids, Jeb's granpop, and the peaches, watermelons, and collards Uncle Abe bought wholesale for his restaurant.

Their kids were always laughing like their mother and running. Jeb and his sisters would stiffen, terrified their uncle would hit their cousins or shout like their own daddy did. One time, Jeb couldn't resist racing against his cousin Henry, excited to have another boy around. And Jeb was winning, which felt good. He got picked on at school for being too slow at games and for having sisters with quicker fists.

When he and Henry rounded the house, Jeb stumbled against the coal chute, smearing black dust on his knickers. His daddy barreled over and raised his fist, but Uncle Abe's shadow fell across them. "Lea that boy alone," is all he said, and Jeb's daddy—taller and older—moved on. Jeb paid for it later, his daddy lashing him with his shaving belt, but whenever Jeb was think of how he skulked away, he smirked.

Then there was the day of his daddy's burial. When Uncle Abe announced at the cemetery after the service that he was going back to Florida, Jeb started to cry. Uncle Abe said he'd witnessed too much death. In his less than two years in the North, the people closest to him died: first his father and wife, then his two children, then his daughter's infant, then Jeb's daddy. Jeb was eight, old enough to control his tears. His daddy would have backhanded him for it. Uncle Abe handed him a blue handkerchief and patted his shoulder, saying, "You gon get through this, Jebby. You the head of the house now. Gotta be strong for your mammy and them." Jeb regretted not asking Uncle Abe to take him to Florida, to free him from that house of mule-headed women.

The memory drove Jeb to rummage for his fireproof box, which he hid from Faye. It housed the most personal of his belongings, such as his lucky fishhooks. His baby teeth. His muh's cornhusk pipe. The Indian head pennies his granpop slipped him, telling him to keep them hidden from Massa Silas. Bunched in the corner was Uncle Abe's handkerchief, now threadbare and gray. It was one of the earliest things Jeb saved.

Seeing that Segregation business in the news used to make Jeb think of his uncle. He'd wonder why a Colored man who'd known the so-called promised land would return to that. After the death of his muh, Jeb understood; without her presence, "home" felt like nowhere. It made him feel lost. He suspected the same for Verna, and he rang her up to tell her he'd go on her trip. Perhaps she had the right idea about getting away. And how *was* the South now, considering that Johnson signed away Segregation a decade ago?

He could also understand why his uncle said the North helped lots of Colored folks, but not enough. His daddy and other Colored men got factory jobs that paid far more than sharecropping, but Jeb could count on one hand the Colored women he knew who weren't domestics for white folks, just like in slavery times. His muh did it practically to her dying day. His sisters were still doing it.

As for himself, his muh used to tell him to study hard so he could become a doctor. He loved math, and his white teachers in Vauxhall suggested he think about carpentry. Then came Black Tuesday. Jeb quit school to make money. The best he could get was the job collecting trash. And those Italian boys he worked alongside? Many were in the same situation schoolwise. Some were newly arrived from the mother country and could barely speak English to boot. But they made twice as much and got promoted to drivers. Mr. Fiorelli praised Jeb and the other Colored men for their work, but they stayed stuck on the back of the truck. Within a few years, those fresh-off-the-boat crackers could afford a fleet of trucks to pass to their sons while Jeb could just give the Coleman name to his.

The major things he owned, after working and saving money most of his life, were a pickup truck and a fishing boat. And things people considered garbage.

Verna's next calls—he'd started answering them again—were to solidify travel plans. First she said they'd go around Christmastime. Then it was the first week of January. Just before New Year's, she fell sick with something undiagnosed that put her in the hospital. A quick calculation told Jeb that Uncle Abe must be around ninety. If he was still alive, he might not be for much longer.

Jeb drove the few blocks to Waldorf Place to search for his uncle's letter. He also hoped to find his muh's wedding ring. It had disappeared long ago, probably thanks to Verna's notoriously sticky fingers.

The house looked impossibly narrow with the yard vacant alongside it. The knee-high grass was flattened in the places where Jeb's things had sat, and there were clods of dirt everywhere. The gnarly oak around back, which had shed its leaves, seemed even more naked without its skirt of spare tires. The whole place had the feel of a graveyard whose headstones had been ripped out.

Shuddering, Jeb rushed into the house. The stillness disoriented him. At its fullest, Verna's and his children would be running in and out, and sometimes Rosine's too. The television would be blaring a wrestling or baseball match from the parlor, which his muh used for her bedroom. The sweetish haze of her pipe smoke would fill the air. The smell was now gone, and Verna had bought new furniture since he last visited. Every windowsill and ledge was crammed with her ceramic and brass figurines, history books, and old greeting cards.

Jeb started his search in the parlor but had trouble staying for long. Verna had gotten rid of their mother's cot and moved in her bed. It was almost as if their mother never existed. The upstairs bedrooms, unlike what Verna had told him, were empty. Thinking he could have very well used them, he fumed down the two flights of stairs to the basement. Crossing to the house's only toilet, he banged his knee. A crash sounded. He fumbled to turn on the lightbulb above the toilet and gasped.

The dank space, with its familiar smell of coal dust, was crammed with boxes, bins, and crates. He'd knocked over one with baby-doll clothes and miniature furniture. They looked too expensive for Verna's domestic's salary. Jeb sucked his teeth and shook his head, remembering how their mother used to harangue Verna about her stealing. As he was replacing the items, he saw what he wanted: his muh's old trunk. He hurried over, opened it, and jumped away. A ghost, is what he thought he saw. He chided himself for being a yellowbelly but his heart was pounding as he crept back. Seeing the pale unsmiling face inside, he forced a chuckle.

It was the large painted photograph of his daddy's mother, Adelaide. It used to hang in the parlor next to those of his daddy and granpop, both of which he found at the bottom of the trunk. Jeb shivered to see how young his daddy now looked. Jeb had outlived him by more than three decades. His granpop's face, on the other hand, used to strike him as ancient. Now, they had the same crevices in their cheeks and foreheads, the thick moustache, and white cottony hair.

Jeb hastily replaced the photos and hunted through the rest of the trunk. Neither Uncle Abe's letter nor his muh's wedding ring was there. The remaining personals were his muh's old pairs of eyeglasses and medical bills. He slipped the glasses into his overcoat pocket. He was no thief like Verna; he considered them heirlooms. Why did Verna need them anyway, after claiming the house and now the yard too?

In one of the boxes, Jeb was elated to find letters, but the first group, tied with a ribbon and thick as a dictionary, wasn't from his uncle. It was from Verna's husband, who'd written to her throughout his service during the Second World War. Jeb's chest tingled when he found more letters beneath, from Campbellton. There were four, postmarked in 1932. Jeb scanned them, quickly frowning. They were love letters to Verna, from a man also named Abe. "Speaking of marrying," he wrote, "you said when you get ready, you are coming home." She must have been lying even back then. What would she, who frequented Harlem nightclubs like the Savoy over Palladino's Bar in Vauxhall, want with a self-described country boy?

Jeb sucked his teeth, wondering if in her summer mood, she'd confused those letters for Uncle Abe's. Or perhaps it was her farmer Abe who she hoped to find in Florida now that her husband was dead, and she'd used their uncle's name to lure Jeb.

Still, he kept searching. Several other boxes revealed items he could make no sense of and which frankly made him feel an odd sort of way. Like one marked "Important!" It was full of blue bottle caps of different shapes and sizes. Another, mason jars, each stuffed with what looked to be saran-wrapped packets of pillow feathers. When he found a box half full of ketchup bottles, including one with a ripped label reading "Vauxhall Diner," it was time to leave.

Jeb was on I-95 headed south and he'd told no one, not even Faye or Booker. The news would surely have reached Verna in her hospital bed, and he didn't want to upset her in her condition. He told everyone he was going to Connecticut to fish.

The highway became one lane when Jeb entered Alabama from Columbus, Georgia, and the gray Buick up ahead was going no more than thirty. Yet he started humming that "Country Roads" song. In all of Verna's stories, she never mentioned the rust-colored dirt, which he'd found himself marveling at more than watching the bumpers ahead of him. The wide blue sky. The rolling green hills and endless pines. The Spanish moss dangling from furry oaks. The roadside signs advertising boiled peanuts and pigs' feet. Such a welcome change from New Jersey. Verna didn't mention the cotton fields either. Their family must have farmed them during slavery and after, but the plowed rows, where scattered white puffs stood defiant, captivated Jeb. There was also the intoxication of January heat and humidity, which he was experiencing for the first time. It soaked through his polyester shirt and forced him to lower his windows around South Carolina. The weather alone might have brought his uncle back.

Verna could have you hanging on to every wild word of her tales, but Jeb thought he might have connected more to where they came from if she mentioned those intimate details. Instead, she insisted on names, like the Alabama town where she claimed he was born. It shared the name of Spain's capital, she said, though she pronounced it more like *candid*. It wasn't on the road map—no surprise.

Jeb's mouth stretched into a smile as he entered Campbellton, Florida—population 316, according to the sign. Upon seeing the lone palm tree at the roadside, he felt the childlike glee Verna had expressed in the diner. He'd never seen a palm tree in person. As random as that one looked, it was an in-his-face message that he'd arrived.

Next to the tree was a small one-story brick building. A hand-painted sign advertised it as both the post office and city hall. As Jeb pulled into the near-empty parking lot, an old white man in overalls who was walking by peered into the truck. Jeb waved with a nod. The man responded by glaring.

Jeb chuckled nervously, telling himself the man was just ornery, not a card-carrying member of the Klan, but his hand shook as he got his brush from the glove compartment. He flipped down the mirror and stared at the burnt-caramel skin speckled with moles, the more-pepper-than-salt hair that had kinked up. He hadn't encountered a white Southerner before now. The gas station attendants along I-95 were all Colored. Would white folks see him as just another unwanted here?

He brushed his hair into something more presentable, the naps loosening and blending into waves. After straightening his shirt, he stepped out of the pickup. He could hardly breathe, and it wasn't just the humidity. He glanced between the two doorways, uncertain which to enter. Finally he decided on the post office. If his uncle was alive, he must still receive mail.

Inside, the white farmer-looking man was chatting and laughing with a postal clerk. Jeb was amazed that the clerk was a Colored girl with one of those Afros. She was dark and heavyset, reminding him of Bertha. Bertha—who he hadn't seen in some three decades, who was still his wife on paper. His stomach curdled as he remembered that Bertha's family was from Headland, about a half hour's drive away in Alabama. He fidgeted with his pocket lint, wondering if Bertha had family left there, if she ever wrote to them about him or his muh.

The postal clerk smiled at him. As Jeb stepped to the counter, the white man remained there with his package. Jeb felt the man's gaze crawl from his head to his shoes. Angling his back to him, Jeb hesitated, not wanting to mention the Coleman name. Somewhere in his mind, he knew that girl couldn't be related to Bertha and that he was trying to delay the inevitable: hearing that his uncle no longer lived in Campbellton or that he was dead.

"Afternoon," he mumbled. Recalling from the gas stations that Southern folks were extra polite, he added a "ma'am." "I'm lookin for somebody. Maybe you knew—*know* him. His name was Abe."

The white man grunted. "This Abe got a last name? Lots of Abes around."

Was I askin you, cracker?

He removed the old gray handkerchief from his shirt pocket, glad he'd tamed the impulse to speak. *This ain't New Jersey,* he reminded himself. *Don't go gettin yourself strung up on your first day down here.*

Running his fingers across the frayed material, he squeezed out his uncle's name. Stopped breathing as the white man told him he died.

The postal clerk shook her head. "Naw, Mr. Hinson, Abe Coleman live up around the old Mill Road."

The white man jammed his thumb over his shoulder. "Laverne, I used to see that man every year on the highway with his peanut stand. Damn near hit him one time." He slid his face into Jeb's field of view. "He'd be about my age, wouldn't you say?"

Jeb's mouth gaped like the many fish he'd caught. His face had started to drip.

"He ain't dead, I tell you! He just don't get out much no more. He married to Doreen from my mama's Bible study." She glanced at Jeb and pointed to the left. "Two blocks up, take the road on your left. Three or four houses past the railroad tracks, you gon see a bright yellow house on the right. Can't miss it."

He thanked her and turned to leave.

"Sir, you kin to Mr. Coleman?"

He paused. "Just passin through, ma'am."

A white woman entered with packages heaped onto a baby carriage, asking Laverne for help. Jeb slipped out and rushed to the pickup, his knees barking. As he backed out of the parking space, he almost collided with another pickup entering the lot.

The face that appeared in his rearview was white and scowling. That face leaned out of the truck, yelling, "Watch where you're goin, nigger!"

So some things hadn't changed.

"Yessir, can I help you?"

The woman's voice was soft and sweet but she blocked the doorway with her stout frame. Her age was hard to discern, but she looked too young to be married to a ninety-year-old. She wore a patterned smock and cutoff dungarees.

The smell of fried chicken punched Jeb like a storm cloud, smelling as good as Faye's. His stomach rumbled. He could see Faye in their kitchen, sulking as he put on his shoes to go to the diner. He missed her food.

As he started to speak, he nearly stuttered like his oldest boy.

"I was told a Abe Coleman live here."

She didn't budge. "Yes?"

He cleared his throat, even though it didn't need clearing. "I'm his nephew. From New Jersey."

Her hand flew to her mouth. She stepped onto the porch and pulled Jeb to her ample squishy bosom, pinning his arms. Her head barely came to his chest, like Faye's, and her hair had that same thick smell of Dax grease. She released him, all smiles.

"My goodness gracious! I never realized he still had family up there. I'm Doreen, his wife. You come on in."

She opened the door wide and Jeb raised his brows. He'd heard about Southern hospitality, and he grew up in a time when it was unheard of to lock doors, even on one's car, but a stranger had never invited him in like that. He felt uncomfortable for Doreen. She should have questioned if he was who he said he was. Or perhaps she saw his resemblance to the man waiting inside.

He took a shaky step across the threshold. It took a moment for his eyes to adjust to the dimness. Then Jeb saw him: a cinnamon-colored man dozing in a rocking chair, a trail of drool on his chin. He appeared to be drowning in his overalls and white long-sleeved shirt. Did all the men in Campbellton wear overalls?

That man looked too fragile to be his uncle. Maybe Campbellton had more than one Abe Coleman? But as Jeb's gaze swept around the modestly furnished room, he saw the enormous framed photograph above the sofa. The unsmiling woman—skin pale enough to make her look white, or like a ghost.

"Nice picture, ain't it?" Doreen said. "That's his mama."

"I know. Adelaide. She was my granma."

Doreen's eyes crinkled as she smiled. "Y'all really is kin."

She walked over to the old man and roused him. He looked around, dazed, clutching the arms of the chair. His eyes were like those of a bird of prey. They homed in on Jeb.

"Who that, Reenie?"

Doreen shouted into his ear. "That's your nephew, sugar."

"Say what?"

Doreen glanced at Jeb. "Son, what did you say your name was?"

The man was pushing her aside and standing up, squinting. Jeb could see plain over his head. Why had he thought his uncle would be taller after all that time? He took a step back, feeling winded.

"That you, Pappy?" the man was saying.

Jeb fumbled for words as Doreen flashed an apologetic look. "He think just 'bout every man he see these days is his daddy."

She grabbed the man's arm but he shook her off. "I know who my pappy is, Reenie."

Jeb gasped as his heel made contact with the front door. He hadn't realized he'd backed up that far. The old man moved in on him. Clasped Jeb's clammy hand. Placed his head against his shoulder. The head had surprising weight and heat. Jeb's eyes watered, and he told himself it was because of the Old Spice. He hated Old Spice.

A sharp pain came to the left side of his chest, just below his clavicle. Before he could worry if it was the first sign of a heart attack, Doreen jolted him again by ringing a bell. Just as fast, the old man released his hand and strode over to Doreen. She motioned for Jeb to stay put as she led her husband down the hall.

Jeb plopped onto the couch beneath Adelaide's stony gaze and glanced at his shirt. There was a half-moon of sweat there, from the old man's head. The pain in his chest had increased, and he felt his heart beating faster, causing him to sweat more. He pulled Uncle Abe's handkerchief from his pocket and stared at it, wheezing. His uncle was nothing like he remembered. His uncle did not—*could* not, perhaps—remember him or anything about the past. He couldn't tell Jeb how he'd fared with the burden of so much loss.

Doreen shuffled back into the room in her slippers and straightened the crocheted throw on the rocking chair, saying that her bell worked like a charm every time. It got Abe to settle down, reminding him that supper was ready. She glanced at Jeb and her mouth dropped open.

"You okay, son? What's your name again?"

He mopped his face, avoiding eye contact. "Jeb."

"Can I make you a plate, sugar?"

"I just ate." He tried to slow his breathing. "How long he been like—" He twiddled a finger next to his head.

Doreen sighed and sat on the rocker, making it creak. "This thing started about ten years ago. But the doctor say he got good health besides. Still get up at the crack of dawn every day to check them peanuts out back." She laughed, staring at her small hands. "You oughta see him go. That's why he was sleep when you came."

After a pause, Jeb said, "So, he never talked about us?"

Doreen looked away, shaking her head. "Naw. He never talked too much about New Jersey at all, and I ain't wanna press him. He said he left a lotta death and sadness behind. I presumed everybody was gone."

Jeb grimaced, folding and unfolding the handkerchief. Doreen honored the silence. Jeb struggled to put together his next question, thinking about what he'd experienced so far in Campbellton: the bigot in the parking lot, the Confederate flags, the way the town's residents changed from white to black once he crossed the railroad tracks.

"What is it—what *was* it—about this place, do you think, that made him want to stay down here? I mean, we had it better up North in some ways, but . . ."

A smile spread across her face, making her seem girlish. "Well, son, he found me."

Something like guilt mixed with jealousy surged through him. He worked his jaw, thinking about Faye. Faye—who had shared a home with him for thirty years, and who was his woman on the side before that, for most of the seven he lived with Bertha. Faye, who continued to cook dinner for him even as he skipped out to the diner. He knew she suspected him of having a new woman on the side, and he hadn't even thought to calm her worries by sharing his true travel plans.

And Bertha—she used to fill him with a lust that scared him. It made him place his wishes above his muh's, and he wasn't used to that. As hot-blooded as Bertha used to make him feel, though, he reunited with her just once after she left.

The only woman—the only person, really—who had had the power to keep him someplace was his muh, and now she was gone. He felt a stinging in his eyes and balled the handkerchief in his fists.

"I spose you must be tired, Jeb, drivin all this way. Wasn't expectin guests, but you welcome to stay long as you need. We got us a spare room in the back. You'll stay, won't you, son?"

His insides screamed no. But he reminded himself of his age. If you didn't count the knees, he felt no different than when he was sixteen, but he admitted to himself how tired he was. There couldn't be a hotel or even motel for miles. He hadn't thought that far in his travel plans.

"Yes, I'll stay. Thank you, ma'am."

He brought in his overnight bag from the truck and followed Doreen down the hall. He glanced around for a collection like his and Verna's, but the house was spare. It had so few furnishings that there was an echo. The back room Doreen led him to contained a twin-size bed, wooden chair, and ironing board. The solitary wall decoration was a wooden cross.

Doreen apologized for the room being a mess, but the only thing out of order to Jeb was the lumberjack shirt tossed over the chair and the pile of folded clothes on the bed. Doreen transferred it to the ironing board. Before shutting the door softly behind her, she told Jeb the bathroom was up the hall next to the kitchen.

A musty smell rose from the crocheted quilt on the bed as Jeb sat on it. He held his head in his hands, thinking about his feeble-minded granpop. Perhaps his daddy would have gone senile too had he lived long enough. He wondered if the same would happen to him someday soon.

More questions that would never be answered ran through his mind. Why had his uncle lied about having no family left? How had he dealt with Segregation after New Jersey? What would Jeb's life have looked like had his uncle taken him to Florida?

I wouldn't have shacked up with Bertha.

Jeb did it because his muh didn't like her, and he wanted to make his own decision for once. Because, while he might have been the sole man *in* the house on Waldorf before his sons were born, his muh never stopped presiding over it. His muh henpecked him over Bertha, and he took to yelling at her for the first time in his life. After Bertha ran off, Jeb couldn't put up with the children crying and carrying on, asking when their mother was coming back. That's why he moved in with Faye, he told his friends. The real reason was too shameful: without Bertha between him and his muh, he might have turned his fists on her, just like his daddy did.

Uncle Abe probably never hit a woman.

But, he told himself, without Bertha, his children wouldn't exist. And even though few of them kept in touch, their visits reminded him he hadn't done such a bad job as a daddy. He'd kept them clothed and fed, and two had finished high school. They were all employed, and none of his daughters was cleaning houses.

And I'd prolly be wearin overalls right now.

He snickered, wiping his eyes. He would also probably have a farm. He wouldn't have become a trash man. Wouldn't have learned to see the value in unwanted things.

The thought of it made him itch to get back home. He could see his collection rotting there in the woods. His stomach growled, and he thought of the Hungry Man Special at the Vauxhall Diner. What he really wanted, though, was Faye's fried chicken. His knees ached for the down-home ointment she made, which cooled and soothed his joints without that Ben-Gay smell.

He grabbed his bag, heaved himself off the bed, then paused. A feeling of unsettlement came over him—the same as when he saw the bare yard on Waldorf. He was about to stuff the lumberjack shirt into his bag when he visualized Verna doing likewise with her baby-doll furniture, the ketchup bottle, his muh's wedding ring. He fingered the soft red material, which had the slightest scent of aftershave, suddenly understanding why Verna stole. And he was no thief.

Remembering his camera, he tossed the shirt back onto the chair and dug through his bag. He told himself that as soon as he got back home, he would fabricate a story for Verna. He would say that their uncle never wrote because he had difficulty establishing himself in Florida, that he wanted no more visits because he was ill, and that he had a good woman looking after him. If Jeb told the truth, Verna might think he was hiding some historical detail their uncle had shared. She might try to come see him herself. Jeb wanted to spare her the disappointment. And who knew what she might try to pilfer?

He'd give Faye and his friends the real version, though, focusing on the heat and how hospitable everyone was, the red dirt, the lone bolls of cotton, and the overalls everywhere. A surge passed through him as he considered sharing the story of the trip with his children too. When they next visited, Faye wouldn't have to prompt him to mention the latest trout he'd caught or the bears and deer he'd felled. Those stories made his children look like they were sleeping with their eyes open. Jeb even considered telling all of his children, whoever was willing to listen, about Uncle Abe. The man was, after all, their uncle too.

He left the room and found Doreen in the kitchen eating fried chicken and mashed potatoes opposite her husband. The old man was slumped over, snoring softly. Spotting Jeb, Doreen put a finger to her lips. She tiptoed out of the room and Jeb followed into the living room.

"Everything okay, son?"

Jeb cleared his throat, which had started burning. "I'm gonna get goin." He ignored her widened eyes. "Best to hit the road before the sun go all the way down. Before I leave, though, can I take a picture of him?"

"You sure? It's so dark out already."

"Yeah, I got a flash."

He pointed at the framed photograph of his granma, knowing Verna would demand hard evidence, which she expected from everybody's stories but hers.

"And I want her in it, too."

Doreen gave him a funny look but consented. He removed the photograph and carried it outside. Like his childhood home, the yard sat alongside the house, but the similarities stopped there. There was white sand, not grass. A vat stood near the back of the house, along with a signboard reading PEANUTS FOR SALE. A hedgerow divided the yard and the field beyond.

Jeb placed Adelaide's photograph atop a chair Doreen brought. She returned inside and led out a sleepy-looking Abe. She motioned for Jeb's Polaroid but Abe scowled, asking why she wouldn't join them. After she left to get a neighbor, Jeb glanced at the old man, who was brushing crumbs from the bib of his overalls. Jeb felt the unanswered questions at the back of his throat. He pulled the gray handkerchief from his pocket and got Abe's attention with it.

"Say, man," he said, his voice hoarse, "you don't remember—"

The old man's brows furrowed but he looked up and smiled at the commotion from next door. Doreen was coming across the yard with a dark-skinned teenage boy as short as she was.

"Reenie! What you doin there with my pappy?"

The pain returned to Jeb's chest. Doreen gently reminded Abe that they were taking a photograph. She positioned him closer to the chair, which she took her place behind. Jeb stood on the other side. The boy told them to cheese but Jeb couldn't bring himself to lift his lips. The three photos the camera spat out, dark despite the flash, revealed that none of them had smiled. Their expressions were just as sober as Adelaide's.

Jeb gave one of the Polaroids to Doreen, who walked him to his truck, saying, "Wish you coulda stayed longer, son. But I understand. You got a wife and kids?"

He nudged a pebble with his shoe and nodded. *Yeah, but . . .*

"That's good. I got a son from my first husband who passed, bless his soul. I wish Abe ain't have to bury the both of his so young. Wish I coulda gave him some more, but we was too old for that." Jeb glanced in time to see her eyes water. He thrust the handkerchief at her but she shook her head and smiled up at him. "Treasure them, mm?"

His throat was on fire. Unable to look at her, he got into the truck, saying, "I never found out why they went up North in the first place. Did he ever tell you?"

"Well, well. I don't quite remember, now. You know, back in those days, with the boll weevils destroyin crops and everythang . . . actually, you know what? I think he said somethin 'bout . . . was it somebody accused him and his daddy of stealin clothes from a white person's yard? Somethin like that."

Jeb's eyes bulged. Verna wasn't lying, for a change? He bellowed a laugh that made his own eyes wet. Doreen looked confused, even more so as his laughter morphed into hacking sobs. Tears were everywhere. Running from his eyes. Slipping into the corners of his mouth. Pooling in his goatee. He scrambled to start the engine so he could hightail it, but he dropped his keys. By the time his frantic fingers located them, Uncle Abe stood at the window with Doreen, holding out a blue striped handkerchief.

Openmouthed, chest still heaving, Jeb took it.

"It's gon be alright," his uncle said, his eyes starting to well.

Chills ran down Jeb's neck. Perhaps his uncle's mind had flashed back, after all the loss of memory. But then Abe looked over at Adelaide's photo, saying, "Mama gone now, but you gon be alright, Pappy."

Jeb felt his lips pulling down. The old man hunched his shoulders and started crying himself. Doreen pulled Abe gently away from the truck, motioning for Jeb to get going. Jeb tore out of the yard, one hand on the wheel, the other swiping at his face. When his sobs had turned to sniffles, he glanced at his hands on the wheel and saw he had a handkerchief in each, one old and one new. He stared so long that he almost swerved across the divider line.

He considered saving them to add to his fireproof box. On second thought, seeing them later would only remind him of what he already wanted to forget: the uncle who didn't rescue him as a boy and can't rescue him now. He considered tossing them out of the window and leaving the past in the South, for good, when he remembered Verna. The handkerchiefs would be worth something to her.

Soon after crossing into Alabama, he was tucking the handkerchiefs into his shirt pocket when he slammed on the brakes in the middle of the road. The car behind him swiveled around him, honking. His heart was racing as he squinted in the rearview, scanning the roadside for what he thought he'd seen. He pulled sharply to the shoulder, then stumbled out of the truck and rooted through his bag. Camera in hand, he jogged back a few paces.

His eyes hadn't fooled him. There it was: a signpost at the roadside with a teeny metal plaque: MADRID, POP. 202. He aimed the Polaroid and snapped a photo but the flash refused to work. Jeb shook the camera, pressed the shutter again and again until he'd used up the last of his film pack. Still no flash. Every photo came out nearly black.

LAUREN GROFF

The Wind

FROM *The New Yorker*

PRETEND, THE MOTHER had said when she crept to her daughter's room in the night, that tomorrow is just an ordinary day.

So the daughter had risen as usual and washed and made toast and warm milk for her brothers, and while they were eating she emptied their schoolbags into the toy chest and filled them with clothes, a toothbrush, one book for comfort. The children moved silently through the black morning, put on their shoes outside on the porch. The dog thumped his tail against the doghouse in the cold yard but was old and did not get up. The children's breath hovered low and white as they walked down to the bus stop, a strange presence trailing them in the road.

When they stopped by the mailbox, the younger brother said in a very small voice, Is she dead?

The older boy hissed, Shut up, you'll wake him, and all three looked at the house hunched up on the hill in the chilly dark, the green siding half installed last summer, the broken front window covered with cardboard.

The sister touched the little one's head and said, whispering, No, no, don't worry, she's alive. I heard her go out to feed the sheep, and then she left for work. The boy leaned like a cat into her hand.

He was six, his brother was nine, and the girl was twelve. These were my uncles and my mother as children.

Much later, she would tell me the story of this day at those times when it seemed as if her limbs were too heavy to move and she stood staring into the refrigerator for long spells, unable to decide what to make for dinner. Or when the sun would cycle into one window and out the other and she would sit on her bed unable to do anything other than breathe. Then I would sit quietly beside her, and she would tell the story the same way every time, as if ripping out something that had worked its roots deep inside her.

It was bitterly cold that day and the wind was supposed to rise, but for now all was airless, waiting. After some time, the older brother said, Kids are going to make fun of you, your face all mashed up like that.

My mother touched her eye and winced at the pain there, then shrugged.

They were so far out in the country, the bus came for them first, and the ride to town was long. At last it showed itself, yellow as sunrise at the end of the road. Its slowness as it pulled up was agonizing. My mother's heart began to beat fast. She let her brothers get on before her and told them to sit in the front seats. Mrs. Palmer, the driver, was a stout lady who played the organ at church, and whose voice when she shouted at the naughty boys in the back was high like soprano singing. She looked at my mother as she shut the bus door, then said in her singsong voice, You got yourself a shiner there, Michelle.

The bus hissed up from its crouch and lumbered off.

I know, my mother said. Listen, we need your help.

And when Mrs. Palmer considered her, then nodded, my mother asked quickly if she could please drop the three of them off when she picked up the Yoder kids. Their mother would be waiting there for them. Please, she said quietly.

The boys' faces were startled, they hadn't known, then an awful acceptance moved across them.

There was a silence before Mrs. Palmer said, Oh, honey, of course, and she shuffled her eyes back to the road. And I won't mark on the sheet that you were missing, neither. So they won't get it together to call your house until second period or so, give you a little time. She looked into the mirror at the boys and said cheerfully, I got a blueberry muffin. Anyone want a blueberry muffin?

We're okay, thanks, my mother said, and sat beside her younger brother, who rested his head on her arm. The fields spun by, lightening to gray, the faintest of gold at the tops of the trees. Just before the bus slowed to meet the cluster of little Yoders, yawning, shifting from foot to foot, my mother saw the old Dodge tucked into a shallow ditch, headlights off.

Thank you, she said to Mrs. Palmer, as they got off, and Mrs. Palmer said, No thanks needed, only decent thing to do. I'll pray for you, honey. I'll pray for all of you; we're all sinners who yearn for salvation. For the first time since she rose that morning, my mother was glad, because a person as full of music as the bus driver surely had the ear of God.

The three children ran through the exhaust from the bus as it rose and roared off.

They slid into the warm car where their mother clutched the steering wheel. She was very pale, but her hair was in its familiar small bouffant. My mother thought of the pain it must have cost my grandmother to do up her hair in the mirror so early in the morning, and felt ill.

You did good, babies, my grandmother said as well as she could, her mouth as smashed as it was. She turned the car. A calf galloped beside them for a few steps in the paddock by the road, and my younger uncle laughed and pressed his hand to the glass.

This is not the time for laughing, my uncle Joseph said sternly. He would grow up to be a grave man, living in an obsessively clean, bare efficiency, teaching mathematics at a community college.

Leave him be, Joey, my mother said. She said in a lower voice to her mother, Poor Ralphie thought you were dead.

Not dead yet, my grandmother said. By the skin of my teeth. She tried to smile at the boys in the mirror.

Where we going? Ralphie said. I didn't know we were going anywhere.

To see my friend in the city, my grandmother said. We'll call when we find a phone out of town. She put a cigarette in her mouth but fumbled with the lighter in her shaky hands until my mother took it and struck the flame for her.

They were going the long way so they wouldn't have to drive past the house again, and my mother watched the minute hand of the clock on the dash, feeling each second pulling her tighter inside.

Faster, Mama, she said quietly, and her mother said without looking at her, Last thing we need's being stopped by one of his buddies. I got to pick up my pay first.

The hospital loomed on the hill beside the river, elegant in its stone façade, and my grandmother parked around back, by the dumpster. Can't risk leaving you, she said. Come with, and bring your stuff. But when she began to walk she could only mince a little at a time, and my mother moved close, so she could lean on her, and together they went faster.

They went up the steps through the back door into the kitchen. A man in a ridiculous hairnet, like a green mushroom, was carrying a basin of peeled potatoes in a bath of water. Without looking he barked, You're late, Ruby. But then the children caught his eye, and he saw the state of them, and put the potatoes down and reached out and touched my mother's face gently with his hot rough hand. Lord. She get it, too? he said. She's just a kid.

My mother told herself not to cry; she always cried when strangers were tender with her.

Put herself between us. She's a good girl, my grandmother said.

I'll kill the bastard myself, the man said. I'll strangle him if you want me to. Just say the word.

No need, my grandmother said. We're going. But I got to have my check, Dougie. All we got is four dollars and half a tank of gas, and I don't know what I'm going to do if that's all we got to live on.

Can't. No way, Dougie said. Check gets sent to the house, you know this. You filled the form. You checked the box.

My grandmother looked him directly in the face, perhaps for the first time, because she was a timid woman whose voice was low, who made herself a shadow in the world. He sighed and said, See what I can manage, then he disappeared into the office.

Now through the door of the cafeteria there came two women moving fast. One was a plump pretty teenager chewing gum, the cashier, and the other was Doris, my grandmother's friend, freckled and squat and blunt. For extra money, she made exquisite cakes, with flowers like irises and delphiniums in frosting. It was hard to believe a woman as tough as she was could hold such delicacy inside her.

Oh, Ruby, Doris said. It got even worse, huh. Jesus, take a look at you.

Shoved his gun in my mouth this time, my grandmother said. She didn't bother to whisper, because the kids had been there, they had seen it. Thought I was going to be shot. But, no, he just knocked out a few teeth. My grandmother gingerly lifted her lip with a finger to show her swollen bloodied gums. When Doris stepped forward to hug her, my grandmother winced away from her touch, and Doris took the hem of her shirt and lifted it, and said, Oh, shit, when she saw the bruises marbling my grandmother's stomach and ribs.

Better go up and get looked at by a doctor, the cashier said, her damp pink mouth hanging open. That looks real ugly.

No time, my grandmother said. It's already too dangerous to show up here.

In silence, Doris took her cracked leather purse from the hook and put all the cash in her wallet in my mother's hand. The cashier blew a bubble, considering, then sighed and pulled down her own purse and did the same.

Bless you, ladies, my grandmother said. Then she took a shuddering breath and said, In a way, it was my fault. I thought I'd stay until we finished the shearing. You know he's rough with the sheep. I wanted to save them some blood.

Mama? my younger uncle said by the door.

No, don't you do that nonsense, you know that's not right, Doris said, fiercely. It's his fault. Nobody else but his.

Mama? Ralphie said again, louder. It's him, he's here. He pointed out the window, where they could see just the nose of the cruiser coming to a stop behind my grandmother's Dodge.

Get down, Doris said, and they all crouched on the tile. They heard a car door slam. Doris, moving faster than seemed possible, went to the door and locked it. Half a second later the knob was rattled, and then there was a pounding, and then my mother couldn't hear for the blood rushing in her ears.

Doris picked up the pan of potatoes and came to the window wearing a furious face. What in hell you want? she shouted. Dare to show your face here.

There was a murmuring, then Doris shouted down through the glass, Not here, up in the ER getting looked at. Quite a number you done on her. Couldn't hardly walk. She said this nastily, glowering. Then she turned her back on the window and went to the stainless-steel table in the middle of the room, where the cashier watched out the window over Doris's shoulder.

They heard an engine starting up, and at last the cashier said in a thick voice, Okay, he got in and now he's driving around. But, like, when he figures out you're not up in the ER he's gonna just come into the kitchen through the cafeteria, you know. Like, there's no lock on that door and we can't stop him.

Doris called for Dougie in a sharp voice, and Dougie hurried out of the office with an envelope, looking flushed, a little shame-faced. He had been hiding in there, my mother understood.

I won't forget your kindness, all of you, my grandmother said, but my mother had to take the paycheck because my grand-mother's hands were shaking too much.

Send us a postcard when you make it, Doris said. Get a move on.

My grandmother leaned on my mother again and they went out to the car as fast as they could, and it started, and slid the back way, down by the green bridge over the river. When they had twisted out of sight of the hospital, my grandmother stopped the car, opened her door, and vomited on the road.

She shut the door. All right, she said, wiping her mouth gingerly with a finger, and started the car up again.

My mother saw on the dashboard clock that it was just past eight. The teachers were doing roll call right now. Soon a girl would collect the sheets and take them to the office, where someone, thinking they were doing the right thing, would notice that all three of the kids were gone, and call their absence in, first to the house, where the phone would ring and ring. But then, getting hold of nobody, they would call it in to the station, and it would be radi-oed out immediately to him. And he would know that not only was his wife gone but his kids were gone with her. They had an hour, maybe a little more, my mother calculated. An hour could maybe take them out of his jurisdiction. She told her mother this, pressing her foot on an imaginary accelerator. My grandmother did drive faster now through the back roads. Gusts of sharp wind pressed the car.

For some time, they were strung into their separate thoughts. My mother counted the cash. A hundred and twenty-three, she said with surprise.

Doris's grocery money, I bet, my grandmother said. Bless her.

Ralphie said sadly, I wish we could've brought Butch.

Yeah, just what we need, your stinky old dog, Joey said.

Can we go back someday to get him? Ralphie said, but my grandmother was silent.

My mother turned around to look at her brothers and said, bitterly, We're never going back. I hope it all burns down with him inside.

Hey, the little boy said weakly. That's not nice. He's my dad.

Mine, too, but I'd be happy if he eats rat poison, Uncle Joseph said. Then he bent forward and looked at the floor, then at the seat beside him, and said, Oh, jeez. Oh, no. Where's your knapsack, Ralphie?

Uncle Ralphie looked all around and said at last, with his eyes wide, I took it into the kitchen but I think I left it.

There was a long moment before this blow hit them all, at once.

Oh, this is bad, my mother said.

I'm so sorry, Ralphie said, starting to cry. Mama, I gotta go pee.

Surely Doris will hide it, my grandmother said.

Hold your bladder, Ralphie. But what if she doesn't find it in time? my mother said. What if she doesn't see it before he does? And he knows that you took us. And he gets on the radio for them all to keep an eye out for us. They could be looking for us now.

My grandmother cursed softly and looked at the rearview mirror. They were whipping terribly fast on the country curves now. The boys, in the back, were clutching the door handles.

My uncle Joey, in a display of self-control that made him seem like a tiny ancient man, said, It's okay, Ralphie, you didn't mean to leave your bag.

My younger uncle reached out his little hand, and Joseph, who hated all show of affection, held it. Ralphie had a fishing accident when I was a teenager, and my cold, dry uncle Joseph fell apart at the funeral, sobbing and letting snot run down his face, all twisted grotesquely in pain.

Mama, we got to get out of the state, my mother said. We'll be safer across state lines.

Shush now, I need to think, my grandmother said. Her hands had gone white on the wheel.

No, what we got to do is ditch the car, my uncle Joseph said, they'll be looking for it. Probably already are. We got to find a parking lot that's full of cars already, like a grocery store or something.

Then what do we do? my grandmother said in a strangled voice. We walk to Vermont? She laughed, a sharp sound.

No, then we take a bus, Joseph said in his hard, rational voice. We get on a bus and they can't find us then.

Okay, my mother said. Okay, yeah, Joey's right, that's a good plan. Good thinking. We're fifteen minutes out from Albany, they got a bus station, I know where it is.

It was her father who had once driven her there in his cruiser, because her middle-school choir was taking a bus down to New York City for a competition. He had stopped on the way for strawberry milk shakes. This was a good memory she had of him.

Fine, my grandmother said. Yes. I can't think of nothing else. I guess this will be our change of plans. But, for the first time since the night before, tears welled up in her eyes and began dripping down her bruised cheeks and she had to slow the car to see through them.

And then she started breathing crazily, and leaned forward until her forehead rested on the wheel, and the car stopped suddenly in the middle of the road. The wind howled around it.

Mama, we need to drive, my mother said. We need to drive now. We need to go.

I really, really have to pee, Ralphie said.

It's okay, it's okay, it's okay, my grandmother whispered. It's just that my body is not really listening to me. I can't move anything right now. I can't move my feet. Oh, God.

It's fine, my mother said softly. Don't worry. You're fine. You can take the time you need to calm down.

And at this moment my mother saw with terrible clarity that everything depended upon her. The knowledge was heavy on the nape of her neck, like a hand pressing down hard. And what came to her was the trail of bread crumbs from the fairy tale her mother used to tell her in the dark when she was tiny, and it was just the two of them in the bedroom, no brothers in this life, not yet, and the soft, kind moon was shining in the window and her father was downstairs, worlds away. So my mother said, in a soothing voice, So what we're going to do is, Mama's going to take a deep breath and we're going to drive down into Albany, over the tracks, take a right at the feed place, go down by the big brick church, and park in that lot behind it. It's only a block or two from the station. We're going to get out and walk as fast as we can and I'll go in and buy the tickets on the first bus out to wherever, and if we have time I can get us some food to eat on the bus. And we'll get on the bus, and it will slide us out of here so fast. It'll go wherever it's going, but eventually we'll get to the city. And the city is so enormous we can just hide there. And there are museums and parks and movie theaters and subways and everything in the city. And Mama will get a job and we'll go to school and we'll get an apartment and there'll be no more stupid sheep to take care of and it'll be safe. No more having to run out to the barn to sleep. Nobody can hurt us in the city, okay, boys? We're going to have a life that will be so boring, every day it will be the same, and it is going to be wonderful. Okay?

By now my mother had pried my grandmother's hands off the steering wheel and was chafing the blood back into them. Okay? All we need is for you to take a deep breath.

You can do it, Mama, Joseph said. Ralphie covered his face with both hands. The grasses outside danced under the heavy wind, brushed flat, ruffled against the fur of the fields.

Then my mother prayed with her eyes open, her hands spread on the dash, willing the car forward, and my grandmother slowly put the car back into gear and, panting, began to drive.

This was the way my mother later told the story, down to the smallest detail, as though dreaming it into life: the forsythia budding gold on the tips of the bushes, the last snow rotten in the ditches, the faces of the houses still depressed by winter, the gray clouds that hung down heavily as her mother drove into the valley of the town, the wind picking up so that the flag's rivets on the pole snapped crisply outside the bus station, where they waited on a metal bench that seared their bottoms and they shuddered from more than the cold. The bus roaring to life, wreathed in smoke, carrying them away. She told it almost as though she believed this happier version, but behind her words I see the true story, the sudden wail and my grandmother's blanched cheeks shining in red and blue and the acrid smell of piss. How just before the door opened and she was grabbed by the hair and dragged backward, my grandmother turned to her children and tried to smile, to give them this last glimpse of her.

The three children survived. Eventually they would save themselves, struggling into lives and loves far from this place and this moment, each finding a kind of safe harbor, jobs and people and houses empty of violence. But always inside my mother there would blow a silent wind, a wind that died and gusted again, raging throughout her life, touching every moment she lived after this one. She tried her best, but she couldn't help filling me with this same wind. It seeped into me through her blood, through every bite of food she made for me, through every night she waited, shaking with fear, for me to come home by curfew, through every scolding, everything she forbade me to say or think or do or be, through all the ways she taught me how to move as a woman in the world. She was far from being the first to find it blowing through her, and of course I will not be the last. I look around and can see it in so many other women, passed down from a time beyond history, this wind that is dark and ceaseless and raging within.

The Hollow

FROM *The New Yorker*

JONAH VALENTE HAD been an object of amusement to Jack and his college classmates, and presumably he had gone on being one to other people ever since. An awkward, intense, muscle-bound young man, the sort you could imagine crashing through a wall accidentally, he had had the dim, muddled quality of students recruited to play football at the school, who either didn't measure up academically or didn't believe they did. Valente's claim to fame, what had made him a *figure* on campus—one of that subset of maybe fifty classmates who, possessing some extravagance of character, defined the larger composite character by which the student body understood itself—came from his having abruptly quit football during sophomore year to take up painting, a passion he had developed apparently out of the blue and with a single-minded earnestness that embarrassed his more sophisticated classmates, who knew to disguise their sincerity. When Valente left the football team, changed his major, and began hanging out with a group of druggy slackers who loitered around the Visual Arts department like sun-drunk flies, the school paper ran a feature on his unusual transformation and he acquired the nickname Beaux Arts. This got shortened to B.A., and then Baa, Balente, Ballantino, the Baleen Whale, simply the Whale, and, by a different route altogether, Picasso. A year later, after spending the summer in Florence on a painting scholarship, Valente got kicked out of school. According to rumors at the time, his expulsion had to do with drugs, but Valente maintained among his friends that it was the school's way of punishing him for quitting football. Jack had no basis for judg-

ment. Nor did he really care. You knew very little about your classmates in the end, their real lives and disappointments and hopes,
and what you did know was mostly hearsay, and often dubious and
even somewhat fantastical.

In the indolent, halcyon days before graduation, Jack had
thought about Valente exactly once. He had been lying completely
stoned in a friend's common room, gazing up at the crown mold-
ings, when he realized that people called Valente "the Whale" not
simply because of the association pattern in certain words but in
reference to the story of Jonah. When this insight lit up within
him, it seemed to glow for a minute with a profound and inartic-
ulable meaning. Then he forgot it, and he probably would have
forgotten Valente, too, if years later he hadn't moved to the rural
area where, according to their mutual friend Daniel, Valente lived
at home with his mother. Jack's house was in the next county over,
half an hour away by car, but he was a newcomer and he didn't
know anyone else yet.

He had moved there with Sophie. "Sophie's choice," he jok-
ingly told people. Really, they had both made the choice. But
then, shortly after buying the house and leaving the city, he had,
in quick succession, lost his new job and lost Sophie. She hadn't
left him because of the job (at a large financial firm), though
she didn't like his new job or believe that he liked it. Apparently, she
didn't like their new life in the country, either. Sometimes
she called herself a journalist, but that wasn't quite right. She
wrote—nonfiction, she had a degree in it—but she picked up magazine assignments infrequently and had trouble finishing pieces.
Some fire was missing in her, she'd be the first to admit. She bit
off more than she could chew, spent months diving deeply into
projects, then found herself paralyzed, unable to write a word. Jack
had long ago stopped giving her advice. He simply assumed that
he would earn the money, and she would (or would not) figure
out how she wanted to spend her time, and either way they would
have kids and a home, a garden, friends, vacations, and so on.
Buying the house had taken the better part of a year. Then in the
space of four weeks everything had collapsed.

Sophie said that her feelings for him hadn't changed, but she
now understood—it had surfaced inside her with a force she could
scarcely describe—that something was wrong, wrong for her, anyway, with the life they had laid out before them, and if she didn't

get out now she never would. Jack pointed out that their new life
had hardly begun. But she was unshakable. "I know myself," she
said. "Once I settle in, once we have a kid and the rest, I'll never
leave." She looked not exactly desperate but as if she were drowning in a substance his words were forcing her beneath. "Please."
She placed her fingers on his forearm. And he didn't argue. Better to give people space. Either they came back to you, he rea-
soned, or they disappeared into their own confusion and misery.
With people he didn't like, he thought of it as giving them enough
rope. With Sophie, it was the usual indecision, the usual flighti-
ness. That's what he believed.

The house was in Trevi, a small hamlet upriver from the city, out
past the suburbs, picturesque and quaint (if not quite as grand as
its European name), with Bradford pear trees all along the main
street, which in spring so filled the roadway and the air with petals
that it resembled a snow scene. A water tower bearing the town's
name and stilted up on arachnid legs, with water stains rusting its
gray-blue paint, dwarfed the two-story houses and brick storefronts
and shops. Years ago, some local wag had christened this Trevi
Fountain, and more recently a group of friends from a nearby college had purchased a disused bank building in the heart of town
and opened a lunch counter of the same name.

Trevi sat on the train line north of the city and laid claim to the
only stop for twenty miles in either direction, and, naturally, this
brought a certain wealth and cosmopolitanism you did not find
everywhere in the region, and certainly not in Rock Basin, where
Jonah Valente lived with his mother. Initially, Jack had planned
to take the train to work. He had been at Tabor Investments only
a short time when he was fired. Before that, he had spent half a
decade in the D.A.'s office and seemed in line for a political career. But he had burned out on that life, or that's what he said,
anyway, and in anticipation of starting a family he had signed on
for what he believed would be a cushier position all around. Perhaps his new employer didn't agree with this interpretation of his
job, because, as soon as he gave his bosses a chance by making an
impolitic remark on a business-news show, they had wasted little
time firing him. No, they had *dangled* the threat. He could have
fought to stay, but, instead, haughty and superior, he had called
their bluff and forced them to follow through.

The house was an early-nineteenth-century farmhouse, fixed up and expanded over the years, painted charcoal following the new style, a color like smoke against the pitch-dark sky. It had clapboard siding and a metal roof, a mostly private small field with an old stone wall and a falling-down chicken coop, a tiny creek, and a wild profusion of ivy and flowers. Toward the main road there was an unpainted barn. Jack, who had been so invested in settling in—furnishing, repainting, touching up the trim, replacing cracked windowpanes, talking to contractors, landscapers, and arborists about what to do with the chicken coop, the yard, the silver maples and pin oaks—found himself overcome with apathy. He could hardly bring himself to wash the dishes or take out the trash. The mail piled up unopened on a chair in the entryway. Not long before, he had been a dynamo, on the phone with lawyers and water-treatment specialists, septic contractors, electricians, and insurance agents. He had learned about ground wells and leach fields, UV water-purification systems, sump pumps, pipe fittings, cell-foam insulation, byzantine tax exemptions and property-tax schedules, the life span of roofing shingles, aluminum roof coating, and septic-tank baffles. *Baffles.* He liked that. That just about said it! Finally, he'd simply stopped.

Daniel, Jack's friend from school, said that Jack's state of mind made a lot of fucking sense. "Jesus, considering everything. Get drunk, get laid," he said. "The French would go out whoring." Jack supposed that he had been the one to phone Daniel, but it no longer felt that way.

He had called for news of Sophie. Daniel was a successful magazine writer and someone Sophie often turned to for professional advice. It was Daniel, in fact, who had written the article on Valente for the school paper ("Portrait of the Artist as a Young Lineman"), and who now told Jack that he should give Valente a ring.

"Any word from Sophie?" Jack asked.

"Soph? She's all right. She's staying at her parents', but I guess you know that." Daniel laughed suddenly. "The last time I saw her, she was hanging out in bars, writing in a notebook, waiting for guys to text her."

Jack responded stoically. "What guys?"

"Dates? I don't know. I think she said she was writing a book. About contemporary dating, or dating apps. Something like that. Maybe she said 'mating.'"

"I see. So she's the one out whoring," Jack said.

"Yeah, you're the only one not having any fun."

Jack could picture her sitting at the bar, her black hair unfurling about her face as she bent over her journal, pensive and daydreaming. It surprised him to find this thought, the image of her sitting there, poignant, rather than upsetting.

Still, when he reached her on the phone, he said, "So I hear you've been out whoring."

She didn't laugh at this but made a noise that suggested fatigue or annoyance, or perhaps both. "What did Daniel tell you?"

Jack gave an inaccurate, largely imaginative account of the conversation. He did not want to hurt Sophie, but at times he felt the urge to be crude, and even sometimes mean. It welled up in him like an irresistible pressure, building behind the prim dishonesty that obscured the raw, dark realities of the heart.

When he had finished, Sophie was quiet for a moment, then said, "I don't want to get in the habit of explaining myself to you. So I guess I'm not going to."

"If it's freedom, it has to feel like freedom," he suggested.

"Something like that."

Later, with nothing to do, he telephoned Valente. "Holy shit! Jack Francis?" Boy, was it Valente—that same deep, echoic, excitable voice. "*Dude*, am I glad you called," Valente said. "My mom is driving me crazy."

It was Valente who noticed the hollow. This was not during his first visit, which he and Jack spent getting very drunk. Jack told him about Sophie, the D.A.'s office, and his brief foray into the private sector—the general cul-de-sac into which he seemed to have driven his life. Mostly, though, he listened to Valente talk about the years he had spent trying to get his artistic career off the ground, keeping body and soul together on part-time work. Valente had been employed by a house-painting crew, but something had happened and now he coached women's rugby at a Catholic college across the river. The school was on spring break that week.

They discussed college, of course, and Jack was taken aback to find that their memories of this time did not align. He shouldn't have been surprised by this—Valente had many strange notions—but it was vaguely unnerving to see that two people could live through the same experience and understand it so differently. Jack said that he had found everyone at college interesting at first—unique and particular and destined, it seemed, for some extraordinary future—but they had all turned out to be dull and conventional, and he increasingly saw himself as dull and conventional, too. Valente disagreed. He thought that their classmates had been deeply weird and had clung to the idea that they were dull and conventional to keep from sliding off the face of the earth.

"Look at you!" he exclaimed. "You tried to be the man in the gray plaid suit, and you got fired for mouthing off on one of those scam shows."

This was only partly accurate. Jack, on that fateful day, had been listening to an overgrown child in what he believed were nonprescription glasses hyperventilate about the earnings figures for a Chinese company that Tabor did business with. While the man grew practically breathless and goggle-eyed at the company's undervaluation, a graphic overlay showing a buy-sell meter flashed "Buy! Buy! Buy!"—and Jack, exhausted by this prattle, sick of Tabor and the expectation that he appear on these shows, the little devil in Jack, with an imperceptible smirk, said, "Well, yes, if you believe those figures."

It would have been a stretch, but he could have told his bosses that he had been confused about which company Tabor was working with. Not particularly plausible, but they would have permitted him the one strike. Instead, he just said, "*You* really believe those numbers?" At times he felt so clear about his rightness and other people's dishonesty that he could scarcely breathe.

He and Valente remembered the aftermath of Jonah's expulsion differently as well. Valente seemed to believe that some sort of popular movement had arisen to reinstate him. Jack recalled nothing of the sort. He remembered *jokes* about Valente, and the sense, if not the outright suggestion, that it was just as well, what had happened, since there was clearly something off about their former classmate. Mythologies about Valente sprang up in his absence, as predictable as they were unlikely, but mostly he was forgotten.

Jack and Valente were sitting outside under a pergola heavy with potato vine and clematis. Jack had built a fire in the fire pit, and the wood crackled and sparked, dashing the flowers and vines in a shifting light. Valente said that he was rereading his favorite biography of van Gogh, and that the artist, who claimed to find the darkness more colorful and vivid than the day, had painted at night with lighted candles in the brim of his straw hat. "A great fire burns in me, but no one stops to warm himself," he recited. "They pass by and see only the wisps of smoke." That was van Gogh. Valente leaned back and tilted his head to the sky. He had lost bulk since college and now was almost thin, carved in intense relief. The light and shadow accentuated the bones and hollows of his face. He told Jack he was saving up for a summer program in France, a painting course. Not the usual bullshit, he said. You studied with some real masters. And they took you to all the famous spots: Auvers, Arles, Saint-Rémy. But it was expensive, and he couldn't save enough unless he lived with his mom. Was he showing work? Jack wanted to know. There was a café in Rock Basin, Valente said. It wasn't much, but it had a little gallery and he had some work up there. He told Jack that van Gogh's first public exhibition had been in the window of an art supplier, a man he owed money to in The Hague. Van Gogh talked the guy into putting up a few of his paintings; if they sold, he said, he would use the money to pay off the debt. Well, they didn't sell, and the dealers who saw them in the window didn't like them, either. Valente laughed. "It just shows you," he said, smiling at nothing but the dark. "Everyone has to start somewhere."

"Dude, what's in the middle of your house?"

This was how Valente greeted Jack on his third visit.

Jack handed him a beer and retrieved another for himself from the fridge. "What do you mean, the middle?"

Valente explained that he had awoken in the night with a strange intuition that there was something wrong with Jack's house. "I kept walking around it in my head. Like circling the downstairs. Then I realized there's an area that's not part of any room."

Jack shook his head; he didn't understand. Valente said he would show him and led Jack to the closed-off section of the house, demonstrating how, approaching it from any of the six adjoining rooms, you wouldn't notice anything odd and might even confuse it for part of the stair column. It was smaller than a room and could, he conjectured, be a sealed-in linen closet or pantry, or perhaps a disused chimney shaft—though when they walked above and below the area on the second floor and in the basement, no vertical element carried through.

Valente asked Jack for a tape measure and a pen and paper and set about sketching a rough floor plan. He drew with surprising efficiency and ease. Jack watched him. The low sun barreled through the west-facing windows, penetrating the colored glass jars along the windowsill and painting forms like watercolor blotches on the wall. Valente guessed that the sealed-off area wasn't much bigger than three feet by six. To know more, he'd have to go through the wall. But Jack had just finished repainting the walls. So there was a hollow, so what?

They moved out into the warm, silken dusk. A golden light crested the hill, attaching to the drifts of pollen and follicles of grass flower that rose and trembled in the air. Valente gazed into the setting sun.

He spoke at times in a way that made Jack think of a boulder tripping down a hill—slow, inexorable, always in danger of veering perilously off course.

"When you said moving here was 'Sophie's choice,' were you quoting that movie?" he asked.

"It's a book," Jack said. "Or it was a book first."

"About the Holocaust."

"So they say."

Valente squinted in perplexity. "What does the Holocaust have to do with moving here?"

"Nothing," Jack said. "It's just a bad joke."

Valente paused and frowned like a mime feigning thought. "When the Gestapo came to Picasso's studio during the Occupation, there was a photo of *Guernica* lying around. They asked him, 'Did you do this?' and he said, 'No, you did!'"

Jack looked at him. "Is that true?"

Valente shrugged. "I don't know. That's what they say. Picasso said art is a lie that makes us see the truth."

Jack didn't respond, and Valente closed his eyes. In the distance, the sunlight caught a window on the toolshed and burned a liquid, blinding gold. Valente's face had folds and pleats like an accordion. He's aged more than the rest of us, Jack thought.

"There's a water tower in Rock Basin," Valente said, "just like in Trevi." His eyes were still closed as he spoke. "For years, Rope Man and I talked about climbing up one night and painting it. Probably we were going to paint some bullshit—something lewd, you know. But now I think I'd just paint big letters that say 'You are free.'"

The wrens made their evening call—*jiminy, jiminy, jiminy.*

"Rope Man?" Jack said.

"Friend from high school." Valente opened his eyes. "We called him Rope Man because he had this Polish last name no one could pronounce. It started with 'rope.'"

"What's Rope Man up to now?"

"He's dead." Valente's voice was flat and he stared straight ahead at the chicken coop with its busted-up lath buried in honeysuckle.

"What happened?"

For a second, Jack thought he saw a savage fire in Valente's eyes, then the fire blinked, settling into mildness, like a star.

"When van Gogh's cousin wouldn't marry him, he put his hand in a lamp flame," Valente said. "Her family wouldn't let him see her, and he said, 'Let me see her for as long as I can keep my hand in the flame.' I guess it was something like that with Rope Man."

"I don't know what that means," Jack said.

Valente picked at the grass where his fingers hung. "Nobody noticed he was burning up."

"And what happened with van Gogh?"

"They blew out the lamp," Valente said. The sun had gone mostly behind the hill. A single ray wavered above the ridge like a filament of glass. "Van Gogh didn't kill himself, you know. Everyone thinks he did, but it was some teenagers that liked to prank him. They shot him—probably by accident."

"I never heard that."

"Look it up."

Jack closed his eyes. A faint residue of red or orange seeped through his eyelids. "Tell me more about van Gogh," he said.

And Valente spoke, of wheat fields and flowers and crows and turbulent skies, of painting loneliness and sorrow and anguish, of moments when the veil of time and of inevitability (to use the painter's own words) seems to open for the blink of an eye, of boats in storms, and boats pulling other boats—towing them, tugging them—and how one boat sometimes pulls another, while that second, helpless boat prepares to reverse roles someday and pull the first boat through a storm, or a time of special need. Valente described an impossible person, a scoundrel, a tramp, difficult and gruff, prone to fighting, taking up with prostitutes, rejected by everyone, repulsive even to his parents, unlovable, homeless, driven by inexpressible love, or love that was expressible only in a particular form that did not allow it to be shared between two people, and that was therefore cursed, a love that was refused while he was alive, and only, when this cretin, this parasite, offensive to every standard of good taste, was gone, did everyone see how much they *did* want his peculiar, displaced, and overripe love, and the same respectable people who had found him so revolting now clutched him to their breast with the fiercest longing, because a certain intensity of color reminded them, or so Valente said in his own way, of intimations of such intensity in moments of their own that they had forgotten or suppressed.

Jack had intended to get past the hollow, but he found that he couldn't. At night, before falling asleep, or having awoken to darkness, he felt the eerie, mystical nearness of it, and this unsettled him. He started, without realizing it at first, to orient himself in the house and on the property in relation to the hollow. "Like Mecca, or Jerusalem," he said, chuckling to himself as if the joke would rob the hollow of its power. Inspecting the walls, he found no crack or crease; the paint and plaster ran flawlessly to the corners, the ceiling, the baseboards—there was no easy way in. He began to feel angry with the sellers. Surely they had known about this secret hollow and said nothing. Maybe they had even closed it up.

Spring break ended, and Valente returned to coaching. Jack saw less of him. Jack did not miss seeing him, but not seeing anyone presented its own problem; namely, what to do with himself. He felt a great restlessness growing inside him, something vast and formless. He lay in the sunlit grass on the hill, watching the leaves migrate in the breeze. The fields and orchards in the distance appeared overexposed, gilded on one side with seams of light.

The days were blending together into one composite day. He was drinking too much, but what else was there to do? He kept thinking about a concert in the city that he and Sophie had gone to over the holidays. It was at a church uptown, somewhere on the East Side. Dark, heavy stones composed the walls and vault of the church—an intimate, tall, solid space. He no longer remembered what the concert was—a mixed program of canonical and newer pieces, played by a spare, shifting ensemble. The church was small, and attendance was sparse. What he remembered was the sound of trucks, garbage trucks, on the street outside, heavy, vibrating, accelerating, braking, letting out hisses of compressed air, and the complaints of their straining engines as they stopped and

started along their route. The sound of the trucks, low and sono-
rous through the stone walls, had made the music more beautiful
somehow, accentuating perhaps the simultaneous existence of the
disparate realities that hold our fragile world together in its brittle
shell. The music tiptoed along the knife edge of its key, its tones,
giving the illusion of freedom when there were always far more
missteps than safe harbors and nimble plunges into grace.

When Valente came over on a Friday evening, his long hair hung
in greasy locks and his face was patched with dirt.

"We had a match today," he explained and took the beer Jack
offered.

"I thought you were the coach," Jack said.

Valente drank deeply, answering too quickly and choking.
"Yeah, but when we win I let the girls tackle me." He coughed to
clear his throat. "*Blood in, blood out,* you know—like the military."

"Blood in, blood out? How many girls tackle you?"

"I don't know. Fifteen? You should see me," Valente said. "I'm
like Gulliver."

Jack pointed at his face. "Did someone punch you in the eye?"

Valente's voice was soft and wistful. "Man, those girls are crazy,"
he said. "They love to beat me up."

A silence fell, and they briefly regarded the birds streaking
through the backlit trees, stenciled silhouettes against an aureate
sky.

Jack coughed lightly in his fist. "So . . . what should we do about
this hollow?"

"Hollow?"

"The chamber in the wall."

Valente seemed not to understand. "Oh, *that,*" he said after a
minute. "But who cares about that?"

Who cares? Jack thought. You were the one who brought it up!

"Here's what you do," Valente said. "Drill a hole in the wall and
run a fiber-optic spy camera through it."

"I don't have a fiber-optic spy camera," Jack said.

"Yeah." Valente nodded. "Too bad."

In the creek at their feet, tiny fish idled and darted in the current. Jack watched them move beneath the braiding water.

Valente finished his beer, crushing the can between his strong,
heavy hands, and grinned.

Jack grinned back. "Hey, why'd you get kicked out of school?" he asked.

Until that moment Jack had felt indifferent to this question, or worse than indifferent: he felt the answer would disappoint him. But a sudden annoyance at Valente had overcome him, a sense of the precise limit to what Valente could be or do, a sense—how to put it?—of some insuperable grossness in Valente's character that would never, even with boundless fellowship and care, settle into sufficient self-awareness. Standing beside the green-violet *Ricinus,* the former football player kicked at tufts of moss and a crust of caked mud that lay along the bank of the creek. He smiled without turning, as if at the little swimming fish.

"I wasn't, you know, 'kicked out,'" he said.

"You weren't."

"I could've come back." Valente gazed at the trees. "Didn't want to."

Why was that? Jack asked.

Valente squinted inquisitively as the leaves above them shook like silver-green sequins. "I was doing so much acid that summer," he said after a minute. "Summer after they told me to take a year off. I don't remember why, but I had keys to George Diehl's apartment. You remember Diehl? I never liked that kid, but he was always down to get high. Well, George was away for some reason, and I'd been tripping all night. I couldn't come down. I remember it was sunrise when I got to his place, and I lay down in his bed, but I couldn't sleep. So I started pacing from room to room. For, like, hours. There were just four rooms, but I couldn't stop. I was getting spooked, so I decided to watch something. George had this projector hooked up to a DVD player, but I couldn't find any DVDs, so I just pressed Play to see what was in there. All of a sudden there were these people dancing and singing. Tons of them, in matching costumes, doing elaborate routines. They made shapes like flowers, geometric shapes. All this stuff. Too much to follow. At first I thought, This is cool, but then I started to get a bad feeling. They were like aliens. Like they were on a different planet, dancing in outer space. Somewhere you could never get to, you know? And then I thought, No, I was wrong. It *was* our world, the dancing planet, and I was the one who couldn't get there."

Jack stared at him. "What the fuck are you talking about?"

"What?"

"I asked you why you didn't go back to school."

"Oh, yeah. Shit . . ." Valente laughed. "I guess that's when I knew I'd never go back. I was covered in dust."

Jack shook his head. "Dust?"

Valente nodded. "Picasso said art washes the dust of the everyday from the soul. You get it?"

A splitting pressure had arisen in Jack's head, and the day's brightness was making him nauseous. "Dude, you got to get off this Picasso and van Gogh thing."

"What do you mean?"

"No one's ever going to take you seriously, going on about Picasso and van Gogh, and wildflowers and shit," Jack said. "I'm not telling you anything you don't know. Find some obscure artist to talk about. Better yet, shut up. Don't say anything. Christ!" he burst out. "You have to show people you can play the game."

"What game?"

Jack massaged his forehead with his hand. "Don't be obtuse."

"But they're the best," Valente said quietly.

"And you know"—Jack continued without really hearing him—"it's not like because some artist was poor or misunderstood, and you're poor and misunderstood, things are going to work out for you. Millions of people fail. Millions for every Picasso. It's not like *failing* means you're the next van Gogh."

"I don't think that," Valente said.

"Good. Baby steps toward sanity. But don't think the people who succeed don't play the game. They all do. Picasso did. They dance the goddamn dance. Purity of spirit's just some shit they talk about once they've made it to make the rest of us believe—"

Jack shut up. Valente looked so dirty and bedraggled, leaves and twigs feathered in his hair and something fierce and sad in his look. Jack could only say, more softly, "Look, kemo sabe. Tell me, where does it go from here?"

Valente didn't respond. That haunted, confused kid they'd once called Picasso, as if in affection, with no affection, with laughter, with doubt, said nothing. He walked off. After maybe ten paces he stopped, as if about to turn, but then continued on to his car.

Jack watched him go.

The ignition sounded, and from the open window of his Toyota Valente shouted, "You're covered in dust!"

"So what?" Jack said

"You covered me in your dust," Valente yelled at him, putting the car in gear and lurching forward.

"I didn't do it," Jack shouted back. "It was those fucking rugby girls!"

But Valente was already speeding down the drive and most likely didn't hear him.

"We've got a hollow," Jack said. He was talking to Sophie on the phone.

"Am I supposed to know what that means?"

"Between the walls. There's an empty space."

She spoke with a certain circumspection. "Isn't that . . . normal?"

"Not like this. It's a big hollow. Not as big as a room, maybe, but close."

A longer pause accreted on the line. "Jack, what's this about?"

"It's your house, too," he said. "I thought you'd like to know there's an unexplained cavity in the wall."

"Is everything all right?"

"Besides the unexplained cavity in the wall? Yeah, everything's awesome."

"You sound . . . I don't know." She sounded tired herself. "Is everything really all right?"

Jack soothed his hot cheeks and brow against the cool wood of the doorframe. "Do you remember that concert we went to over the holidays, Soph? Somewhere uptown, off Park maybe. There were these trucks moving in the street. You could hear them through the walls while the music played."

She didn't respond for so long Jack thought the line had gone dead. "I remember the concert," she said finally. "I don't remember the trucks."

"There were trucks."

"All right, there were trucks."

"And the sound of the music . . ." He no longer knew what he meant to say. The scope of something inexpressible, a mammoth, ungraspable intimation, had overtaken him.

Jack called Valente to apologize. He had heard nothing from him in a week. To his surprise, Valente's mother answered the phone.

"Jonah's in the hospital," she said. "He's all right, don't worry, but he's not supposed to see anyone yet."

"What happened?"

There was a pause. "How do you know Jonah?" she asked.

Jack told her they were old college friends, and that he'd recently moved to the area.

"Maybe Jonah would like to tell you himself, when he's feeling better," his mother said.

Jack pondered this briefly but soon turned his attention to other things. A week later, quite unexpectedly, he received a letter from Valente in the mail. It was written on brown card stock in a large, handsome hand:

Hey Jack,

First off, don't feel bad when you hear what happened or like you owe me an apology or whatever. We argued, so what? I don't take it personally. But don't add this to your list of reasons I'm crazy. I'm not that crazy. Just a little crazier than you. Or maybe not—ha-ha!

I never told you this but sometimes I get pretty low. Van Gogh's last words were "*la tristesse durera toujours*," which in French means "the sadness shall last forever." But he died with a smile on his face, they say, and sometimes I think about that and think life isn't so bad.

You're right, I talk about van Gogh and Picasso a lot. What can I say? They're my heroes and it gives me comfort to keep them close. It isn't cool, but I guess I'm not cool. When I try to be, I feel like I'm suffocating, you know? I told myself, I'll just say what's on my mind and people can think what they want. Dumb, huh? I don't think I'll ever learn to play the game you were talking about, but maybe that's okay, too, do you think?

The doctors say my main issue is a lack of proportion. Well, I can't argue with that. I get strange notions and it's like I can't resist. After our argument I was thinking about Rope Man, and I got it in my head I was going to climb the water tower and paint it, like Rope Man and I always talked about. I guess I was pretty drunk. Everyone says I'm lucky I didn't hurt myself worse. Rugby's out for a while, but the doctors are coming around to the idea that I'm not a danger to myself.

One more van Gogh story, if you won't chop my head off for telling it—ha-ha! I don't have my books here so it's from memory. In a letter to Theo, van Gogh says he knows he's a nonentity, a bum, basically, in the eyes of the world. And despite that, he says, he'd like to show in his work what's in the heart of such a nobody. I think that's pretty cool.

The rugby girls came to see me the other day, six or seven of them. They're crazy, those girls! They brought me brownies they baked. I wish I'd known they were pot brownies before I ate so many. . . . I think the girls felt bad they couldn't fight me, 'cause two of them started wrestling right there in the hospital until Nurse Ratched kicked them out. (Actually, her name's Sally and she's all right.) But it cheered me up to see the girls. Hey, don't worry about me! In no time at all I'll be back out there painting with birthday candles burning in my hat.

Your bro,
Jonah

It was two years before Jack saw Valente again. On the day in question, he and Sophie were across the river, poking around in antique shops and cafés while their infant daughter napped in her papoose. In Chandor, a town just north of Rock Basin, Jack found Valente at a craft fair, working one of the stalls. All around him were small garish canvases, showing still lifes and cottages and bright flowering bushes.

"Jack Francis!" Valente bellowed when Jack approached.

"Hi, Jonah." Sophie was in a different part of the fair, looking at jewelry, or retailored vintage dresses.

"What's crackin'?" Valente appeared genuinely pleased to see him. Jack, at least, read no trace of their last encounter or the intervening years in his look, just that restive quality, as if every instant teetered on an uneasy precipice.

"Nothing," Jack said. "Driving around. I'm here with Sophie. And a little human that popped out of her."

Valente grinned. "Sophie finally made her choice."

"Yeah, I guess." Jack had forgotten his old joke. "These yours?" he said and pointed to the paintings.

"These?" Valente's face went blank and a sudden humorless fire appeared on it. The shift was so precipitate that Jack wondered for a second whether he had, in fact, said something different and unforgivable.

"What?" Jack said.

Valente threw his head back and laughed. "Man, you must really think I suck at painting. This shit?" He cast a hand about. "I'm

just doing my friend Raj a favor. I wouldn't be caught dead painting this bullshit."

"I see," Jack said, not entirely sure that he did. "How's your stuff
going?"

Valente shrugged. "I'm not in the Louvre yet."

"No." Jack picked up and put down a canvas that seemed to
show a strangely colored child or doll, or possibly a clown.

Valente was asking him a question. It took Jack a moment to
realize that he was asking about the hollow. What had happened
with it. "Hollow?" Jack repeated. The word triggered something
in him, a sense of déjà vu, but he couldn't quite catch the recol-
lection. He hadn't thought about the hollow in months, years. It
seemed much longer ago than it could have been that Valente had
brought it to his attention, a memory far more deeply buried in
the past than the facts allowed. He stared at Valente impassively,
although some slight mirth may have danced in his eyes. "What
hollow?"

Valente narrowed his eyes, trying to assess what was taking
place. He held Jack's gaze, then he smiled. A snort erupted from
him, a laugh, and then Jack was laughing, too. They laughed with
a gathering force, truly cracking up. Jack didn't know the last time
he'd laughed so hard, or why, really, they were laughing, but they
were roaring, fighting for breath.

"What's so funny?" Sophie was tapping Jack on the shoulder.
"What are you laughing at?"

Jack turned, grinning, and was about to shrug, when Valente
cut in and in his loud, abrupt voice answered, "Sadness."

Their laughter petered out. Jack studied the thinning, wrin-
kled skin around Valente's eyes, waiting for something to happen.
Valente was smiling broadly, entirely in earnest. It was the earnestness of a large, clumsy person, crashing through a world of glass
doors and gossamer screens. Jack realized that he was waiting for
Sophie to suggest that she had misheard, but she said nothing.
Only pursed her lips. He breathed quietly. The day was crystal-
line, blue, touched by clouds. Cool. A light breeze. The market
hummed. A burble of chatter. Dogs' barks. The smell of cut flowers, of burning. Colors. Crushed leaves. Exhaust. A chime, tin-
kling. A yellow shawl. Time pooling. Opening. A moment, before
anyone spoke.

Detective Dog

FROM *The New Yorker*

"NO POLITICS, JUST make money," Betty's mother, Tina, liked to say. And when it came to China: "See nothing, hear nothing, say nothing. Do you hear me?"

"I hear nothing," Betty had wanted to say sometimes. Or, well, many times, really. But instead she'd said nothing and, as directed, made a lot of money. After all, she was the good daughter.

And that was how it was that when umbrellas took over Hong Kong she had a nice place in Vancouver. And that was how it was, too, that when racism took over Vancouver she could up and move to New York. It was convenient to be rich, you had to say. In New York, she didn't even have to buy an apartment. She and her husband and the boys just moved into her sister's old place, which they liked so much that they bought the apartment next door, and then the apartment on the other side, too. They figured they'd turn the extra kitchens into bathrooms.

"Buy another one!" Betty's father, Johnson, bellowed over FaceTime from Arizona. "Buy the whole floor!" Johnson, who had always loved acquisition, had recently started a list called "Ghost Towns of the World." One of these days, Betty's husband, Quentin, said, Johnson was going to buy them all up. Corner the market.

"Every time he says, 'Too many people in China,' I can hear his pitch," Quentin said, with a hint of awe in his voice; he did think Johnson a genius. "'Now people who don't like where they live can move somewhere else. No problem.'"

Betty laughed. "Does that mean there'll be a ghost town for us?"

"Maybe." Quentin seemed to be considering this seriously.

But never mind. "Three apartments for four people is enough," Betty told Johnson now, smiling but firm. "We are not buying any more." And, when he continued arguing, she shrank him down from full screen to half.

In Vancouver, her neighbors had complained about her. "The Chinese are taking over," they said. "The Chinese are buying up everything." That was when they weren't yelling, "Go back to where you came from!" Betty had tried to reason with them. If she were the sort of Chinese who wanted to buy in Vancouver but not live in Vancouver, if she were the sort of Chinese responsible for Vancouver's empty houses and empty apartments, she wouldn't be standing right there for them to yell at, right? And she was not an invader, by the way, she was a parent who had worried that her eleven-year-old would go out protesting on the street with his friends. And then what? Then he would get teargassed, that's what. And, by the way, tear gas wasn't so great for the baby they'd adopted during the 2012 unrest, either.

But a Chinese was a Chinese was a Chinese to them.

"When people want to yell, all they can hear is what they want to yell," Tina liked to say.

Which was why, after five years, Betty and her family had moved from Vancouver to New York, where all anybody said was "We are so happy you are willing to chip in for the new elevator" and "Did you know the building needs a new roof?"

"Yes," she said. "Yes, yes." And, "Anything else?"

Now, in the gilt lobby mirror by the striped chairs, she looked happier to herself. A little plump, it was true; she did not like her chin joining up with her neck, as if they just needed to be together. But she liked her short-short hair and her cheery cashmere hoodies, and look how she could just push her oversized sunglasses up onto her head—no puffy eyes to hide. When the Hong Kong police stormed the universities, she and her family just sat here in New York on their lilac leather couch and watched on their computers. Lined up like ladies at a hair salon—one, two, three, four. Even when COVID came, at least they worried about sickness and death but not jail.

Of course, Theo, now seventeen, was upset all the time. All his old Hong Kong friends were involved in the protests; sometimes he thought he spotted them on his screen, although it was hard to say for sure because they'd grown up and because everyone was wearing gas masks. Really, it was crazy to take screenshots and zoom in the way he did—running his fingers through the long hair on top of his head and scratching the short hair on the sides. "Is that Victor? Is that Pak? Don't you think that's Pak?" he'd say. Or "That must be Wingman, I recognize that scar."

Whether Theo would have been so riled up were it not for the ambulance sirens going and going was hard to say. It shook Betty up, too, that even nine-year-old Robert knew "ventilator" was spelled with an "or"; she was just glad he wasn't sure how to spell "morgue." Although, as imaginative and intense as he was, he was writing a story about dancing morgues for the mystery unit in his English class. It was a murder mystery, he told her, in his quiet, unnerving way. He was not like the other boys at all. The last story he'd written was about mind-reading hats that looked like regular fur hats but then stole your thoughts right through your scalp. How they did it was the mystery.

Betty herself almost never told stories, but, having read a book about Western creativity growing up like a flower out of the soil of curiosity, she was trying to at least ask a lot of questions, and not just any questions but the right questions. Meaning, not questions like "What do you mean you were out all night? Where were you?"—the sort of question she was prone to ask Theo—but questions that showed interest. Like "Do the morgues ever stop dancing?" Playfulness, too—she had underlined that in her book. She tried to ask questions that showed playfulness.

"Do the morgues ever stop dancing?" she asked now.

"Yes, and when they stop dancing all the people are going to come out, alive again," Robert said. He had what would have been a perfect bowl cut if he hadn't started trimming his hair himself. Now he looked as if he'd been transitioning into Mark Zuckerberg, only to change his mind halfway.

"And then what?" Betty asked. She relied a little heavily on "And then what," she knew, but she couldn't think of anything else to ask. "Will they breathe okay?"

"Yes, but they'll be a little dizzy," he said.

"Interesting." Another thing she said too much, but oh well. "And what will the people say?"

"They'll say, 'It's great to be alive, what happened to my phone?'" he said. "But I'm not sure what the morgues will say back." He touched his tongue to his nose; he had a tongue like a dog's.

"How about 'We're not responsible for personal effects'?" she said—thinking that he wouldn't know what that meant. But Robert, being an avid chaser of what he called true facts, did know. He retracted his tongue and laughed as he wrote—by hand, as he liked to, with a pencil:

> "It's great to be alive, what happened to my phone?"
> "We're not responsible for personal effects."
> "What kind of a morgue are you? Didn't your mother teach you anything?"
> "No, we're the worst of the worst. Because of the virus, they had to scrape the bottom of the barrel."

Betty laughed. "Great!" she said.

"I still have to figure out what the mystery is."

"The mystery is how this whole COVID craziness could be happening," she said.

Robert's handwriting had deteriorated since he had come to the U.S., but if Betty had ever had the energy to nag him about it she did not anymore. Remote learning! Robert's school theoretically went from 8:25 to 2:25, but that included ninety minutes of independent study, thirty minutes for lunch, and thirty minutes for recess. Why did the kids get a break when it was the parents who needed a break? And how could the teachers still be complaining about how much they worked? Why did they not even make the kids show their faces on Zoom? Right now, for example, Theo was playing Liberate Hong Kong on his computer while in trigonometry class at the same time. How could that be okay?

"You realize that stories about morgues are not normal, right?" Theo said, looking up from his game.

"So? It's not normal to be jamming virtual surveillance cameras as if you were a real protester, either," Robert said.

"I am so a real protester."

"The kind who shouts 'Gaa yau!' from the couch, you mean."

"If I were there, I'd be on the streets," Theo said.

"Not now during COVID, you wouldn't."

"Even now, I'd be there. And as soon as things really started up again I'd be throwing petrol bombs, don't worry."

"You can tell we're not really brothers," Robert observed to the air. "I would never say something violent like that."

"Adopted brothers are still brothers." Quentin's nostrils flared when he was being serious, and today this did make the boys settle down. When Theo started up Animal Crossing, with its desert islands full of protest banners, Quentin was even able to say, "Aren't you supposed to be in class?"

Theo switched sullenly back to full screen.

But what Robert had said was true. He wasn't violent like his older brother. He didn't say the sorts of things that made Betty and Quentin thank the Lord they were safely on the other side of the world, far away from what their friends in Hong Kong called "protest trouble." "This generation, they are like firecrackers. One explodes, and then the whole string goes," they said in WeChat posts. And "Do they realize they are not dealing with a paper tiger? This is a real tiger, with teeth. They are going to get themselves killed." There were friends who approved of the protests: "I give my kids food every day to take with them to share. Bottled water is also important, and when they come home I wash their clothes right away to get the smell out." But others wished they had gotten their kids interested in sports. "Better for their health, better for their college applications, better for everything," they wrote. "However, you need to be athletic."

"You know what your grandmother always says," Betty told Theo. "No politics, just make money. That's good advice."

But although she had listened, Theo did not. Theo was her biological child, but his outrage reminded her of her older sister, Bobby—Bobby, who had, unbelievably, tried to send them a letter last week. After all these years! Betty was shocked and apprehensive. And, maybe because she was worried, annoyed. Who sent real letters anymore, much less a letter via a personal family messenger? Only Bobby would somehow enlist Uncle Arnie, through his Shanghai factory, as if they were all in a spy movie. She had apparently even instructed Uncle Arnie to hide the letter in his shoe, which he did not do in the end; he was afraid airport security would make him take his shoes off. Instead, he tore it up and flushed it down a toilet—because he knew it was trouble, he told Betty later, and because he didn't want to upset Tina and Johnson. As for why he had even told Betty about the letter, he claimed it was because he was too honest, but Betty knew the truth: there was something in the letter that he couldn't keep inside. He swore he hadn't read the thing before tearing it up, but of course he had. He had! And where was Bobby? she demanded. Her parents had been desperate to know for years, she said, the whole family had. Uncle Arnie insisted that he didn't know. The letter and some instructions had been left for him in a plain envelope, he said, and the security cameras had found no trace of whoever had sneaked it into the factory.

"Anyway, no politics, just make money. Isn't that what your mother always says?" he finished.

In other words, the letter had to do with politics. Probably, if she were Uncle Arnie, she, too, would have thrown it out.

It was amazing how many things her mother's words could mean. To Theo, for example, they meant that Betty and Quentin were going to hell.

"Is that how you want to live your life?" he yelled. "Is that your motto? Just make money?"

"All it means is that that is the way to be safe," Betty said. "It is like 'The tallest tree catches all the wind.' That does not mean a short tree is a good tree. It means that a tall tree pays a price for sticking up."

She didn't know how to tell Theo that when a son yelled at a mother the mother cried for a week. She kept that inside, though she was sure that Robert knew anyway. Never mind that he was the adopted child—Robert would shoot her that quick look of his, like a flash of light in the dark that could only be a signal. He understood her, while all Theo understood was his opinion of his family.

"I hate you," he would say, for example. "I hate your values and your way of life, and I do not respect you. What have you ever done but look the other way no matter what was going on? Did you ever tell the truth? Did you ever speak up? No matter who was being killed and who was being jailed? You know what the word is for people like you? The word is 'complicit.' I bet you don't care about the Uighurs, either."

So he ranted—ranted and ranted—as if he had not been the first to complain when Betty said that because of COVID there would be no maid and no cook. Even though there was pretty good takeout in New York and she knew how to make a few dishes herself, he had objected. And now every day Theo brought up colleges farther away than the colleges they'd talked about before. Colleges in Alaska. Scotland. New Zealand. He wasn't applying until the fall, but still they discussed the possibilities constantly.

"How about a semester in Antarctica?" Quentin suggested at dinner. "There must be semesters abroad in Antarctica."

Betty glared, but Quentin just winked and kept going.

"You can study penguins," he said, showing Theo an article on his phone. "Did you know they poop out so much laughing gas that their researchers go cuckoo?"

"They do?" Robert said. "Let me see, that's so cool."

Theo, though, stood up without a single bite of the Oreo mousse cake Betty had made specially for him, from a recipe he'd found and asked her to try.

Should they buy one more apartment after all? For the sake of family sanity? Quentin and Betty talked it over. But just when they had decided yes, Theo needed more space, more independence, more something, he got the hang of online poker. Betty had heard about online poker from her friend Susu, whose son had made a lot of money playing it, which you wouldn't think would upset Susu but did. Because once her son made a lot of money she lost control of him, she said; she just hoped he wasn't doing drugs. Hearing which, Betty had shaken her head in sympathy—and later, when she told Quentin the story, she had said how glad she was that Theo was no good at math.

"Although sometimes a quick calculation can mean millions," Quentin pointed out.

"Still," she said. "Poor Susu."

"Poor Susu is right," Quentin agreed.

But now it seemed that Theo was better at math than they'd thought.

"I underestimated myself," he said. "I guess I did just need to work harder." And, "All I needed was to put more time into it."

Time that he had now, thanks to COVID.

It was hard to know whether to cheer or to worry when he won a hundred dollars. Then he won a thousand dollars. Then he lost five hundred dollars.

"Thank God he learned a lesson," Quentin said. "In Macau, at least you have to book a hotel room to gamble. On the computer you can gamble with no overhead."

"Terrible," Betty said.

Then Theo won five thousand dollars. Then he won ten thousand dollars. Then he won another ten thousand dollars.

"Beginner's luck," he said modestly. And, to be sure that he didn't gamble away all that he'd won, he bought a car.

"A car?" Betty said. "How did you buy a car?"

"With cash, that's how," Robert said, when Theo didn't answer.

He'd picked a little red Miata with a pop-off roof; it got great mileage, he said, and Susu, too, said it was an excellent deal, a real COVID deal, which she knew because her son had cosigned the papers—which he could do because he was old enough, and which he had thought was okay because Theo had a license he'd gotten before COVID so that he could go visit friends in the suburbs.

"At least it's not drugs," Susu said.

As for whether Betty and Quentin preferred Theo angry or rich, they could not agree.

"It is as if his heart is hidden. Disappeared under a blanket where no one can see it," Betty said, adding, "I think he just wants to get away from us."

"Away from us?" Quentin said, astounded.

"Susu says this is what seventeen-year-olds are like, especially in the U.S. They are separating. It's their psychological stage."

"Away from us?"

She didn't answer.

"And when do they stop?"

His question hung in the air like the kind of smog that used to drift down from the Mainland and choke them. They tried to sleep.

It did not occur to them that Theo would use his car to leave them. There he was, though, two days later, packing up.

"Where are you going?" Betty asked.

"You cannot use our charge cards," Quentin warned.

But, having his own money now, Theo just knit his eyebrows and kept packing. One duffel bag, two, three. Children his age did not believe in suitcases.

And, the next morning, he really was gone.

"He made his bed," Quentin said quietly.

Of course, they were shaken up anyway. But the bed! They hadn't even known that Theo knew how to make his bed.

"Complicit," he had called them. Complicit. And what was it that he liked to yell?

Betty remembered. "I think it was 'Did you ever tell the truth?'"

"What truth?" Quentin said.

Betty kept it inside that she kept a lot of things inside.

Instead, she asked Theo's bed, Where are you, Theo? She asked the kitchen counter and the apartment buzzer, too. Where are you? Where are you? She did not tell any of her friends what had happened. Nor did she post anything about it on WeChat. She told his school that he was sick. A fever and a cough, she said, no loss of taste but they were having him tested. And yes, yes, of course, confining him to his room. The school was mostly interested in the confinement part of the story.

Besides that, she and Quentin simply watched their chats and email, hoping. Theo would be back soon, they agreed. And just about any place was safer than New York. So that was good. If only they were among the friends on his Find My Friends app.

"He went to visit someone," they told Robert.

"But he was supposed to stay home," Robert said. "Everyone is."

"You're right," Betty said. "He was. I hope he brought enough masks. I hope he is being careful. I hope he is using hand san."

She hoped, too, that Robert would know enough not to ask whom Theo was going to visit. And, thankfully, he did know enough.

Instead, he said, "I'm sick of COVID. I want to play soccer. I want to see my friends." And, "I want a new dog."

"Is there something the matter with Bongbong?" Betty asked.

"I want an upgrade."

"An upgrade?" Quentin said.

"I don't want another of the same kind of dog. I want, like, an original dog."

He said this because Bongbong was not their first dog. Bongbong was a replacement dog they'd gotten after Yappy died, you might even say a carbon copy of Yappy, whom everyone in the family had loved. But, of course, "everyone" had not included Robert, who hadn't been born yet, much less adopted. Betty could see his point in a way. Still. An upgrade?

What a way to think.

When Robert had wanted to be paid for making his bed, they had paid him. Because the maid used to get paid, he had argued, and that was true. It seemed fair. Then he had wanted to be paid for getting out of bed in preparation for making it. To which

Quentin said okay, without even asking Betty. Now Robert wanted to be paid for brushing his teeth.

"Does your price include flossing?" Quentin asked.

Meanwhile, Tina and Johnson were so upset when they heard about Theo that Betty did not even tell them about Bobby's torn-up letter, much less that Bobby had once told Betty she had written a last letter, the way many of the Hong Kong dissidents had, just in case something happened to them. The letters declared that they were protesters and had not died by suicide—that being what they'd felt they had to write, given how many more people had been detained than were in jail. Given, that is, how many people had disappeared.

And, later, Betty thought she should have told her parents all this during their FaceTime call—she should have! But at the time she didn't see how she could—they were so busy reassuring her that Theo wasn't going to disappear the way Bobby had. He wasn't, they said. He couldn't. Although—five days? She should hire a private detective right away, the way they should have with Bobby. "Before she got too far away." Even after all these years there was a catch in Tina's voice.

"One good thing is that it is very difficult to transport a Miata to Hong Kong. So Theo probably didn't go there," Johnson said.

"If you don't want to call a detective yourself, we can call for you," Tina said.

"In fact, we can call right now," Johnson said.

It was all Betty could do to divert them to the subject of Robert's demanding to be paid for everything. Finally, though, Tina said, "You know who gets paid for everything?"

"Who?" Betty said.

"American children," she said. "And let me tell you, if you allow Robert to become American you will regret it."

"Do you think so?" Betty said.

"You will! Your mother is right!" Johnson thundered. "Become American citizen is great. Hold American passport is great. But do not let Robert get American ideas. You know what they are, those American ideas?"

Betty waited.

"Twentieth century," he said. "They are one hundred percent twentieth century."

As for whether she should have told her parents that what Robert wanted money for was to support Black people, why would she do that? Knowing that they would have said, "Black people! Only Americans are so concerned about Black people!" But this was what happened when you sent children to school in New York—they joined the People of Color Club. No politics! Tina would have said, and Betty herself wanted to tell him, We are not people of color, Robert. We are rich.

But unfortunately he was the president of the club. Thanks to COVID, the kids had nothing else to do but to Zoom and discuss whether or not they were racist, as a result of which Robert was elected president because everyone agreed that, being of Chinese origin, he was probably the most racist. "The Chinese are the worst!" they said, to which Robert happily agreed.

Betty was happy for Robert that he had found a kind of acceptance Theo never had at his age. Still, like Susu, she wished they could all have just stayed in Hong Kong. In Hong Kong, there was no People of Color Club, because they were all the same color, and if you said bad things about white people it wasn't racism, it was resistance, unless you said it to their faces. Then it was speaking truth to power.

Now Quentin mused, "If I pay Robert five dollars to get up, and five dollars to brush his teeth, at least he will have some pocket money and not take up poker."

But Betty did not like Quentin's approach.

"In my opinion, it will make him as money-crazy as everyone else in the family, including you," she said. "Please, please do not pay him anymore." But what is a mother but someone who cannot stop anyone?

Before Theo left, they had noticed the ambulance sirens mostly at night. Now that there was less yelling, though, the sirens seemed to go on all day as well. How long was this going to last, this New York "on pause"? And why was wearing a mask such a big deal in America? In Hong Kong, people didn't complain about their glasses fogging up; they just wore their masks, and not in such a way that their noses stuck out. Of course, as Quentin pointed out, their noses were smaller, and flatter noses fit better under the masks. Still.

Betty wrote to Robert's teacher, "Could you give him some extra work? Because your homework about the Canarsee tribe of the

Lenape people only took him a half hour to complete. That was better than the gravity assignment, which took fifteen minutes, but never mind. Please—we parents are going crazy."

Of course, she knew that Miss Strange was just going to say what she always said to what everyone knew she called "pushy Asian parents"; namely, "The curriculum is age-appropriate." And so she did, though this time she added that there would be "NO CHANGE" to the no-grades-this-semester policy no matter how much extra work the kids did. Which Betty couldn't really blame her for saying, since some of the Asian parents really were complaining. What's more, as Miss Strange herself complained, it had been everything she could do to shift her entire class online. Parents had no idea how stressful it was, she wrote, especially since she had three children, four dogs, no husband, and a phobia about technology, which was why she had gone into teaching to begin with. However, just this one time she would provide an extra-credit assignment for interested students.

"Thank you," Betty typed. "Thank you." For she really was grateful.

If only the extra-credit assignment was not to tell a family mystery to a pet.

"To a pet?" Betty said. "You have to tell a mystery to a pet?"

"It doesn't have to be a real pet," Robert said. "It can be an imaginary pet." And, "Miss Strange said parents could help."

Betty sighed. It was revenge. It was the revenge of Miss Strange.

"How about a story about your grandpa," Quentin said. "How about a story about Yeye and Bongbong meeting in heaven? Yeye could feed him people food, and Bongbong could ask why he never got to eat food like that on earth."

"That's not a mystery," Robert said.

"It's a mystery to Bongbong," said Quentin, at whose feet Bongbong was even now sitting obediently, looking hopefully up at a cookie. His white tail thumped as if it had a special chip in it.

"And I don't want to use Bongbong anyway," Robert said. "Bongbong is a lapdog. I'm going to use an upgraded dog."

"Like?" Betty said.

"Like a German shepherd Seeing Eye dog," Robert said.

"Do you know what a Seeing Eye dog is?"

"It's a dog with superpowers." And, true-fact finder that he was, he spoke with an air of authority.

"Well, a Seeing Eye German shepherd would make the story more interesting," Betty conceded. It was going to be a long homework session, she could see.

Quentin left the room—having work to do, he said. How was it that he was now the boss of the business that she had founded over his strenuous objection? His bottom left an imprint on the leather stool seat, which was lilac to match the couch; the decorator had done that.

"What's the dog's name going to be?" she asked, trying to be playful.

"His first name is Detective."

"And his last name?"

"Dog."

"So—Detective Dog?"

"Yes. His name is Detective Dog, and he is interested in missing people." Robert raised a big round magnifying glass to his eye— one of Quentin's, which he kept on the kitchen counter in case he ever wanted to do a crossword puzzle.

"Theo isn't missing," Betty said calmly. "Theo is coming back."

"From his friend's house," Robert said.

"Yes."

Robert gave her his quick look. Then he squinted through the magnifying glass, which fit right into the gap he'd cut in his hair.

"I want you to tell me a mystery so I can solve it," he said.

Betty sighed. With Theo gone, it was as if she and Robert were on a desert island in that Animal Crossing game, except that, instead of protest banners, they had sirens. He was so quiet and intense, the whole apartment was quiet and intense.

"Is it my job to help you solve a mystery or my job to tell you one?" she asked.

"To tell me one."

"Are you sure that's what Miss Strange said?"

"Yes."

Betty sighed again. "I don't know how good a mystery it will be, Detective. I'm not a storyteller like you."

"It doesn't have to be good," he said. And, "We can start today and finish tomorrow. I'll ask you questions."

"Well, okay." How could she say no? She thought, then began, "Once upon a time there was a number-one daughter who everyone agreed was the best daughter in the family."

Robert cocked his head. "What do you mean, 'the best daughter'?"

"I mean that, out of three sisters, she was the smartest. She got into all those top schools. Andover and MIT and Harvard Business School. In fact, everywhere she applied she got in. She got an internship on Wall Street, and then she got a job on Wall Street. She was making a lot of money. But, all of a sudden one day, she dropped out and ran off with an American. And not just a regular American. A drummer."

"Why a drummer?"

"I don't know. All I know is that, when her family later heard that she had left the drummer, they celebrated! They had a dinner for her, even though she could not come. But after that she disappeared completely."

"Like Theo?"

Theo has not disappeared, she wanted to say.

Instead she said, "She went somewhere—no one knew where. For many years her parents cried. Then one day, guess what? I saw her again."

"Are you in the story?"

Quentin came back into the kitchen for a bag of chips, and not a lunch-box-size bag but a large one—meaning, Don't bother me.

"Are you in the story?" Detective Dog asked again when Quentin left.

"Yes, Detective," she admitted. "It was almost by mistake that I saw her a couple of years ago. We were about to move to New York, but we still had a business in Kunshan and sometimes stayed in Shanghai, as you probably remember. In the French Concession, where there are a lot of old European buildings, and restaurants and cafés and yoga studios. Do you remember?"

He nodded. "Shanghai was great."

Betty smiled. "It was. And, well, one day I went out to a café, and who did I see? She did not look the same as the last time I saw her. The last time I saw her she had blond hair and tattoos and a gas-mask pouch. Now she had plain hair and plain clothes, as if she were in disguise. We had some coffee. Of course, she was surprised to see me, too. I waited for her to tell me what she was up to. But she did not tell me right away. Instead, she raised an eyebrow and tilted her head. Meaning, there were cameras everywhere. I told her I needed to stop by my apartment, which I did, so that I could 'forget' my phone there, and no one could trace me with it. Then I met her in a park. I was not surprised to hear that she was trying to evade the police, because actually I had seen her once before, when she was involved in the protests in Hong Kong."

"You saw her before but didn't tell anyone?"

Betty looked away.

"Why?"

"Because I promised."

"So you knew other people she knew. Who would have wanted to know."

Betty hesitated but finally nodded.

"But you're telling me now."

"It's your homework," she said. Though what she really wanted to say was "Because you'll find out one day, I can see. Because you are like a mind-reading hat." And, "Because I don't want you to leave one day, like Theo."

"And why didn't she want you to tell?"

"Because the Chinese government likes to know all your family members. So if it isn't enough to pressure you, they can pressure them."

"Meaning, it was her family you didn't tell."

She nodded.

"Who were your family, too."

She nodded.

"Meaning, she was your sister."

Somehow it was a shock to hear it aloud.

"Yes," she said bravely. "Who, you know, did not want to be in trouble anymore. Or at least that's what she told me. She said she had come to Shanghai to try to give up her dangerous work. In fact, she had been effective—very effective, I think. She was so smart. And for a while she had believed that things would work out—as a lot of people did. So many people were involved in the protests. How could Beijing arrest them all?

"But now all she could think about was 2047, when Hong Kong would be swallowed up by the Mainland forever. Of course, back when the Mainland first started to rise up, we were proud to see Chinese people stand up to the West. Talk about bullies! The West always had to humiliate everyone and, by the way, now that Hong Kong needs help, do you see them? But in the end the Mainland turned on us, too. They attacked us the way they fired on their own people in Tiananmen. Of course, you were a baby, so you didn't know too much about what was happening."

"I am a dog," he reminded her.

"Oh, that's right. I mean, you were just a puppy," she said. Playful, the way she was supposed to be.

He gave a woof.

"You were only two and a half. But Theo never got over leaving his school and his friends, especially since he got bullied in Vancouver."

"That's why he became a bully himself."

"He's not a bully."

"And how was Shanghai going to help her give up her work?"

"I think we should take a break here." Betty glanced at the oven clock. "Time to start dinner."

They made an American-style tuna-noodle casserole with cream-of-mushroom soup. Then they played video games and looked for new recipes to try. Robert wanted to make peanut-butter-Snickers-cheesecake whoopie pies, which Betty said they could if he would do a yoga video with her once a day without pay. He said he would.

"Of course, the real mystery is where Theo is," she told Quentin in bed that night.

"He'll come back."

"I don't know. He has all that money." She pulled the quilt up under her chin. Though it was nowhere near summer, Quentin liked the A.C. up high; he said it reminded him of Hong Kong. "And now another headache: Robert's homework."

"Why don't you charge Robert for every five minutes you help him?"

"I can't charge him," Betty said. "I'm his mother."

"Mothers should charge," Quentin said, yawning.

The next day, Robert ate his cereal without a spoon, with his snout in his bowl.

"Detective Dog here, reporting for duty," he said. He licked his lips.

"In this house, dogs eat dog food," Betty warned. "Purina Puppy Chow."

"Not detective dogs," he said, crunching. "Detective dogs eat granola. So why did your sister move to Shanghai?"

Betty sighed, adding a scoop of vanilla ice cream to her decaf.

She used to allow herself this only in the afternoon, but ever since Theo had left she'd been allowing herself to have it in the morning, too.

Detective Dog raised his magnifying glass. "Why didn't she just move to New York?"

Betty drank—slurped, really. "Because, Detective, even if, way back when, she had married the drummer and become a U.S. citizen, which anyone else would have done, she could have had trouble getting an exit visa. And, anyway, she hadn't. She had to hide in China someplace. And so she thought she would hide with her boyfriend's family outside of Shanghai."

"She had a boyfriend?"

Betty drank, then answered, "He was also a dissident—played the guitar and apparently knew how to talk to journalists and get them to write things. I guess you could call him a kind of press agent. But his family was originally from this little village. And so the plan was to go live there for a while—to retire from protesting and live a simple life with chickens and a garden. Of course, a lot of the protesters were worried about getting arrested; they were worried they would be tried in a court on the Mainland. Some attempted to escape by boat to Taiwan. But she thought that, if she and her boyfriend just kept quiet, the government might realize they were done causing trouble. And then she thought she might finally be able to reconnect with our family. She said that it was torture being separated, and that she had never imagined we would be separated for this long."

"And then what happened?"

"Well, the boyfriend's family had no money. So she decided to do some teaching, first in a little school, and then in an international school. English language and U.S. history, since she had, after all, studied in the U.S. And these were international kids who could use some history beyond, you know, George Washington and Abe Lincoln."

"And then?"

"Well, she had a spy in her class. The spy was up front about sharing things with her father. 'My father this, my father that,' she would say—not to scare Bobby, exactly, really just to say, 'Someone is watching.' Bobby shrugged it off. She said there were informants in all the classes."

"So this was Aunt Bobby?"

Betty started a little but nodded. There it was. She had not meant to say Bobby's name, but she had.

"The missing one no one talks about?"

Betty nodded again.

"Can I have some milk shake?"

She pushed her coffee forward. It really was practically a milk shake, what with all the melted ice cream.

Detective Dog slurped. "And so, what about the spy?" he said.

"Well, one day, Bobby taught Thoreau's essay 'Civil Disobedience'—a famous essay about disobeying the law when your conscience won't let you just go along with it. She did not think this was so sensitive; after all, the point of the discussion was not whether the Chinese should disobey the law—she knew better than to encourage anything like that. The point was how important that idea was to some Americans, and how not all Americans agreed with it. And she was cautious. She did not use the words 'civil disobedience' in the file name, for example. She called it 'Thoreau.' Luckily, too, the spy happened to be absent the day she taught the essay. But then the spy came to office hours. And, as Bobby explained the essay, the spy recorded her. With the result that she was invited to tea by the authorities." Betty paused.

"So what's the matter with that?"

"Tea is never just tea. It's intimidation. Which worried her enough that she asked me not to tell anyone. Though she wanted me to know."

"That?"

"That they might think she would never stop being a dissident. That they might think she was the kind who would always stoke the fire under the cauldron. The kind who would not only make trouble but also spread trouble."

"And then?"

Betty got herself another scoop of ice cream.

"And then?" Detective Dog asked again.

"Well, and then I believe she was arrested. Every now and then, I wrote to her boyfriend and asked if he had written any new songs. And, if he had, I asked, Were they happy songs or sad songs? He always answered, Not too happy. Then he asked what you were up to."

"Changing the subject, you mean."

Betty drank.

"And what about the letter?"

She startled. Had Robert overheard her and Quentin talking? "I have not received a letter," she said.

"Interesting," he said.

She said it again. "I have not received a letter."

But there was his quick look, and finally she admitted, "There was a letter. But I did not receive it, because it was torn up."

"Do you know what it said?"

As Detective Dog held the magnifying glass up to his face once again, Betty heard Theo. *Did you ever speak up? Did you ever tell the truth?* Outside, the sirens went on and on.

"In Shanghai, Bobby told me that she had once written a letter to say goodbye just in case, and that she had told her boyfriend to make sure we got it if the time came. A last letter, she called it."

"So was that the letter?"

"I don't know, Detective."

"Why was it torn up?"

A ghost town. She wished they could all move to a ghost town.

"I think because Uncle Arnie knew it would break our hearts," she said finally.

"Uncle Arnie was the messenger."

"Yes. Also he maybe knew in his heart that in our hearts we already knew."

"So why did he tell you that he had it at all?"

The ambulances. The sirens. "Now you know why your grandmother always says, 'No politics,'" she wanted to say. Because that was the moral of the story. No politics.

Instead she said, "Because some things you cannot keep inside." She watched the strobe lights move along the tops of the window frames. They sped up, then slowed, then sped up again as Detective Dog pressed his nose to the magnifying glass.

"Why do you always call me Robert?" he asked, his nose flat and distorted. "Why do you never call me Bobby?"

If she wasn't crying, she might have been able to answer.

"Is it because you promised my mother?" he asked. He was still holding up the glass.

"She was the best of us," Betty managed. "The smartest and the bravest."

"Was." Robert put down the magnifying glass, pulled at his shirt sleeve, and wiped his eyes on the stretched-out material.

"We don't actually know," she said. "We may never know." She tried to hug him but he struggled away.

"My name is not Detective Dog," he said, his nose in his shirt.

"No," she said. And, trying to be playful, she said, "To begin with, you are a boy, not a dog."

"My name is Bobby Koo," he said.

"She was trying to protect you."

"Maybe Uncle Arnie will tell us where she is."

She tried again to hug him but hugged his shirt more than his small body. "And maybe Theo will come back," she said.

"The Chinese government likes to know all your family members," he said.

"Yes. And here you are safe. So it worked. But she loved true facts, you know. She spoke up. She wasn't like me."

"You speak up, too," Robert said.

But Betty shook her head no. "Not like Bobby. She was the best of us. And you," she said, "you, Detective Dog, are her son."

Sugar Island

FROM *Ploughshares*

MAGGIE AND JOAN took the two o'clock boat to Sugar Island. A man was supposed to show them his camelback sofa: green velvet upholstery, scrolled arms, feet like talons. Seven hundred. The ad said it dated back to 1908. This struck Maggie as disgusting—a hundred years of butts—but Joan loved old things, and she wanted to buy Maggie a sofa, somewhere they could sit together and read when Joan visited. Joan's love language was gift-giving. Maggie's was gift-receiving.

This was years back, when Maggie was still a phlebotomist. That's how they met—Joan had suspected she was deficient in Vitamin D, and Maggie was the one who stuck her vein and sent away her blood. Some patients were difficult: Maggie had to stroke their hands, and ask them to make a fist, then make it again. Often, she had to tie rubber tubes around their arms. And then she stabbed them, sometimes more than once. But Joan wasn't like that. She was easy—her cephalic vein was plump and bright, and Maggie stuck it on the first try. By the time she'd taped gauze in the crook of Joan's elbow, Joan had asked her out.

It was convenient to sleep with a woman whose bodily fluids she'd already handled. It turned out to be much less convenient for Maggie once Joan moved to Ohio a few months before. They took turns making the 445-mile trip, and with each trip, it took Maggie longer and longer to get there. She would park at the rest stop in Ceylon, get a car wash, do a crossword. One time, she pulled off the turnpike to play eighteen holes of mini-golf. She could not identify the exact moment at which her love for Joan folded in on itself. But somewhere on the turnpike, while she was going the minimum speed in the rightmost lane, she found she could not make it sit up straight.

Joan was the most generous woman Maggie had ever loved. She'd given her everything: A down jacket, chicken dinners, potted plants. Supplements. Cocktails. A haircut in the bathroom, orgasms in the middle of the day. And now the promise of a couch. But more than any of that, Joan gave Maggie a sanctuary from herself. She'd supplied the certainty that someone safe waited on the other side of the ceiling—and, now, the interstate. It soothed a racket inside Maggie, knowing this.

Being in love with Joan wasn't something Maggie wanted as much as it was something she let happen. Sometimes Maggie blamed the recession, or the election—who could expect her to be alone in these conditions? They kissed and then kept kissing, fucked and then kept fucking, and Maggie accepted everything Joan had to give. It was the perfect storm of loneliness and coincidence. Maggie did not have a knack, historically speaking, for objecting to the events of her life. She did not have a special talent for being alone.

Sugar Island had a population of 683. When they stepped off the ferry, Joan looked at her map and walked briskly in the middle of the street, ahead of Maggie. There was more land than houses, and the land looked hungry, a little desperate. There were no stop signs, but this didn't seem to matter, because there were no cars to stop.

"Are you okay?" Joan asked, looking back. She asked this during every lull.

"Yeah," Maggie said. "Fine."

They arrived at a sloping driveway and walked down a gravel path, and there they were, at the house of the man with the sofa. The house was one story, the color of pale urine. Thick vertical blinds on the windows, a Buick parked out front.

The old man who opened the door had a face so gaunt his cheeks looked vacuum-sucked. His gray hair was combed and gelled. He was smiling as if he'd been waiting for them all day. Maggie considered how many miles they were from anyone else.

"You're here for the camelback," he said, and looked between them for confirmation. Joan nodded. "I'm Bagley," he said, and stepped back to let them in.

Maggie blinked in the light and saw that the walls of his front room were filled with art.

"Please," he told them, "have a look around."

There was a portrait of a sad young girl holding a fat fish. There were landscapes of wreckage, farms painted from the sky, a cactus next to a telephone booth. There were houses in disrepair. Then there was the one Maggie would think of for years, long after she and Joan broke up: a small oil painting of a green bottle of Pert shampoo that had been squeezed so much it was crimped in the middle.

"No way," Joan said. She squatted low before a painting of a dog smoking a cigarette. "Is this a Griffith?"

Bagley got a naughty look on his face. "It's a Griffith."

Joan squealed. "I love him," she said. "He's one of my favorites. Is this from his—"

"His Pet Peeves series, yes," Bagley said.

"Oh, my god! I'm in awe!" Joan said.

Bagley offered them white wine or Coke or something called Rumchata. Joan said she'd love a white wine. Maggie wanted nothing. When Bagley returned with the wine, he took a seat in a high-backed chair and asked them what it is they do.

"I'm an artist," Joan said. "A painter."

"How wonderful," Bagley said. "How perfect!"

"And I'm a phlebotomist," Maggie said. "I draw people's blood."

"You're an artist too, then," he said. "She paints, you draw."

At this, Joan laughs too much. "You're right!" she said.

Maybe Joan was just being polite, Maggie told herself. But still, she felt her heart dip into envy. We will be here all day, she thought, Joan in rapture, carrying on with this strange man.

Bagley wanted to know about Joan's work, so Joan pulled out her phone and sat next to him. Maggie watched as Joan thumbed the screen, and Bagley's face changed again and again. "Oh, how lovely," he said, and "Incredible," and "It reminds me of Pachowsky, in the best possible way."

Back then, Joan was using a lot of gold leaf. A few months before, the people at the Sandusky, Ohio, Merry-Go-Round Museum hired her to restore a herd of antique wooden carousel animals. Joan chiseled off inch-thick layers of old paint and epoxy, then applied fresh color and varnish. At first, Maggie found the animals creepy, garish, but she sensed Joan's work was respected by other artists, and this inclined her to say she respected it too. The things Maggie knew about were crude—blood, plasma, veins. She was always mindful that her work was easily mastered, while what Joan had—talent, acclaim—seemed a result of magic and luck.

"You would not believe the money a grown man will pay for a painted pony," Maggie said, but neither Joan nor Bagley seem to hear her.

The last time Maggie tried to end things, she practiced what she would say during the 445-mile drive to Sandusky. She'd decided to tell Joan the truth. "The trouble is," she would say, "I don't care what you have to say about anything at all."

But when Maggie let herself into Joan's apartment, Joan wasn't there. Maggie ate a string cheese and lay on her mattress. After a while, she called Joan. Joan told her she was in the hospital. At work she'd dropped the body of a wooden elephant on her foot, and the doctors couldn't reattach the severed portion of her second toe. She was waiting to get the wound sutured. "My god," Maggie said, opening another digit of cheese.

At one point, Bagley placed his hand on Joan's shoulder, and something petulant caught in Maggie's throat. She stood up. "So, the couch," she said. "You said seven hundred?"

He didn't even glance at her. "I dabble in art too," he told Joan. "I like to mess around with charcoal. Let me just—" He stood then and went off in search of something.

When he was gone, Joan whispered to Maggie, "Are you okay?"

Maggie could only shrug.

Bagley came back with a drawing and showed it to Joan first. "That's my wife," he said.

Joan looked and her eyes went dreamy, deep in some sort of feeling. "Gorgeous," she said.

After a minute, Bagley sat down next to Maggie and showed her the sketch. It was a naked woman, legs splayed. Straight nose, shut eyes. Enormous breasts and bush. She was lying in some kind of meadow, surrounded by grass and lilies. He'd bungled the hands, but the other details were neat, proportional, exact.

Bagley looked at the picture again. "You really think it's good?" he said to Joan.

"Yes," she said. "You have quite the eye." She smiled at him, then said, "I painted Maggie once," and turned to look at her for confirmation.

Maggie nodded. "She did." The morning after they first fucked, Maggie told herself it wouldn't happen again. But then Joan knocked and wanted to show her something she'd made. "Come outside," she said, and Maggie followed her to her fire escape, where Joan had attached a long tube of ripstop to a fan. The tube inflated and seemed to sway, like an air dancer, and Maggie saw that Joan had painted the tube to look like her. The ripstop woman was wearing the same striped shirt she'd worn the day before. Maggie watched her nylon self lean one way, then the other. Her arms swung wide, and when wind blew, she kinked at the waist and bent low, then stood up again. It was so startling, so moving, that even now, years on, Maggie's pulse still quickens when she drives past a car dealership.

Bagley smiled, sensing unease. Then he set his drawing on the coffee table and looked at them. He said, "So. Let's have a look at the camelback."

Joan squeezed Maggie's hand and Maggie pulled it free, put it in her pocket. They followed Bagley through the bright kitchen into his bedroom. The shag carpet was Kelly green, the four-poster bed dark oak, the walls papered in garish florals. And opposite the bed was the camelback.

"It's lovely," Joan said, and the springs made a sound when she sat.

"This baby is a real find," Bagley said. "Perfect condition, save for a little stain here, on the other side of the cushion." He lifted the fabric and showed them a small pen mark. "I've got a couple guys who'll bring it over on the ferry," he said. "No extra charge. White glove delivery. Great guys."

"I live on the third floor," Maggie said.

"That's no problem!" Bagley said. "They'll do as many flights as you got."

"Come sit," Joan said, and patted the seat next to her.

Maggie did. "Stiff," she said.

"Firm," Joan countered.

Bagley pointed to a scroll carved into a leg. "What I love most is all these beautiful details in the woodwork."

Joan was thrilled about the scroll. "They don't make them like this anymore," she said, and Bagley nodded.

He said, "I'll throw in a slipcover. And a matching pillow."

"A slipcover," Maggie scoffed.

"It's for preserving it," Joan said. She was trying to skim impatience from her voice, Maggie could tell. "What do you think?"

Maggie said, "I don't know. It's very ornate." She thought of the stuff in her apartment: the bookshelf made of imitation wood, the single straight-backed chair, the mattress made of poly-foam that came rolled up in a box. She had to unroll it and let it rise, like dough. She has since menstruated all over it.

The couch would fit better in Joan's apartment, where the furniture is expensive and attractive. Joan's mattress cost eighteen hundred dollars. It was so luxurious that it had a woman's name. The Layla. When Joan moved, Maggie helped her carry the Layla in and out of a truck and then backward up her new stairs. This was the first time it was clear to her they would not last: they were stuck in the stairwell with one hundred pounds of foam and steel coils between them, and they could not find a way to make it around the corner.

Maggie considered her options. Accepting the couch, refusing the couch—every possible decision would give Joan the wrong idea. Maggie would feel cruel either way.

She knew it was past time to take an active interest in the events of her life. All day, she poked people's arms and watched blood leave their bodies. These people were willing to endure a little pain. They were ready to get better. "Tell me," they said to their doctors when the results came in. "What should I do? What is the way to mend myself?"

Maggie was not so brave.

Yes, okay, yes, let's get the couch. Yes, I love the couch, Maggie said, and as Joan filled in the blanks of the check, she almost believed it herself.

"Do you want to walk forward or back?" Joan asked. The couch was a different color in the sun; the velvet shone and looked almost wet.

"Whatever," Maggie said, so Joan took the front end. Opposite each other, they crouched in Bagley's driveway, and Joan reminded Maggie to lift with her legs.

"You have to be my eyes," Joan said, stepping backward. "Tell me if I'm going to walk into something."

The camelback was more cumbersome than heavy, and Maggie shifted her hands to accommodate the bulk. She'd insisted they take the couch today, rather than schedule a time with Bagley's great guys.

"You got it?" Joan said when Maggie moved a hand under the front leg.

"I got it," Maggie said.

They walked in time, each step agitating the couch. Past Joan, Maggie saw fields of rushes and creeping thistle. There was so much nothing. The street was flat and seemed deserted, but then Joan said, "Hello," and a boy in big jeans pulled up next to them on a bike, no helmet. He nodded as he glided past them, and ped- aled with lassitude, knees wide, aimless. The only sound was his bike chain slipping over the sprocket.

At the dock, they bought the camelback a one-way ticket.

The boat ramp was too narrow, and they had to hoist the couch onto their shoulders to clear the railing. Maggie was depleted. Her arms trembled and her tennis shoes slipped a bit with each step.

A man in a red vest coached them through it. "Keep going," he called, when they were halfway up the ramp. "Keep going. A little farther. A little farther. A little—okay, stop," he said, when Maggie let go of her end.

Panting, she bent at the waist and put her hands on her knees. "I just need a minute," she said.

"Would you like some help?" the vest-man asked.

"No," Maggie said. "I'm fine." Then: "Yeah, okay. Sure." She stepped aside and watched the man lift the back half with ease. He and Joan walked off—jauntily, it seemed to Maggie—and set the couch on the ferry deck. She could have done that, she thought. She wished she hadn't given up so quickly.

The boat left Sugar Island with a lurch, and Joan put an arm around Maggie. Joan smelled like sweat and Bagley's wine. They sat on the camelback, looking out over Lake Michigan, and it was nice, after hauling the couch, to be held by Joan. More than the material goods and the attention and the eye contact during sex, Maggie expected she would miss this the most: the way Joan clung, close as plum to pit.

She expected, too, that only she was capable of ending things.

She fancied herself imperious. It was just a matter of time, she thought, until she had the gumption necessary to leave Joan. But she was still waiting for the gumption when, months later, Joan met Aimee. Aimee, who taught ESOL and who Maggie determined, from a series of searches online, had a septum piercing, and was impossibly pretty and fun.

After Joan left, Maggie became sick of venipuncture, of easily mastered work. She wanted more for herself. She spent thousands of dollars applying to medical school, and did not get into a single program. No magic, no luck for her. The rejections came swiftly, one after another, and she told no one, because no one knew she'd applied. The next year, when she was accepted to nursing school in Illinois, she decided to go.

In the years that have passed since the trip to Sugar Island, Maggie has moved in and out of seven different apartments and two small one-story homes. Each time, without remorse, she's thrown away many things: pit-stained T-shirts, travel tubes of toothpaste, the orange and yellow Skittles in the bottom of a bag. Magazines read long ago, socks missing their mates. Birthday cards from aunts who've since died. It is like getting rid of evidence, she feels—evidence that she's ever been anyone other than who she's become.

After they break up, it pains Maggie to see the couch in her living room, where she and Joan set it down. "It's perfect," Joan had said, and then knelt and stuck small felt discs to each foot. It is this image that Maggie returns to: Joan in dirty sneakers, on her knees, holding half the couch aloft. Maggie hardly believes she'd wanted to leave a person like that.

After they break up, Maggie pushes the couch from one end of the room to the other. She makes it face the window, then the bookshelf, then the door, but decides to leave it where it was. Over time, the couch becomes common, ordinary, part of the background of her life. And when she is many years older, when she has become someone she can live with, she will come home from an overnight shift to find that her sweet, well-adjusted partner has unwittingly sold the camelback for twenty-six dollars in the neighborhood garage sale. "Do you know the name of the person who bought it?" Maggie will ask, trying to sound indifferent.

ELIZABETH McCRACKEN

The Souvenir Museum

FROM *Harper's*

PERHAPS SHE SHOULD have known that she would find her lost love—her Viking husband, gone these many years—in Sydesgaard, on the island of Funen, in the village of his people. Asleep in the hut of the medicine woman, comforted by the medicine woman, loved by the medicine woman, who was (it turned out) a podiatrist from Aarhus named Flora. The village itself was an educational site and a vacation spot where, if you wanted, you could wear a costume and spin wool for fun. As for Aksel—was he Joanna's common-law ex-husband, or ex-common-law husband? Eleven years ago they had broken up after living together for ten. "Broken up"—one summer Aksel left for Denmark, and she never heard from him again.

Not *never*. He sent an apologetic postcard from London. But never after that, nothing for eleven years. She'd married, been made a mother, lost a mother, been legally divorced, finally was fully orphaned by her father's death. Her father, who had been heartbroken when Aksel disappeared, for his own sake. Who else would breakfast with him on white wine and oysters? Who would discuss the complexities of savory pies: pork, kidney, the empanada versus the Cornish pasty? They had adored each other. Enormous and bearded, condescending and fond, ravenous, sad-eyed, the pair of them. Mortifying, when Joanna thought about it, how alike they were—her friends had commented on it. It was her father who referred to Aksel as a common-law husband, when he was in every way a boyfriend, including the way she thought about him years later: with a lechery untouched by having to legally untangle.

After the funeral, her father's cluttered bedroom was like the tank of an animal who perhaps had died or perhaps had fallen asleep behind the greenery. She looked and looked for him. Nothing felt definitive. The watch was in the nightstand drawer beneath an expired passport, heavy and silver, a steam locomotive on its case, a yellowing sticker on the back: *Please bring to Aksel.* She read and reread the sticker. Leo, her son, was like his grandfather, drawn to long-ago things, though nine-year-old Leo particularly loved weapons and had nearly every morning for two years drawn in pencil an armory. He liked blades best: swords, bayonets, the occasional flail. He was not allowed toy weapons, though they came into the house the back way. That is, in Lego boxes: bows and arrows the size of safety pins, pistols that snapped into the tense and insatiable hands of Legomen.

She turned the watch over in her palm. Perhaps Leo could get interested in horology. She pictured him hunched over a watchmaker's bench and thought about tossing the note and keeping the watch. Instead, she transferred it from her father's nightstand into her own. *Bring,* he'd written. Not *mail,* not *get.* The sticker was as close to a will as he'd left, goddamn him. She should probably— she thought, aware of the daft expression already on her face— attempt to honor it.

It took a year to settle the estate, sell the condo, come into the little bit of money that would allow them for the first time to travel abroad. Joanna bought Leo the bunk bed that she had wanted as a child. When she went to wake him up for school in the morning, she never knew at what altitude she would find him. That morning he'd hidden himself in the top bunk among the stuffed animals and the alligator-patterned comforter cover, which had disgorged its comforter. Then she saw one bare heel. Even his heel was fast asleep and dear.

"Leo," she said.

The heel disappeared. He balled himself up under the covers as though winding himself awake. Then he sat up and blinked, bare-chested and skinny.

"What do you think about Vikings?" she asked him.

"They're not my favorite," he said, and put out his hand. "Glasses?"

He was newly bespectacled, having failed a vision test at school. Because he hadn't cared, she'd picked him out a pair of square black frames, so that he looked not like the bookish skinny wan pubescent boy he was, but like a skinny wan eighties rocker. *Wow,* he'd said, stepping out of the optician's, scanning the parking lot, the parking lot trees, the Starbucks and the Staples. *Wow.* Just like that, both he and the world looked different.

She found his glasses on a bookshelf and handed them up. "Vikings aren't your favorite?"

He scooted to the end of the bunk and climbed down the ladder. "I like Romans." The underpants he'd slept in were patterned with lobsters, too small. "Vikings didn't *really* have horns on their helmets. Did you know that?"

"I did not," she said.

For a year and a half, before Leo could read but after he'd begun to talk, Joanna had known everything in his head, thoughts and terrors, facts and passions. He'd belonged to fairyland then; afterward, to books and facts. Now he had thoughts all the time that she hadn't put in his head, which she knew was the point of having children but destroyed her.

"So," she said. "I have a friend in Denmark. I was thinking we might go there this summer."

Leo sat at his desk and picked up a pencil. In the voice he used for lying, or when he cared too much about something, he said, "If we go, could we go to Legoland?"

"I thought that was in California."

"Real Legoland," Leo explained. "*Danish* Legoland. Denmark's where Lego was invented."

"You're not too old for all that?"

The glasses magnified his incredulous look. He was like a mid-century TV journalist who knew he was being lied to. "Mommy, you *know* I like Lego."

"Yes," she said. "Of course." Lego: its salient angles, its minute ambitions. On her own childhood trips, Joanna had been at the mercy of her father's interests. He drove the car; he decided where to stop it. Not amusement parks, not tourist traps. Instead: war museums, broken-toothed cemeteries, the former houses of minor historical figures, with tables set for dinner—soup tureens and fluted spoons—and swords crossed over the fireplace. Joanna, aged nine, ten, forever, had wanted to go to Clyde Peeling's Reptiland. To the Mystery Spot, where ball bearings rolled uphill. To Six Flags over Anywhere. A sign for Legoland would have driven her mad with longing, would have made her whine, even though whining—her mother would point out—had never gotten her anywhere. Her father would have driven on to some lesser Civil War battlefield to inspect an obelisk.

Leo was a child of divorce, and all his own vacations were airplane volleys from Rhode Island to California and back. The two of them had never really traveled together.

"All right," she said. "We'll go to Legoland."

She had already renewed their passports, bought the tickets, reserved a Volvo with a GPS. But you had to give a child the illusion of choice.

Legoland was overwhelmingly yellow, and Leo, abashed, hated it. The rides had electric signs that estimated how long you'd have to stand in line to ride them. The log flume was a forty-five-minute wait. The polar roller coaster, an hour and five. It was an ordinary overcrowded amusement park. They had flown through the air, Boston to Paris, Paris to Billund, to end up at *this* place, the first day of their vacation. He wondered how long they would have to stay for his mother to get her money's worth. She could be grim about expensive fun. The crowds of children upset him, blonder than the blondest American blond. *Flaxen hair,* he thought. Like from a book. Flaxen hair and cornflower-blue eyes, though he'd never seen flax or cornflowers in real life. If he had, he might have thought, *Blue as a Danish child's eyes, pale as a Danish child's mullet.* The blondness itself seemed evil to Leo. A blond child who screeches and steps on your foot is compelled by its blondness; a blond mother who hits you with her stroller—here comes another one, rushing after her child, attempting to climb into the lap of the life-size Lego statue of Hans Christian Andersen—does it out of pure towheadedness.

In America he would have cried out, but in Legoland he felt he had to bear it.

Even the gift shop was disappointing. He'd been imagining something he couldn't imagine, some immense box that would allow him to build—what. A suit of Lego. A turreted city big enough to live in. Denmark itself. He did not dream in Lego, not anymore, but sometimes he still raked his hand through the bins of it beneath his bed as a kind of rosary, to remind himself that the world, like Lego, was solid and mutable both.

Joanna, too, found Legoland terrible; Joanna, too, could not confess. It was a kind of comfort, because Aksel had always been exhausting on the subject of Denmark versus America. Denmark was beautiful, and so were Danes; America was crass, and every moment of American life was a commercial for a slightly different form of American life; you could not so much as enjoy a hamburger without having your next hamburger advertised to you, though the hamburgers would be exactly the same: spongy and flavorless. "Americans have garbage taste," he would say, tucking into an American banana split. "Not you, Johanna." He always added a spurious *h* to her name. "But someday you will go to Denmark, and taste the ice cream, and you will understand." Clearly the man had never been to Legoland, where even ice cream required a half hour wait in line, and then was a tragedy of dullness.

They stopped at a self-serve slush stand that allowed you to mix any flavors you wanted in a tall plastic vessel that looked like a bong. Leo's personal cocktail came out army green. This always happened to his Play-Doh too when it got mixed together. He drank it with his eyes closed and winced. He most resembled his late grandfather when unhappy.

"Poor bunny, you're jet-lagged. Here. Let's sit." They sat on the bench next to the Lego Hans Christian Andersen, and Joanna had a sense that they shouldn't, they should leave the space clear for people who wanted pictures of themselves with a Lego Hans Christian Andersen. But why should those people get their way?

"I'm not jet-lagged," he said.

"Do you want to just go to the hotel room?"

"Is the hotel room in Legoland?"

"Yes," she said.

"Oh." Then, "I hate it here."

"Denmark?"

He looked at her aghast. "This isn't *Denmark*," he said. "Can we go? It's not what I thought it would be like."

"Yes," said Joanna, grateful and motherly, a *good* mother, indulgent. "What did you think it would be like?"

But she knew. In our private Legolands we are the only human people.

"I'll tell you what," she said, and she handed Leo her phone. "You choose. Wherever you want to go, we'll go. I know Vikings aren't your favorite, but I have a friend at that Viking village—"

"What Viking village?"

"A Viking village," she said. "We'll go at the end of the week. In the meantime, do some research. Plan the next three days. If you want, we can come back to Legoland—"

"I'm never going to come back to Legoland," he said passionately.

When our children love what we love, it is a blessing, but oh, when they hate what we hate!

Denmark was studded with little museums dedicated to misery and wealth and the unpleasant habits of men, and Leo wanted to go to every one. He was warming to the Vikings. There was a kind of gentle boredom to Denmark, which was in itself interesting: archaeological museums whose captions were entirely in Danish, with displays of pottery shards and nails and swords and bits of armor. To become interested in a boring subject was a feat of strength. A splinter of Viking armor was more interesting than the whole suit, to Leo, because even though it was in a plexiglass box it might fit in your pocket. Perhaps he liked bits because of his nearsightedness—now that he had glasses, it was alarming what loomed on the horizon—but entire objects told the entire story, and therefore belonged to everyone. Looking at a piece of a thing, he might think, deduce, discover something nobody ever had, which was all he wanted in the world.

They took a ferry to the island of Ærø. In the old shipyard, Leo made rope using a crank-operated machine and, with the help of a blacksmith, forged a plain iron hook. The blacksmith was a lean man with a sad, rectilinear face and hair the color of clapboard. The black iron glowed orange when you put it in the forge, and when you hammered it orange sparks flew off, and then you were left with something so black and solid you couldn't imagine it had ever been otherwise.

They went to the Welfare Museum, three maritime museums, the Danish Railway Museum. Of course, Joanna missed her father, seeing his dullest passions alive in his grandson. Who else could love trains so much that they were still interesting in a museum, where they were robbed of their one power, movement? Not Joanna, but she could love somebody who did. She felt a useless pride in Leo's peculiar enthusiasms; Leo's pleasant father liked action movies and video games, like any American boy.

Joanna had arrived with three pieces of Danish: *Taler du engelsk?* (the answer was always, Yes, I do); *tak!*; and the phrase for "excuse me," which she remembered because it sounded—she thought it sounded; she had a terrible ear—like "unskilled." Unskilled! *Taler du engelsk? Tak!* Soon she picked up the vocabulary of ice cream— Aksel was right, vanilla ice cream in Denmark was hallucinogen- ically delicious—*kugler, vafler, softice, flødeboller.* Though a month after they got home Joanna would wake up in the middle of the night wondering, Is the Danish word for thanks pronounced *tock* or *tack?* And which pronunciation had she used? The wrong one, she was sure.

Aksel's watch was in her pocket. She'd put it in a Ziploc bag to keep it clean and hadn't so much as wound it. It wasn't hers to wind. She liked the weight of it about her person.

Did she still love Aksel? No, but the memory of him came in handy sometimes.

They found the Souvenir Museum the old-fashioned way, first one roadside sign, then another. The museum was on the grounds of a modest castle. Like Legoland, the name was full of promise. Sou- venir: a memory you could buy. A memory you could *plan* to keep instead of being left with the rubble of what happened.

A teenage girl with a drowsy, dowsing head slid a pamphlet across the ticket desk, and then pointed to the door to the mu- seum. Leo opened the pamphlet. The museum was made of six rooms. He was startled to see that the last room was called Forbid- den Souvenirs.

A year ago Leo might have asked his mother what *Forbidden Sou- venirs* meant. Now he was seized with a terrible, private fear that he didn't want her to disturb or dispel. He read books about war; his mother didn't. Soldiers took souvenirs: ears, teeth, shrunken heads, scalps.

His mother, innocent, admired the first glass case, which was filled with salt and pepper shakers. Two Scottish terriers, black and white. One Scottish terrier (salt) lifting its leg in front of a red fire hydrant (pepper). The next glass case was also filled with salt and pepper shakers. There was a density to the collection that felt like a headache, or the physical manifestation of dementia, where the simplest items had to be labeled for meaning: china Eiffel Towers marked *Paris,* pot-metal London Bridges marked *London.* It had clearly been somebody's private collection, a problematic Dane's hoard. Surely all the salt and pepper shakers had been made in one vast factory in Japan or China, then stamped with geographic locations and shipped off.

"After this," she said, "we'll go to the Viking village. Your grandfather would have hated this place. What's the matter?"

I don't want to see, he thought, but also he did.

He was stepping into Forbidden Souvenirs. It took him a moment to figure out what he was looking at: coral, ivory, alligator shoes, exotic game of all sorts, pillaged antiquities.

"Are you all right?"

"Yes," he said.

A faceless mannequin wore a leopard jacket over nothing, its skinny white featureless body obscene. "Grandma had a mink stole," Joanna said. "I can't remember what we did with it."

Some of the objects flaunted the original animal: the head of an alligator biting closed a pocketbook, the paws of a white fox dangling from a stole. Was that better or worse than the elephant carved out of an elephant tusk, the tortoise incised into the tortoise shell?

"I thought there would be ears," said Leo. "From the enemy."

"What enemy?"

"I don't know," said Leo helplessly. "The enemy dead."

"No ears," said Joanna in an improbably cheery voice. She gestured at the glass case. "Nothing to worry about."

"I wasn't," he said. But he had been, the worry was in him, the fear of seeing something he shouldn't have, human, severed. The feeling was traumatic and precious.

"Anyhow," she said.

"Do they pretend there?" he asked.

"Do they what where?"

"Pretend at the Viking village. Dress up and say they're Vikings."

"Oh. Not sure. Why?"

"The Renaissance fair," he said darkly.

They'd gone to a Ren fair when Leo was four. He'd gotten lost in an iron maze of child-size cages and began to sob—she had a picture of him that she'd taken before noticing the tears—and a man dressed as an executioner had to talk him out, gesturing with his plastic axe. Leo liked to bring it up from time to time, evidence of Joanna's bad judgment. He liked history. He did not like grown-ups in fancy dress.

She said, "It'll be great."

"That's what you said about Legoland."

Had she? "Leo—"

"I *said* I didn't want to go."

"No, you—"

"Yes I did," he said. The words were underlined, she heard it, and later she would understand it as the first sign of adolescence, and she would forgive him, but she didn't forgive him now.

"Well," she said, "we're going."

The eyes of a half-dozen taxidermic animals were upon them, as though betting on who'd win the argument and who'd end up in the museum. Then the humans turned and wordlessly went from the room.

In the morning they drove to Odin's Odense, their bags packed in the trunk of the rented car. That night they would go on to Copenhagen, then fly back to the States. Joanna looked in the rearview mirror at sulking Leo. Next year he would be tall enough to ride up front, but for now he was in the backseat. *You get to choose*, she'd said, and she'd hoped to finagle him into believing that a trip to the Viking village had been his choice. What she'd endured for him! Three days of stultifying museums. They had traveled together beautifully, sleeping in the same room for the first time since his infancy. Ruined now. She knew the ruination she felt was her own treacherous heart.

The car's GPS brought them deeper into the suburbs, red tiled roofs, no businesses. "This doesn't look right," said Leo from the back, hopefully. But the GPS knew what it was doing, and there they were. Odin's Odense.

They had to pass through a little un-Viking modern building that housed admissions, a gift shop, and flush toilets. Joanna wondered whether she should ask after Aksel, but what if he had a Viking name? The old woman behind the counter thrust a map at her and frowned encouragingly. The museums of the world are filled with old women, angry that nobody listens to them, their knowledge, their advice. She hadn't told Leo why they were here, in case it came to nothing.

Joanna gave him the map. "Here. It's in English."

He consulted it and said, casually, "There's a sacrificial bog."

"That might come in handy."

They walked into the Viking village on one of those days of bright sunshine, the sky so blue, the clouds so snowy white, everything looked fake. Though why was that? Why, when nature is its loveliest, do human beings think it looks most like the work of human beings?

Was her detection system still tuned to Aksel's frequency? At one time, she could walk into any room and know whether he was there. Now she detected nothing.

The Viking huts were 89 percent thatched, like gnomes in oversized caps. A teenager in a tunic and laced boots ducked out of one, his arms laden with logs. He gave Joanna a dirty look, and she understood that he was mad at his mother, wherever she was, in whatever century, and therefore mad at all mothers.

Leo, too. He pointed to a small structure with no roof and said, gloomily, "I think this is the old smithy."

There was nothing smithish about the old smithy. Joanna put her hands on her hips as though she were interested in smithery, though all she could feel was her heart beating warrantless through her body. She knew she and Leo would forgive each other. She knew that it was her duty to solicit forgiveness from everyone, but just then she was tired of men whose feelings were bigger than hers. She felt as though she'd grown up in a cauldron of those feelings and had never gotten out.

"Okay. What's next?"

"The medicine woman's hut."

Inside the medicine woman's hut, a squinty, hardy-looking woman of about sixty sat on a low bench, stirring an open fire with a stick.

"*Hej,*" said the woman. This was the jaunty way some Danish people said hello, and Joanna always felt exhilarated and frightened saying it back, as though she might pass for Danish a few seconds longer. Which was worse, being found out as an American or as a fraud? It was a big space, illuminated by the fire and the sunlight coming through the front and back doors. The fire was directly underneath the highest part of the thatched ceiling: Viking fire safety. "Say hello," said Joanna to Leo.

A preposterous command. He didn't.

The medicine woman gestured to a low, long bench across from her. In English, in the voice of the Iron Age, the woman said, "Welcome. Where do you stay?"

Were they supposed to be ancient, too?

Leo tried to feel it. Before Denmark, he hadn't realized how much he wished to be ancient. To be Danish. To be, he thought now, otherwise for a reason.

His mother said, "Last night, near Svendborg."

The medicine woman nodded, as though approving of this wisdom. "It is beautiful there." She withdrew her stick, inspected the end, stuck it back in. "You have been to Langeland? The 'big island,' you would call it?"

"No."

She nodded again. "You must."

She was the medicine woman: everything she said had the feel of a cure and a curse. Yes: they would go to the big island. It was inevitable.

On the big island, thought Joanna, she might forget her big mistakes; on the big island, they would scatter their memories, if not her father's ashes. They had not brought his ashes. There were too many of them.

"There is an excellent Cold War museum," the medicine woman said.

What was a cold war, in the land of the Vikings?

"It has a submarine," the medicine woman said to Leo. "It is the largest in Europe, I believe. I took my son. Also mini-golf close by. A good place to holiday, if you do not come here. Wouldn't you like to come to holiday here someday? That is what we do. We put on the clothes and *puh!* we are Vikings."

"Yes!" Leo said. "You mean, you stay here? You *sleep* here?"

"Of course!" She turned to the corner of the hut and said a sentence or two to a pile of blankets. Perhaps it was an ancient incantation. Nothing happened. She said it again. They could not find a single cognate among the syllables.

The pile of blankets shifted. An animal? No. The blankets assembled themselves into a shadow of a man.

The shadow became an actual man, sitting up.

The actual man was Aksel.

He was eleven years older and much thinner, and he had shaved his beard, even though he was now a Viking. He'd always had long squintish eyes; they had acquired luggage. He yawned like a bear, working all the muscles of his jaw; that is, he yawned like Joanna's long-ago love, the foreigner she'd fallen for when they had worked together on a college production of *True West*. Joanna had been prop mistress, and had collected twenty-seven working toasters from yard sales and Goodwills. Aksel directed, and had broken every one of those toasters during a single impassioned speech to the actors, sweeping them off a table while declaring, "I don't want you to act, I want you to react, I want you to *get mad*."

The medicine woman said, "Aksel's mother told us you were coming here with the boy."

Joanna nodded. She still didn't know what millennium they were supposed to be in. "You get mail here?"

"She texted." The medicine woman mimed with her thumbs.

"Johanna," said Aksel. That needless, endearing *h*.

How many time frames was she in? College, midtwenties, the Iron Age, the turn of the last century. He was recognizable to her—she'd worried he wouldn't be—and beloved to her too.

"What are you doing here?" he asked, in a serious voice.

It was a good question. He didn't look like her father. That might have been what brought her here. The watch could be mailed; Legolands were legion; but where in the world was a man like the man she'd just lost?

Her actual heart found the door behind which her metaphorical heart hid; heart dragged heart from its bed and pummeled it. Years ago she'd wondered what, exactly, constituted love—the state of emergency she felt all ten years of their life together? Not that the building was on fire; not that the ship was about to sink; not that the hurricane was just offshore, pulling at the palm trees: the knowledge that, should the worst happen, she had no plan of escape, not a single safety measure; she was flammable, sinkable, rickety, liable to be scrubbed from the map. That feeling was love, she'd thought then, and she thought it now too.

"My father died," she said.

"Ah, Walter," said Aksel, and he rubbed his jaw dolefully. "I am sorry. Recently?"

"A year ago. I have something for you. We decided—this is Leo—we decided it was a good time to come to Denmark, to deliver it."

"Hello, Leo," said Aksel, who looked half in dreamland, populated as it was by ancient Danes, long-ago girlfriends, and preteen American boys. "I am very glad to meet you."

"You know my *mom?*" said Leo.

"That friend I mentioned." Then to Aksel: "I Facebooked your mom, but I guess you're off the grid."

"I am very much upon," he said. "You just don't know my coordinates." He looked again at Leo and nudged the medicine woman's back with his knee. "This is Johanna," he said of Joanna. "This is Flora," he said of the medicine woman. "Shall we go for a walk, Johanna? Just for a moment."

The medicine woman turned to Leo. "Do you want to play a game? My son is doing so. Come, he will teach you." She got up and ushered Leo through the front door, and Joanna and Aksel went out the back, the fire smoking, a fire hazard, but the Vikings must have known what they were doing.

"I've thought of you often, Johanna," said Aksel. In the sunlight he was shaggy, his color was not so good, but he was beautiful, a beauty. His clothes smelled of smoke. He seemed a victim of more than recreational Vikinghood.

"You're on vacation," she said. "I thought perhaps you'd become a professional Viking."

"Ah no. I am a software developer. Flora, she is a foot doctor. And you?"

"Bookkeeper."

He nodded. "You were always a keeper of books. Let us discuss what you have brought me."

The minute she pulled the watch from her purse she missed its weight. She opened the Ziploc bag, suddenly worried that watches were supposed to breathe.

"Ah!" said Aksel mildly. He took the watch and immediately put it in a pouch he wore tied to his belt, as though any sign of modernity were shameful. "Walter knew I admired this watch. That is what you came to give me?"

"It's what my father wanted you to have."

"And only this."

He started walking and she followed, her long-ago husband, her lost love, to the banks of the sacrificial bog, if bogs had banks. Aksel said, "But not the boy."

"Not the boy what?"

"He isn't my son."

"What? No! He's *ten.*"

"Ah!" said Aksel. "My mother said you were coming with a boy, and Flora thought maybe. She has a keen sense for these things."

She saw on his face an old emotion, disappointment shading into woe. "What did *you* think?"

He turned to the bog. "I might have liked it. Flora has a son. It might have saved me."

"Saved you? Viking you, or *you* you?"

The bog said nothing. Aksel said, "I can love anyone," and took her hand. It was the first time he had touched her. A moment ago she'd thought that would be the last step of the spell, the magic word, the wave of the wand. But it wasn't.

I could lie, she thought. She'd never really lied, not like that, a lie you would have to see through, a first step on the road to a hoax, an entirely different life, where facts and dates and numbers would have to be fudged. Leo *did* exist because of Aksel. He would not otherwise.

But then Aksel dropped her hand, as though he'd been joking. "Women are lucky. God puts an end to their foolishness. But men, we are bedeviled till the end of our days."

She said, with as much love as she could muster, quite a lot, "Fuck off."

"All right, Johanna."

"Why did you leave?"

"I didn't want—" But there he stopped. The Viking village was all around them, smoke in the air, the bleating of sheep that didn't know what millennium they were in, either. Or perhaps they were goats. She couldn't always tell the difference.

"What didn't you want?" she asked him.

He shook his head. "A fuss."

"Jesus. I want the watch back."

"We might have married," he said. "But then it seemed as though we should have done it at the start."

"Give me the watch. I'll sacrifice it to the bog."

"It's worth rather a lot."

"Then Leo should have it. My son. I mean, we spent four hours at the railway museum. I don't know what I was thinking, giving it to you."

He retrieved the watch from his pouch, his Viking pocketbook, and weighed it in his hand as though he himself would throw it bogward. Instead he wound it up—later, when Leo *did* become interested in old watches, she would discover this was the worst thing you could do, wind a dormant watch—and displayed it. First he popped open the front to exhibit the handsome porcelain face, the elegant black numbers. "Works," he remarked. Then he turned it over and opened the back.

There, in his palm, a tiny animated scene: a man in a powdered wig, a woman in a milkmaid's costume, her legs open, his pants down, his tiny pink enamel penis with its red tip tick-tock-ticking at her crotch, also pink and white and red. It was ridiculous what passed for arousing in the old days. She was aroused.

"Old Walter," said Aksel. "He lasted a while, then. He started taking care of himself?"

"No. He got worse and worse. He was eighty."

"He never wanted to be," said Aksel, in a sympathetic voice.

"I know it."

He offered the watch. "In four years perhaps your boy will be interested."

Ah, no: it was ruined. Not because of the ticking genitalia, but because it was somebody else's private joke, and she the cartoon wife wanting in, in a robe and curlers, brandishing a rolling pin. Even a cartoon wife might love her rascal husband. She did.

"He wanted you to have it for a reason," she said.

Flora's son and Leo played a Viking game that involved rolling iron hoops down a hill. Flora's son was sullen and handsome, with green eyes and licorice breath, terrible at mime, and so he put his hands on Leo's to demonstrate how to hold the hoop and send it off, then looked Leo in the eyes to see if he'd gotten it, all with a kind of stymied intimacy that Leo understood as a precursor to grown-up love.

I will learn Danish, thought Leo. *I will never learn Danish.*

He turned to let the hoop go, and there was his mother, striding up the hill. Bowl her over for ten more minutes with this boy, ten more minutes in the Iron Age—where they had no concept of minutes—ten more minutes of this boy scratching his nose with the back of his wrist then touching the back of Leo's wrist with his Viking fingers. Bowl her down and stay.

No, of course not. The stride told him that they were leaving.

Would he have wished her away? Only if he could wish her back later.

And would she, Joanna, have wished her beloved Leo away? Only if she could also wish away his memory. To long for him forever would be terrible.

"See you later," said the Viking boy, who spoke English all along, running to gather the hoops.

ALICE McDERMOTT

Post

FROM *One Story*

"MAYBE BRIMSTONE," MIRA said. "Smoky, cloying. Tincture of something rotten. Flesh, maybe."

Adam paused. Pulled down his mask, sniffed the air. He had a lovely nose. Small and neat, slightly pinched. Pale, even delicate, above the black face mask and the auburn indications of his patchy beard. She had told him this once, that she loved his nose. He'd said, "Only cartilage."

He readjusted the mask. His eyes were smiling. His eyes were now all she had to go on.

"It smells like pot," he said. "Same as ever."

She had brought him to this corner of the park as if to share a new, as yet undiscovered view. But it was all familiar to them both: the yellowed grass of the softball field, its ring of pathways and benches and scattered trees, the motley apartment buildings all round the periphery, made to seem distant by the open space. It was March, and although the air still held its winter chill, a wan sun had brought people outside. Runners and bicyclists—she could hear them struggling for breath as they passed, everyone grown heavier, out of shape—small, hell-bent children on scooters, and couples with strollers: sleeping pandemic babies or tentative toddlers holding out their little hands, feeling the cold breeze on their palms—their first encounter with the wind, no doubt. A revelation after a life-thus-far all indoors.

These little ones were the only creatures with fully human faces. Except for the trio of maskless crust punks who were sharing a joint at the dusty far end of the field. Somewhere, a drum beat a dirge. A guitar made an attempt to follow. The blue sky above it all was as listless as the distant music.

Mira and Adam stood together, still and attentive, chins raised as if trying to recognize the tune. But it was the odor she had brought him here to identify.

Like something decaying in the woods, she had told him. Carrion. Poop. Gaseous. Animal not vegetable. Not industrial. Definitely animal. Some bloated body of something or other, melting into the dirt, turning to tar.

She said now, "I think I'm going to be sick."

He took her arm, moved her along the path.

"Well, that's a shame," he said after they'd walked a while in silence away from the field. She had dressed too lightly for the weather, rushing the season along, and he put his arm around her when he noticed her shiver. Then he paused to take off the jacket she had just returned to him, insisted she slip into it. "You always liked the smell of pot," he said.

"Not anymore," she said. "Not if it smells like this."

"Well, that's a shame," he said again.

They passed a young woman with a pouched baby pressed against her chest. It wore a little yellow cap, like a sprung crocus. Instinctively, Mira smiled under her mask. She had always smiled at babies. The mother, masked, hooded, ear-budded, walked by, all unaware. Everyone had grown a little more oblivious.

She told him, "I really thought it was just a bad batch. It smelled so awful."

"No," he said, thoughtful. "Same as ever. It must be you, post-COVID."

She took his arm. "I knew I could rely on your expertise."

He said, "Happy to consult."

They had weathered it together. Inadvertently, it seemed. Their relationship had mostly ended in early February, weeks before the shutdown began. A mutual lack of enthusiasm, they'd said. Which was too bad. They had gotten along so well, pre-passion, as they called it then, well before they were saying pre-pandemic, back when they were just friends. They'd remained apart through the hellish spring and the long summer and the spiking fall, with only reports from mutual acquaintances that they'd each stayed in town, managing. In early December, he sent her a text, *How are you doing in all this?* She'd replied, *Scratchy throat, fever, going for a test.* Three times, he texted the single word: *Results?* Until she finally wrote: *Positive. Sleeping.*

The nook where she'd placed her bed got the morning light from the next room, and then just a sliver of sunset between the buildings that were her west-facing view. It seemed farcical, in retrospect, the way the shortening days of midwinter, what, prior to this, would have been any normal stretch of shorter days, made a caricature of themselves as they came and went across the foot of her bed. Like an old-time comedy sketch featuring a long corridor with multiple doors: A peep of pale light, then a burst of madcap yellow, then gloom, then fiery red, then the same darkness out of which the mischievous morning would once again appear, cartwheel evilly across the foot of her bed, glower, vanish. She watched all of it from under the heaviest sleep she had ever known—a dream that she'd pulled a slab of sidewalk up under her chin. At one point, she said out loud, having no idea how many days had gone by, "This is hilarious."

The sirens, not nearly as bad as they were at the beginning, compelled her to get up now and then, take an Advil, eat some toast, get back into bed.

Adam was there, in her tiny kitchen, one morning—the light said it was morning—in the midst of this. Two takeout coffees on her little table. "Your phone died," he said. Masked, but clean-shaven back then. Her phone was recharging on the kitchen counter. She had left it on her bedside table. Ages ago, it seemed.

"You came into my room?"

He nodded. "You were zonked." He still had her key.

"Call your mother," he said. "And your sister. They're frantic."

"They called you?"

He shrugged. The mask made it difficult to tell if he looked good. She thought, yes. "Guess I'm the boyfriend of last report. Or resort. They called your friend Angie."

"She's in New Hampshire."

"And your downstairs neighbors."

"Roy and Carol went home to Virginia."

"Your landlord. Who's in the Hamptons."

"I know."

"And then me."

She held out her hand. "You shouldn't be here," she told him. "I don't want you to get sick."

He pointed to the mask. "I'm careful." He began to unpack from two canvas bags all that he had brought her. He wore a parka, jeans, hiking boots. Strange visitor from a world where people needed thick-soled shoes, outerwear. "Oranges, blueberries. Tea." He placed them on her counter. "Bagels. Yogurt. You want me to get you a pizza?"

She shook her head. The little kitchen got the full morning light, and usually, in the before times, even a hint of sun hitting the wide, worn floorboards—as it was hitting them now—evoked the perfume of the century-old wood, all the beauty and mystery of it. A scent that always reminded her of what she loved about this little apartment, this small building, about Brooklyn itself. Despite the garbage and the crust punks and the occasional electric bolt of fear, or loneliness, there was always, in Brooklyn, this companionable sense, scent, of a past; not of ghosts—everyone was too busy for ghosts—but of bustling past lives, bodies, some warmth from them, some breath, a kind of history left invisibly on the fragrant air. Mira thought of it as a landscape comfortably worn—worn out in places, sure, but also worn in, companionable, peopled.

Of course, this morning she could smell nothing at all.

He pointed to the coffee. "Almond milk latte," he said. "Still hot."

He had brought her as well an oversized box of Advil, a four-pack of Gatorade, and a little white pulse oxygen meter that he offered to her rather sweetly. "I did my homework," he said. He reached for her hand, held it lightly in his, and clipped the thing onto her fingertip. She turned her head away like a shy bride while they waited for the beep. He frowned as he read it. "I always thought you were a nine or a ten," he told her, "but this thing says you look like shit."

"I'm not laughing," she told him. She removed the lid from the coffee, felt the steam rise. "Not smelling. Not tasting, either."

She drank it to please him, although it tasted like nothing, slightly metallic. She drank it from the couch on the far side of the room. And then apologized and took herself to bed.

Night had returned, the day banged shut again—funny stuff—when in the tremulous darkness she heard him say, "I don't think you should be alone."

*

From the park, they walked down to the waterfront. Briny, yes, she told him, her masked nose in the air. The scent of cold water. Got it.

"Can you smell the dead fish?" he asked her. "The industrial waste?"

She shook her head, a little startled. "No."

"Neither can I," he said. "It's a myth."

Certainly life was returning; there were bicyclists here too, and more babies in strollers. Six delirious mutts bouncing through the dog park. And yet, the Manhattan skyline, flat-faced, without dimension in the pale sun, seemed deserted. She nodded toward it. "Do you think there's anyone left, over there?"

He squinted across the moving water—sequined sunlight, scrims of foam, black reflections that flashed like skimmed stones, indicating darker depths, and then slid under again. "I can see a few little cars," he said, peering across it all. "Little beetle shells. They're still escaping."

She told him about a film project she'd worked on in college: a Manhattan skyline made from pale crackers—saltines, matzo, Carr's biscuits. Put together with baking soda glue and painted with baking soda paint and placed on an upside-down baking tin in the middle of a baking sheet filled with a shallow layer of water. Backlit, so there were shadows. "We thought it was genius." They set up their cameras at eye level with the water, breathless for fear that the whole thing would collapse. And then they introduced three gray rats—pets belonging to a sad and eccentric housemate—who crossed the shallow water and devoured the skyline, even as it collapsed around them.

"We set it to *Rhapsody in Blue*," she said.

He nodded. "What else."

"We'd all get high to watch it. Over and over. We thought it was a riot."

They'd shown the video in a sketch comedy class she was taking, back in the day when she thought she was going to be a comic, or an actress, or the author of witty and sardonic essays about the foolishness of life. (She'd even had a title for her first book, back then, *The Casual Comedy*, which only Adam had recognized, pre-passion but not by much, as words borrowed from Yeats.)

"Some people in the class found it offensive—although this was a good decade after 9/11. Some suggested we should have used cockroaches instead. Someone said ants. I told them, 'The rats were available.' The professor called it amateurish, with terrible production values, but prophetic nevertheless." She paused. Pulled at her mask. The fabric had grown clammy with her breath. "Maybe he knew something."

Adam was looking out over the water. Gone to her, she thought. He seemed always to disappear whenever she spoke for too long. An underlying condition of their inability to stay together. Some lack of attentiveness on his part. On hers, some tendency to make every conversation a monologue. They had both, in the end, accused the other of being emotionally withholding.

He put his arm across the back of the bench and she reflexively leaned into him. She could smell the detergent on his T-shirt. The boy musk of his sweater. Unchanged. Her nose would know him anywhere.

"Have you been over?" he asked her. And nodded toward the skyline.

She shook her head. "In the beginning, I pictured my office every day. Eerie and empty. My desk, the bathrooms, the elevators. Now I'm having trouble believing they still exist. Or ever existed. Over there."

"I miss the place," he said.

"Me too."

The water lapped, silver and black against the apron of rough stones. There were the usual odd bits of wood, the ugly brown tatters and frills of what might once have been seaweed, a rolling plastic bottle, a Starbucks cup. "We sound like refugees," she told him. "A couple of lonely immigrants."

Distractedly, his thumb brushed the shoulder of his own coat. "Exiles," he said.

His symptoms began just as hers were beginning to subside, and her response—she heard herself cry, "Oh now I feel guilty"—filled her briefly with self-loathing; making it all about her. Another underlying condition of their inability to stay together.

"No telling if I got it from you," Adam said. "I probably brought it with me."

Mira had finally found the strength to move from her bed to the couch, where she was now wrapped in the garish blue-and-yellow *SpongeBob* blanket she'd carried into her Brooklyn life from her Dayton childhood.

Just that morning, he had helped her take her first shower in days, lifting the limp T-shirt over her head, bending so she could steady herself, a hand on his shoulder, as she slipped off the flannel bottoms. In the before times, this would have been prelude to wild pleasure, his tight curls in her hand, his lips brushing past her navel. But in her fragile exhaustion, nakedness was as dull, as inevitable, as a b.m. A consequence of inhabiting a body, no more. To expect pleasure to follow something as necessary and wearying as the discarding of clothes seemed now a peculiar kind of misunderstanding. A delusion even.

Standing naked on the black-and-white tile, she told him, "It's like my body is saying, 'I'm fighting a virus here.'" She thumped his shoulder. "'What more do you want from me—fun?'"

He laughed, ruefully, perhaps. As he helped her step into the tub, steadied her arm, poured shampoo into her hand, he said it was more like they had gone from young and hot to fragile and very old, without all the living that was supposed to come in between.

Whatever Netflix he had chosen was now nattering at the far side of the small room. He had stopped shaving, but his cheeks and his neck, always a little florid—he was Scots-Irish—looked pale. He said, "Just a headache. Some congestion. I'll be fine."

"You should go get a test," she told him.

He smiled at her. He had dispensed with his mask at some point. She couldn't have said when. "I'm afraid you'll change the locks while I'm gone."

That night his coughing woke her. He was sitting on the edge of the couch where he'd been spending the nights, lit only by the streetlight, his head nearly between his knees. She put a hand to his cheek. His skin was clammy and hot. She went back to her little sleeping nook, quickly stripped her bed, fumbled in her closet for a fresh set. In her hurry, she'd flipped on the harsh overhead light. It was the worst kind of light—a couple of bare bulbs surrounded by an old-fashioned wreath of white plaster—a historical flourish, her landlord had called it, like the wide floorboards, the tin ceiling in the kitchen, the glass doorknobs. He'd said, showing her the place, the people who built these old buildings couldn't help themselves. Compulsively artistic, he'd said.

She never turned on the overhead because it reminded her of the explosion of yellow light that used to drag her from her nightmares when she was a child. Those horrifying seconds when her startled parents, their pajamas, their bedheads, their pale fear, were swept into the last moments of the dream. It was always the same dream when she was a kid: she was running along a dark highway, beams of headlights bearing down on her, her foot suddenly slipping off the curb.

When the bed was made, she turned on the low bedside lamp. And then led him in to lie down, covering him up to his chin. He was shivering.

"Goddamn," he said, teeth chattering. "This sucks."

"I know," she told him, as if soothing the terrified child she had been. "You should never have come. I should have made you go home." She could hear the once familiar sound of the bed frame rocking—how they had once set this bed to rocking—now with his chills.

"You were alone," he told her. "I hated thinking of you alone."

She took his temperature, 103. Clipped the oxygen meter on his finger—ninety-six, no, like a digital roulette wheel, the numbers went teasing back and forth and settled on ninety-four. She gave him Advil and Gatorade and then spent the next hour as he slept searching for all the information she could find, information she had been too weary to seek for herself. Antioxidants. Vitamin D. Wave the arms to clear the lungs. Eat eggs. Walk around. Head for the hospital if oxygen drops below ninety.

"I can get you gummies," Adam said. "Edibles." They were waiting in a short but block-long line for coffee, the fact that they were shoulder to shoulder making them a pod among the other single and socially distant customers. A pod, if no longer a couple. "I mean, if the smell stays bad to you. There are other ways."

She shook her head. "I'm old school. As in, what we used to do when we cut classes in my old school. I like the rolling and the inhaling and the passing around. I like the smell. Chewing a gummy." She drove her hands into the pockets of his coat. "What's the point? Why not a Pinot Noir gummy, a Burgundy, a Beaujolais— get your buzz without all that swirling and sniffing, without those long conversations over dinner. Without all that taste." Together, they stepped forward a few paces. The breeze tossed some grit.

"It's not the getting high," she went on. "It's the memories. The fragrance of my crazy youth. The olfactory soundtrack to a lot of laughs."

"Except now it smells like death." He paused. "To you. Post-COVID."

She nodded, pulled at her mask, looked ahead to the line of coffee-seekers moving in solemn procession over the broken sidewalk. One or two jogged in place, but most were hunched, stooped, huddling against the rising March wind, looking neither right—where each thin tree in its square of dirt had been well-visited by the neighborhood dogs—or left, where the brick and brownstone and aluminum-sided row houses were tightly sealed.

She wondered how many of these caffeine supplicants were COVID survivors; how many of them knew that what they so patiently sought had actually lost all flavor. She said as much to Adam.

"And yet," he said. "Here they are. Seeking it still."

They exchanged a glance, but it was eyes-only above their masks. Hard to read.

He had a virtual office visit with a doctor his insurance company assigned him. Neither Adam or Mira could identify the man's accent, but the window behind him in the Zoom featured sunlit greenery, perhaps palm trees. The doctor prescribed an inhaler, an antihistamine, and laughed dismissively when Adam, at Mira's urging, asked about the benefits of eating an egg a day or waving his arms. When Mira called her own group, she spoke to a young doctor who looked like a twelve-year-old in purple, oversized glasses. This one shook her head, skeptical and amused, when Mira mentioned the inhaler and the antihistamines, and said of the eggs and arm-waving, "Whatever you want to do." She advised staying off the internet. She said, finally, biting her brightly painted lips, "We don't know. No one knows. There's just so much we don't know."

The doctor signed off with a wiggle of her fingers. "Feel better."

Mira closed her laptop. She and Adam were side-by-side at the small kitchen table—no need to keep their distance now.

She'd write a screenplay, she told him. Sci-fi. There's a meteor heading for Earth and the President goes on television to say, "I don't know. What do you want to do?"

He nodded. "Here we are then."

"Just us," she told him.

Now she slept on the couch, her own weariness gone from concrete slab beneath her chin to concrete shawl across her shoulders. One morning she woke to a subdued light: a cold rain at the windows. The gloom gave her rooms a solemnity they hadn't had before, back when dawn and dusk and darkness had gone tumbling in and out, slamming doors. (She understood now that it had been the sound of her remaining neighbors, headed elsewhere.) She threw off her blanket and went to the bed. He was awake. "Lousy," was all he said. She made him get up, walk around. His blood oxygen level was ninety-three. His temperature, 102. Last night, she'd ordered Pedialyte. Too much sugar in Gatorade, the internet had told her. On a hunch, she opened her front door. It had been a long time since she'd glimpsed her own landing with its dirty skylight haze, watery now with the rain. The bottles were lined up on the threshold, although no one had pressed the downstairs buzzer and there was no one else left to let anyone in. She poured a glass. Made him drink.

He said, "Hard to get too worked up over front door security."

"Wave your arms," she said when he began coughing again.

She ordered chicken soup from the deli—this time the buzzer rang—and he drank a bowl, although she tasted only something vaguely salty at the back of her throat. By midafternoon, he was feeling better. His fever was down a bit. When she took the oxygen meter from his finger—back to ninety-five, good—he held out his hand and made her measure her own. Ninety-seven. Brilliant. "We're going to get through this," she said.

"Never doubted it," he told her.

But as the day moved toward night, he began to hold his head in his hands once more. Nothing seemed to help him. Unbearable, he said at one point, it must have been past midnight. Everything hurts. At three A.M., his temperature was 105. He sat in her living room chair, afraid, he said, to lie down. She studied him from the couch, where she was once again wrapped in her girlhood blanket, fighting her own weariness, her own impulse to stretch out and go back to sleep. Leave him to his own battle. "Why afraid?" she whispered.

There were new circles beneath his eyes, a certain gauntness just beginning. "Because there's so much we don't know."

He was a thin and narrow-shouldered young man with a head of thick, curly hair, broad cheeks, and brown eyes. A friend of some friends, a *just down the block* neighbor. They now had only a vague idea of when and where they'd been introduced, which meant neither one of them had taken much notice at the start. They met, most consistently in those early days, on the street, shopping bags or coffee in hand, at the deli or the bodega, or heading for the subway. They both ran in the park every morning at around seven and took to looking for one another for the walk back. They both were dating someone else in those days. Each one believing the other's relationship was long-term and serious. They discovered only later that both were not either of those things, but the mistake made their friendship easy.

They rode the subway to Union Square together one Saturday morning—this was late September, 2019—and then walked through the market. She was meant to meet friends for brunch, and it was clear he'd had something else he was meant to do as well. But they found themselves, each of them, pretending to shop, buying vegetables and cheese and the raspberry cornmeal muffins they had sampled from a basket—as if sampling these muffins and bringing home a half a dozen of them in a plastic bag had been the goal they'd both woken with. And then, when their lingering together, unremarked on as it was, began to feel awkward—"You need to bring your own carryall," one of the vendors told them, as if they were tourists—they parted. He turned back. "You want to grab a drink tonight?"

The days—neither could say how many—now seemed to move through her rooms at an executioner's pace. Every morning he said he might be better, and every afternoon, he seemed convinced of it. But then with the dreaded dimming of the sun, his fever spiked again, the headache returned, his oxygen level hit ninety-two, ninety-one. The cough grew deeper.

The sirens, too, that last spring had been ubiquitous both day and night, now faded from the daylight hours, only to echo again as the light faded.

She did a search. "Melatonin's involved," she told him. "This is really, literally worse at night."

She found herself trying to delay the closing of shades and the lighting of lamps. "It's this damn Earth," she joked. "Always turning. So annoying." The internet said he should lie on his stomach, and she took the pillows from her couch to make the position bearable. After an hour of this, he began to cough up quarter-sized discs of white phlegm. She handed him a box of tissues, touched the back of his neck, and then, as the night wore on, brought in her spaghetti pot. "A spittoon," she told him. "I always thought this apartment should have come with a spittoon." In the bedside light, the phlegm against the stainless steel looked like circles of finely shattered glass.

They both knew how this virus could go from bad to very bad in an instant—a foot slipping off a curb.

When the coughing subsided, when he was still flushed and sweating with it, he said, "Stay a minute."

She sat on the edge of the bed.

They found themselves returning to the kind of conversations they'd had, pre-passion, certainly pre-pandemic, in the before times when they hadn't a second thought about taking a sample from a communal basket of broken muffins; when, convinced as they both were that the other was in love with someone else, they had freely named their disappointments and their fears.

Both had begun their decade in New York as, they agreed, cartoon hipsters. He was going to play music. She was going to write screenplays. But a cousin of his, in real estate, had asked him to show a few properties, and he found he was good at this, personable, instinctively honest. She had taken a pay-the-rent job with a cable network. ("Close to screenwriting, right?" she had said, when they were merely friends and so easily self-deprecating.) Ad sales, nothing creative. But she was good at this, too, quickly promoted.

Now they both found themselves with an expertise about things that held little interest or delight. Day jobs that offered them only the pleasure of knowing what it is to be a person with expertise.

Adam said, sitting up in her bed, the pillows and sofa cushions boxing him in, the stainless-steel pot nestled against his hip, that when the gigs disappeared, back in March, he'd begun to wonder why he was staying. In the weeks before the shutdown he had noticed how the city's young musicians were getting younger. How the old guys who showed up for every session were beginning to look foolish. Gaunt. Long-haired. Out of shape. Still sounding like stoners. Now he wondered how many of them would return, when things opened up again. He wondered if he'd be the one to replace them. An old guy haunting his own middle school dream.

His cousin had offered him a place in their office in the Dela-

ware Valley, where the real estate market was booming, folks flee-
ing the city. New houses being built. Closer to his parents.

"I go there," he said, his voice hoarse from the coughing,
"What's my life?"

She said simply—simply because the virus had left her dull-
witted, inattentive, tired, "I don't know." And then tried for more
sincerity, touching his hand, those familiar calluses on his fingertips. "It could be nice. Trees, grass, running streams. Houses where
you can't see your neighbors."

He laughed. "When was the last time you saw your neighbors?"

She looked toward the alcove's one dark window. It reflected
back the dim room.

"You mean, other than you?"

She tried again, stretching out as she spoke, along the foot of
the bed. Under the quilt, he lifted his knees to accommodate her.
A vague ache had settled in her spine. She was still so very tired.
"New construction," she said. "Nice big kitchens. A car. Everything
in working order. No rattling radiators. No historical flourishes.
No ghosts in the machine."

He said, "Leave the city." It seemed neither a question nor a
statement. He might merely have been testing the words, posting
them on the still air. She thought of her work-life cliché: Just putting this out there. An annoying expression, pre-pandemic. Com-
ical now.

She put her cheek to the duvet. Put her folded hands to her
chest. Drew her knees up. From above, she thought, she would
look like the toppled figure of a praying child.

She told him it had always been easy enough for her to forget the
trivial hours at work—meetings, calls, clients, office intrigue—if, at
the end of the day, she encountered a rain-slicked Park Avenue,
or a blood-orange sunset down the gentle rise of a cross street. If
friends called to her from the shining corner of a crowded bar. If
on her phone she had tickets to something really good.

She could be content if the dull days were balanced by an equal
number of hours when everything was lit like a scene from a movie.

In the before times, she told him, she could come up from the
subway at the end of certain days, days when all of ragged Brooklyn smelled like the sea, and believe she belonged here, home,
grounded, geographically content.

But after all these months confined to her cute little apartment, with its old wood and its glass doorknobs and its past lives—the comforting sound of her neighbors, before they fled, the opening and closing of other people's doors—she was beginning to fear this busy procession of days and nights might be bringing her to something she'd failed to anticipate, something that could slip, in an instant, into the farcical, the absurd.

She feared she might become, with her stale expertise and her witty Instagrams posted on the fetid air, like the drunken lady in the chorus, still singing at the top of her lungs when everyone else had stopped.

"What do you want to do then?" he asked her.

She rolled onto her back. He moved his feet again to give her more room. On the ceiling, the plaster wreath, delicate and precise, finely wrought, quaint. It hovered above them in the dim light like a ring of leaf-shaped smoke. "Who knows?" she said. "Stop time. Bar the door."

She sat up suddenly, her pulse pounding and the neck of her T-shirt damp with sweat. Even in the bluish, streetlight-stained darkness, she could see the silhouettes of bowls and glasses along her sink and across the room's various tabletops. Empty bottles of Pedialyte and orange juice, mugs, teacups, the glass jar of the blender furred with the gray remains of a day-old smoothie, the stalagmites of the sick room. If she could smell, she knew, she would have to open a window. There was a siren, faintly howling. Adam called to her again—she knew it was again although it was the first time she heard him—and then there was a heavy crash, furniture, a glass, what she knew was his body, his skull, hitting the wide wood floor.

He was lying in the arched doorway of the sleeping nook, sprawled like the murder victim in some cheap film noir, lit only enough to clarify the scene.

She cried out. Went to him just as he was stirring. Not dead—she had the thought, just the two words, clearly, even calmly, but without any good sense of their meaning. She helped him to his feet and then she felt the weight of him as he fell again, a cross-body fall, striking her chest and her thighs and her feet. She managed to grab his arm, but it might as well have been the remnant of an empty sleeve. She reached down again, struggling to lift him. He clasped her wrist. There was a tremendous counterweight, as if something was pulling him from her, not mere gravity, but a force, invisible, demonic even—something that had wrapped itself around him in the dark, that had his waist, his thighs, the back of his head, and was pulling against her. She said his name again, as if calling to him from a great distance. She felt the grip of his hand on her arm, felt him slipping away from her, going under.

In all their hot and spirited lovemaking, back in the old times, his body had never felt so heavy, so ungainly, in her arms. They had never struggled like this, panting together, more limbs, it seemed, than should belong to just two. She had never known, even in the throes of the best of it, a power, a third presence, so tangible that the weight of it might have crushed the breath from them both.

She moved him to the bed somehow, got him to sit, anyway, on the edge. "I'm calling 911," she told him. For help, yes, but also, she knew this clearly, for another presence in the room, another living person. She wanted to help him, but, more than that, she wanted the company of other people, any stranger would do—someone to rush into the room, snap on a light, dispel the terrible dream.

He said, "Shit." And began to cough. "I'm a dead man," he said.

The ambulance sat at the curb for what seemed an outlandishly long time, the red light turning and the motor running, the surreal crackle of the dispatcher's voice reaching her through the sealed window long before she saw anyone emerge.

"Glad I'm not having a heart attack," he said from the bed. He was alert, a little bruised, a little ashamed.

And then the back doors of the ambulance were opened and she saw they were donning their protective gear, moving like space-suited astronauts in the dim streetlight, turning this way and that in their swollen shoes, nodding, and—languidly, it seemed to her—gesturing at one another as if to approve some sartorial daring. *Oh, I like that. Yeah, you can pull that off, for sure.* Then moving like moon walkers across the sidewalk to her building.

Although she had watched them approach, the harsh sound of the buzzer startled her. "Masked." A voice said through the static of the intercom. And she nearly said, I know you are. "Please wear a mask."

She turned on some lights—it had seemed necessary to watch for the ambulance in the dark—and found her box of paper masks. She gave one to Adam, slipped on her own. The apartment was a walk-up, but they were dressed for stealth, she was certain, and moved silently up the stairs. There was only, out of the silence, a knock at the door, low down, made with the toe of a shoe.

She was surprised by the tears in her voice as she described what had occurred. One of them took the information while the other two took his temperature (they had flipped on that terrible overhead light) and checked his blood oxygen—ninety-two, "not great"—and then asked him the same questions she had just been asked, as if they were checking for accuracy, inconsistencies.

"We're required to take you to the nearest ER," one of them said—it was a woman's voice that came from behind the mask and the plastic shield and the crinkling yellow robes, high priestess of the night's ordeal—but, she told him, he was not obliged to be taken if he preferred not to go. "The ER's a shit show tonight," she said. "You'll be there for hours. You'll see things you don't want to see."

Adam's eyes above the mask were darkly troubled, black, feverish.

"But if it's the right thing to do," he said, hesitant. "If I need to go."

The woman—Mira had thought she was middle-aged, even matronly, until she said "shit show"—shook her head. She might actually have been quite young.

"You're sitting here. You're talking, you're breathing. You've got a fever and a cough and your oxygen's not great, but I've seen what people look like when they need to go to the ER. You're not one of them. Probably just dehydrated. That's why you passed out." She shrugged. As she spoke, her face shield caught and reflected the overhead light. On the other side of the bed, the face shields of her two companions did the same. It looked to Mira as if some weird communication was taking place among them, an alien, flashing exchange. She couldn't tell if what they were silently conveying to one another was amusement or compassion or disdain. I've seen worse.

"It's your call," the woman said.

Later, Mira said it was symptom-shaming. As if she and Adam were too young, too healthy-looking, too privileged to be at risk, to merit their concern, not after these many months of universal trauma, not after all these three had seen.

Even standing there, just outside her own bedroom alcove, she felt the impulse to rise to Adam's defense, or to the defense of this insidious virus—his lungs were filled with shattered glass, for God's sake. She wanted to tell them again—had she told them already?—about the counterweight that had pulled against her as she tried to lift him from the floor.

And then, weirdly, weightlessly, one of the figures raised its arms, held out blue gloved hands as if for a benediction. She would not have been surprised to see the shapeless yellow feet slowly rise an inch or two above her floorboards. "We're here to take you if you want to go," the figure said calmly, kindly. "You might want to go. Just to be safe."

Their brightly lit face shields signaled agreement. "Your call," the third one echoed. All three stood there for a moment, huge and yellow in this small space. Stirring, almost imperceptibly, as if in some vague breeze.

Adam's eyes above his mask moved beyond them, seeking her out in the awful light, as if she were the last one of his own species. "What do you think?"

The three EMTs turned as one to look toward her, their protective gear crinkling. It was a constrained, infinitesimal shifting, a planetary motion, that nevertheless made her suddenly conscious of her own thin layer of clothes, her own body beneath, recovered, recovering, although, at the moment, she was nauseous and trembling. In the brief silence, she was aware of another siren wailing elsewhere.

She told him, speaking past them. "Only you can decide."

In retrospect she wished she had cried out, I don't know. No one knows. Wished she'd wept with indecision, or struggled, with him, against the weight of it all, the uncertainty, the mystery, so much we don't know.

But she said, Only you. She said it coolly, believing it was true. (The flashing, bobbing nods of the three as they turned back to him assured her it was true.) Believing too that some door had forever closed between them with her words.

He said, "I guess I'll go then, just in case."

Once more she watched from the window, the apartment behind her dimmed, empty. As they slid the gurney into the ambulance, she glimpsed his bare foot, uncovered, blue in the streetlight. She put her forehead to the cold glass and cried, at last, with open-mouthed, childish abandon. When she looked out again, she saw that there was a string of crooked Christmas lights framing a dark window across the street. She could not say if they'd been put up too early or too late.

Walking back through the park, she asked him, "Where are all the old people?"

He shook his head. "When were there ever old people in McCarren Park?"

"Weren't there?" She was suddenly uncertain. "Old men playing chess. Nanas in their black dresses, dark stockings, thick ankles, taking some sun. Didn't we use to see them?"

"Here?" he said, eyebrows raised. Skeptical.

"Maybe I'm thinking of Prospect Park. Or some movie. Maybe they were extras for some movie."

"Maybe," he said. "Maybe they'll emerge when the weather's a bit warmer."

"If they're still available," she said. And then wished she hadn't.

At her building, she asked if he wanted to come in and he looked up toward her window. What blue there was in the sky, and it wasn't much, the windows caught and reflected back as pale white.

He had not been inside since the night they brought him down the stairs to the ambulance. When they released him later that morning—the paramedic had been right, he didn't need hospitalization—he'd returned to his own place to recover. She'd felt a little hurt by this, but he said, "You don't need to find me dead on your floor." And then he added, "Not twice."

He said, Bogart style, before she could say it herself, "We'll always have COVID."

"Probably not," he said now, titling his head back farther than necessary to see her window. "PCSD." And he shivered, comically, casual comedy, reminding her that she still wore his jacket. She slipped it off and handed it to him.

He said he had a gig that night, in Greenpoint. Outside, limited capacity.

"I'm not ready to be social yet," she told him.

He nodded to say he understood. He said, "Soon as I got to the ER that night, I asked the doctor, I said, 'Doc, will I be able to play the guitar, post-COVID?'"

She laughed. She knew the punch line. *Funny, I couldn't play the guitar before.*

He said, "I realized that if I had to do it all over again, I'd do it all over again. In my next life, I want this one."

Not the Delaware Valley then. Running streams, green fields. New construction, no neighbors, no ghosts.

It was what she had wanted to ask him as they walked, what she had, in fact, called him to discover. But she hadn't found the chance. As they'd walked, the question—what now?—had become a betrayal of something, some intimacy, some fear or despondence, that was too fragile for this emerging post-pandemic life.

She said, "I'm going home for a while. Breaking my lease. Putting my stuff in storage."

"For good?"

"No, just for a while."

He laughed behind the mask. "I said, do you good."

Now she looked up at the blank and featureless spring sky. "Christ," she said. "That's all I need. My hearing changed too." She touched her face. "Ears, eyes, nose, all changed."

He bent down. She could feel the warmth of his breath through his mask. Through her mask. They were two bodies, breathing, recovered, returned.

"Changed utterly," he said, and kissed her goodbye—cloth against cloth.

Bears Among the Living

FROM McSweeney's

THEY CALL OUR town the City of Trees because of the trees. Along Harrison Avenue, sycamores with their tops sheared to accommodate power lines overhead. On Foothill, massive peeling eucalyptuses. On Mills, prim maidenhairs dropping their rancid berries. Our town is a page, its streets are the lines, houses are words, and the people: punctuation. Trees are just trees. We hear church bells on Sunday but never see anyone coming out or going in. The Church of Christ has a new sign in front that says HE'S STILL LISTENING, which makes me a little sad. It makes me want to say something worth listening to. Less and less, I'm in control of what I broadcast. At a park the other day I was reading on a bench while my wife pushed our son on the swings. A woman walked up to her and said, Just a heads-up: There's a man reading over there on the bench and he's not with anybody. We're all keeping an eye on him. His zipper's wide open.

It was true. I mean, it's true. Lately, while walking, I'll sometimes feel a suspect breeze on my groin and look down to find my zipper open and I haven't used the bathroom in hours. Either the craftsmanship of zippers has declined or I've been neglecting to zip. A friend tells me not to worry, that it's an evolutionary adaptation, like pattern baldness or the gluey odor certain old men acquire. My friend (his name's Andrew—calling him my friend makes him sound imaginary) thinks it's a way of keeping undesirable DNA out of the gene pool. Besides, there's no law that says you have to keep your zipper up, he says.

I'd never thought there was, but he says it so defensively, as if he were dispelling a widely held opinion. Sunday mornings, we walk our dogs together, and whenever a car in a driveway is blocking part of the sidewalk, he'll kick the bumper as we walk past.

Bad car, he tells his dog.

The limits of my language, Wittgenstein said, are the limits of my town. Something to that effect. We are bisected by freeways, circled by helicopters, tilted up toward the foothills, snug in our stalls. Will we die in our beds? Will we die in our cars? Will loved ones surround us waiting for frank instructions? Our town: a blend of street noise and birdsong, a flurry of signs, an algebra problem. People call it a bedroom community, a phrase I used to repeat because it sounded kind of lurid until I finally looked up what it meant. Asleep at night, I plot and replot my jogging circuit. Seventh to Mountain, Mountain to Baseline, Baseline to Mills, Mills to Bonita . . . I wake up exhausted.

Mornings, when my family's still asleep, I survey my modest claim, purposeful and sincere as a lighthouse keeper. I walk Otis into the park across from our house and we watch the overtrained border collie fetch Frisbees, catching them, stacking them one by one, and then carrying them home in his mouth. You're a good boy, too, I assure Otis, even though both of us know the only thing keeping him from sprinting toward the foothills, never to return, is the frayed orange leash clipped to his collar.

Yesterday a local man was arrested for lewd and lascivious conduct. The newspaper said that after getting a *personal body part* stuck in a park bench, he needed the help of some bystanders to free it. Such a strange euphemism: *personal body part*. Isn't every body part personal? No wonder schizophrenics think newspapers transmit coded messages: there's too much casual ambiguity. Before I learned to read, I remember seeing a grainy photograph of a teenage boy on the front page of the paper. I asked my mother what the story was about, and she skimmed it and said, He won a prize at school. For what? I asked. Her eyes were fixed on the boy's picture. For some vegetables he grew, she said finally, and folded the newspaper and tucked it under her arm, but I could still see the doomed boy peeking out, and for the first time I noticed how the seeds of future misfortune are hidden in photographs. Only in retrospect can they be detected.

I don't have all that many memories of my father. He died a few weeks before I turned eleven. I remember him sitting in a La-Z-Boy and laughing loudly at the nightly news, and feeling kind of resentful because I couldn't figure out what was so funny. I remember overhearing him say to a friend from the track: I don't like being drunk. But I do like getting drunk. I also remember trying to watch Halley's comet with him. He woke me at three in the morning and we sat on cabana chairs in the driveway, him sipping from a tall glass of Regal Blend, trying to get drunk but not be drunk, and me shivering and anticipating the moment the comet would scream across the atmosphere, spraying shards of fire and dust and ice. The stars pulsed. An hour passed. The moon hung there, dumb as always.

He woke me again at dawn and pointed to a faint blue scribble in the sky. Barely scratched us, he said. He handed me a chunk of charcoal, freezing cold. I found this in the front yard, he told me. I held it to my nose. Charred rock, a molar plucked from the jaw of an old god. I carried it to school in the side pocket of my backpack but forgot about it until after lunch, and by then the chunk was lost, dust.

Probably just a briquette from the grill, my mother says when I call to ask her about it. She's been drinking Gallo wine again. When she's been drinking Gallo wine, she tends not to indulge my sentimentality. Your father always had an antisocial sense of humor, she says. One summer the singer Freddy Fender performed at the horse racing track he managed, and she couldn't go, but she really wanted a signed picture. Though my father didn't want to ask for one, eventually, he gave in and got one for her: *You're the Tear in My Eye. With All My Love. Freddy Fender.* Later, years after he died, she looked at it more closely and realized it was my father's handwriting. Simply to amuse himself, he'd asked Freddy Fender for the picture but not the signature.

Laughter's supposed to be shared, she says. She tells me she accidentally watched a documentary about it. It's like a universal language, she says. Even before humans could talk, we laughed; I can't remember why. Something to do with showing we mean one another no harm, or surviving danger, the overwhelming relief of it.

She tells me how on their second date, he suddenly started laughing, and when she asked what was so funny he said, Nothing. She kept pressing him and he finally told her he'd been thinking about the sun. Whose son? she asked. No, *the* sun. What about it? she said. I just realized there's an object in the sky that will blind you if you stare straight at it. And? she asked him. You don't think that's a little amusing? he said.

And that, she says, was your father. It's how she concludes every story about him: And that was your father.

What else? she says to fill the silence (when she's been drinking Gallo wine, it's difficult to get her off the phone), and she waits and I wait to see which of us knows the answer.

The summer he died is a smear of wildfires and hostile fauna. Miles north of us, the pinewoods burned, clotting the central coast of Florida with a scorched haze. My mother, sister, and I moved to a cul-de-sac of gravy-brown condos, drew straws for the smallest bedroom (I lost), sat inside awaiting instructions from the proper authorities, and watched pine ash fall and fall. Then it rained. The fires smoldered and finally went out, and I spent the summer selling off my baseball cards and hunting snakes in the palmetto scrub behind our condo. When I came home one night covered in chigger bites, my mother brushed clear nail polish over the welts and I lay shirtless and miserable as the chiggers suffocated in their hidey-holes. My body was a decoy, a trap made of meat. I scratched off the scabs of dried polish one by one. Years later someone told me chiggers don't burrow inside skin, and that the welts, which were actually full of chigger saliva, would've healed quicker if we'd left them alone. The summer he died, I watched the retired bail bondsman next door bludgeon a cottonmouth with a shovel—the snake's severed head kept snapping while its headless body slithered away, and the retired bail bondsman grinned and gestured with the shovel as if he'd orchestrated this educational display just for me.

A sign in front of the Methodist church: GOD ISN'T ANGRY. Whenever I pass it, I say it aloud, God isn't angry, adding the unspoken verdict: He's just . . . . disappointed.

*

Lately I've been thinking about the ice cream man. The ice cream man, he tunnels into our town, solves our streets, turns on his music, and waits like a spider. Nothing's more inscrutable than a darkened house. Nothing except a whole street of darkened houses. Some of us sleep, some lie in bed counting their resting heart rate. Every website agrees: its rhythm is unusual. This isn't good. We like our refrigerator magnets and our dental hygienists' hairstyles to be unusual, not our resting heart rates. I remember when sleep was so easy, a nice calm pool warmed by humming turbines . . . now sleep is a panicked rabbit clutched tight to my chest. Just keep still and I won't hurt you, I tell my rabbit, but you can't calm the thing you're clutching. That's been true for years. If we let him, the ice cream man would notice even the faintest tremor of need and drive toward it at once. What a fireman is to a burning building, an ice cream man is to our desire for ice cream.

Coyotes eat the cats, cats eat the songbirds, songbirds eat the morning quiet. Nothing eats the coyotes. Last year some homeowner tried poisoning them but only succeeded in making them more ornery. Our coyotes are not noble mascots. They look like starved and hunted dogs.

My son plays a song that goes, *I am, I am, I am Superman, and I can do anything*, and he asks if the singer is saying *can* or *can't*. Can, I say. The chorus repeats and he asks me again and I reassure him again. He has no tolerance yet for brooding superheroes who can't do certain things. He likes Superman. He suspects he's only pretending to be scared of Kryptonite, the way he pretends to be Clark Kent. The characters in his cartoon shows never use words like *kill* or *die*. We must eliminate them! says the skeleton lord. Punish them, destroy them, vanquish them. Temporarily, of course. Even the worst villains survive into the next week, and the next. When the skeleton lord's air fleet is brought down, the sky blooms with the black parachutes of healthy skeletons. My son leans closer to the television, willing each of them safely back to their evil lair.

I was standing around with some other parents, waiting for the kids to be released from school. I miss maps, one of them said. You know, the kind you kept in the glove compartment and had to unfold, and when you were done with them you could never quite figure out how to refold them. We all remembered those. Then everyone started sharing nostalgic artifacts from childhood. I miss thinking Columbus discovered America, someone said. I miss using my mom's makeup mirror to pretend I was walking on the ceiling. I miss getting lost. I miss feeding my neighbor's dog chicken bones through the fence. I miss carrying money loose in my pocket, back when three or four dollars was so *powerful.* I miss invisible ink. I miss feeling loyal toward my breakfast cereal. I miss getting all dressed up to have my picture taken. I miss friendship bracelets, extra credit, merit badges, participation trophies. I miss being rewarded just for following along. I miss ant farms. I miss having my foot measured. I miss thinking every rabbit I saw was the Velveteen Rabbit.

I miss when my future was more interesting to me than my past, I thought. The other parents paused and looked at me, which meant I'd said it out loud as well. They waited for an explanation. The least I could do was tell them how I used to dream of being a landscape architect, as opposed to dreaming of when I used to dream of being an landscape architect. Dreaming ahead instead of dreaming behind. I kept my eyes on the sidewalk and finally said, I also miss scratch-and-sniff stickers. Sighs of relief from the other parents, robust communal nodding. It felt good to think about things you hadn't thought about in a while. Harmless, nearly forgotten things. Some of the stickers smelled like what they were supposed to smell like and some didn't, and every time you scratched them the smell grew fainter. Remember that? You had to make sure to ration it out because the stickers wouldn't last long. It was an object lesson. Remember? Scratching and knowing that every time you scratched you were erasing the very thing you were savoring.

Where were we? That's another phrase my mother repeats when we talk on the phone. Now, where were we? As if conversation is this punishing labyrinth we're navigating together. Careful not to lose our way, careful to measure where we're going against where we've been. Oh, now I remember, she tells me. I was telling you about those sounds coming from the roof. I thought something was trying to claw its way in—turns out something was trying to claw its way *out.* . . .

*

A friend gave her a book called *When Bad Things Happen to Good People* after he died. She never read it. She put it on the only bookshelf in our house, which happened to be in my bedroom, next to the only other book we owned: *The Good Earth* by Pearl S. Buck. I must've scanned its title a thousand times before falling asleep. As a kid I imagined it as a jingle: *Bad things happen to good people in monsoons, hot-air balloons. Ancient tombs, hospital rooms.* Another friend came to the house during the funeral and took away all my father's clothes, donated them to the Salvation Army. She thought she was doing us a favor, scrubbing our closet of unwanted reminders. Years later we'd still see his golf shirts all around town. On a man pumping gas into a motorcycle. On a supermarket bag boy. Another friend leaned in close to her after the service and whispered, They say the grieving process lasts six months for every year you were together.

She was forty-two years old when he died and she never dated again. She begrudgingly went to one Parents Without Partners meeting and came home with some pamphlets and a coupon for three free karate lessons. She had eight hundred dollars in the bank, monthly social security checks, a job at a betting window at the racetrack. Everyone at the meeting seemed so plodding and glib, brimming with false light. Boys need positive male role models, a fellow partner-less parent told her at the meeting. She thought at first he was hitting on her, but it turned out he was recruiting boys for his martial arts dojo. Relieved, disappointed, she took the coupon he offered her. At River of Tradition we teach the four pillars of respect, he said, pointing to the patch on his coat, where the four pillars were listed. She wasn't wearing her glasses so she couldn't make them out, but it looked like one of them was CUSTARD. He's at an age where he should be working hard on his belief system, the man said, though she'd never told him how old I was.

My birthday parties, until I stopped having them, were always at Top Dogs. It had a special party room in the back and everyone got a footlong except the birthday boy, who got a birthday footlong, which was just a footlong with special birthday toppings. I remember eating at Top Dogs a lot as a child, but I don't think we went there an unusual amount—I just remember every single trip there. The greasy, ass-buffed smoothness of the booth seats, the ritualized dressing of the footlong. Years after he died, when my mother was going through her born-again phase, she made us pray before we ate them. No one ever explained the mechanics of prayer to me, so I treated it like a wish list, closing my eyes and telling God everything I wanted. We quit one church for another and then quit church altogether, but the idea that I was born incomplete and that my natural inclinations are faulty, damnable even, has always rung true to me. Especially when I'm inside a Top Dogs. Our town council banned all fast-food chains within city limits, but the nearest Top Dogs isn't far. Just across the border in a grubby, makeshift red-light district: strip club, suspect massage parlor, marijuana factory outlet (ice cream man idling in the parking lot), Top Dogs. I eat quickly, hunched like a scavenger bird, and tell no one I've gone. I don't pray before eating my footlong but I tell myself that tomorrow I'll atone by running six miles instead of three. In my head I'm already running, absolving myself stride by stride for my casual trespasses into nostalgia.

In a booth nearby, a woman wearing a shredded golf visor says to another woman, Did you hear about the boy whose last wish was to die in Santa's lap? Turns out he was faking. It was just something he started saying and his parents went along with it. The other woman considers this and I sense everyone in our jetty of booths leaning in to hear her response. Top Dogs isn't the sort of place that abides deliberation—the woman's silence pulls at us like the branching limbo before a diagnosis. She reaches behind her ear and brings a tress of hair to her nose and sniffs at it. You know, she finally says, it's almost impossible to actually smell yourself.

Here's what I've been wondering, my mother said to me once over the phone. Here's what's been bugging me. Do you think he'd be dead by now if he didn't already die?

One year my sister and I dressed as boxes of laundry detergent for Halloween. She was Rinso, I was Biz. We made the costumes ourselves out of old cardboard boxes. Our mother thought it was so clever she sent a photo of us to the multinational conglomerate that manufactures Rinso and Biz and received, in return, a coupon for $1.50 off her next purchase. She was livid, she ranted about it for years afterward . . . but what had she expected? Free Rinso for life? She never could shed her unblinking faith in products she saw advertised on television. She knew Ivory was 99.44 percent pure and Calgon would take her away. When I was an infant she fed me Tang in a baby bottle because the commercials said it was healthy. The astronauts drank it, she'd say whenever she was pressed about feeding a newborn sugar water. That neon orange space powder rotted my baby teeth down to the root. Nowadays she watches the wholesale jewelry network, where the commercials are the show, and all the shows are about jewelry. She still wears her engagement ring, which she's had resized twice to fit her shrinking finger. The only other keepsake she has of my father, besides pictures, is his name on a yellowed slip of paper. After their first date she wrote it down and wedged it between her mattress and box spring because she heard that's what Janet Leigh did the night she met Tony Curtis.

Listening to my wife and son try to reach a compromise about how many toys he's allowed to bring to bed with him, I think: The sheer number of words it takes to raise a child—it's absurd. *Can,* I repeat when the song comes on. He *can* do anything. Escorting him through childhood on a flotilla of words. I remember the wannabe Amish guy who tended the video store cash register while his daughter lay next to him in a playpen. One night I came in and he was showing her trading cards with pictures of crying dwarves on them. Silently he'd hand her a card and silently she'd study it and hand it back to him. When he noticed me he said, I want to teach her that the world isn't as uncomplicated as she thinks it is.

A worthy enough goal, I guess. My son says he and a friend watched footage of ocean trenches, and there are these blind white eels that break apart if you bring them to the surface—they're held together by water pressure—and they terrified him. I tell him he shouldn't worry because he'll never have to go to the bottom of the ocean. You're better off worrying about the DMV, I say. He walks off without asking what *DMV* stands for, because he doesn't need to. His sense of danger is prehistoric, wiser than words.

And what to say about my half brother, my father's first son, who showed up at my college graduation and gave me a hundred-dollar bill in a bank envelope? He's ten years older than me, and I'd only met him a few times and haven't seen him since. He looked unnervingly like our father. He had a thin scar on his cheek and the skin on either side of it was misaligned, like patterned wallpaper not quite matched at the seam. The thing you should know about our dad (he told me when we were alone)—and you might not remember this because you were pretty young when he died—but that man was hung like a goddamn grandfather clock.

On my morning run, I often imagine myself at age eight watching me run past. There he goes again, I think of me thinking. When I was eight I found a switchblade in a crumpled paper bag. I also found, in the glove compartment of an abandoned mail truck in the woods, a porno magazine full of pregnant women. Something like that is bound to leave a permanent stain . . . and now that I'm thinking about it, what was a mail truck doing abandoned in the woods? I remember how on my school bus someone wrote *Black Sabbath Rules* on the back of the seat in front of mine, and every day I returned to check if they'd written anything else. I wanted a list. I wanted to know exactly what the Black Sabbath rules were.

I called a phone sex hotline I found in the magazine, made my voice good and deep. When the woman came on the line she said, *Well, well, well, well, Mr. Motherfucker.*

Our streets, they were here when we got here. They channel us, keep us from scribbling in the margins. Just before two city buses cross paths on Indian Hill, there's a moment when it's unclear whether or not the bus drivers will wave to each other. It lasts for about two seconds. When they do wave, the moment is neatly resolved, allowed to vaporize. When they don't, it lingers like a failed sneeze and expands into an omen, a placeholder for everything dreaded, all the things that could end badly and do. Next to my father in his Skylark, I used to signal to semitruck drivers on the highway, trying to get them to blow their air horns. I wanted influence, I wanted to be recognized by the biggest things on the road. I did this recently with my son in the car, and when the truck driver answered with a sustained honk, my son sank low in his seat, mortified. He made me promise to never do it again. I promised I would try. My son tells me I say *maybe* too much. He tells me that *we'll see* is not a satisfying answer. He's already eight years old, older than I was when I started to understand the subtle language of the road, the exonerating and implicating notes passed wordlessly from driver to driver to driver.

At IKEA he asks why there are so many pregnant women shopping and I tell him I'm not sure. He asks if women go to IKEA to get pregnant, and although I'm intrigued by the idea of women going to IKEA to get pregnant, I restrain myself from telling him that yes, they do. I say maybe they do. He asks if I knew that French women are naked 30 percent of the time, and I tell him I did not. Where did he hear this? He says it's just something he knows. He says he knows a lot of things his mother and I don't. It seems like lately he's been trying to keep himself a mystery. When I tell him he needs to go brush his teeth, he says, Does a tiger brush his teeth?

I know there are other things I should be showing him—truths, values, important concepts—but how can I if I'm still not clear on the particulars myself? The other day he asked what Captain Hook's name was before he lost his hand. I checked into Hook's details and read out his birth name to my son: James Aloysius Hook. His name was Hook before the hook—having his hand cut off and fed to a crocodile was a terrible irony. Or a coincidence. Or an ironic coincidence.

In college, I tell him, I had a friend named George Blaze. Guess how he died? My son covers his ears. He doesn't want to guess, or know, how George Blaze died. Later he asks me if there's such a thing as a monster planet. I ask him to clarify what he means and he says, A planet with only monsters on it. How am I supposed to answer a question like this? I answer yes. Which makes him happy (I knew it would) and a little apprehensive. How close is it? I pause for some quick calculations. At least ninety-seven light-years away, I tell him. Which is very far, I say. A light-year's like a normal year but much longer because it's a distance. You know how long a year feels, January to December? Okay, so imagine that but you're walking the entire time, through space. For ninety-seven years. That's how far.

He asks why it's called a light-year and I say, No one's really sure, and put my hand on his shoulder, consoling him about all the things we want to know and cannot.

*

When my wife and I first met I told her I used to be pen pals with former president Ronald Reagan. She asked where the letters were and I tried to remember, growing annoyed at myself for being careless enough to misplace personal letters from former president Ronald Reagan, before remembering there were no letters. Truth is, I'd written to him once, after he tested the microphone at a radio address by saying, I've signed legislation to outlaw Russia forever. We begin bombing in five minutes. For a newly fatherless kid living fifty miles north of Cape Canaveral, which was a primary Russian target, who kept himself awake at night worrying about flash burn, air bursts, blast waves—phrases even the most unimaginative child could conjure viscerally—Reagan was a terrifying clown. The least he could have done was to write back and reassure me, tell me my fears were unreasonable. About a week later, I received a form letter on White House letterhead. I don't remember what it said. I read it quickly, licked my thumb and rubbed at the signature to see if it was real, then threw it away.

We are bears among the living, agile and fearsome. We range and rut. We hunt. We return to our dens to sleep and let torpid winters seal our wounds. When we die our pelts are stripped from our bones, draped over plausible likenesses, nailed to pedestals in telltale poses. Children still flinch at the sight of us, though our eyes are flat and lifeless. For now death seems to have perfectly arrested our essence. One day we're moved to the garage, replaced by a Christmas tree, and we stay there, surviving, yes, but shrinking. Time declaws us, softens our contours and our blood-matted fur, and it gives us a bow tie, and one day, where a life-size bear once stood, there's a cute little plush toy stuffed with foam and air, a harmless abbreviation consigned to spend a third life in the land of make-believe.

Sometimes I think I can I still summon the sound of his voice. A thin, distant rasp. My childhood is a song I've heard so many times I've stopped listening to the words. Probably half the things my father said to me he never said to me.

You're the man of the house now. Your duties consist of inward foraging, incubating petty grudges, and eating food before it expires. Fear not, I'll be watching over you until you're old enough to watch over yourself. Don't let that stop you from doing what, to the best of your knowledge, boys do. Become what you are, become what you are pretending to be. Learn something about everything and everything about something. Don't linger before mirrors. Appreciate rain. Take what scraps you have of me and raise them as a scarecrow against aspiring father figures. Make up some good shit. Never trust anyone who owns a reptile or a riding lawnmower. Is it my voice you're hearing right now or someone else's? And how old are you now? Old enough to watch over yourself? Old enough to watch over someone else? Children, and I quote, are the living messages we send to a time we will not see. Something along those lines. So what are you trying to say and why are you still trying to say it? Do you think this is a game, Kevin? Do you think you are winning?

GINA OCHSNER

Soon the Light

FROM *Ploughshares*

IN THE OLD Clatsop story, God pinched the mud of the north
Oregon shore into mountains, carved rock to jagged crags. That's
how he cut his hands and his blood stained the flats of the north
plains. Every autumn, as if remembering this event, the soil north
and east of Astoria pushes forth blood-bright cranberries. That's
the way Jaska heard Indian Jennie tell it, anyway. Because God suffered, those who work the north plains harvest suffer. This part
Jaska could vouch for. Thirty years of hauling fishing nets had
pulled his chest toward his hips and put a thick hump between
his shoulders. Thirty years of work had turned his bones to chalk.
That's the reward of hard work, Mother says in her many letters,
but he knows fear has stove him up as much as the work.

Not hospitable waters, these. Forty gillnetters had been lost
this year alone and it was only May. Forty reasons to content himself with his single net tied to a piling and his weir set along the
quivering flats. "Set-netters don't drown like the gillnetters do,"
his spinster sister, Kaari, had said on his fifty-fifth birthday. They
kept house together. She cooked and cleaned, did laundry. Gave
advice. And so, from that day on, he fished the flats where the
sandbars glistened at low tide and he could look north and west
and watch the gillnetters fishing the mouth where the river water
met the ocean. He could look and thank God he wasn't out there
with them.

"It's women's work, what you're doing," his friend Lasse teased.
Lasse had lost a leg somewhere in France during the war and now
anything other than war or gillnetting was women's work.

"I'm not so young," Jaska said.

"Yes. But you're a Finn. How can you live with yourself?"

"I don't. I live with my sister," Jaska replied.

Kaari. Mother wrote to him every other week, asking about her. *Jaska, is she eating regular-like? Is she working? Any unattached men showing interest?* Yes. Yes and no. He never wrote to Mother about that trouble in the woods some thirty years ago. Typical trouble single girls working a kitchen camp might get into. But they were Finns and Lutherans; Kaari should have known better. She should not have been surprised when she got pregnant or when her man—Bucky or something like—didn't rush to the altar. About the man's untimely death: cut from crotch to crown by a haulback, he never wrote. Nor did he remind Mother that Kaari was fifty, well past the notice of men, that she'd been measuring sugar, salt, and flour at Gundersen's for twenty some years. Instead, he wrote to Mother about the forty men lost, the desperate search by Peacock Spit, the treacherous sandbars that shift without warning. He wrote about a man who had lashed himself to the boards of his boat with leather straps. He washed ashore on a single beam. His tongue hung out of his mouth, and his eyes had been pecked out. Mother possessed the unflappable Finn nature. Little shocked her. She lived through the lean years, she liked to remind him. The hard years in Finland that drove so many of them to Minnesota and North Dakota where, she assured them, the living was easier, the winter lighter, the cold warmer.

It was this Jaska thought of as he threaded through the dark toward his single net and weir. The easy living in Astoria. Twenty-seven canneries, fifty-two saloons. Twelve churches, two of them Finnish Lutheran. A movie theater, a union hall, four saunas. This abundance would kill a woman like Mother. All those houses painted in bold blue, rose, or yellow set like thumbtacks pinning the fir-covered hillsides. An excess of cheer, Mother would say.

Jaska picked his way through the bull kelp. Behind the eastern hills a long silver wrinkle widened, throbbed with light. That would be dawn. Beside the piling his lone net lay flaccid. But the weir, the hoops of which jutted from the sand like ribs, rocked, wriggled. Thrashed. Too strong for an eel or salmon, these movements. And the noise coming from the weir? Too human to be anything but a child.

Jaska hurried for the weir, flung open the lid. Inside, mired up to the waist in mud, was a boy. In an hour the tide would have taken him. "Stop flailing about," Jaska said. He dug at the mud around the boy's waist and thighs, scooping with his trowel, cursing under his breath. A minute, two, and then he freed first one leg and then the other to the shin. "Grab tight," Jaska said. The boy wrapped his arms around Jaska's neck, his one leg around Jaska's waist. With a grunt Jaska pulled. A loud slurp and the mud released its hold. Jaska tumbled, heels over head and the child laughed. Laughed. Jaska's first thought: how shall I write about this to Mother?

Jaska figured the child to be seven maybe eight years of age. Not from these parts, he was sure of it. "How do they call you?" He asked in Swedish, English, Spanish, and Finnish. A chunk of horehound candy lured the boy into the metal washtub. The boy squirmed beneath the pitchers of warm water Jaska poured over him, as if the fresh water were acid. "Settle down," Jaska murmured, pouring with one hand, holding the boy in the tub with the other. Layers of bladder wrack and seaweed clung to his back, torso, and limbs. More warm water, more candy, and a good long sit before the greens peeled away and the boy beneath the mud slowly emerged.

Jaska rested on his heels, blinked at the creature before him. Hard to believe this was the same child pulled up from the marl. So beautiful now to behold. A cherub, like something from a fine painting that belonged on the vaulted ceiling of a cathedral somewhere. If God existed, he existed in this boy; that's how beautiful the child seemed to Jaska. And yet, he could not discount the otherworldly quality of his alabaster white skin, hair white as dry clouds, eyes an odd cornflower blue. Well. Did not Jonah step out of the open mouth of the whale, his skin blanched blister white? Did he not stumble upon that shore, dumbfounded and disoriented? The boy, Jaska decided, must have suffered a similar fate. We do, after all, still live in the age of miracles.

Jaska pulled the boy out of the tub, rubbed a towel gently over his shoulders and back, his skinny legs. His feet. Only his feet were imperfect. One foot twisted inward at the ankle, the other foot had no arch. Kaari squinted at the boy from her perch by the hearth. He could read the look in her eyes. He brought the child in; this was a mess she wouldn't clean up.

Kaari approached the boy. So white, the child, like he'd been drawn up from a big vat of bluing. And the eyes! Dull and oddly nonreflective. Like they would swallow her up in darkness. Kaari bent and ran a finger along the boy's bony shin, touched the twisted foot. "Someone put him in your nets. He's not right and they wanted to get rid of him."

Jaska gave the boy more candy. "Does not every creature bear the image of God?"

"Surely they do." Kaari glanced at the hard light in the boy's eyes. Not dark now. Light as if a twilight sky full of stars, icy cold and distant, passed through them.

"We cannot fathom the mind of our creative God," Jaska continued. "Did not St. Paul say we are made perfect through our imperfections?"

That's a question she's spent thirty years tiptoeing around. Better to turn her hand to what can be touched, gathered, cleaned. Kaari gathered the wet towels. "If you're going to keep him, you ought to fit him for shoes. Like those special ones they make in Portland."

"He's fine just the way he is." Jaska scooped up the boy, flung him over his shoulder. The boy shrieked with delight as Jaska plodded up the stairs. Laughed and ran his hands over Jaska's hump.

In Mother's most recent letter she made requests. *Tell me the untellable story. Tell me a story that outstrips time.*

She wanted a love story. She wanted joy. Those are stories Kaari can't tell. About love she never wrote. About Bucky she never wrote. She wrote about the woods, the way they swallowed her up. The darkness brewed within them—that was her meat, her milk. Her music. Darkness, she wrote, made a clean heart in her. About her own child, who lived for only a day, she never wrote. Only Indian Jennie and Liila, the pastor's wife, knew about the infant she put into the water down by the docks. Liila said, *God understands all,* but the look on her face said *that's what you get for chippy-ing around with men in the woods.* And sure, she was forgiven on Sunday, but Monday through Saturday nobody wanted a thing to do with her. Those were the bad years, thirty of them to be exact, consisting of calendar days, tide schedules, letters from Mother.

Mother writes: *Bolsheviks. They creep through the wheat fields. At night. Singing Soviet hymns. Good songs, lousy lyrics. Those godless Bolsheviks; they ruin all that is right and beautiful. Are there Bolsheviks in Astoria?*

There are, in fact, a few. The Red Finns, Kaari tells her, meet in the Socialist Hall on Front Street. They even have their own newspaper. Some of them are leaving for Karelia, a Soviet promised land in what was once a part of Finland. They are helped along by cannery bosses, who are only too happy to pay their passage if it gets talk of unionization out of their mouths. Mother describes the ballet in Minneapolis. The way the girls mince about on tippy-toe baffles her.

Why don't they just hire taller girls so that they can walk normal-like? Mother asks.

"Heh-a!" Jennie yelled from the porch. "You seen my man? I've looked all over for him." Her eyes roved aimlessly.

Kaari put the kettle on the stove. "He's gone, Jennie."

"Yeah. But I've got supper ready for him. If you see him, tell him I'm looking for him."

Kaari motioned to the chair in front of the stove. "Come in, Jennie."

Jennie dropped a large burlap sack on the porch, scraped her boots on the step, and crossed the threshold.

They had to get this conversation out of the way before Jennie would come in and drink the raspberry tea Kaari kept at the scald for her. Indian Jennie. Bucky's Jennie. Kaari wanted to hate her. Bucky had left Kaari for Jennie. But Jennie was so simple these days, childlike and forgetful, and it seems wrong to hate a child. Grief had scrambled Jennie's brains. But somehow she remembered to stand on Kaari's porch at least twice a week and ask after Bucky.

Kaari set a mug on the table.

"Torger was found dead this morning. Someone set fire to his shed with him in it." Jennie reached for the mug. A loud slurp. "And you know old Hans."

Kaari nodded.

"Taken off by a cougar." Jennie set the mug on the table, leaned toward the staircase. "White!"

The child had crept down the stairs and fixed his gaze on Jennie. Jennie shuddered. "The devil is white, white."

White and reeking. The smell of marl, the rank and rot of things that wash up onto the rack line filled the room. And this after a full bath.

"He's lost, I think," Kaari said. "Jaska says he's a prophet. Like Jonah."

Jennie surveyed the chalk-white hair, the misshapen feet. "My mother knew a prophet once. At night he closed his eyes. His body lay on his mat, but his spirit was in the stars. He died twice. Then came back to the living. With messages from bears. Heaven is full of bears." Jennie stood and nodded toward her sack on the porch. "Daffodil bulbs. We could plant them along the cow trail. We could wait for Bucky."

Not the right time of year for planting bulbs. Not on the trails. Not with all the rain. So much of it that the hoofs of the cows have turned up like snowshoes. Their bovine instinct for safety has kept them off the hillsides. Not so for Jennie. The hills could slide right out from under her, the mountains crumble. Nothing will keep the woman from her rituals.

"Let's go," Kaari said to the boy, pulling on his arms. He wriggled away. Kaari tried again. He sank to the floor, a heap of dead weight. Kaari dragged the boy to the door. He could walk. She knew it. This was a game and she was having none of it. "Walk," she commanded and the boy flailed and carried on with a god-awful racket that put the crows to flight.

Jennie scrutinized the boy. Then she hoisted him into her arms as if he were no heavier than a sack of potatoes, carried him up the trail on her short, sturdy legs, leaving the bag of bulbs for Kaari. Kaari followed, her gaze on Jennie's stubby legs. Jennie had the strength for hauling nets. Also, she had her own mesh boards and could tie good knots. Maybe this was what Bucky saw in her: a woman who would be at home on a boat, would work and work and never stop to ask why.

At the trail's summit they had a regal view of the bay to the south, and to the west and north the shipping channel and the river's wide gray mouth. Behind them was Sugar Loaf Mountain and a scabland of bare rock and scrubby pines.

Kaari hunkered over her knees and pushed bulbs into the soft mud. Daffodils. A ridiculous prospect. Nothing grows well here. The wind and salt and stabbing rain stunted everything, bent all life on the hills to horizontal lines. Everything but the razor grass nattering and whistling, slicing the wind to jagged slivers. The boy hummed. The wildness up here seemed to calm him, but then he spied a Swedish tanker gliding along the lane. He scowled, threw rocks over the cliff.

Jennie crouched in front of the boy, her eyes sparking bright. "What will you do with him anyway?"

As if awaiting her reply, the boy turned his gaze on Kaari. The directness of that gaze, raw and open, set her teeth on edge.

"I'd put him in the water," Jennie said. "It's kinder to them that way." Then, as if touched by electricity, she straightened. "Did you hear that? Bucky—he's calling me."

Kaari peered down the trail. "Sure," she said as Jennie lumbered down the path.

It's a kind of love, these lies. What harm is there in weaving loose fictions. Bucky's at sea. Bucky's in the woods. Bucky is the wind. "Bucky should have been a wolf," Kaari tells the boy. Well, he should have been given a wolf's name. That's what you do if you want someone to live a long life. What kind of name, after all, is Bucky?

Kaari reached for the boy, who allowed her to pull him up on her back. She had not named the baby. It could not have lived with or without a wolf's name. Sure, she'd said the prayers you were supposed to say for newborns. But what words for an infant turning blue? Then wracked with a jagged breath—one, two—punching the air with tiny fists. Then silence. Gone.

She does not remember the weight of that other child in her arms. The sweet smell of his hair. The color of his eyes. She was tired of tending messy memories. Besides, this boy on her back was here now and needing her. And Jaska was right. He was beautiful. Except for the feet, beautifully perfect. "What will we call you?" she whispered, knowing he would say nothing. The boy dug his heels into her stomach, wrapped his arms tighter around her neck. The heat of his body against hers loosened something below her stomach, a liquid pressure from between her legs. Kaari raced down the trail. Past the hedgerow, the Scotch broom, Jaska's old nets. As the boy slid off her back Kaari bolted for the biffy. That pungent odor of ammonia carbide? She knew it was the smell of her monthlies even before she pulled up her dress and sat on the wooden ring. What to make of that thick dark stain on her underwear, she wondered, she a woman who's not had monthlies in over five years?

Jaska didn't know socialism from rheumatism. The meetings in the Socialist Hall, what they talked about he didn't know or much care. Not a Hall Finn and not a church Finn. He kept to himself. His hump saw to that. It started as a knot of muscles that wouldn't unclamp.

Round like a steel trawl float and anchored between the shoulder blades, it ached when the weather changed, when it rained, when the fogs rolled in thick. Thirty years in the making, this hump, this reminder of a body bent by gravity. His hump provoked perfunctory sympathy from the elderly Finnish women, so sorry, so sorry for him, kindly jokes from the men, unguarded looks of fascination from children. But not from the boy. He licked his index finger and traced the bulging outline. As if to say *there*. Or *now*.

Jaska stood before the mirror and lifted his shirt. *There. Now.* The hump was there. He turned sideways. Now it wasn't. A trick of his changing sight? Jaska arched his back, reached with his fingers. There, but just. He pulled his shoulders back. Always, when he did this, hot searing pain stung from vertebra to vertebra. Now it didn't. Jaska dropped his shirt. And began the longest letter he'd ever written to Mother. He wrote how at low tide sunrise pooled in the litter of clam shells glowing wet and pink. The boughs of Douglas firs were scythes whittling the sky into pieces. He wrote of the freckled globes of the violet foxglove, how they held an interior light of their own. And yet for all this natural beauty, nothing, he wrote Mother, compared with that of their new lodger, a boy. Such a beautiful child and so light. When he carried him on his shoulders he seemed to weigh less than Gundersen's sacks of meal or salt. When he lifted the boy his back didn't ache a bit. His step was strong and sure. He had the strength of his youth. The boy had given him this, he wrote.

Mother wrote: *Are you reading your Bible regular-like? Are you training up the child right?*

Jaska reads the gospels in their mother tongue. On this he and Kaari agree: Jesus sounds smarter in Finnish. Kaari reads to the boy from the New Testament. Accounts of miracles and healings. Sight to the blind. Strength returned to the halt and the lame. This earns a sly smile from the boy and nothing more. His stubbornness she believed to be evidence of some Finnish in him, though his hygienic habits spoke otherwise. He wouldn't use the outdoor biffy. He wouldn't use a fork or spoon. Though his fingernails were long as claws, he wouldn't let Kaari near them with her file. And of course, he wouldn't speak.

Of Jaska's love for the boy there is no limit: this is the enchantment of children. They reveal a capaciousness we didn't know we had. With the utmost care, he mixed flour and glue to make a mold of the boy's feet. For hours he boiled leather to render it soft and supple. With infinite patience, he sewed strips of leather to fashion shoes with a long, firm tongue running from the heel to the calf. That the boy shows no interest in these proceedings bothered him not a bit. It is a kind of love to do for someone what they don't know or care needs doing: washing him, speaking gently, showing him the mesh and how to work the wooden tongue and mesh board. He loved to surprise the boy with gifts. He brought him floats from Soviet Russia and Japan and sweets of all sorts from Gundersen's, like double salted black licorice, ribbon candy, sticks of striped horehound. "Who you buying this all for? You got a girlfriend?" Gundersen liked to joke and Jaska, not a smiler by nature, could not help laughing. Yes, laughing.

One night, Jaska dreamed the town shook loose from its moorings. The hills turned liquid. The canneries, houses, docks—all heavy as granite—slid into the muddy water. The walnut-size stone between his shoulder blades grew. Small scales of flint wrapped his ribs, crept over hip bones and along his groin. For a few glorious seconds he lay flat on the water, marvelously buoyant in his flint skin. And then his body, which was not a boat, but a coffin, sank. Save me! Jaska gasped, bolting upright. The boy, sitting on Jaska's legs, stared calmly at him. A puddle of rank seawater pooled beneath the bed.

"Where do you get to at night, Boy?" Jaska whispered.

And the child, turned alabaster in the moonlight, merely smiled.

Though it is well into spring, the sky didn't know it yet. Darkness rained in long silver needles. Darkness rolls over the clouds in thick tufts of storm. The wolves' anguished melodies knocked from hill to hill, tree to tree.

"The wolves are in the walls," Kaari said to Jennie during Jennie's customary visit. "The wolves make all this wind." At the sound of her voice the boy, sitting in the metal tub, laughed and splashed about in the soapy water. She'd given up on him, left him there to bathe himself.

"No," Jennie said. "It's him," and pointed to the boy. "This is what happens when something is brought to a place where it shouldn't be." The boy, naked and dripping wet, now sat at the kitchen table stroking the shiny scales of a salmon Jaska had been keeping alive in the kitchen sink. Spellbound, they watched his hands. Flick. Flick. His long fingernails, sharp as knives, flashed. Scales flew through the air. They could not take their eyes off him, even as he boiled the fish, its body jackknifed in the water and the head sticking out of the pot. He ate it like that, one half of the fish cooked, the head still alive.

At last Jennie spoke. "If he were mine, I'd pour vinegar in his eyes. If he doesn't blink, then you'd know for sure."

"Know what?" Kaari asked.

"If he's really a devil or not."

That night, Kaari wrote to Mother. *What is happening to us, oh Mother? Kalle's horse shattered Kalle's back with a single kick. The crows have augered themselves into the windows of the canneries, driving their beaks into their brains, dying even as their wings flapped powerful strokes. Each night, the wolves come down from the hills and choir their sad canticles. Their forlorn ululation pierces the fogs. We are changing, Mother.*

They awoke the next morning to bad news: all the milk at the dairy had gone on the blink, curdled even as the cows stood in their stanchions. The Chinese at the cannery were on strike. Pastor Juha's horse had been houghed. But it was the news about the twelve men lost at sea that put everyone on edge. From the Bible Jaska read to the boy about storms and seas and Jesus who calms such things. Kaari looked at the boy. In his eyes she discerned a preternatural coolness, a distance that suggested indeed, they were of two separate worlds that were only just now intersecting.

A smile twitched at the corner of his mouth. "Mother," he said. One word. What cruel power that word wields. How it tugged on a thread from a deep, dark center of herself where she is wilderness, empty and wild. "Mother," he repeated.

Kaari lunged, her hands circling his neck. Jaska leaped from his chair and shoved her, hard. Kaari fell to the floor and stayed there. Pretended to be more hurt than she was. But it was the boy Jaska looked after, making him tea and speaking to him in soothing tones as he hoisted him on his back and headed out into the widening night. That's the way it is between some brothers and sisters. Washed with different waters, that's how different they are. She was surprised it took this boy to show her that.

Kaari pulled herself from the floor. She would apologize later. Blame it on her monthlies. Outside, the clouds had thinned.

The moon bobbed timidly in the black sea of sky. Kaari pushed through the underbrush for the footpath. Outside Jennie's place, she stood and hollered. Waited. Then knocked on the door. Long tongues of water stood in the troughs of the cedar planking of the porch. Which struck her as odd. It was not laundry day and the cedar shake overhang, though wobbly, was sound enough to keep the porch dry. "Jennie," Kaari called as she pushed open the door. From within the interior gloom, she spied a small fire guttering in the grate. It was not like Jennie to leave a flame unattended. Kaari took a few steps toward the fire. The stench of marl overwhelmed. And this too was odd. Jennie might be simple, but she kept her place clean. "Jennie!" Kaari crossed for the kitchen. And there she was, sprawled on the floor, her face buried in a thick slick of mud.

Every night, darkness knocks on my windows. It wants to build a house inside of me one splintered stick at a time. Like the turning and lengthening of a lock's tongue finding rest in its ward, darkness turns and lengthens. Closes. I am quite shut in now.

    P.S. There is something wrong with the child and I do not mean his feet. What are you going to do??

Kaari set the letter aside. Jaska sat by the fire with the boy. So much trouble, this boy. And now Jennie. Dead and it made no sense. Nor did the riot at the cannery or the murder on the docks. Kaari looked at Jaska. "We are changing," she said.

The boy found a stash of Mother's letters, had them spread out, had folded them into shapes. His hands danced through the letters. Which ones, his hands seem to say, shall feed the fire?

Jaska sat watching the flames rise and fall, rise and fall. A letter sailed into the grate. Then the leather shoes and straps. The boy laughed.

"Do something. Do something," Kaari said. Once to herself, the second time to Jaska. Jaska nodded slowly, though she could see that his eyes were wet with tears.

They agreed they would take him to Seaside. They'd go early the next morning. They'd say they found him, abandoned. They would say he was touched, one of God's simples, in need of aid. Perhaps an orphanage in Portland would take him. Surely, a child this beautiful would be adopted.

Kaari rose first. She listened to Jaska and the boy breathing quietly beside each other. So beautiful, so beautiful, this boy. In the weak light, his skin seemed to glow translucent. Jennie was right. Better to put such creatures back where they came from. *Mother,* she would like to write, *did Christ our Savior forgive us of every sin? And did he, Mother, forgive us of wrongdoing we knew we would commit and were not in the least bit sorry for?*

Kaari bent over him, her shadow clothing his body. She put her mouth near his, took in the sweet breath. His dark eyes snapped open. "Mother," he said. Kaari fell back on her heels, scrambled down the stairs and out the door.

When Jaska woke, the fire had burned to glowing coals. Outside the kitchen window the moon bobbed luminous on the dark water of the bay. In an hour the water would swallow it. Dawn would break in a gray wash. *Take me, pull me out or under. I'm ready.* He'd tell the boy they were on a journey. They'd make a special visit for horehound candy in Seaside. Be it right or wrong, a crime or an act of kindness, he would not let himself think.

"Boy?" he called. The child liked to sleep. Sometimes in the bathtub, sometimes under the bed. "Boy?" Jaska hoisted himself from the chair, up the stairs, down again. To the porch, yard. "Boy?"

What new trouble he would or had already caused, this, too, Jaska did not want to think about. Kaari's voice rang in his ears: *Do something. Do something.*

Kaari groped through the waist-high sword fern, plodded along in darkness over the trail and toward the cliffs. The caviling of the owls wobbled low and ominous. Nattering rattle, whickering wind, how to harvest this darkness? She'll put it on her tongue, like castor oil. Swallow it down. That's what she'll write Mother. The brittle fog gloving the trees, she'll write about that. And dawn. How it draws darkness to itself. Neither a blessing nor a curse, it simply happens; their only job is to navigate it.

Near the top of the trail, Kaari allowed herself to lie on a bed of moss and watch the sky warm from pigeon gray to eggshell blue. All around her, green shoots of the bulbs she'd planted knifed through the mossy sward. Kaari rolled to her elbows, stood, and peered over the edge of the cliff.

The fog thinned to scraps of cloud and the distillation of light through it, radiant. A drawstring pulled on her abdomen. Wasn't that Jaska down on the flats? He'd not brought his thin planks to walk on, or a pole for balance. Just Jaska ankle deep in the marl. And the boy! His white hair danced in the wind. He hopped about in the mud farther away from shore, farther from Jaska. *Oh, you fool,* she wanted to shout. *Why is the child here? Take him to Seaside, or give him back to the water, for this land surely cannot abide him.* Instead, she cupped her hands around her mouth and shouted Jaska's name.

Tiny sand flies, sharp as grit, hurled themselves at his face. A litter of mussel shells split open glowing lavender, glistening wet like eyes. All that separates us from where we want to be is a bit of water, bits of glass. Mother wrote this in her last letter. *We must walk on water,* she wrote. *Walk into that light.* And so light, this silver glass, this water, so strong surely he will walk on it. Before him, in the shallow surf the child stood. Rising through the platen silver, so perfect and so perfectly needing him.

Jaska's feet moved of their own accord, carrying him closer to the child. The flats shone like a mirror. The child stood gazing at him. Brilliant light everywhere. Jaska shielded his eyes from the glare. Only then did he notice the child cast no shadow. Oh what, Mother, oh what, would you say about this? The child beckoned with a hand, urged him into the water. And then a voice, sharp and shrill from the heights: "Jaska—Don't!" A dark crease, a crumple to the light, that voice. At the sound of it, he shook his head, as if it were, like these flies, a mere irritant.

Jaska took another step toward the boy. The water lapped at the boy's knees, then his thighs, his waist. The water lapped at Jaska's ankles, shins, knees. *The trick,* Mother wrote, *to walking on water has to do with faith. I'm blind, quite blind now. And I can tell you this with certainty. You close your eyes and you keep walking.*

Dizzy with light, blinded by the glare off the wet sand and shells, Jaska walked with the hesitant toddling steps of a small child. How far would faith take him? A game, a trick. The child, now past the safety buoy, was playing with him. Beckoning him. Pretending to be caught up in a net, then jumping free, splashing, calling gaily. He'd not figured the boy would be so quick and agile in water. But just as he was about to grasp something solid, an arm, a leg, the boy swam beyond Jaska's reach. Not a good game, not with tide coming in.

Jaska waded farther. The water heaved. The boy plummeted. Then reappeared. Not smiling now, but thrashing and flailing; it seemed now he really was tangled in the net. "Father!" he cried, his voice thin and spectral. "Save me!"

"Hang on!" Jaska called even as another swell lifted and dragged the boy under.

"Jaska!" Kaari's voice again, this time much closer. Jaska turned. She was setting planks, a rope over her shoulder. "Help him," Jaska called. She had the strength of three women now. The boy had given her that. She could get the rope to him, he knew. "Throw!" he hollered, pointing to where the boy's head crested briefly, then vanished.

Kaari looked at the child, gasping and choking, and at her brother, mired thigh-deep in the mud. *Oh, Mother! One rope and two in peril. Is it a sin to let go the one you shouldn't have?*

Kaari set another plank. One end of the rope she tied around her waist, the other she looped as a lasso. She had lost Bucky because he had wanted to be lost. She had lost her child because he was never hers to have. The boy in the water, he wasn't hers either. But Jaska, to his hips now in the mud, he was a different matter. For what she was about to do he would not forgive her. That would be her burden to bear. But it's a kind of love to do what must be done because no one else can or will. And it's a kind of love to let go. Kaari swung the lasso once, twice. On three she let it sail where it landed true. Impervious to his noise, his threats, his anguish, Kaari cinched the rope tight. And hand over hand she started the long haul.

OKWIRI ODUOR

Mbiu Dash

FROM *Granta*

WE WERE ALL there the day Mr. Man came to town, driving that blister-colored tin car. It looked like he had scrounged the dumpsters for scraps, like he had welded them together under a flaying sun, building an automobile out of tractor parts and posho mill parts and old radiator and washing machine parts. We thought to ourselves, "A man like this must have a good story lodged beneath his tongue." We knew that we wanted him to stay for as long as it took to get that story out.

It was the first of December, Epitaph Day in our town. That's the day of the year that we set aside for remembering our dearly departed. In the morning, we went to Our Lady of Lourdes, and Father Jude Thaddeus called each of our dead by name, and we blinked tears into our canvas shoes and swallowed the Communion host and said to each other, "Take heart, my dear, take heart."

And afterward, we went to the brewhouse, and Mama Chibwire dipped into her barrels and handed out mugs of mead. That's what we were doing when Mr. Man came to town. We were sipping on mead and sniffling into our sleeves. Thinking of the way Salama used to cut chunks off the cow's rump right while it grazed on the field, thinking of Aminata's funny skulking walk, thinking of GodblessAmen's way with cane rats, how they followed him every which way he went, like he was the Pied Piper, how the neighborhood children took to saying that GodblessAmen himself looked like a cane rat, and when they said this, the grown folk started to see it too, and we all believed that no doubt GodblessAmen had once been a cane rat himself and no doubt he would turn into one again when he was done with this wearisome life.

That's exactly how it happened in the end. GodblessAmen was riding his motorcycle when he got waylaid by a boda boda thief and received a machete blow to the neck. Someone telephoned the police. They arrived to find him no longer a man, just a mangled rat trying to dig itself into the murky ground. The police were frothing at the mouth. They would not believe that a dying man had just up and turned himself into a cane rat. They smacked the bystanders with clubs, saying, "You dare waste the government's time?"

We were at the brewhouse that Epitaph Day, and we were sipping on mead, and thinking of all the ones we had lost. Then Mr. Man drove by in his tin car, squinting, forehead scrunched, looking like he owed us a story. Mama Chibwire poured him a mug, and we all scooted over to make room for him and for that wretched soul that followed him around. And Philomena sat in his lap because she was already drunk and when Philomena is drunk she's truly mannerless—she will climb atop of tables and piss in soda bottles, or she will grab a hog by its corkscrew tail and drag it, grunting and tottering, across the town, until the apothecary runs out of her wood cottage, waving a cast-iron pan, saying, "Philomena Nanjala, let that poor devil go or I will wreck your medulla oblongata!"

Mr. Man gulped down his drink, mouth twisted on account of the floral notes of the mead—the lilacs and the lantanas that the honeybees had suckled. Or perhaps just on account of the mead's cloying sweetness. He did not seem to like what Philomena was doing on him, either. She was writhing, her eyes closed, looking like a woman deep in the throes of childbirth. She acted like she was doing something sensual, like she was trying to seduce the poor fellow, trying to make him say, "Haki ya nani, you're finishing me!" But us, we knew the truth. She was only trying to feel for his wallet, to learn how fat its contents were, so she could make up her mind whether he was worth her time or not. We were horrified at her guts. We said, "Philomena Nanjala, behave yourself!"

Philomena's sister, Petronilla, was there with us too. She grew vexed. She jumped up from her stool, grabbed Philomena, and tossed her out the window. Philomena fell into the puddle below, where she promptly blacked out.

We felt ashamed, like we had let Mr. Man see us with snot smeared across our cheeks, or with holes in our bloomers. We felt we ought to apologize for Philomena's gaudy behavior. So we gave Mr. Man ingratiating smiles, and complimented him on his shirt, which read United Colors of Benetton.

"Where are you from?" Mama Chibwire asked, filling Mr. Man's mug.

He pointed over his shoulder with his gnarled-up thumb, toward the wispy, mint-colored horizon. We wondered to ourselves if he meant just over the valley, or if he meant a place like Sudan or Manitoba or Kyoto. A man like that really could have come from anywhere. And with that wretched soul, too, following him everywhere like a haggard shadow. We looked at it, all curled up at Mr. Man's feet. Where had Mr. Man picked it up? Had an old hag given him the evil eye? Had a beggar asked for a coin, and then cursed him when he'd refused?

We looked pitifully at Mr. Man.

"Stay," we said to him. "Stay for as long as you want."

Me, I always thought of my mama on Epitaph Day. Now I wanted to gulp down a mug of mead in her honor. I wanted to pour some on the ground and say, "Dottie Nyairo, you old scoundrel." But Mama Chibwire wouldn't let me drink any mead. She said, "Mbiu Dash, you're only *thirteen*."

They made a mule out of me every chance they got. Everyone in the town did. They said, "I see you're headed toward the marketplace, Mbiu Dash, be a good girl and take this bag of charcoal with you to the maize-roaster." They said, "What's an orphan like you running around for? You've got no place to go, and no people to see either. Here, scrub this bucketful of bedsheets. And mind, I'll be checking your pockets later, so don't think you can pinch any of the Omo." They said, "Mbiu Dash, hop on over and fetch the apothecary. Tell her that the rabbit keeper got that dirty thing of his stuck inside maid's hole again."

When they had things for me to do, no one gave a squirrel's tail that I was thirteen. And when I was darting through the streets, knocking on their doors, saying, "Please-please-please you've got to let me in before they catch me," no one minded that I was thirteen either. They only tugged at their curtains, and said, "Not my problem."

Well, let me ask you, whose problem was it, then, that the police and the preacher men and the busboys wouldn't leave me alone? That they were always trying to sneak up on me, trying to stuff their fists in my mouth and do me the dirty? Whose problem was it that there were throwaway kids like me all over town, hiding in the gutters because no one wanted to see their grimy faces, stealing dried sardines from the fishmonger's stall, and running, constantly running, so as not to get dragged into the alleyways?

You're only thirteen. Fair enough. But I had seen much since that day my mama robbed the bank. This made me *big* thirteen, the type to be able to drink mead on Epitaph Day if I wanted. Still, Mama Chibwire slapped my hand if I reached for any of it. She gave me bone soup instead, and not even salted bone soup. I sipped glumly and I thought of my mama robbing the bank, how she laughed and laughed until no more sound came out of her throat.

Every Epitaph Day, Sospeter Were took out his PA system and played "Vunja Mifupa," and we all spilled out of the brewhouse and did the chini-kwa-chini dance for our dead ones. We thought of how someday it would be us gone, and how some other people would be the ones twisting themselves and turning themselves upside down and inside out for us. It was a sweet thought, one that made our toes curl with glee. To be dead someday, and missed, and held tenderly by those we'd left behind—that was our greatest aspiration in Mapeli Town.

I got up too, to go dance for my mama. But the townspeople shook their heads at me and said, "Mbiu Dash, you had best sit here and keep our guest company."

I clicked my tongue to the roof of my mouth. "Look what you did," I said to Mr. Man, when everyone else was gone.

"You like to dance?" he asked.

"What type of question is that? Everyone likes to dance."

"Well, dance for me then I see."

And I curled my lips. I was *big* thirteen. I knew what men were like. I said, "Don't speak such mud to me. You think I'm a puppy dog, to do things for you just because you asked?"

Mr. Man frowned, chastised.

I said, "Why don't you ask *him* to dance for you?"

I was pointing at the wretched soul at his feet. It was a boy. Well, what was left over after the boy's boyhood was plucked away. He was all shrunken and empty and limp, like a squishy rubber toy. He wore an ivy cap, plaid shirt and corduroy trousers. He had glass shards for eyes, cobalt-colored, sparkling even in the muted light of the brewhouse.

"Who is he?" I asked Mr. Man.

"That's my son Magnanimous."

Mr. Man pushed his brew mug over to me, and said that I could have as much of his mead as I liked. I knew that a gesture like that was awfully suspicious. A grown chap like him, trying to intoxicate a young girl? I said, "Shame on you, Mr. Man."

Then I got up and left, jumping out the side window so that none of the dancing townspeople would see and make me stay. I stumbled over Philomena, who was still lying in a muddy pool. I squatted down beside her. I studied her face, memorizing the arch of her eyebrows, the curve of her cheekbones, the bridge of her nose. I pushed her lips back and studied the inside of her mouth. Her gums were orange like a drying river, like henna on the fingernails of the women who sold baobab seeds outside the town mosque. A praying mantis hopped onto the sharp edge of her chin. I flicked it away before it could crawl higher, into her nostril. Then I lay down in the crook of Philomena's arm, with my ear pressed to her chest. I listened. It sounded like a seashell in there. White noise.

I pinched my eyes shut and pretended that Philomena was my mama. I pretended that it was the old days, before my mama ever robbed the bank. I pretended that my mama came home from work, and that we ate coconut rice with curried chicken, and that I had rubbed her sore back with oil of calendula and peppermint prescribed by the apothecary. And now we were lying together in the bed that we shared, my mama's soft snores making the chiffon canopy above us tremble.

My mama worked as a tooth doctor. Each evening, I ironed her white scrubs and set them ready for her. Now they dangled on a hanger behind the bedroom door. Sometimes, in the afternoons, she came to fetch me from school. I would find her standing by the barbed-wire fence, wearing her scrubs and a bear-fur trapper hat that she once found in a Moscow flea market. She would be smiling coyly, her eyes glowing in the sun, her pockets bulging with sweets.

My mama was not finicky like other tooth doctors. She always let me eat as much Goody Goody and Chupa Chups as I wanted. And she never once made me brush my teeth before bed. We had an understanding: I could ruin my teeth, perforate them with holes big enough to lose five-shilling coins inside, and she would patch them up for me with silver amalgam someday.

Every evening, as we lay in bed together, I chewed on bonbons and ball gums and gobstoppers. I chewed them until my jaws ached. I chewed them until the flax of the pillowcase stuck to my face. I chewed them and stared out our bedroom window, watching as men hobbled by, hawking a type of rhubarb which gave a person's virility back to them, and as women wheeled handcarts filled with sour flatbread and canisters of camel's milk. Busboys clambered onto the roofs of their fifty-seaters and lay there, smoking Lucky Strikes and singing "I Shot the Sheriff."

And my mama, she was lost inside herself, surrounded by a clammy, half-fragrant, half-pungent devil-wind that spun fast and flung rotted tonsils and misaligned jaws and Kalashnikov rifles at her.

"What are you doing?" someone asked.

I opened my eyes and was dismayed to find that I was not in the flat that my mama and I had once shared, but rather, in a puddle, cradling a drunken woman's head, pretending like she was my mama. Mr. Man was watching me. He leaned out the window, with his mug of mead pressed to his hairy bottom lip, and with that wretched soul—that leftover boy Magnanimous—clinging diagonally across his body like a satchel.

"Nothing," I said, and got up, and began to walk away.

"Wait," Mr. Man called. "Wait, please." And he scrambled to jump out of that brewhouse side window, same as I had just done.

I looked over my shoulder and saw that the townspeople were dancing a little ways off, their limbs melting in the heat like sticks of butter. They were drunk, every last one of them, and now they tottered, and they contorted themselves, and they hooked onto each other like parts of a chain-link fence.

I knew peril when I saw it. And here it was—a godforsaken man, prowling about, trying to ensnare a throwaway girl. He knew full well that the entire town had lost its mind to Mama Chibwire's mead. He knew that he could do anything to me no problem, there weren't any witnesses.

I said to myself, "Mbiu Dash, you witless dunce, don't just stand there!"

I took off running toward the yellowwood trees. I quickly lost Mr. Man—he did not know the way through the clock tower, or the boatyard, or the old cemetery, or the schoolhouse. Now I was in the town, and I went from window to window, peeking in. That's what I did on most days—pressed my face to dusty panes and squinted, watching as the townspeople drank masala tea and listened to *Je, Huu Ni Ungwana?* on the radio.

I started peeking through windows after I lost my mama. I was full of fear that I would wake up someday and find that everyone else was gone too. That I was *truly* alone. So, I watched the townspeople through their windows, to make sure that they were all still there, and that their hearts were all still pounding in their chests.

Currently, no one was home. The entire town was at the Epitaph Day dance by the brewhouse. I looked inside the empty houses, and it occurred to me that absence was just as meaningful to observe as presence. Each of the houses had its own muffled vivacity: shadows climbing up the walls, sitting in the rafters, chewing khat. Mice hobbling out of cracks and rolling like bowling balls across cement floors. And the ghosts of the dearly departed, returning briefly. Sitting in rocking chairs to darn threadbare coats. Swirling soups of pigs' feet that were simmering on unattended stoves. Writing letters to loved ones they had left behind. Saying, *In the long of night, I walk the navy sky and count the stars with my own hand, naming each after you.*

Mr. Man came driving in his jalopy, sticking his head out the window, saying, "Wait, please!"

I took off running again. Past the tin houses that crinkled in the heat. Past the fields of bristle grass and juniper bushes and sunflowers. Past the papyrus reeds and sycamores and wattle trees. Up the hill that sometimes wobbled on fatigued feet. To the vulgar house where my darling lived.

There was a rickety gate flanked by stone angels with severed heads. A yard full of tangled balls of thorn trees and wild flowers and barbed wire and stiff yellow grass. An awning, double doors, a chimney. I pressed my face to the windowpane and stared into her kitchen. Fruit flies darted over the wicker basket on the table, inside which a speckled mango decayed. A bird smacked against the pendant lamp hanging near my head. It was a rufous-naped lark. Its dull eyes glazed over in a momentary daze. Then it got its wits back and lurched away, leaving a tuft of tawny feathers on the stained glass.

Where was she, my darling? I started to panic. What if she had gone outside, and got caught by Mr. Man? What if he had stuffed his fist in her mouth and dragged her into an alley and done her the dirty?

"Ayosa Ataraxis Brown!" I yelled, turning away from her kitchen. I looked through another window. She was not there, at the groaning staircase where she sometimes sat. I ran around to the butterfly garden that was overgrown with weeds, and I found her by the broken tiered fountain. She sat prim, her white lace socks pulled up to her thighs, and her knees hugged to her chest. Her taffeta dress crackled with static. The ruffles in them were stiff, gorging alleyways into her skin.

She was all greasy pigtails and vapid face. Her mouth was red around the corners. The day before, we had gone to the marketplace to get clementines for the marmalade she wanted to make. The clementine seller took her money and said, "Thank you, pretty girl."

And Ayosa had recoiled. She had squared her jaws and dug her hands in her pockets. All the way home, she would not talk to me—she was seething with rage. Later, she scrubbed her face raw with a pumice stone. She scrubbed her chin and cheeks and forehead, scraping off any encroaching prettiness.

When I found her in the butterfly garden, she was watching stink bugs and wax worms reel on the hot, cracked stone of the fountain. She looked up at me, and waved me closer to look at the insects too.

"It's Epitaph Day," I said to her.

I said it with my eyes. My darling and I, we never talked to each other with our mouths.

She said, "You want to build a bicycle?"

She showed me a dumpster in the middle of her yard, filled with scrap metal. We sifted through the pieces, ripped out the wires and fashioned them into a tandem bicycle. Then we rode the bicycle from one end of the yard to the other, our palms callused and our temples taut and our frocks withered in the moist air. Our right feet pounded the pedals and then our left feet pounded the pedals and then right-left, right-left, until our movements, and our noses, were filled with the scent of lavender, and our faces were raw from the thorns of prickly pears.

Then Mr. Man found us. We did not see him until it was too late, until he was grabbing our bicycle by the handlebars, and saying, "Wait, please!"

"Run!" I said to my darling. She made toward the apothecary's cottage to get help. Me, I did not wait for any type of help. I knew that there wasn't anyone out there who could save me from the monsters. I knew that all I had was myself. I closed my eyes and turned myself inside out, so that my soft parts were tucked away and my hard parts were outside, and then I was coursing through the air and I was hacking at Mr. Man and he was wailing and wailing.

"I don't mean to hurt you," he cried. "Look, look, I only want to show you this!"

He reached inside his breast pocket and held out a photograph. In it was my mother, wearing her bear-fur trapper-hat, and a down parka that swept over her ankles, and she was smiling that coy smile that I knew so well. Mr. Man had tears trembling in his eyes, shining like opals. He said, "Here, take it. I will get into my car and go away now."

This time, I was the one that ran after him, saying, "Wait, please!"

He was tired, he said, and needed a place he could lay down his head for a while. He had driven for days to find me. I showed him the way to the shanty by the river. It was decrepit, lopsided, leaning against a parasol tree. From its porch steps, you could see the water lapping at the rocks, and the grebes and albatrosses pecking at the writhing fish, and the jacanas sunning themselves in the sand.

The shanty had belonged to GodblessAmen. He had lived inside it with his cane rats, snagging eels in the river and eating them raw, carving voodoo dolls out of wood and standing them everywhere. The voodoo dolls were still here, even though GodblessAmen and his cane rats were gone. The dolls gave me an eerie feeling, as though they were watching intensely and wielding daggers behind their backs.

"You can stay here," I said to Mr. Man. "No one ever comes this way."

He took his son Magnanimous off his shoulder, and slung him over a threadbare chair. He walked over to the stove and fumbled about, searching for matches, a jerrycan of kerosene, a dusty saucepan. He found lemongrass growing out back, and fetched it, and made us sweet, aromatic tea. He said, "I met her in Moscow. Your mother, I mean. We studied at the same university. She and I, we started as comrades, and ended up as . . . Quite frankly I don't have the proper word for it. Soulmates?"

I bit my lip. "Mr. Man, are you my father?"

"Lord, no!" he said, curling his mouth as though in unimaginable horror. "Dottie Nyairo was my sister. No, that will not do. She was not a sister at all. She was more, much, much more. A part of my soul, inhabiting a body separate from mine. Our love for each other was spiritual. It is eternal."

I said, "I'm awfully sorry for you. Me, all I lost was a mother. You lost a part of your soul."

Mr. Man laughed, even though I had not meant to be funny.

We sat in silence for a long while. Then Mr. Man got up and lit a tea light, which was the only sort of candle he could find. "Epitaph Day," he said in explanation, and set the light down before us.

I stared out the window, at the jacanas. I was thinking of a dream I had recently had. In it, my mother's laughter rolled out like a great sea spreading as far as the eye could see. It was an angry sea swatting at the bustards and the finfoots and the thick-knees, sweeping them all away. Knocking dhows over and drowning those red-eyed fisher-people with dirges on their tongues. And I found a blue marlin, whose belly was inscribed with old prophecies. Saying, *Mother is made of gold and daughter is only of tarnished copper.* Saying, *Mother has a field of poppies growing on her bosom.* Saying, *Look what you did, Mbiu Dash—you spilled all her patchouli oil, now she'll never return to you.*

Mr. Man squatted down at my feet, and touched my knees. "If you don't mind, would you tell me about that day?"

"What day?"

"The day she robbed the bank."

I did not like how close Mr. Man was, so I pushed my chair back and stood up. I walked to the door and leaned against the jamb.

"Please," Mr. Man said. "I've got to hear it."

"I was there with her. I was in the front seat of her Volkswagen. I saw her kill two policemen with her Kalashnikov. She jumped into the car with her sack of money. We drove through the streets, and my mama tossed money notes out the window for the townspeople to take. The police were chasing us with rifles of their own. My mama tried to lose them. But they got her, in the end. She was hit twenty, thirty times. The bullet holes had her looking like a carrot grater." I sighed, and said, "You know the story, Mr. Man. Everyone knows the story. It was all over the news."

Mr. Man stood next to me, and gazed at the paper wasps and owl flies at our feet.

"The thing I came all this way to ask is, did she *suffer*?"

I shook my head. "I guess she did not. She laughed a lot, even when she was getting hit. She held me and laughed until all the laughter inside her was finished."

Mr. Man went and poured himself more lemongrass tea. He took a huge swig. Then he said, "You've got to be careful. You've got to give the guilt only a knuckle, not the whole finger."

"I've got no guilt. *She* was the one that robbed the bank.

"Why should I have any guilt about it?"

"Survivor's guilt."

"You're speaking mud, Mr. Man."

"Maybe I am," he conceded. "In any case, I've got some."

"Mine follows me about like a stray mongrel."

He was talking about his boy Magnanimous, I knew. I said, "Tell me your story, Mr. Man."

"It's the same story as your mama's."

"You robbed a bank?"

Mr. Man shook his head. "No, that's not what I meant," he said. "The lot of us, we came back from Moscow. Engineers and doctors and lawyers. All perked up and full of beans. Ready to lead our people to the promised land."

Mr. Man fell silent, lost in his thoughts. He was silent so long I thought he'd fallen asleep standing.

"Mr. Man?" I said.

He blinked, and saw me, and saw where he was. He climbed down the porch steps. He said, "Wait here a moment, I'll be back."

He started toward the river. His son Magnanimous got up from the floor and began to follow him.

"Hey!" I said. "Hey, Magnanimous?"

He paused by the lemongrass bushes and turned to regard me. "What happened to *you*?" I asked.

He shrugged. "The police came for my papa. They called out his name and then they started shooting. My papa wasn't home, thank goodness. It was just me, doing homework at the table. So I took all the bullets for my papa."

I twisted the corner of my frock round my index finger. I said, "What did it feel like, taking all those bullets?"

"The sky was yellow, like gooseberry. The clouds were turning, making shapes. I saw minarets, and strings of Chinese lamps, and canary birds big as airplanes. There were cowbells on my ankles and tambourines on my wrists. When I moved, there was song, and when I stopped moving there was song too. I saw pixies in cotton-candy skirts, twirling to the music of my bones. And I was laughing, and my body was falling apart, turning to millet grains, and the snipes and the wagtails were pecking at it. It felt like hallelujah."

Mr. Man returned, carrying a pair of dead, bleeding ducks. He set them down on the low table, and boiled a pot of water, and began to pluck them. He hummed as he worked, that song that went *something-something-here's-the-story-of-the-hurricane*.

"Mr. Man?"

He looked up from the onion that he was dicing into quarters. "My name's Gregory. Grey for short."

"What happened after you returned from Moscow, all perked up and full of beans?"

He crushed a head of garlic with a hammer. He tossed the lacy garlic peels at the floor, and Magnanimous lunged at them and stuffed them into his mouth.

"They said that we got indoctrinated while we were studying in the USSR. They said that we were communists, planning a coup, supported by our Soviet sponsors. They spied on us, and stalked us, and blackmailed us, and sidelined us. Some of us got disappeared. Most of us went into hiding. Dottie, she was proud, scarlet-chested, like a parakeet. She would not come with me, no matter how much I begged. She said she was tired of playing cat and mouse. So she stayed behind to fight."

I grimaced at his words. I could not bear to think of my mama this way, as though she had not been the type of woman who lined her eyelids with kohl and wore silk camisoles on Saturdays. Who let me have sips of her red wine as we watched *For Your Eyes Only*. Who drove out with me to the hills, so we could lie under the fever trees and eat butter cookies and read Enid Blyton books. Dottie Nyairo, who always snipped my fingernails with her front teeth. Who wore her permed hair in a beehive. Who let me stare at the sun too long, so I would get floaters in my eyes. Who made rice with fried egg for dinner most nights of the week.

Dottie Nyairo, who had been mighty proud of her name, so proud that she had taken it with her when she laughed her way out of this world. With her, I had been Mbiu Nyairo. Afterward, the name just did not fit me right, like a cardigan that had got shrunken in the wash. Now I had a blank space where my mama's name had been. Mbiu *Dash*.

I watched as Mr. Man dropped sprigs of rosemary and thyme into the bubbling pot. "You enjoy your meal, now," I said.

He looked up at me, his eyebrows furrowed with astonishment. "Won't you eat?"

"I never once chewed on duck. Don't intend to start now."

I hopped down the steps of the decayed, termite-chewed porch. Mr. Man and his son Magnanimous came to the door to watch me.

"Where are you going?" Mr. Man asked.

"Home."

"Where's that?"

Look, Mr. Man might have been a part of my mama's soul, but that did not mean that I was about to have him sneaking up on me in the dead of night. So, I did not tell him that I lived in the bullet-riddled Volkswagen that my mama had laughed her way out of this world in. I did not tell him that I lived with a horse called Magnolia, which I had found in the trash somewhere near Lucky Summer. I did not tell him that I lived with two hundred or so pigeons. That they were all huddled in the backseat of the Volkswagen. That I liked the way the pigeons looked—their understated elegance, the iridescence of their dress, their glossy, watchful eyes.

I shrugged, and said, "How about you mind your own business, Mr. Man?"

ALIX OHLIN

The Meeting

FROM *Virginia Quarterly Review*

IN THE MEETING, James Halliday announced the company was being sold and then he couldn't stop coughing. This was bad timing—both the sale of the company and the coughing—because everyone, including Mallory, had a lot of questions about the sale and the coughing fit seemed a little too prolonged to be real, theatrically timed and thus suspect, though James was well-liked overall and thought to be a straight shooter by the kind of people who used the term *straight shooter* and believed in such a thing. Mallory was also sick, though she wasn't coughing. She had multiple doctor's appointments scheduled but she kept canceling them and coming to work instead, because she, like everyone else, knew the sale was coming and wanted to be there when the news came out. She poured James a glass of water. He drank, his eyes wild and red and teary, then said, "As I was saying—" and started coughing all over again.

Mallory exchanged glances with Simone across the table. Simone looked panicked. Technically she was second in command because a sudden string of executive departures had left her there, designated-survivor style, but she was twenty-five and had confided to Mallory in the restroom, after asking her for a tampon, that she was applying to law school.

"I think what James was saying," said Shyama from HR, "is that we deeply value everyone's contributions here and the company will be looking to make this transition as smooth as it possibly can be."

There was a silence strewn with James's continued, though quieter, coughing.

"When?" Mallory said.

"When what?" Shyama said.

"When is the smooth transition? When is the sale? When is our last day of work?"

James Halliday finally subdued his cough. "It's today," he said. "It's happening. It's now."

Some facts about James Halliday: He was exquisitely good-looking. He had high cheekbones and green eyes with notably long eyelashes. His mother was a Peruvian human-rights activist and his father was a cardiac surgeon who had met her while volunteering in the Peace Corps and the whole family, including James, returned to Peru for a period of time each year to do good works. Everyone at the company knew this from reading media profiles of him, though he never discussed it himself. When he was in Peru doing good works with his family, he was still accessible by email. He was always accessible by email. Mallory had never known anyone to return emails faster, on a regular basis, than James. On the evening she received her diagnosis, she wrote him at ten P.M. to say that she would be taking a couple of personal days. She didn't say why. He replied at eleven. *I hope everything is right with you and the world,* his email said, a message Mallory archived immediately so she'd never have to look at it again.

James Halliday, now recovered, fielded questions. He shared that the digital-media conglomerate buying the company had some thoughts about their profit-model scalability. He said that in the interim there would be triage. Eventually, he said, new positions would become available, though he was careful not to promise they'd be available to anyone in particular. On questions about severance and benefits packages he deferred to Shyama, who passed out glossy folders containing exit surveys and 1–800 numbers. On questions about project management he deferred to Simone, who looked stricken and unable to answer them, and so James took them back and answered them himself. The meeting was over in an hour and Mallory returned to her workspace. Next to her, Bryan Das cursed softly into his cell phone. "Can we reverse the sale? I know I signed the paperwork—I want to *unsign* it." To Mallory he said, "I just put a down payment on a fucking condo."

Shyama came through the office balancing a tray on her upturned palm like a waitress. On it were wheatgrass shots in paper cups. Her HR portfolio included wellness.

"Seriously, Shyama?"

"It was in the fridge," Shyama said. "I didn't want to waste it."

Mallory's phone rang. It was a client—the news was getting out. Mallory said, "In the interim there will be triage," and hung up.

She opened the brochure. Her health insurance would be good until the end of the month, following which she would be eligible for COBRA coverage at a cost she wouldn't be able to afford. At the end of the month she was supposed to fly to Denver for an experimental protocol that she also wouldn't be able to afford. At least she hadn't put a down payment on a fucking condo.

She clicked through her email, forwarding client contacts to her personal inbox. She messaged a headhunter. She posted an article about viral marketing on LinkedIn. Bryan and Simone and some others headed to the Mexican restaurant downstairs to get drunk. "I'll be there in a few," she promised, and Bryan said, "Just want to steal a last few office supplies?" and she said, "I've been coveting your Swingline stapler for months," and he said, "If you touch my Swingline I will cut you," and put it in his messenger bag. Everyone laughed hollowly and loud. There was a last-day-of-camp feel to things, an extravagance of emotion, hugging where hugging had not previously been condoned.

Then stillness settled. At the other end of the room someone's computer speakers broadcasted the tinny bass of classic rock on 101.5 The Hawk. As she often did, Mallory gazed out the window at the office building across the street. She could see a whiteboard where people in meetings drew graphs and brainstormed with dry-erase markers, and she could never quite decipher what they wrote and found herself trying to, all the time, despite not really caring and knowing it wouldn't, ultimately, be very interesting. Her preoccupation was as pure a waste of time as existed in this life, and therefore was a luxury. She walked to the window and pressed her palms to the glass. On their whiteboard an orange arrow intersected a green rectangle inside which sat a single blue word.

"It says *deliverable*," James said. "Inside the box it says *deliverable*."

When she turned around, he was sitting in Bryan's ergonomic chair, looking more impeccable in his T-shirt and jeans than she did in her office-casual wear. Until she came to work at his company she hadn't known there were expensive T-shirts tailored to look impeccable. She knew it now because James had once been photographed for a men's fashion magazine that listed the prices of the clothes. The hoodie he wore in the picture was cashmere and cost nine hundred dollars. As head of brand management, she enclosed PDFs of the piece with their market-share reports and also framed the article and hung it in the hall by the elevator until James, who was modest, asked her to take it down.

"How do you know?" she asked now.

"I called over there and asked them," he said. "It was driving me crazy."

Of course he would have called and asked them. James Halliday would never have luxuriated in weeks of wondering about a word on a whiteboard.

"Not that I know what the deliverable *is*," he added, and coughed.

He looked around, spotted a box of tissues at someone's work-space, and blew his nose. Another fact about James Halliday: He suffered from lung irritation and was especially sensitive to indus-trial particulate. She knew this, as everyone in the office did, be-cause Shyama had circulated an apologetic memo on his behalf explaining why they weren't allowed to open the windows.

"You didn't ask?" she said when he was done blowing.

"We have to keep some mystery in this life," he said. "Also, they probably think it's proprietary. Come sit."

She sat down next to him, in her own ergonomic chair. He leaned toward her, tented his fingers beneath his chin.

"How are you doing? I've been worried about you."

"Me—why?"

"You know."

She didn't. She didn't know what facts, if any, James Halliday knew about her. She'd worked for him for eighteen months un-rolling a content strategy for the company that had not succeeded. Because of this, she believed that the failure of the company to thrive was in large part her own. She didn't feel that badly about it, though the loss of the job itself was catastrophic. She took hold of her ponytail and pulled at her split ends, an old habit. In a month, when she began the experimental protocol, she would lose her hair. The results of the protocol were uncertain, the doctor had said, but the hair loss was a definite outcome—a deliverable.

James Halliday studied her with rare, considered attention. He said, "I know you always thought the XFC distribution strategy was a mistake. I suppose you think I should have listened to you."

Mallory couldn't, for a moment, remember what the XFC distribution strategy was. Then she couldn't believe that he thought she still cared, at 1:30 on a Tuesday afternoon on the last day of her job, as the company emptied to a shell whose constituent parts were downstairs ordering watermelon margaritas and shrimp nachos. But of course he thought that, because he still cared. A steadfast and imperturbable earnestness, an implacable refusal to acknowledge the superfluity of his company: These were keys to his success. Because if James Halliday thought the company mattered, James Halliday with his good works and his good looks and his smartness and sincerity—if *he* believed it, then couldn't it be true?

Mallory said, "It doesn't matter what I think."

He leaned back, crossed his legs at the ankles. "No," he said, "I guess not. Man, I hate this song." She'd forgotten the music was playing, but he got up, strode down the row of computers until he reached the source of "Scenes from an Italian Restaurant," and clicked the sound off. She thought that would be the end of it, but as she was packing her bag, he returned.

"What are you doing now?" he said.

"Putting off the inevitable drunken afternoon at Nacho Mamacita."

"No, I mean after that."

She didn't say: *I'm going to look for another job while pursuing an experimental protocol in Denver that will certainly lead to hair loss.*

She said, "I might get a cat."

"I'm going to Galisteo in the morning," he said. This made sense; Galisteo, in California, was the campus headquarters of the digital-media conglomerate that had bought their company.

"Okay."

"Why don't you come with me?"

"Me? What for?"

Although they'd collaborated on the company's brand story, Mallory and James weren't close. At the last company barbecue, they'd spoken for five minutes about their shared affinity for vinegary German potato salad. Encouraged by his agreement, Mallory had declared mayonnaise-based potato salad "a monstrosity," at which point James excused himself from the conversation.

"I'll be there for meetings. You can connect with Arthur—he heads things out there. You can advise us on the content strategy for the transition."

Mallory felt, as she often did lately, lightheaded. The doctor said this was not necessarily a symptom of her illness, though it could be. Eat small, frequent meals, the doctor said.

"I have the discretion to keep a few people on payroll beyond today," James Halliday said.

Once, leaving the office, she saw James Halliday hail a cab in the rain, notice an elderly woman beside him who needed it, put her in it, and walk away, umbrella-less, with his hands in his pockets.

"Surely," he said to her now, "the cat can wait."

That night she skimmed some articles about the conglomerate, how they were industry disruptors altering the digital-media landscape while at the same time becoming fixtures of it. Arthur McLellan, the CEO, was the opposite of James, at least personality-wise: He was brusque, twice-divorced, with garrulous ex-wives who gave interviews about what a self-absorbed person he was. His self-absorption equated to absorption in the company he built and was therefore only a positive where stock valuation was concerned. Instead of focusing on the articles, Mallory found herself texting people from work. Bryan hadn't managed to unsign the mortgage on the condo but after the watermelon margaritas had gone home with Dmitri from IT, a long-held goal of his, so he was in good spirits. *Why didn't you come out with us?* he wrote. *We did karaoke and Shyama sang Purple Rain. She's kind of sexy in an Ann Taylor way.* Then he started texting about James—*He's probably on a private jet to Lima. He's forgotten all our names already*—and Mallory stopped answering.

Some other facts she knew about James Halliday, from media profiles, office documents, and general gossip: He was a Virgo. He had completed two years of a PhD program in American studies at Brown before going into business instead. His college girlfriend was now a well-known actress making the leap from indie films to superhero movies. His current girlfriend was the executive director of a nonprofit organization that made microloans to women in Kenya. He considered himself a feminist. He didn't eat red meat. He believed it wasn't too late to change the world.

*

She landed in Sacramento to a heat wave, Northern California style: a wall of drought that prickled her skin and made the distant air crease. At the extended-stay hotel, she checked into her suite and threw up in the bathroom. Her face swam green and pale in the mirror. She threw up a lot lately, a symptom the doctor ascribed to stress related to the illness and not to the illness itself. The view from her window was a parking lot flanked by parched, spindly palm trees. Her cell beeped with a text from James, and when she got down to the lobby, he was on his phone. He paused briefly to look at her and asked, "You okay?"

When she nodded, he gestured for her to follow him outside to a rental car, and he drove them in air-conditioned suspension along freeways and up through twisting, arid canyons pockmarked with brown pines and scrub oaks until they reached the Galisteo campus, which was spread like a Spanish villa across plots of watered green lawns. Set away in the hills, off a private road, the place looked majestic and secretive, like a supervillain lair. Arthur McLellan ran company buses from Sacramento and paid his employees enormous salaries to offset the commute. She'd read that many of them shared tiny apartments that they hardly saw, because they spent all their time on the campus.

Inside, the building was hushed with special quiet, like a museum. Wherever she looked people were working, but everyone was wearing wireless headphones and not speaking. They entered a boardroom with floor-to-ceiling windows, through which Mallory could see tennis courts, a pool, a gazebo—all deserted. James murmured, "Just listen for now," as if she might have done anything else.

The first meeting was with a Swiss executive who was there to discuss, if she understood correctly, a newly invented tool for cardiac surgery. It wasn't clear to her if he was a doctor or a salesman for the tool or both. Cardiac surgery had never been part of the brand story at James Halliday's company and she wasn't sure how it connected now. She felt drowsy and useless. After this meeting was coffee with a team promoting holistic pet care. Then, a webinar titled "Next Generation Wellness." In the late afternoon they drove back to the extended-stay hotel and separated to their rooms, and the next day went exactly the same: the drive to the villa, a sequence of meetings, Mallory politely introduced at the start and then, just as politely, ignored. She was given no instructions, was asked no questions. It was strangely exhausting to accompany James this way, though James himself seemed always bright-eyed, engaged in each meeting, often tapping on his phone, presumably returning emails at his usual pace. Despite his cheerfulness a ripple of unease snaked through her. *Why was she here?* She'd thought that James would have tasks for her, a project to manage, but there was only this: meetings and conversations, James and his phone, handshakes and smiles, charming his way through each day.

On the fourth day, Arthur McLellan, the CEO, returned from a trip to Dubai. Arthur, like James, was in his thirties, but looked older—balding, with protuberant, asymmetrical features, like a poorly assembled baby. She'd read that he dropped out of Berkeley to start his first company, and that he still lived like a student, caring little for material things. She'd also read he was quick to anger, and that although the Galisteo campus was set up in open-concept spaces, each floor held a curtained and soundproofed room where he could yell at people without slowing the general workflow. She hadn't seen the yelling rooms.

At noon she and James arrived at Arthur's office, where turkey sandwiches were laid out on a coffee table. They were plain, on whole-wheat bread; Arthur McLellan was known for food aversions. Arthur was wearing a red golf shirt, which did not look as though it had cost nine hundred dollars, and tan pants. Between him and James she could detect neither tension nor warmth. As they took their seats, the conversation sped through quick introductory chatter—the weather, the drought in Northern California, climate change in general, they all shook their heads—then James passed her a lime LaCroix and a small bag of Terra chips.

"Okay, Mallory," Arthur said as she held these items, "what are your thoughts?"

"My thoughts," she echoed.

"You've now had a chance to be in the room," he said. His eyes fastened onto hers, steady brown and unblinking. His Terra chips sat untouched. He said *be in the room* with emphasis, as if it were a privilege, which of course it was. "What do you see? What's the strategy? Where's the story?"

It was the first time all week that her opinion had been solicited, and she was in no way prepared to offer one. In another version of her own story, Mallory thought, she would rise to this occasion. She would wait a beat, let the silence gather, and then issue brilliant answers to these questions. But instead she felt bile rise into her throat, hot and acidic, and she swallowed it down. She looked at James Halliday, whose expression seemed carefully neutral. She'd seen him look this way before, in meetings: It was meant to communicate *your honest input is desired.*

She sipped her drink, swallowed again. "I've been in the room for a lot of meetings," she said, "but it was pretty high-level, I think? Pretty diffuse?"

"Diffuse," Arthur repeated, frowning.

"I guess I don't really understand what you guys are all about," she said. "You know, on the ground or whatever."

"On the *ground?*" Arthur asked. He glanced outside at the land-scaping—by his window was a large bird-of-paradise plant, its poky orange heads dipping in the breeze—as if this was what she meant.

She felt clammy in the armpits, and at the same time feverish. "It's a little all over the place," she said.

"It's called diversification," he said. "Appetite for growth." He looked down at his sandwich.

"Appetite isn't just what you eat," Mallory said, "it's why you're eating. That's the story you need to tell."

"I believe that's your job," Arthur said. He seemed repulsed—by the sandwich, by her, by the meeting. His gaze flicked over to James. "James thinks wellness is the story, isn't that right, James? Media as medicine. Media as *self-care.*" His voice was edged with disdain.

"I think—" Mallory said, and then James Halliday coughed into his napkin, phlegmily and at length. Arthur's brown eyes flicked with annoyance. She'd read he was a germaphobe who refused to shake hands with anyone. Her vision fuzzed. She couldn't get pur-chase on her own thoughts. She was failing James, and also herself. She'd questioned why he'd brought her here, and now she under-stood: Because his company was fighting for its life. He'd thought they shared the same story—the same brand.

Arthur threw his sandwich in the trash, uneaten.

"Let's pick this up later," he said, dismissing them.

Mallory and James stood up, James's green eyes shining with wet tears that looked like they came from emotion but were more likely due to his cough.

*

That night, she dreamed of rain. In her dream it was raining steadily and sideways, sheets pelting the glass, and she'd always slept well when it rained. When she was a child, in New Jersey, she'd open her window whenever it rained, and the sound would muffle the traffic outside, the neighbors' shouting, her own parents' shouting, and now she dreamed that she was a child again and opened the window, the rain soaking the sheets, warm and oddly comforting until it wasn't, and she woke up and discovered that she'd wet the bed.

Outside it hadn't rained at all, in fact the opposite: The dry air carried the tinge of wildfires. Nothing like this had ever happened to her before, even as a child, and she sat in her urine, perplexed. She thought of calling her doctor, but what could the doctor say? That it was a symptom of the illness and not the illness itself; the illness hid in the recesses of her body, lurking, indecipherable. She pulled the sheets off the bed and spent the rest of the night in an armchair. So in the morning she was less than wide awake when James texted that they'd be leaving in five minutes. They were going back to the Galisteo campus, though she didn't now understand what the point would be, after the previous day's disaster. Hadn't she already proved how little use she was? But James greeted her with the same friendliness as ever, a friendliness she now perceived as relentless, even pointless, determination. She'd thought of James's charm as integral to his success, but after meeting Arthur, who wasn't the slightest bit charming and didn't try to be, she wondered whether it was a detriment; or, what seemed somehow sadder, an irrelevance.

As he drove, the sky ahead of them brown with smoke, James took hands-free calls, and she realized that he was speaking to Simone, instructing her on the disposition of the office.

"We don't ship personal effects," he said. "If they didn't leave with it, we assume it's not wanted." She couldn't hear Simone's voice but took, from his soothing tone, that she was upset.

"You found *what?*" he said. "Okay, stop opening drawers. Custodial will take care of it. As I said, we don't ship." Mallory admired the way he phrased this, as if it were a long-held policy or law and not a decision he was making in real time, while maneuvering a Nissan on a twisting highway. She could hear a bleat of protest that must have been loud in James's ear and he grimaced. "I have to go," he told Simone.

"What did she find?"

"You don't want to know," he said.

"She should never have been put in that position," Mallory said, surprised to hear herself say it; she'd never criticized James to his face before, although he didn't seem to mind.

"Office materials fall within her portfolio," he said.

"I don't mean cleaning out the office. I mean being a VP. She's just some kid who's going to law school."

"Simone's going to law school?"

"She's applying."

"I thought she cared about sustainability. Is she going into environmental law?"

"She said corporate something." Once, at happy hour at Nacho Mamacita, Simone, Bryan, and Mallory had discussed signs the world was about to end. Arctic ice floes melting, plastic molecules damaging fish DNA. Simone had said, "I have ten years to make enough money to see me through the apocalypse."

Bryan said, "What use is money going to be after the apocalypse?" and Simone said, "It will buy land where I can homestead with my people."

It wasn't Mallory's own plan, but she could see the logic of it.

As they drove farther into the hills the air darkened. Just last week there had been a fire that took several days to contain; firefighters were still battling the last of it. Now the smell of smoke filtered sharply into the car.

"Should you be driving out here? With your cough?"

"That's very kind of you to ask," James said, without answering the question. "Wildfires are actually how my lung sensitivity began. My mother was working to evacuate villages near La Merced during a fire. I was on her back, an infant. She carried me through all the smoke. There's a strong chance I'll be looking at a lung transplant at some point."

His tone was not emotional; he was only stating another fact.

"I grew up on a Superfund site," Mallory said. "Playing in a polluted river. That might be why I have . . . what I have now." She could remember dipping her toes in the water as it flowed red with chemical effluviant from the paper plant—the color seemed magical to her then.

They left the main highway and took the smaller one that led to Galisteo. On either side trees spread their branches in a sharp,

shadeless canopy. The sun recessed in the haze. James was coughing again and she wondered how well he could see. She offered to
drive, but he shook his head. He pulled out an inhaler and used it.
There was an uptick in traffic going in the opposite direction, cars,
more cars, then buses. They saw helicopters in the sky, and the
smell of smoke intensified. The sky grew opaque. James's phone
chimed, and he handed it to her; she read that their meetings had
been canceled. The campus was being evacuated.

James pulled over to the side of the road and made a three-
point turn.

"The fire is here," he said.

They turned back in the direction they came. James's phone
was beeping constantly, a cascade of notifications, and Mallory
turned the ringer off and gripped it as it vibrated again and again
in her palm.

When she looked in the rearview mirror, she saw great plumes
of smoke with fire entrails. The sky looked like a piece of paper
being incinerated: a rim of red licking at the horizon, black ash at
the center. The smoke was in the car now, and the heat was too,
pressing their faces with gravid force. James began to drive faster,
missing the lane boundaries, grinding against the gravel shoulder,
then correcting. It was hard to see the road at all. Mallory thought
of a children's story she'd read once, where all the animals came
running out of the forest in advance of a fire, because they'd
sensed it coming. Nothing like that was happening now. There
were no animals anywhere. Somewhere someone was speaking,
a small panicked voice. At first Mallory thought it was the radio.
Then she realized that it was coming from James's phone, which
she must have answered by accident, and picking it up she heard
Simone's voice saying "What should I do with—?" and she pressed
End Call.

Then James braked to a halt. All around them cars were parked
and burning, and people had gotten out of them and were running. The cars cluttering the road made it impossible to continue
driving. Mallory unbuckled her seat belt, opened the door, and
looked at James, who shook his head. His cheeks were contorted
with constant coughing; he couldn't run anywhere.

She closed the door. James was pointing furiously at her, telling
her wordlessly to get out and run. She shook her head; she took his
hand. She knew he wouldn't leave her if their roles were reversed.

That was a fact. James's shoulders rippled with convulsions. She squeezed his fingers and he squeezed back. She breathed in the smoke and ash, sediment growing in her lungs. Once, as a child at the Jersey shore, she'd fallen beneath an ocean wave and swallowed water and sand, and even after she picked herself up and staggered to the beach, she felt herself weighted with everything she'd taken inside. Breathing the fire was almost like that, and then it was like nothing except itself. The fire met the horizon, wild heat and appetite for air, and it met the melting, blackened car, and at last it met the two of them where they sat, together, and gone.

KENAN ORHAN

The Beyoğlu Municipality
Waste Management Orchestra

FROM *The Paris Review*

SELIM THE HALF-WIT hoarded everything—that was the story they told me my first day in waste management. Selim had lost his wife, and I guess everyone figured he took up hoarding as a way to fill the void. It started out with stuff his wife might have liked—small earrings, a tea set, owl statuettes—picked out of garbage bins. Well, Selim ended up with a house packed to the rafters with trash he thought was gold. He tucked it onto shelves and into stacks, put it in cupboards, crammed it under floorboards, couch cushions, and the mattress, until there was no space left but overhead. Then he installed a system of boards and beams into the frame of the house, with maybe two or three inches of clearance from his head, in order to pile trash above him. More and more he took from the waste bins: old, tattered books, bicycle bits, apple cores, orange peels, broken printers, smashed-up furniture, crumpled cartons and boxes, hundreds of pounds of paper, pens, eyeglasses, eggshells, water bottles, shoes with holes, sleeping bags with urine stains, jackets too small, jackets too large, bed frames, filing cabinets, coffee mugs, coffee grounds—on and on an impossible list of trash weighed down on those boards and beams until at last, while his dreams of finding his wife in all this waste were licking the night sky, the house's framing broke and the collected works of the city's refuse crashed down upon Selim the half-wit, killing him not instantaneously, but swiftly enough to confuse him into believing in his deliverance.

The garbagemen laughed at the end of the story, and then the oldest one, without a hint of jest, indeed with genuine concern, said to me: "And you are doubly at risk, because a woman hoards more than a man."

And the other garbagemen stopped their laughing and nodded solemnly. The nearest to me said: "We make light of a truth; it is easy to find the merits in another's garbage if only because it reminds us of the mortality of our own legacies."

I smiled and laughed and so did they, and they all went out to their tasks. I found my assignment: a truck helmed by two men named Hamdi and Mehmet. I hopped into the cab. The older man, Hamdi, drove us off to our route, and as he did Mehmet said that I shouldn't take anything the others said seriously. "Garbagemen, for who knows why, make up myths and tales more readily than any other profession. Still, it is not good to take from the trash. Once you start, there's no stopping. Eventually you'll find yourself buried under it."

A day became a week, became a month, became a year, as it happens. Mehmet and Hamdi made me go down the thinnest alleys of Beyoğlu because they had round bellies they couldn't squeeze between the buildings, and they laughed at themselves so that their laughter accentuated their jiggling bellies. They gave me a slender handcart to navigate and said, So long, we'll see you at the end of the maze.

I went down the alleys because I was the thinnest, but it's not hard to be the thinnest garbageman when you're a woman. My small handcart scraped its sides against brick and stucco and stone—sometimes my shoulders, too, would scrape the walls, and I worried that over time I might erode a small, Fatima-shaped tunnel into the alley, or worse, that the alley would grind me down into a rectangle.

I stopped at the back doors and loading zones, the garbage bins always stuffed to overflowing, but really only half full because people are very bad at the economy of space. I emptied the bins into my handcart and continued on to the next little station, on and on all afternoon until I came out the other end of the labyrinthine alleyways soiled and sweating and reeking. Then I waited for Mehmet and Hamdi to finish their route in the truck and pick me up. They didn't make me squeeze between them in the cab. Always whoever was in the passenger seat moved over to let me sit by the rolled-down window.

In a sunny corner crooked between a kuaför and a pizza place was a bin packed with sheet music. Every day it was full up with sheets, not the kind printed in a book and tossed out by someone quitting the piano but handwritten compositions, sometimes crumpled in disappointment, sometimes scribbled over with one, two, three layers of corrections. The man who lived on the second floor was a composer, that explained it. I knew little about listening to music and even less about reading it. But you can tell a lot about someone by the way their trash comes to occupy a bin. From the state in which I found the pages, I could tell the man was tortured by the impossibility of translating what swirled around his soul into a symphony that would render the same swirlings to the soul of a listener, and that was enough for me to know that his music was beautiful. I told Mehmet about the composer, even showed him a few sheets of music, and Mehmet shrugged. "Or else a piano teacher, or else a student, or else a lunatic. How can you know if you don't read music?" He went back to arguing with Hamdi over the reinstatement of the death penalty.

Without any reason, I promised myself I'd find something to convince Mehmet it was a beautiful composer's trash bin. But the next week I found nothing in the bin, and the week after that, nothing again. Not so much as a single note scratched onto a napkin, or a used-up resin block, or even a banana peel with fret marks pressed into its skin from distractedly being eaten during practice. No, the old man must be sick, I thought, come down with a summer cold. It was a shame; I enjoyed collecting the composer's trash if only for the reprieve of tending to something precious, of being entrusted with the death of the beloved machinations of someone's art. You look for small grandeurs in my line of work. A month here and you'd be singing odes to those rare crumbless toasters.

Trash, just trash, unadorned, unloved. Scorned because it announces decay and decay is the product of time, and time is the fear of all living things. Layer, layer, layer, layer.

"Do you think he's died?" I asked Mehmet. We were in the cab of the truck, watching Hamdi drag a large bin full of sardine tins across the street.

"Who?"

"The old composer."

"Old men are in the habit of dying," he said.

Somewhere a faucet was loosing dribbles of water over the flagstones of the alley, and above, the muezzin's call to prayer slid
over the grooves of the sky. The heat had me with my uniform off
and over my head. My undershirt was soiled, the cuffs of my trousers slicked by the puddles. I dragged my cart behind me to the
next bin: the composer's. I lifted the lid, expecting to find nothing
once more, and so resigned to my worst fears, but instead, deep
in the receptacle, I spied a small instrument laid gingerly over a
pile of clean newspapers, more precious than a pair of china cups
in packaging.

I pulled the instrument up and knew at once to save it from the
trash, knew at once to commit the only sin of a garbageman and
keep this piece. The violin had obviously been loved. I took the
instrument into my arms. The patina held that precious luster of
esteem that seems to catch the light in even the darkest nooks—a
compass for the sun, as liquid as the glow of a freshly skinned
onion.

I had before prized a few items I'd found discarded, keeping
them in a pocket or sneaking them into the cab of the truck only
to find them broken and dingy in the light of my apartment, and
so I'd later place them in my own trash bin or leave them along
the side of a road or buried under the retaining wall of a cemetery.
But when you come across a truly unbroken thing, it is a miracle,
blessed, pure.

There was a new instrument in the composer's trash bin each
week. I would, excited as a young girl on her birthday, run up to
his bin, peel off the lid, poke my snout inside, and fish out either
an immaculate violin, or a viola, or a bow, or a hand-carved music
stand, or once even a cello, always placed delicately on a bed of
clean newspaper. Mostly, it was easy sneaking them home—I was
the last person to put anything in the back of our truck, and would
hop out of the cab as fast as an eel when we arrived to the dump so
that I could retrieve my newspaper-wrapped treasure before anyone saw it. Then it was quick goodbyes, see-you-tomorrows, and I
was off for home with my bundle in the seat beside me.

I lived in a closet turned studio in an old Ottoman mansion that had been partitioned into apartments many decades ago. There wasn't space enough in there for me and my thoughts at once; however, one claustrophobic afternoon, while cleaning each crevice and corner in my studio, I found a small hatch. It was in the top of my wall, behind a layer of wood panels that were under a covering of stucco. I pulled down the hatch, revealing a ladder. The ladder led me up into the framing of the old house, what you might call an attic if there had been anything but timber and shingles, indeed if there had even been a few floorboards. I crawled from beam to beam like an insect. It was a cramped little attic, spreading out over only a small portion of the center of the mansion—most of the upstairs rooms had the roof of the building as their ceiling. Only in the very center was the space tall enough for me to sit upright. I resolved to make the attic the home for my collection of string instruments, and over the next few days, I took up a few plywood panels and a box of nails. "Quite a racket the birds are making on the roof," said a neighbor. I agreed and speculated it might instead be a large owl or a rodent or even a child climbing around. Over the weekend, I cleaned away the cobwebs and dust, brought up a battery-powered lamp, and constructed a display case. As soon as I finished my renovations, I tucked the instruments into neat and tidy order. I spent my evenings after work sneaking up into the attic to pull one instrument down and back into my studio, where I studied it for hours, with no thought in my head other than to marvel in its beauty.

One morning, I showed Mehmet the latest violin from the composer's trash. He told me the city's orchestras and philharmonics had been ordered to compose and perform with uniquely Turkish instruments. "Every day it's something new stolen away from us," he said. I thought he was being dramatic but I remembered now a few things—tampons, waffle makers, coconuts—and then just as quickly reforgot them. As we rode along the Golden Horn toward the dump, we passed at the shore a building that had not been there yesterday. They must have thrown it up overnight, or else when my back was turned. Enormous, gray concrete reached from the water to the sky.

Next in the old composer's trash, I found an oud, then a saz, then a ney. I worried what it meant that even these traditional instruments were being removed. Was it an act specifically against the old composer?

The city of Istanbul woke knowing that books were now banned. We did not talk about it; we did not complain in the markets or at the office about how much this would put us out, but we felt it right in the sockets of our hearts. We simply rose from our beds and set about adjusting, some of us living now as if completely amnesiac regarding the reality of before, drowned in a blue fluid of forgetting.

Then the morning was filled with hundreds, thousands of narrow columns of smoke creeping up through the cracks of the city to hide the sky in black. People burned their books, but not everyone. Some forgot to do it right away, they were late for work, and so burned them later at the stove while making dinner. Some didn't want to burn them, trusting them instead to the cycle of nature, leaving them to decay in their gardens or in the gutters of Istanbul, flowing then in scraps to the Bosporus and washing away into the sea. Frugal ones used their pages as toilet paper. Not all books had been banned. The last line in the presidential decree read: "Exempting all religious books, histories of religions, works by religious figures, spy thrillers, murder mysteries, and science and mathematics textbooks unless containing lines of poetry or else whole poems."

There rose for three days large columns of black smoke that painted the reflections in the Golden Horn very, very dark. I returned from work one evening to find the six or seven books I had space for in my studio had mysteriously disappeared. Even the cookbook that was not an actual published book but merely a folder of my mother and grandmother's recipes was gone.

I tried picking up the bin, but it wouldn't budge. I squatted and tried lifting with my legs, but it was no use. So I dragged the bin into the alley from its perch, scraping it over the flagstones and into the sun to have a peek. The lid popped off easily enough. Curled up inside, with his knees into his chest and blinking quickly in the light, was the old composer.

"I'm the trash today," said the old man.

"All right," I said. "But climb on out and get in my cart yourself or I'll hurt my back lifting you."

The old man did as I told him, and after some huffing and grunting he was tucked into my handcart, not saying a word as I continued on my route, not complaining in the least as I made my stops and piled more trash atop him. We went like that until the rubbish was up to his neck, only his pointed head poking over the pile. Though he didn't complain, he wore a harsh frown, one that doubtless took great effort and concentration to maintain. I'd just collected the last bin of the day when the old man said: "Well, off to the incinerator, I suppose."

"Yes," I said. "I suppose."

"Will it be quite hot?"

"Oh yes, quite hot," I told him, and this seemed to bring him relief.

"It's just been so damn cold in my apartment. I could do with a change of temperature."

"You might not fit through the slot."

"I'm not so fat," he said. He was very slim.

"It's a narrow slot at the incinerator."

The old man nodded with a strange sadness. He must have shrugged his shoulders, because some of the trash around his neck curled over and fell out of the cart.

"It's terribly hot in my attic," I said, trying to console him. "You could go there instead." This struck me as a perfectly logical suggestion, in part because while we had been going along, I had grown nervous over explaining to Mehmet and Hamdi, as well as to our supervisor, why there was a live body in my handcart. It didn't seem like the sort of thing people wouldn't notice, or that they would ignore. And just how had I planned to stuff him in the incinerator anyway? The more I went like that down the alley with the old man in my cart, the more I realized he'd become a big headache, because though I admit I'm not very cognizant of the goings-on in my country, I didn't think having a composer in my trash heap was a good thing. That's the way Turkey seemed nowadays—it was impossible to keep track of what could get you in trouble. I resolved then to pile trash all over the old man, to hide him from Mehmet and Hamdi when they picked me up. I loaded him into the back of the truck myself, telling him to stay quiet, and I offered to drive the truck back to the dump, dropping Mehmet and Hamdi off at their homes on my way. It took some extra care at the dump, but mostly nobody pays much attention to trash, and so with a quick bit of shuffling and waiting for the right heads to turn away, I had the old composer in the trunk of my car as I zipped home through the hills over Beyoğlu and into Kuştepe.

I pulled down the ladder to my attic and shoved him up the rungs. He was taking his role as garbage very seriously and hardly employed his legs or arms; his movements were halfhearted. When he stepped up into the attic, though, everything in him changed. The lights were out—the space was made darker by the single cataract of sunshine coming from the transom on the far wall. I pulled the hatch closed behind us and heard, in the darkness, the small sounds of secretive, embarrassed weeping.

"You are safe here," I said, trying to console the old man, but he shook his head and slumped to the floorboards, reaching his arms out in front of him.

I had to crawl on my hands and knees to get to the light switch. When I threw it on, I found the old man bent over one of the violins.

"My violin," he said. He held it to his chest, clutching it fast and wiping his tears away. "I thought it had been burned, or broken, or compacted into a small cube. My violin . . ."

His two cellos, the other violin, the viola, the saz, the oud, the ney—they were there, waiting for him in the dark, waiting for him to notice each of them in turn and display the same tenderness in their reunion ritual. He did so, not quite petting them, but running his hand over their bends and grains the way one reassures a lover of one's presence.

Mehmet had been saying for weeks now that it was dangerous. I never listened to him. It's strange to me, how much people want to talk when they are nervous. But then the grocer started saying it, and my neighbor in the stairwell, and the postman, and the baker—it was dangerous to keep some things. They had all seen people taken by the police for having hidden things they should have discarded. They all swore they were witnessing more crimes. The baker said someone was smashing her windows. The neighbor said someone had mugged him. Maybe Mehmet was right, the city was becoming dangerous. He said it with a nervousness of the vocal cords, a chirp in their vibrations like the scrape of a coin over a cello's string.

*

The composer didn't stop playing. Even in his sleep (which was infrequent and often upright in his chair), he made faint gestures of bow over strings. All week his was hurried, ravishing playing, making up for lost time, which of course is an impossible game, especially for the elderly. The old man went about his life as garbage in my attic as though nothing had changed. He asked for paper and pencils, and then for the rest of his instruments, something I could not do because he was no longer in his apartment throwing them out. We speculated that perhaps the government (who had thrown him into the trash bin) might return to his apartment (maybe when they went to seal it up) and throw away the rest of his instruments, but until then he would have to be happy pent up in my attic, bent over and cramped with his remaining instruments. That was until, when making my route through the veins of Beyoğlu, I came upon a violinist in a trash bin. Just as the composer had been, she sat hugging her knees to her chest. She said: "Hello, I am the violinist of the building. They've thrown me out."

Then in other trash bins I found other wonders. A glittering snare drum, two honey violins, a dented oboe.

It was like that for weeks; I found more and more musicians and instruments in the trash and stuffed my attic full with them. They all hunched under the pitched roof; only the cellist could stand with her back straight in the low attic.

One Saturday afternoon I took a nice meze up to the attic to have a little celebration with the musicians. When I stepped up into the space, an incredible symphony picked me up and swallowed me. Loud, oh so loud, as if I were directly behind the conductor at a concert hall. It was a brooding piece with heavy brass (where had they found a trombonist and a trombone?), and as they played I felt I'd been made incredibly small. The walls of the cramped room sighed out and folded back a little. The musicians floated up from their seats. The objects of the room shrugged off gravity. Even divorced from its function, each instrument was a masterpiece, but I learned now that especially in use they were devices of great beauty, expressing their songs into a growing bubble that threatened to consume the musicians and the composer and the meze and even me into its membrane. But I rubbed my eyes and the illusion dropped away, and seated at a stool right in front of me, the old composer spun the music out into a magnificent tapestry.

"Please," I said, setting the tray of food aside, "the house is very old. The walls are thin as silk. Everyone will hear you. The whole neighborhood will hear you." But why hadn't I heard them as I put together the meze?

The musicians understood, and nodded with somber faces. "But please, we have nothing else to do." The composer did not acknowledge me in any way. I felt a shift in my stomach and wanted to leave the musicians in peace. I descended the ladder as they returned to their music that shook loose the silt in the canals of my soul, but as I pulled the rope down, the trapdoor closed and made silent throughout the whole mansion what was in fact a dramatic symphony in C.

We were in the cab of the truck coming back from our route, with the windows down and listening to the birds hang their songs on the breeze, when Mehmet said that we'd be busy tomorrow, and the day after, and the day after that. He said they might even assign a fourth person to our truck, but where would we put them? He said the government had issued another, even more austere decree, and so people would have no choice but to throw away half of their lives. I asked Mehmet if I would have to throw away anything.

He and Hamdi both laughed. "You don't own anything," said Mehmet. "I, on the other hand, will have to burn a few of my books. A pity, to have saved them only for this."

"You didn't throw them away?" said Hamdi.

"No, but some went missing anyway, as if vanished by a ghost, and I wept all night for them."

Hamdi, easily nervous, realized he, too, had kept some books, a few exempted spy thrillers, but it didn't matter to him. He should have burned them all, he said. He knew better than anyone about hoarding, which he defined as any attachment at all to an object. "Everything is eventually trash. It is the natural order. I shouldn't try to intervene." Hamdi's thoughts, like an oil tanker, did not change course easily, so he spiraled down a whirlpool of worry and proverbs.

"I'm afraid for my books," said Mehmet. He had hidden in his apartment, even from his wife, a few very special books, things he said were worth collecting, worth holding on to if only to allow another generation to view them. He went very quiet telling me that they were more than books, instead masterpieces of space, magnificent to behold.

"I didn't know you could read," I said, only partially in jest.

Disregarding my teasing, he said: "It is not about reading only."

I took only a few of Mehmet's books at first. I promised they would be safe with me. I didn't tell him about my own books going missing. Since the attic seemed to have been spared the disappearings, I didn't think that was important. I placed the volumes on top of the display cases I'd built for the instruments. The musicians immediately began to read. In fact, the composer complained to me that now all his musicians were reading instead of playing their instruments. I told him not to worry, there's only a few books, they'll finish them soon, and they did, but then they asked me if there were any more. "These are marvelous, I haven't seen books like this in months. Haven't you got any more?" Instead, I brought back a few more instruments, and another musician. No one was throwing away books anymore. The musicians eventually went back to their symphonies, and the composer was happy again. He seemed to think life was better for him after his removal from the world. Still, I smuggled in an odd book or two from Mehmet, if only to give the poor creatures something more to do than play their songs. I worried somehow the word would spread that I had a tiny library in my attic alongside the concert hall. The musicians, you see, were very loud in their discussions of the books, and who knows how it is that the government finds you. Sometimes I held my breath just to escape the anxiety. But the attic proved immune to the police raids that were now a regular occurrence for Istanbul's population.

While I was away on my route, the composer had managed, don't ask me how, to install an upright piano in my attic.

"The floorboards are bowing," said the old man.

"They're only plywood."

"Plywood this strong, eh?" he said, happy.

I worried my orchestra was escaping. I worried someone would see.

*

From my window over the kitchenette sink, with a small cup of coffee at my lips, I watched three policemen get out of their van, saunter over to the median shaded by a long row of Judas trees, and handcuff the nearest one. They stood there, one of the policemen with his wrist in one loop of the handcuffs and the other loop around the lowest branch of the Judas tree, waiting for the municipal forestry department to send out a couple of men with a chain saw. I spent the afternoon at the window as the men from the forestry department set to work felling the tree. The policemen took over from there and stuffed the tree into the back of their van, but not before informing it of its rights.

I prepared a tray of boiled eggs, slices of white cheese, olives, and loaves of fresh bread. I balanced the tray on my head as I crawled up the ladder and through the trapdoor into the attic, where I found not only the old composer and his orchestra but also a dozen strangers. While I was away, the musicians had descended from the attic and into the streets, taking up as many things as they could. Already the only air in this tight space came from the lungs of the person next to you, and now there were so many more lungs thirsty for breath.

"I tried to stop them," said the old composer. He curled up on his stool, as downtrodden as I was stupefied. The musicians had put up shelves in the far end of the space and stuffed them full with books. And now these strangers were joining them as they perused the books and discussed recommendations and prejudices. It was dangerous to have the instruments, they made sound, but this was worse! Who were these strangers, I wanted to know—who knew if they could be trusted? But was this on my mind while a bile of anger slicked my throat? More than anything I was furious that my musicians had stolen away some space from my attic that could have been used to house more of those beautiful instruments, more of those magnificent musicians, and yet, as I went to the strangers to kick them out of my attic, I found that they were a long walk away, that the piano was no longer overflowing with sheet music and musicians, that there was now a semicircle of folding chairs around a podium somehow tucked into the attic, and beside me was a table of refreshments and coffee. How had all of this fit into the attic? How had the seams of the roof not come undone? How had the eaves not shot right out of the building?

*

It was just an old woman at first, wrapped in a ratty blanket that maybe her mother had made decades ago. She stayed under the piano bench. But this one guest turned into two who turned into three, then five, then twelve, then an artist who had watched his portfolios being dismantled by police. "Each page of my drawings, each page of my studies. I thought they would set them on fire, but instead they took them gingerly into their own binders, marking each page and recording the contents before sealing them up in special containers they use with incredibly old documents, and that was worse, worse to know they were being preserved for the bowels of a registry. Who knows if they will use it against me one day, or else work to dismantle it in some metaphysical way, more permanent than burning."

And then came a sculptor and a farmer and a baklava baker and two professors of literature and a French teacher and a pregnant woman and a man in a wheelchair and a family of Syrians, until the whole attic took on the strange and anticipatory pressure of a liminal station and filled each of us to the core with expectation.

They built the massive concrete structure up another level. It was so tall now one had the sense that it was growing rather than being constructed. If you blinked too long, it would expand right over you, swallowing you whole. Not a window to be found. I heard a rumor they were trying to grow space in there. They were trying to compact air so incredibly dense that you could put it into your pocket and chip away at it with a chisel anytime you needed a breath. I heard a rumor that they were storing all the things that had been banned. "What about everything that has been burned?" I had asked a gossip, but she only shrugged.

I heard a rumor that it was a catacomb they were building, with each of us assigned a shelf.

Then, and you might not have noticed anyway with all the public works under construction for the past decade, all the trees were gone from Istanbul and the city was no longer emerald and azure but instead the temper of sunbaked limestone.

I was picked up by the police in the morning, without much fuss. They found in my bag a tube of red paint I'd saved out of the garbage for the painter. It wasn't Turkish red, they said, by which they meant it wasn't the red of the flag, but instead a boring, lifeless red. It was on the latest ordinance's list of banned items.

At the police station, I was delivered to a special officer in charge of the contraband division. "What's with the paint?" he asked me.

I shrugged.

"You an artist?"

"They are banned," I said.

That wasn't exactly true: old Ottoman artists and nationalist artists from the sixties were still celebrated, their works remained in museums and galleries, while contemporary artists had been rounded up, their work removed from the public eye, their tools thrown into the sea. But the officer didn't argue the point. He sighed.

"I've got a drawer of paint myself," he told me.

"Evidence."

He shook his head. "I couldn't paint a straight line if I dedicated my life to it. Still, just having it around makes me think I could, makes it a possibility."

I understood him.

"Is it like that for you?" he asked, holding the tube of paint up to me.

"No," I said honestly. "It's just a tube of paint."

"Hmm."

He put the paint into his desk drawer, then pulled from a file a few pages and held them close to his face. I noticed he needed glasses but didn't have any. I thought maybe they'd been banned. It was possible, they made people look old, weak, the opposite of what a Turk should be.

"There's concern in the department that your neighborhood is deviant," he said. "How'd you get the paint?"

I hadn't heard anything about the neighborhood through the grapevine. Did he mean me? I felt incredibly naïve then, stupid for having believed no one had noticed the orchestra in my attic. But perhaps they hadn't. The officer told me about the tips they were receiving: the rumors had nothing to do with music, no one had complained of any sounds coming from my building. But it was standard to search someone's house after picking them up—there were probably police in my apartment now looking for the attic, or else just looking for anything. Undoubtedly, the musicians were playing, the artists were painting and hammering and molding, and the intellectuals were debating and laughing and writing, and the whole attic was a racket, racket, racket just a few inches over the heads of a half-dozen policemen.

"I saw the paint in the trash," I said.

"You're a garbageman."

"It's a habit," I said.

"You have a habit of taking things from the trash."

I invited only suspicion with my answers. What did he know about me from that file there? What did he know about my apartment?

"Not my habit. I mean, it's sort of an understood nature of garbagemen. We warn each other not to take things. It becomes hoarding quickly."

"And the paint?"

"My first transgression," I said, trying not to sound any particular way, trying very hard to sound like I wasn't trying at all.

He nodded. I remembered the few books I'd owned that had disappeared from my apartment. Surely he knew, maybe he was the one who ordered them taken, and had them now in a desk drawer to show me. Maybe he knew about the attic. I was struck by the horrible idea that he had let the attic operate as a trap. I told myself that they wouldn't waste time like that. If they knew about the attic, this wouldn't be an interview. This wouldn't be about paint. I would be in handcuffs in an interrogation room rather than at a chair across the desk from the special officer.

"And where were you taking it?"

"Home," I said.

"You haven't got even a windowsill to put it on."

I nodded. Were there still police in my apartment? Would the attic, now unbearably packed with people and things discarded, come crashing down on them?

"Two years can feel like a long time," he said. "It would be a shame to spend it in jail if there were someone else who belonged there instead."

I didn't bother answering. The officer seemed somewhat relieved. I'd spared him some extra work, I thought.

He put all the papers back in the file and said that because of my inability to reduce my life along the guidelines of presidential decrees, I would be sentenced to two years' imprisonment. He told me that with the nature of everything there would be no trial, but there would be a court date set at which I could issue a formal statement for the record. I would be provided a lawyer to help me word my statement before the judge, and then I would be taken to the prison and processed. I'd be held in the police station until my court date.

Everything went pretty much how he said it would. At my hearing, my lawyer was exasperated, no doubt swamped with court dates for people like me. Instead of offering any help, he told me not to worry so much about jail, it wasn't so bad. All the people in there had changed. All the people outside had changed.

They put me and a dozen other people in handcuffs and drove us in a windowless van to the enormous concrete building along the shore. It was growing up the face of Istanbul, taking over the skyline like a creeper reaches up the side of a house. I looked for its shooting tendrils, its grasping fingers, but saw only straight lines, ninety-degree angles, flat concrete into the sky. How did it hoist itself up farther over the city?

Yet inside there was hardly any room for us. We stood single file in the hallway leading to the processing center. One of the guards pressed between the wall and our line to pass ahead of us. We were guided to a room with a camera in the corner. After some shuffling, one of us would stand in front of the camera while the photographer crouched beside it and took our pictures. Then in the next room a woman with an ink pad and clean sheets of paper took our fingerprints, but the room was so narrow that we stood in the hall and put our hand through the door while she did this. After processing and a shower, we were given our jumpsuits and directed toward our cells. The cell block was similarly cramped, the atrium a cross section of tightly stratified floors. The ceiling felt very close to me.

A guard escorted me down a third-story catwalk. Up ahead a young woman with her face jammed between the bars, her cheeks red from pressure, called out to me: "Do not worry. It's your first day but don't worry, there are more criminals out in the city than there are in here. It's safer in here than it is in the streets."

The guard leading me nodded his head in agreement. "I'm practically getting my bachelor's degree just by hanging out in here—so many professors and writers, you know."

At last we stopped at my cell. It was not all that large; in fact, when considering the space the building took up, it was surprising how small and how few the cells were. Despite its size, though, there were with me in my cell a few old women, a young man, a child, a backgammon board, a teapot, and a toy car—and I knew the items were in here with us rather than for us. In the nearby cells were a forest and a flock of academics giving lectures to each other. The guard who had escorted me was now halfway down the catwalk, stopping in front of another cell. A different guard came to him and shrugged his shoulders and relieved the first guard of his hat and his baton and his radio before locking him up behind the barred door. Then that guard continued down the catwalk, stopping before another empty cell where another guard met him and relieved him of his hat and his baton and his radio before locking him up and moving on down to another empty cell. I lost sight of anything else.

KAREN RUSSELL

The Ghost Birds

FROM *The New Yorker*

I LED THE way through the woods because I didn't want my daughter to have her first encounter with the ghost flock alone. We were trespassing, but it seemed highly unlikely we'd be caught—the school had been abandoned since the previous century, when ash from the Great Western Fires made most of the region unlivable. My daughter had never set foot inside an old-fashioned brick-and-mortar school, and seemed more intrigued by the idea of seeing a chalkboard than by the birds. The school was on the outskirts of a Red Zone in our family's ancestral breeding grounds—"Oregon" on the older maps, the ones from my boyhood. An evocative name, a name I loved and mispronounced with reverence at age eleven. I grew up in a town called Eugene, in the shadow of mountains that were unreachable by my third birthday. Ore-gone.

We were going in heavy, geared up. The blood kept jamming in my head. My daughter, Starling, looked so small in my viewfinder, struggling under the weight of her spectrograph. She is turning fourteen in November, and she has never seen a bird offscreen. Two milestones for me that dusk: my first visit to the world's largest known roost of Vaux's swifts, and my first trip with my daughter post-divorce.

As we pushed on toward the chimney, I wished that I had invited Orrine. I hadn't wanted my new girlfriend to intrude on my time with Starling, but now that our trip was under way I regretted the decision. I could have used the extra set of muscles. Another paranormal birder's expertise. Orrine has the most extraordinary eyes, the burst purple of a calliope hummingbird's throat feathers.

We've been dating for three months now, if you define dating as sleeping under bridges hoping to glimpse a colony of ghost swallows; I do, and, fortunately for me, so does Orrine.

The school's eighty-foot brick chimney was the tallest man-made structure for miles. It would be difficult to escape if the Surveillers took an interest. Orrine was shot in the former Okefenokee Swamp, while searching for traces of the ivory-billed woodpecker. Another birder in our network, Suzy, had been held for ransom after being caught by Surveillers in the Monteverde Cloud Forest Reserve while mapping the migration of the resplendent quetzal, a bird that's lineage dates back forty-nine million years and that has been extinct for the past twenty. Popple lost his pinky to a Surveiller's laser while taking speed photographs of the ghost of a cedar waxwing.

The Surveillers aren't much for small talk. They won't hesitate to put a trespasser in a bag. Orrine was lucky that day in the swamp—she clung to a branch on one of the few living cypress trees, pulling herself up into its saving arms. The A.Q.I. was such a nightmare that the Surveillers left her behind.

Once the sky became deeded property, Surveillers started patrolling the hazy air above the lonely scrublands and evaporated lakes. Their employers are paranoid in proportion to the suffering that surrounds them; they seem to feel that anyone who casts a shadow in a Red Zone is an "ecoterrorist." We joke that they must want to keep the escape routes to the moon clear. "You'd think they'd look the other way," Popple huffed to me during our spring count. "What's it to them if a pair of paunchy loners are out here collecting songs? It's nothing *they* can profit from."

My daughter mercifully missed the land grabs and the water wars fought above the rasping aquifers. The sky is what has been colonized in her lifetime—a private highway system branching out of Earth's shallows into outer space, its imaginary lines conjured into legal reality and policed with blood-red force. A single human being now claims to own all the sky that lifts from the Andes to Mars.

I'd had a recent run-in with a Surveiller myself. I had not mentioned this to Yesenia, my daughter's mother. She is a worrier by nature, and I did not want to kindle that fire. I did not want to be consumed by it, either. My pilot friend, Stu, a cheerful alcoholic with a Humming Jet license, had flown me to the Red Zone south of Mt. Hood, where I'd spent three weeks camping out and listening to the fuzzy music of a dead vesper sparrow. I escaped the Surveiller in the conventional way, via a blood bribe. Cash is not a resource I have much of, but my blood type is rare and beautifully oxygenated.

To be a kid requires difficult detective work. You have to piece together the entire universe from scratch. I tried to remember this when Starling turned three and her questions evolved from "Who that!?" and "When snack?" to that developmental rocket booster "Why?" No adult is ever more than three "why"s away from the abyss.

Children wake up to the knowledge that they have missed almost everything—millennia of life on Earth, and the blank blooming that preceded us. All children are haunted, I'm sure, by the irretrievably lost worlds behind them. My generation felt this vertigo keenly. By the time I was born, half the world's ten thousand species of birds had gone extinct.

I was the kid who loved baseball cards and antique globes. Vintage newspapers and paperback novels, the arterial reds and blues of old surveyors' maps. At Don's Pawn, I bought a partial encyclopedia set that on my shelf looked like a boxer's toothless grin—I left hopeful spaces for the missing volumes. My father called my bedroom "Jasper's library of rags." Well, I was ten. I could not explain why it was thrilling to spelunk backward through time. I became aware of the past as a vast and mostly unmapped space, still shimmering with the inlaid mineral of the unknown possible. The cooled magma of a finalized reality. When I became a teenager, real lava was flowing in our streets. Phreatic eruptions had become commonplace, along with food shortages, tsunamis, hurricanes, and wildfires. History was my sanctuary throughout the whirling and burning of the 2040s and '50s.

By the time I discovered the Paranormal Birding Society, extinct bird species outnumbered living ones. I should have been collecting feathers in 2040, not Orioles baseball cards and rotary telephones. I never suspected that every bird would disappear in my lifetime. Wavelengths of color and song. Ice pigeons. Yellow-eyed penguins. Great blue herons. Purple gallinules. Red-throated sunbirds. Somali ostriches. Rock doves. Day-old chicks, accumulating damage with each smoky breath. There was a last nestling of every species. On the nightly news, and outside our sealed windows, we watched birds dying from the smoke waves and the fast-moving plagues, from habitat destruction and hunger, from triple-digit temperatures and neurotoxic metals powdering the air. When I was Starling's age, I did not understand, somehow—even as I lifted the greening copper of a twentieth-century telephone to my ear—that our time would end as well.

The fires spread to every continent. The air turned a peppery orange, making each unfiltered breath a harrowing event. A straightforward solution, for any winged creature, would seem obvious: climb higher.

But many birds that headed for the cleaner, thinner air responded to extreme hypoxia just as their human counterparts did when moving from sea level to the Rockies and the Himalayas. Millions died from clotting blood. They fell from the skies in trickles, then torrents. The variegated laughing thrush. The blue-fronted redstart. Obituary writers for *Nature* could not keep up. Human beings, with our infernal ingenuity, adapted. We found ways to survive the death sentence we'd delivered to our gasping cohabitants of this planet.

Nobody I know is traveling to the future anymore. Not Earth's future. Some die-hard optimists enlist as sailors on the trillionaires' intergalactic fleets. My sister Dolores signed her twins up for eight-year terms as indentured servants on the floating starships. Of course, they call it something else, you know: "Emi and Luna are joining the Star Guild!" Air has become damn expensive in the past decade. I hug my daughter tighter to me, flooding her respirator. I want Starling to stay on Earth with me. I worry that she is losing her dreaming eye—the conjuring eye that is hers alone, the one that can see beyond appearances, into the ultraviolet.

It meant a lot to me that Starling had agreed to come on this trip. Now that she's a teenager, it's hard to get her unhooked from her Hololite, and even harder to get her to take an interest in nature. We've had a version of the same argument for years now:

"Dad. I'm fine with a world without birds. Anyhow, if I want to see one, I just ask the Hololite to show me a flame-go, or whatever I'm into."

"A flamingo."

"Exactly. Show me a flame-go, I say, and then one appears with its weird pink candy-cane neck in our living room. And you can program it to fly, or have sex with another flame-go, or eat shrimp cocktail, or whatever you want to see."

I swallowed. "It is not the same. These are real birds that have gone on swimming and singing beyond extinction. They are independent spirits."

Two weeks before our trip, I'd learned on the Ghost Bird Alert Network that the tiny, intrepid ghosts of Vaux's swifts appeared to be following their old migration route down the Pacific Flyway, using the decommissioned chimneys of churches, military bases, and mental asylums as truck stops on the sky-road to Venezuela. In late August, Wanda had counted five thousand ghosts rippling like a single wing and dropping into the chimney of Old Northern State Hospital. Thermal readings suggested that eleven thousand spirits would soon be haunting the chimney of Chapman Elementary School, their numbers peaking in mid-September and declining until the last stragglers left in early October.

I told Yesenia that we'd be visiting my mother in La Grande; I told Starling to get familiar with her early birthday presents, an E.M.F. detector and a pair of Nighthawk binoculars.

"Oh my God, Mom is going to give you so much shit if she finds out. What if Mom keeps calling Grandma and we're not there? What if Grandma breaks?"

"Oh, she'll make it to Tuesday, at least. Your grandma is an *excellent* liar."

Yesenia refuses to let me take Starling on my bird-watching excursions. She barely lets me take her out on our balcony in full protective gear. When we first fell in love, Yesenia saw ghosts of golden-winged warblers and tundra swans, but gradually it seemed as though the power left her. Sometimes I wondered if Yesenia was afraid to see the ghost birds, and had passed that fear down to our daughter. Certainly she resented the time I spent away from home, waiting for the birds to materialize.

Here is the beautiful thing, the maddening thing, about paranormal bird-watching: you can make your eye available to them, but they have to choose that sky.

People assume that to haunt means to stay rooted to one coordinate, like a star in heaven, or a murdered gangster pacing around his last Chicago hotel room. But, if there is one myth the ghost birds have exposed, it's that death means stasis. The flocks we track continue to cross oceans and continents, and the Paranormal Birding Society has been collecting fresh data on their distribution patterns, undead coloration, and evolving calls and songs.

The Paranormal Birding Society sounds awfully official for what amounts to a rumor mill of several hundred people in four hemispheres. We are working to recruit new members. It's a challenge to convince people that the study of ghosts is worthwhile. Why collect data on the dead? A haunting is an opportunity, as Orrine likes to say. Who could watch a murmuration of ghost starlings iridesce across the city skyline without wanting to know where the birds are going, and why? We have so much more to learn from them. How to pierce the smoke wall of our dulled senses and lift into the unknown. How to navigate the world to come.

The very first paranormal bird-watchers rarely understood what they were seeing and hearing, naïvely believing they'd spotted the last surviving snowy owl in a car-wash rainbow, or heard the call of a living whip-poor-will. In the years following the Great Death, grief-mad humans reported sightings of extinct birds on every continent. A bar-headed goose was allegedly seen by a spaceship captain eighty kilometers above the Indian Ocean.

Gradually, as people accepted that the birds were gone for good, the Paranormal Birding Society took flight. But so many questions remain. The most profound of these is the one a child would ask: Why are the ghosts still here with us?

If you want to find birds in 2081, you need to befriend the mechanical ones. Humming Jets are the slender, solar-powered daughters of the helicopters I grew up with. Stu took us over the Cascades. He can turn all the water in his body into red wine and still fly straight—it's his Bible magic.

"Nobody lives down there anymore, right, Dad?" Starling asked reluctantly, when we were about an hour away from the collapsed bridges that bracket the still-burning fires around the ruins of what was once Portland. I wondered what she was seeing with her inner eye. I'm sure they show the kids holo-reels of the Great Western Fires, no doubt heavily edited.

"Nobody is alive in that city," I confirmed.

She nodded, doing her best impression of the blank mountains below us. Maybe she'd decided to feel her grief and horror when she returned home. Starling, like me, is a master procrastinator. I can put off feeling things for years at a time. She looks like me, too, with that face like a blasting cap. When we do erupt, watch out. Yesenia told me as I was packing my things that she'd had an epiphany: "I used to think that you were crazy about me, Jasper. But now I understand that I made a grammatical error. I am not the object here. When I delete myself from the sentence, guess what? You're just crazy."

When Yesenia suggested that I look for a new place to sleep, I felt an avian calm come over me. I used old coordinates to navigate through the blinding storm.

"Do you remember," I asked her, "when I opened the bedroom window in our first apartment, in subzero temperatures, to let in the ghost of a female nightingale?" It was one of our touchstone memories. Her gasp of joy had been as beautiful as the night song.

"I was always pretending," she said. "But you make it so we have to pretend. You're like a little boy that way, Jasper. I'd rather smash my own thumb with a hammer than see the face you make when I tell you I don't see the ghost birds in the eaves of the St. Francis cathedral." I'd never heard a sadder laugh in my life. "Not one dead pigeon, Jasper."

On one of our last nights together, Yesenia and I had it out; she refused to let me take Starling to hear the ghost of a hermit thrush which had been singing late into the evening in the sunken multiplex.

"She is happier than you and I will ever be in this world we made, and you resent her for it! Jasper, what kind of father wants to turn his daughter's body into a haunted house?"

"Your bird-watching crew is totally unhinged," Starling once told me approvingly.

Her mother said a version of the same thing in a different key.

Two weeks after the Surveillers released Suzy, she killed herself. All the hundreds of readings she'd taken, and risked her life to smuggle home from the cloud forest, had come back bone-white. Nobody knew if there had been a problem with the exposure or if the Trogonidae family of birds was leaving us for a second time.

One song had survived—Suzy's recording of a violaceous trogon. Twelve down-slurred notes, repeated with a plaintive intensity. An ancient song forged in Eocene sunlight.

I played the ghost-audio recording for Starling and her mom. Both listened patiently for the first twenty-two minutes, and then Yesenia stood up and pantomimed a scream.

"Jasper," she said. We would be separated in three months, although I did not know it at the time. "To me, this sounds like a horny Chihuahua."

"I like it," Starling said from the sofa. She tends to side with whichever of her parents seems the most downtrodden on that particular day. Even knowing this, I felt my heart lift.

"I knew you would, honey," I said, beaming at her.

"What did you like about it?" her mother said. "To me it sounded like, *cow-cow-cow.*"

Starling looked from Yesenia to me, and I was struck once more by the mature sadness in her dark, enormous eyes.

"I like watching Dad's face while he listens."

To be safe, I'd had Stu take us in three hours before sunset. We had seen the domed compounds of some of the wealthiest people alive, glinting on the bald slopes of the eastern Cascades, spaced with desolate evenness above the scalded valley. "They covered these mountains in bubble wrap," Stu said, an analogy that was lost on my daughter. A new fire was burning in the Great Scar, formerly Southwest Portland. Wind turbines turned below us like huge flaming dandelions. None of this surprised my daughter. What raised her from her stupor was a flash of green. "Are those real trees, Dad?" More mysterious than the choking dust storms and orange skies, harder to comprehend than the Great Scar or the Red Zones, these pockets of inexplicable green health baffle us all. "Rapunzel, Rapunzel, let down your hair," Stu said, hovering over a small hilltop clearing half a mile from the school and tossing out the rope ladder.

After Stu flew off, we made camp, "we" being a touch generous; Starling kept jumping from rock to rock, staring into the canopy of leaves. The plan was that we'd spend the night here and get picked up by Stu at dawn. I felt almost giddy—we were far from the sweep of her mother's monitoring eye and the blue sinkhole of the Hololite. The toppled firs and pines had made a path for us—a raised walkway through the undergrowth. I watched with a rush of pride as Starling stretched out her arms to balance on the wild red trapeze of a quake-felled ponderosa.

When the carbon sinks of the world's forests began to burn—exhaling centuries' worth of carbon, in a protracted death rattle that continues to this day—millions of birds were dispossessed. Now the ghosts return to nest in their old homes. With the right equipment, you can sometimes hear them, even in the domed cities. Often a ghost sings for months and never materializes, and a paranormal birder must make the identification from sound alone. This is a skill that I hope to teach Starling. Not just the waiting and the listening but the openness to revelation. Which is another way of saying, to being wrong about what is possible and true.

We began our descent down the low hill toward the pale-brick ruins of Chapman Elementary. The front entrance appeared to have caved in a long time ago, the once white columns leaning like green dominoes, but I was reasonably confident that we could get in through the gymnasium. The building was constructed in the Classical Revival style, I told my daughter, America's loose interpretation of Europe's severe ideals. I pointed out the broken pediment over the entry door, the double-hung rectangular windows through which we could see shining leaves in the second-story classrooms.

"Geez," Starling said. "Who went to school here? Future senators? Fern-eating dinosaurs?"

Chapman Elementary had not been destroyed, and this had everything to do with humans' love of Vaux's swifts. Birds were the reason the chimney still grazed the clouds, a factory-style smokestack with a Dickensian vibe, far better preserved than the ruins of downtown Portland. Thick silver cables made a triangle around the smokestack—the seismic-stabilization system that had saved the school when Quake 7 flattened the city.

"Why do these ghosts like chimneys?" Starling asked me, and I explained that the swifts had been forced into the arrangement by humans, who clear-cut the woods and encroached on their homes. When the birds were unable to locate old-growth snags, they adapted to a stone forest of millworks and smokestacks. Later, small bands of humans worked to protect the "chimney corridor." Layering their feathery bodies over one another, the swifts huddled together on cold nights, revived at daybreak by the sun-warmed bricks.

"You turn that boiler on, and you're going to kill fifteen thousand swifts," a biologist from Portland Audubon told the Chapman

Elementary schoolchildren. So they voted to retire their furnace, piling on parkas and shivering at their desks until the last birds left. The children changed their plumage to save the swifts.

Starling yawned at me, theatrically unmoved by this fable. Before leaving on our trip, we had sat on Starling's bed and watched footage of the swifts from the early 2000s. A gift from Portland Audubon, transferred to holo-reel by someone's great-granddaughter. In the clip, thousands of Oregonians gathered on this hillside to tailgate the Vaux's swifts' descent. Everyone gasped and applauded when the flock first appeared on the purple horizon line, materializing in twos and threes, then tens of hundreds, around the slender brick tree of the chimney. We heard people shouting encouragement to the balletic, evasive swifts, while others cheered on the hungry raptors that chased them—a whirlwind that was part Tom and Jerry, part sky horror.

An hour before sunset, in the late-September light, the tiny swifts began to congregate, diffuse as autumn leaves and seemingly directionless; at some inscrutable signal, they sped into a dark blue cyclone and began to drop in an orderly frenzy into the open chimney. Even on the grainy holo-reel, it was clear that we were witnessing a miracle of coordination. The Vaux's swifts turned from leaves to muscle. From fog to rope. A lasso formed in the sky, made of ten thousand rotating bodies. By the time the moon had risen, the final swifts had been inhaled into the chimney.

"How do they decide who goes in first?" my daughter asked. "And last?" Vaux's swifts were mysterious aerialists of the western woods; they had died out before researchers could answer that question. Perhaps she would be the one to make the discovery, I'd said, maybe a little too eagerly. Starling had rolled her eyes. "I have enough homework, Dad."

We reached the school with a golden hour to spare. Our silence changed color a dozen times. Arrival. Elation. Anticipation. Nervousness. Itchiness. Impatience. Dismay. The red sun that would have cued the living swifts to descend made nothing happen. The ghosts failed to materialize. The evening blue was fringed with a deep maroon, and we stared at the trees inside the school windows. Nothing called to us from the surrounding foliage or the jungle of rust. Nothing came here to roost.

Stars were beginning to appear in the sky, blessedly smokeless tonight. On such evenings it's hard for me to stay suited up with my mouth glued to my respirator, even though my gauge assured me that toxins were hiding in this air.

"What if we missed it, Dad? What if they funneled in while we were standing here and never showed themselves to us?"

It was possible, of course. Backlit ghosts don't show up in my scope, and the sunset had seemed to follow me and my spectrograph to every new angle. Could eleven thousand ghosts hide from us? What a silly question. How many billions are hiding from us now?

"You might be right, Starling. Do you want to have a look?"

I hadn't set foot in a school in three decades, and the child in me shuddered. It took us a long time to reach the hollow shell of the gymnasium at the base of the hill. There was a stretch of exposed blacktop with faint yellow markings which might have been an ancient basketball court; this was where we'd be apprehended, I thought, if there were indeed Surveillers. Starling followed me, zipped into her white Tyvek suit with the dull-red face shield that made her look like an astronaut on our own planet; whatever she might be thinking about, it was not the fresh-pencil-shavings smell of September, bound books and bullies and locker codes.

Starling started ninth grade last month. She exists for her teachers as a lollipop-headed projection in the make-believe agora of the virtual high school, a flickery publicly funded arts magnet. Only the wealthiest kids can afford private in-home tutors; my daughter and her moody, multiply pierced friends recite Neruda sonnets into their Edu-Helmet microphones. Snow days have been replaced by electrical storms at the server farms. Starling's log-in seems to fail every other week, to her great relief.

"Did you like school?" Starling asked me. I was scanning the windows, wondering what might cause the plants to sway on a windless indoor night. It was a subtle, unmistakable movement.

"I can't say I did. I was more of an autodidact. I made my teachers nuts."

My daughter smiled inside her mask.

"That doesn't surprise me."

Sometimes I think I should have left Yesenia years earlier. Sometimes I know I should have fought harder to stay. No scenario seems fair to Starling. Even though the verdict is in and the papers are signed, I still run with the hypothesis that we could patch things up. I love being a full-time dad to Starling. Loved, past tense—that can't be right.

Starling claims not to mind "splitting time." It sounds so violent. I picture her in safety goggles, bringing the axe down on a block of hours. She says she wants us all to be happy. Happiness for all three of us? None of my experiments has yielded any insight as to how this might be accomplished.

The rubble was daunting. We had to crawl on our hands and knees around the broken columns, and it was my daughter who found the hole in the eastern wall that we half-wormed, half-sledded through to get inside, to the ground floor, rousing decades of dust; just when I decided that we ought to turn back, the ceiling abruptly soared away from our heads. "Wow. It feels like someone took the lid off a box," Starling said. We stood and spun our headlamps through what must have been the school auditorium—I had the exciting, upsetting sensation that we were being swallowed by the school, transported from the building's throat into its belly via a kind of architectural peristalsis. Above us, the hallways crimped and straightened. I had always intended to call off our expedition at the first sign of danger, but in the putty-gray lighting of our headlamps nothing felt quite real, and it became harder and harder to imagine crawling backward in defeat when the swifts might be glowing just around the next bend in the elementary school labyrinth. It took effort to imagine that generations of children's laughter once echoed here. Or birds' chirping, for that matter.

"Do you want to keep going, Starling?" I asked, and she grunted yes, or possibly the school itself did. The pipes seemed to be running, somehow. Or to be alive with a watery echo. The light was almost nonexistent, and I helped Starling to switch her headlamp to night vision.

"Starling?" I called into the spandrel under the school stairwell where she'd been standing only a heartbeat earlier. "Stay where I can see you. . . ."

Starling decided not to listen. Even as a small girl she had a maddening talent for tuning us out. She'd stare into the sky-blue glow of her Hololite with the lidless focus of a fighter pilot and ignore a hundred repetitions of her name. "Why can't you be a good listener?" her mother would warble. Once, around age seven, she'd turned our voices back on us: "When you say listen, what you really mean is obey."

I hope that you'll believe me, even if Starling's mother one day tells the story of this night as if I were a criminal, using a verb like "kidnapped," a noun like "danger." I never imagined our trip could torque like this.

First, my headlamp went out. I still have no idea why—I've used it on half a dozen counts, and I've never had any issues. The pink perigee moon was visible through the windows, floating beside us like a loyal owl. But Starling was by this point a little freaked out. I could understand that, of course. She didn't want to give me her headlamp, and so reluctantly I let her take the lead. "Look, Dad," she called, fixing her low beam on two heavy doors. "Seems like something you'd be into." The doors were bracketed by a beautiful W.P.A. marquetry mural, with two human figures cast as guardians of the portal. A young barefoot girl stood under the tree of life with a dove on one arm, and I swear she looked just like Starling. The wood grain turned an undersea green and mauve as she spun her light over the doors' engraving: "Send Us Forth to Be Builders of a Better World."

We reached a stairwell filled with four inches of gray ash; Starling autographed it with her sneaker toe. "Look up, honey," I said, tipping her chin until the lantern beam reached the far wall. A replica of the chimney rose out of the shadows, and dozens of kiln-baked birds hugged puffy clouds. Of all the things to survive. Ash had buried half the staircase, but some fifth-grade classroom's ancient mosaic still clung to the wall, sweetly misshapen swifts that retained the doughy imprint of their ten-year-old creators' fingers.

Next we made our way through the silent museum of the gymnasium, the scoreboard still legible:

SWIFTS 36—LIONS 28

"An unlikely win for the swifts," Starling mumbled. We paused to take a water break. Most of our supplies were back on the hilltop. I hadn't imagined we'd spend so much time in the school; had I known, we could have spent the night here, and waited to see if the ghost swifts would leave the chimney at daybreak. Starling wanted to take her mask off—so did I, to be honest—but I thought of Yesenia's horrified face and said no, better to be safe. We sat on the bleachers and drank through our straws; I started to tell her about the desalination glands that once extracted salt from albatrosses' blood. "Don't gulp," I said, but of course she did not listen, and now her water was gone.

"Oh my God, Dad. You know the difference between a Buller's albatross and a Salvin's albatross but I bet you can't name three of my friends."

"Sure I can. Diego."

"He was my best friend in *kindergarten*. He joined the Star Guild years ago."

"Amy?"

"Dead," she said, with a gloomy satisfaction.

"Okay. I'm not playing this game."

Starling stood up from the bleachers, wheeling on the court. "Well, I hope we can find at least one swift tonight. Do you know how bad it's going to feel if we get stood up by eleven thousand ghosts?" She made a face.

"Oh, believe me," I told her. "I know."

Her goofy, real laugh was a gift to me. One of the rarest sounds in the galaxy.

We searched the ground floor for another hour. I'd expected an entrance to the boiler room, access to the chimney; instead I found a two-by-two panel in the wall beside the old janitor's closet, which opened outward like an oven door, and fed into a terrifyingly narrow chute with a ninety-degree bend. The old dinosaur of a steam boiler waited after the bend. Were we going to cram ourselves inside the chute, like a letter through an old mail slot? I couldn't settle on the best order of operations—if I went first, I might get stuck, leaving Starling alone. But if she went first worse might happen. Only now do I wonder that I did not consider a third option: leaving the building. I swore I could hear a chirping, dim and repeated. "Do you hear them, Starling?" She cocked her head, staring at me illegibly under the headlamp's halo. "Maybe," she said at last. "Maybe I do. Should I go in, Dad?"

"I'll go. I might need you to pull me out if it gets any tighter—"

Decades of dried bird shit filled the chute. We scooped out guano with our gloved hands, watching it crack and plume apart; at last I was able to wedge myself in up to my waist and shove myself forward, holding my breath out of habit, as all humans instinctively do when entering an unknown element. Now I was grateful for the bulky Tyvek suit, which I ordinarily despise. Starling was right behind me. "Wait, honey," I called uselessly. She grunted as she pulled herself through the chute, and then we each turned a slow circle in the closet-size room. Two hulking steam boilers, unused for almost a century or more, glowered at us. Ancient red-and-green pipes. But then we looked up. Rising for what felt like miles and miles above our heads was the chimney, like an eighty-foot telescope.

"Dad! Dad!" Starling reached both arms into the chimney and closed her fingers around the lowest rung of a rusted maintenance ladder. Our eyes flew up the tunnel together, a heavy dark where no ghosts roosted, hemmed in by blank brick, out the top of which we could see the deep-black sky and the rippling light of stars.

I smiled tightly, trying to conceal my disappointment, because what I saw was only what anyone would expect to see in a decaying chimney: exposed rebar, calcium-eaten brick. Not a single feather in sight. Nothing opaque or glowing, dead or living. The outrageously thick paste of excrement was the only proof that Vaux's swifts had ever roosted here. The chirping had ceased as abruptly as it had begun. No bodies, no spirits.

"Okay, Dad," Starling was saying behind me. "I'm feeling a little claustro. Sorry we didn't find any ghosts. I'm ready to go back now."

I gave the ladder an inquisitive shake. I thought I might climb a little way up, to investigate—sometimes a ghost bird is camouflaged in dense shadow, waiting for living eyes to strike it like a match head and send it leaping into view.

"Dad?" my daughter called from the shadows. "Can you help me? The chute won't open."

Panic had already infiltrated her voice by the time I reached her.

"Let me try, honey," I said, and together we failed for a quarter of an hour. The chute that led back into the wider hallway wouldn't budge. I made a bad mistake then, hurling my full weight against it like a linebacker, hoping I might force it inward and instead sealing it completely.

"Is something holding the door shut?" Starling cried. "Are the ghost swifts blocking it?"

And I told her no, the ghost birds were not responsible. It was her father who was the warm-blooded dummy to blame.

"So we can't get out?" She was breathing too rapidly through her respirator, although I did not mention this, because I was matching her breath for breath.

"For the moment. Only for the moment," I said, a lie that did nothing to slow my own heart.

We were trapped in an oven. My headlamp battery was well and truly dead. Starling's had begun to flicker. We were out of water. We could survive a few nights of dirty air, but water was going to be a problem.

Mrs. Adwoa had assigned "The Cask of Amontillado" to Starling's freshman English class. Starling was writing a pretty terrible paper on it, the thesis statement of which seemed to be that friends should not let friends brick up one another while drunk. I'd made the mistake of sharing some reservations with her after reading a draft. I'd offered my help several times. Then Starling, for some reason, had started crying, and Yesenia had accused me of "crushing her spirit."

I worried now that Starling was thinking about the terrifying scene in Poe: the live burial behind the wall. "Baby," I promised her, "we're not going to die in a chimney."

Perhaps this was the wrong choice of words. I'd meant to reassure her, but as often happens with Starling and her mother I seemed to accomplish the opposite.

"Goddammit, honey. Please don't cry."

"Fuck you, Dad," she screamed, swinging her headlamp around like a bull in a pen. She was moving away from me, her voice pawing the walls. "Fuck you. Fuck you. I want to go home now."

I reached out and spun her around to face me; she was trying to squeeze between the boilers, looking for some secret exit concealed behind the pipes.

"Dad? Why did we risk our lives to see a bunch of dead birds?"

I struggled to formulate a true answer that would not push her farther away from me. I couldn't tell her: You are growing up numb to the universe, numb even to your numbness. You don't know the difference between a screen and a portal. Your eyes cannot distinguish between a digital hallucination and a real ghost. A critical window is closing, Starling. I am trying to hold it open for you, so that you can enter the night.

Instead, I put the question back to her: "Why did you come tonight? Why did you board the Humming Jet with me?"

Her shoulders shook so rhythmically that at first I thought

she had a bad case of the hiccups. A moment later, she was still. Distantly it occurred to me that I was very proud of my daughter for budgeting her air. A crying jag was a conflagration we could not afford.

"I came because you asked me to come. I came because I'm sick of you leaving us." She did a funny thing then—she pushed her face shield right against mine. We were as close as the bumper cars of two hooded faces can come.

"Because I don't want you to be crazy, Dad. I'd rather be wrong. But I don't see them—" Her voice snagged on some inner hook. "I can't see what you see."

Her eyes regarded me opaquely behind the red screen. I embraced Starling, but I came no closer to guessing what was in her heart. While we were holding each other, aware of each breath depleting our tanks, I wished, if I'm honest, for the Surveillers to come. I would have given them a gallon of blood, whatever they wanted, to fly us out of this dungeon.

"Can you radio Stu? Can you call for help now, please?"

Stu and I do things the old-fashioned way—we pick a meeting time and place. I've never wanted to risk any devices; I don't want to be tracked by satellite. The plan was that he'd return at first light to pick us up from our hilltop campsite. But I had no way to contact him, I admitted. Starling stared at me, her eyes ruby-tinted.

"Great. Well, I guess your swifts can always fly him a message, maybe do a little glow-in-the-dark skywriting. 'S.O.S. Dumbasses Trapped in School.'"

Starling's laughter had a hysterical edge that scared me more than what she was saying.

There is no Plan B, I did not tell my daughter. No backup to the backup, nothing to save you but our rickety arrangement.

"Listen," I said. "I need you to wait here. I am going to climb out and get us help."

The pitiful gurgling I heard I first tried to assign to a bird. Brown-headed cowbird. Gunnison sage grouse. Pain came to inform me that these were my own calls. Blood-bubbled speech. Starling was on her knees beside me, trying to give me water.

I'm not sure what caused my fall. Starling said I'd climbed less than halfway up the ladder when I lost my footing. She watched my palms open and shut as I plummeted, grasping at the railing. She heard the bone break and screamed for me, she said, because I wasn't moving or speaking. Another night had enveloped me, more vibrant than anything in the dark boiler room.

"Wake up," I heard a voice calling down to me from the roof of the world.

Let me dream, I groaned inwardly, but she would not give up.

"Daddy! Dad! Jasper!" Jingling the key ring, trying all my names. "Don't leave me alone!"

She began shaking me angrily. Her pitch rose and broke, and I remembered that this stern nurse was in fact my frightened daughter.

When I tried to stand, it felt like walking on stilts of bone. My left leg had become a torture device, built from my own flesh and wired to my screaming brain. Nothing had ever made less sense to me than the sight of the white knob jumping out of my thigh, blood hiccuping around it.

"Starling. I'm sorry. I'm so sorry."

"Stop apologizing, *please.* It's better when you're screaming."

Starling had abandoned all restraint, huge phlegmy sobs rocking her back on her heels. As frightening as any of this night's evil surprises was the speed with which my worst fear became, in a heartbeat, our best and only hope.

"You'll have to go alone," I said. "I'm so sorry, Starling. I can't move."

Paddling in lakes. Seizing prey. Climbing trees. Digging holes. Bird's feet are adapted to so many marvelous purposes. Vaux's swifts are ideally adapted for life in the air—so lightweight they can't perch like most songbirds, or even walk. Instead they hang down, down, down. I closed my eyes and saw the swifts getting sucked into the chimney. Faster and faster they spiraled inward. Spinning on a vortical current of their own creation and vanishing into a dark hole. *Stop dying!* I commanded my leg angrily, which was pumping out a shocking quantity of my lucrative blood onto the boiler-room floor. Stop dying and I swear I'll do a better job at living.

"Dad? What should I do? Tell me what to do."

I could not remember the last time Starling had solicited my advice on any subject. Ordinarily she saved her urgent queries for the Hololite.

"Go," I said. "Climb out of here. Morning is coming. Stu will see you on the rooftop at dawn."

Would he? No better plan suggested itself.

For what seemed like a very long time, Starling stood staring up the flue. Holding onto the *H* of the maintenance ladder. Waiting, deliberating. I confess that I saw how small she was against that epic climb and I did not think, *My daughter is as bright and fleet and brave as a bird. Of course she'll make it out.* I thought something inarticulably sadder.

But then she looked back at me, and I struggled against the headwinds of the terrible pain, my killing fear, and tried to steer my thinking in another direction: I imagined the Humming Jet rising over the hilltop on a tide of sun, a silver bird coming to carry Starling home.

"You can make it, Starling," I said.

She started to climb. The beam from her headlamp traveled away from me, pushing up the chimney. "Be careful," I called after her stupidly.

Then came the lacerating light. It was as if someone had switched on the moon.

Two ghost swifts were lighting the passage out of Chapman Elementary School, back to the upper air. Feathers came dazzling down around them. I stared up the flue and watched as they illuminated the rungs for Starling, their bodies burning so much more brightly than the dimming bulb of her headlamp. When I looked again, the chimney was shaking apart. Bricks began to lift and dizzy around the cylindrical walls. Blue and gray in the moonlight, course after course of glowing bricks growing wings before my eyes. The bricks were swifts, I realized. More swifts began to awaken and rise from the rough masonry, as if a single bolt of shining cloth were unscrolling itself, a bunched and unbelievably long dark blue scarf with thousands of knots, the tiny beaky faces of Vaux's swifts pointing upward at the low enormous moon. So many sleek wings opened at the same instant. One brain coordinated it: the shared mind of the ghost flock.

Could Starling see them? Her face was invisible to me, but I saw her pause on the ladder. I watched my daughter watching the ghost birds. She was still forty feet below the open concrete cap, gripping the rails, her suit crosshatched in a wild ricochet of beating blue light. More incandescent swifts gusted up around her, chirping at an ultrasonic octave. She began to climb after them. Their light was guiding her out. A held breath of swifts exhaled skyward in a rush, and my daughter was among them, pulling herself onto the school's roof. Stenciled against the stars, she knelt and waved down at me; and then even her shadow was gone.

The spectrograph and the electromagnetic field detector and the ghost-box recorder are still, as far as I know, sitting on a collapsed desk in a classroom in the ruins of Chapman Elementary. We'd abandoned them all, ballast that we could not carry into the chimney. So the only devices on hand to record the transformation were my squinting eyes.

A paler light spilled around the swifts' cobalt wings as they exited the chimney, the same otherworldly sapphire hue you could once see shining through crampon holes in glaciers. A light that opened up not only my field of vision but my mind itself. The blackout I feared did not come. So much remains to be seen.

SANJENA SATHIAN

Mr. Ashok's Monument

FROM *Conjunctions*

THE SUMMER OF 20—, when all this strangeness struck, was a
hectic season in New Delhi. It was particularly busy in the Department of Symbolic Meaning, which is situated in the Ministry of
Culture, National Identity, and Historical Interpretation. That year
I was serving as Undersecretary of Historical Records, working beneath a Symbolic Meaning official named Mr. Satya Mishra, whose
first name means Truth. Mishra-Sir, as we knew him, had not been
in the office much of late, as he had been traveling the country
in order to improve public confidence in the nation's ITIHAS
(GLORIOUS HISTORY). Mishra-Sir had on his person at most
times a number of ITIHAS-Preservation Campaign pamphlets,
which he distributed wherever he went. The pamphlets, translated into regional languages, read something like: IS IT TRUE
THAT OUR ITIHAS (GLORIOUS HISTORY) IS IN DANGER?
and included instructions on WHAT TO DO IF YOU ENCOUN-
TER AN UNPRESERVED/DAMAGED/AT-RISK ELEMENT OF
ITIHAS (GLORIOUS HISTORY).

The campaign was rolling on with so much forward motion as
to imply predestination. Temple priests, chai sellers, schoolteach-
ers, rickshaw drivers, common men and women alike were seeing
imperiled elements of the nation's ITIHAS everywhere. ITIHAS:
often personified in the pamphlets as a boulder-built man with a
viripotent head of hair. Our hero, ITIHAS, is shown clambering
out of a hole in the dusty ground while a spindly male villager
resembling Gandhi-ji (oversized spectacles, white dhoti) proffers
his cane. It is a very nice image that spreads the message that even

a feeble-looking villager can help our eminent ITIHAS rise from obscurity.

If anything sells in our nation, it is a story of heroes, and of history.

But pamphlets are insufficient for educating the illiterate, the apathetic, or those glued to their phones. Mishra-Sir kept an eye open for something else. Signs or symbols with greater reach.

That summer of 20—, our department had taken calls responding to, among other things:

1. A footprint known to belong to the monkey god Hanuman as he crossed from the southern tip of the subcontinent to Sri Lanka to rescue the captured Sita, as in the *Ramayana*—now enclosed in a glass case in its forest setting.
2. A shard of elephant tusk belonging to the beast whose head Lord Shiva eventually placed on his son, Ganesha. Currently under examination by a zoolorchologist working closely with the Department of Symbolic Meaning.
3. A slab of rock containing etched annotations believed to be the work originally discovering the number zero—before the Arabs exported the concept west—now displayed in the entrance hall of the mathematics building at IIT-Kanpur.
4. Three drops of confirmed holy water from the ancient river Saraswati.
5. The wheel of a Vedic-era flying chariot, found wedged behind an Audi dealership in Gurgaon.

But most curious of all, that summer, was the business of Mr. Ashok Jagtap and the sacred E—caves.

I am not a famous man. I am merely a record keeper, one of many bureaucratic stewards of ITIHAS. We have been, for many years, making and remaking the country, perhaps unbeknownst to you. We write the textbooks and obsessively chronicle the history that was quashed by years of colonial rule. Of late, we also liaise with Mishra-Sir's public relations officers, whose job increasingly requires them to understand and propagate an accurate and communally inspiring story of our collective past. We leave the messaging to them, but we give them essential material.

My relevance to the tale that follows begins with the interest I took in Mr. Ashok's case. The morning he changed was a morning that history—that great swathe of meaning that precedes us—

revealed itself as the living, still-present creature our prime minister has always sworn it to be. So, let us begin in the small room where Ashok Jagtap lived, alone, having recently been left by his wife.

Mr. Ashok slept on a mattress on the floor. His room had one window, and a mirror barely wide enough to frame one's face, which hung beneath a leaky roof. After several monsoons, it had rusted so heavily that anyone who sought his reflection would find himself staring at a creature with a complexion the color of exhaust smoke.

The mirror is one explanation for why, when he woke on that hot, dry May morning, Mr. Ashok did not initially see what he had become.

That day, he got himself ready, as always, to go to his venerated job as the best English-speaking tour guide at the holy caves E—. "Mr. Ashok," by the way, was how he introduced himself to foreigners, as he felt he could not force them to call him Ashok-*ji*, using our honorific.

On that morning in May of 20—, Mr. Ashok *did* register certain elements of the change: he ascertained a stiffness in his joints, and caught sight of his palms and knuckles, which were a horrid, grayish color. He felt very heavy. But Mr. Ashok needed and had never been given spectacles, and the lights in his room were out, as he had not paid the bill, so he could not see the extent of the discoloration. Mr. Ashok had been ill for weeks—coughing, aching, sleeping poorly if at all. He attributed the new weight and ache to the pain of his wife's absence. My body, he thought, wants me to die.

With effort, he made his way down the stairs, past the kirana shop above which he lived, and found that the eyes of the neighborhood were upon him. People were still gossiping about his wife's departure a few weeks prior. While he was at work, she had hopped on the back of her sister's bicycle in broad daylight, like the star of some Hindi serial. It had happened just after the NGO people passed through town, with their little white tent that taught women all the things their husbands should require permission to do. A man could not even kiss his spouse without her yes, Mr. Ashok's wife had said to him, using the voice a child uses to recite times tables, when she returned from the tent.

Let the neighbors stare! He had a job to do at one of the most important monuments in the nation.

Arriving at the E—caves, he saw his young friend Babu, the balloon seller, leaning against the front gate, his bloom of pink balloons bobbing above him. Mr. Ashok squinted. Babu gave him a puzzled look. Mr. Ashok bent over a few feet in front of the gate, struggling to take full breaths. His body felt strange in other ways: the slight paunch in his belly did not fold in on itself as it normally would have, and his ribs, which had been feeling rigid for some weeks now, rested stoically within him, like a heavy block.

Then, with his face closer to his hands, Mr. Ashok saw his skin for the first time that day.

His first thought was: *it is extremely unlikely.*

He straightened. Babu stood in front of him.

"Ashok-ji," said Babu. His pink balloons were blown up so large that the white polka dots they bore looked pallid, resembling a skin infection. "You're looking very sick. Actually, you're looking a little like a *statue.*"

Mr. Ashok was staring, transfixed, moving his eyes from his fingers to the wide splay of the basalt cliffs, home to the E—caves, behind Babu and back again. In the center, just behind his hand, was the intricately carved dome of the Kailasa Temple, the centerpiece of the caves. On either side of it stretched primitive Shiva temples, spare ascetics' meditation cells, towering figures of Prince Siddhartha, erotic couplings of everyday people and of gods in tantric sex positions, all of which Mr. Ashok showed visitors each day. Above the caves, the sun beat down; all around sprawled drought-yellowed wheat fields, tamarind and neem trees.

Mr. Ashok was looking at these caves—at the rock that comprised them—and then again at his own body, and he thought again, more forcefully, that *it was impossible. . . .*

"Yes," Babu was saying, circling him. Babu reached out a fist. Mr. Ashok would have flinched if he were able to feel the smaller muscles in his face, but Babu was not coming to hit him, only to knock on Mr. Ashok's shoulder as though he wished to be let into the mystery of the situation. The sound of Babu's knuckles rapping on Mr. Ashok's body made the older man feel distant. "Yes," Babu said again. "Very clearly, you are made of stone today."

For the reader unfamiliar with the sacred caves where Mr. Ashok worked, I will provide some background. Some five hundred years after the birth of Christ, a number of conquering Hindu rulers decided to build some holy temples. Putting to work their artisans and prisoners of war, they sculpted gods and goddesses into the rocks; years later, other parts of the cliffs were turned into meditation cells by Buddhists. For a time, the caves were sites of prayer, ritual, and peace.

Then, in the era of the British Raj, the caves were forgotten. Fringe types recalled them—poets and bards, historians like myself. The sacred E—caves *wished*, you might say, to be remembered, for they whispered to anyone who came within earshot, as though they were begging to have their stories set down.

However, of late, as the nation has decided to stop forgetting its history, and in fact has begun remembering with a vengeance, the sacred caves at E—became important, not only to us at the Department of Symbolic Meaning, but to the common people, who were (as the prime minister has more eloquently explained), *made of history*, of ITIHAS, for the past runs through our veins and keeps us alive.

I had one crucial interview with Mishra-Sir before he hired me, after I passed my narrative patriotism polygraphs. Mishra-Sir asked after the source of my interpretive convictions. Breathing deeply, I told him of my aunt and sister, and the small bomb blast in the marketplace. My sister was very small. The two of them had gone to the market with the maid and the Kashmiri driver. "I understand," Mishra-Sir said instantly. "That driver believed in the wrong history, isn't that it? And he blew everything up over this symbolic confusion."

I found myself weeping before my new superior. A terrorist who lusted after the wrong map. The symbols and the signs mattered. Mishra-Sir is a great man. He studied economics, government, history, and politics abroad, in America and in England, returning home upon the prime minister's election. He told me, during that meeting, of the moment he chose his homeland over that much-lauded *abroad*. The prime minister, he said, offered a better, stronger story of the nation.

Mishra-Sir spoke too of our mandate. There is much magic and myth dotting the national landscape, he said, waving in peon after peon bearing cups of chai. Mishra-Sir and his clerks made the difficult interpretive choices. Some stories confused citizens spiritually or morally—like that fabricated map that killed my sister—while others renewed public confidence in the nation's glorious history.

I noticed after I started, though, that despite Mishra-Sir's clerks' high marks on the civil service exams and stunning scores on the narrative patriotism polygraphs, they still often erred. For instance, was the footprint found in the southern forest really Lord Hanuman's, or had it been carved into the ground by a group of enterprising villagers seeking some pilgrim-tourist traffic? Or what of the prime minister's claim that our nation had birthed plastic surgery—was our department to cite as proof the evidence of early medical practices a thousand years before Christ, or were we, instead, to directly affirm the prime minister's argument that Lord Ganesha had received his elephant head via the first operation in history?

When the employee failed to discern, Mishra-Sir, with his peerless intuition, was called in; the answer, he often said, in determining whether something was truly an ITIHAS artifact, was one he borrowed from that time studying American jurisprudence.

"I know it," he would say, "when I see it."

"Not stone *precisely*," Babu amended, as he guided Mr. Ashok, who had fallen silent with shock, to the shady spot beneath a scrubby neem tree where the Hanuman langur monkeys swung lazy and low from the branches. "Stone, after all, cannot walk and talk and move." He said this as if it ought to give Mr. Ashok some comfort.

But what if he suddenly transmogrified, becoming a *true* statue at any moment?

"Shoo!" Babu shouted, clapping at a gray monkey trying to perch on Mr. Ashok's head. The fluff of the creature's tail drooped in front of Mr. Ashok's eyes. He could not feel the texture of the primate's fur, or the scratch of its claws.

"Ask me," Babu said, "you look much better in stone than in flesh. Bit ugly you were before. Now people will think you've got a more serious air."

Then Mr. Ashok had an urgent thought. He needed to know if *all* of him had turned to stone. He directed Babu to stand behind him, using the balloons as a bulky curtain while Mr. Ashok made his investigation. He stretched the elastic band of his gray slacks in front of him, stuck his hand down, and was met by a smooth, rocky pelvis and upper thighs but a fleshy penis and testicles.

Mr. Ashok may have had a higher tolerance for otherworldly logics than the reader does, and so he accepted what he found:

that on this morning, all of him save his genitalia appeared to have turned to stone. What it meant he could not say for sure, but he had his job to do. Duty persisted.

He readjusted his pants and turned to the morning visitors filtering through the front gates. Schoolgirls decked out in blue-and-white salwar kameezes, their plaits running long down their backs, followed their young female teacher to the slippery stone steps sculpted centuries earlier. A group like this would follow the numbered route prescribed by the government's ITIHAS pamphlets for schoolchildren.

On a normal day, Mr. Ashok stood hawking himself: "English-speaking tour guide?" On a bad day, Babu helped: "Free balloon with English tour, very good, yes, which country from?"

On a good day—there were not many—a few foreigners would come take photographs with the caves and with Mr. Ashok himself, and a pretty foreign wife might knock her shoulder against his and he might feel the heat of her near him. On one of those good days, Mr. Ashok might receive a tip, and in the days before the NGO came around, Mr. Ashok might go home warm with the tip, knowing that a few more such days might allow him to buy his wife a new sari, and hold it against her skin, and then they might do their man-wife business with the fervor of his generosity driving them together.

"It's going to be a good day, Ashok-ji," Babu said now, because the visitors were stopping, pausing, lifting their cameras. "Look at all the business your change will bring!"

"Is that man dressed up like a *statue*?" an Asian woman said, halting, pushing her sun hat up as she leaned close to Mr. Ashok.

"Isn't that paint bad for him?" her husband, a white man, said, placing a firm hand on his wife's elbow. "Step back, Eunice. It may be poisonous."

"Picture, picture, picture!" cried their son.

"Balloon?" Babu said. "Free balloon, with English-speaking tour guide!"

"Good morning," Mr. Ashok said, hearing his voice emerge more somber than before. "Welcome to the very famous caves at E—. Which country you're from?"

Without answering, the man lifted his son up and held him in the crook of his arm; his wife lifted their selfie stick, snapping the photograph quickly: three foreigners, the strange man dressed as a statue, and the bobble of a pink balloon in the corner of the frame.

As the day went on, Babu fetched Mr. Ashok a chai (which trickled down and out of his mouth, as his teeth and lips and tongue and uvula were all stone as well), waved balloons at potential customers, and maintained a merry disposition, as he had when he nursed his ailing kaka. But privately Babu was wondering whom he could call on his friend's behalf. A priest? A doctor? Then Babu's mind fell on the political factions that had recently taken up residence in his slum on the outskirts of A—, where, in the lead-up to the next election, the Party had come through bearing rice, distributing pamphlets for the literate, painting graffiti on the walls for the illiterate. A man had introduced himself as the Party's ITIHAS liaison and explained the importance of reporting strange occurrences.

He had the man's number in the phone he had saved months to purchase. While Mr. Ashok stood baking in the sun, standing, well, stone-still, Babu crept behind a tree. The ITIHAS liaison answered on the third try. He listened to Babu's description of the event carefully, then burst into laughter. Babu heard him call someone else over. The man put his colleague on the phone and Babu told the whole story again. The laughter recommenced. On the other end of the line, it seemed the Party members were preparing to call over a third person. Babu hung up. He took a short walk around the caves, to see if he could find the couple who had snapped the photograph of Mr. Ashok. These odd foreigners had proof. They might be of some help.

That day, Mr. Ashok attracted a European couple, who were so busy putting their hands all over each other's hands that they seemed untroubled by Mr. Ashok's stone composition. The woman wore shorts. The man touched her hips, her waist, her bum. They did not even look titillated when Mr. Ashok brought them to his favorite cave, the one featuring the various incarnations of Parvati— Lord Shiva's beautiful consort—and their various naked breasts.

"Nothing dirty, you see," Mr. Ashok said to the woman.

"Your religion is very modern," the man said stiffly.

Mr. Ashok tried again: "It is all natural. All about the cycle of birth and death, creation of life and end of life."

He did not want to escort this unimpressed couple to the edge of this cave, where the most erotic carvings lay. On the single occasion his wife had consented to come on a proper tour with him, he had pinned her here, against part of the unfinished cave, the uncarved stone . . . and though her eyes had widened when he expertly maneuvered her petticoat and though she at first felt like sandpaper, it was one of those rare times when she released into him. No, Mr. Ashok did not take these Europeans to *that* corner.

The woman grew dizzy as they emerged from the Parvatis' den, and the man decided to rush her to the air-conditioning. He pressed a tip of one hundred rupees into Mr. Ashok's stone hand and said, "You are very committed to your costume, mister," at the feel of the rock on his flesh.

Alone, Mr. Ashok wandered back to that part of the cave where the depictions of Parvati ended. The cave's ceiling dipped low, turning from man-made temple back to original cliff. Just there, at that border between the carved and the uncarved, was one more Parvati—Mr. Ashok's favorite. There was a dispute about this Parvati. Some said she was not at all divine, but rather a depiction of the wife of one of the artisans, who adored his partner so dearly that he wished to sneak her in among the goddesses. She lacked the typical Parvati indicators; her son Ganesha was nowhere near her knees, and she had only three arms, none of which held a conch or rosary. There was no cow in sight, no husband loitering. She was alone, neither mother nor wife nor lover, hands splayed as though taking in the sun or dancing to faraway music. Her face was incomplete, and featureless.

He laid his forehead against hers, stone on stone.

Down below, Babu was fumbling with English as he tried to explain to the foreigners that he needed the photograph of Mr. Ashok. The trouble was how to get it to him. Babu, like many of the poor of our nation, had a smartphone—it is easier to get a phone than a working toilet—but he had no more data. He negotiated with one of the guards to receive the photo on his behalf. The foreigners, looking skeptical, sent the image and departed. The guard turned to Babu and grinned toothily. He held out a palm. Defeated, Babu paid him ten rupees to send the photograph to the ITIHAS official.

As soon as Babu left, the guard began blasting off the photo of Mr. Ashok to everyone he knew. It was one of those things one simply had to share.

*

Now I must let you know of Mr. Ashok's misfortune regarding his living situation. On that first day, when Mr. Ashok returned from the caves, he found the kirana store owner, who was also his landlord, packing his things in a soggy cardboard box. The neighbors had reached a decision about the karmic meaning of his change, and they did not judge it positively.

"You've been cursed," the owner said. "Can't have you bring bad luck on the rest of us."

So out Mr. Ashok went, carrying his box. He tried to sleep on the bus-stop bench that night, but could not lie comfortably, and so he sat upright, struggling to shut his eyes.

In his youth, Mr. Ashok had ridden buses through the rural parts of the state to the city of A—, where he found a job sweeping an English tuitions center. He listened in on classes and made his way through the government examinations to become an official tour guide (paying a bribe, borrowing money from unsavory people, to have his educational credentials forged). And so he became a respected man. A guide. A government servant. A servant of history.

He used to see the girl who would become his wife walking each morning to her job as a maid. She had almond-shaped eyes and walked with a limp, which made her attainable. They married quickly.

Their first fight came when Mr. Ashok agreed to drink alcohol— the only time he ever touched the stuff—with Babu after work one day, and admitted to her, through moonshine breath, that he had forged his credentials. She burned his papers that night and left a small pile of ash next to his head as he slept. He did what he felt was necessary in order to keep the architecture of the union intact and hit her across the jaw with as much confidence and as little force as he could manage.

Mr. Ashok believed in duty and karma and yet had escaped the life for which he seemed predestined—a chaiwalla in a small town. For this reason, he admired the nation's prime minister, himself a former tea seller. But unlike the prime minister, Mr. Ashok never aspired to be a great man. All he wanted was a son, and his wife failed to provide him with that. Once she had even told him, in shrill singsong, that she prayed he'd fall sterile so she'd never have to bear his children, for he was a monster, for she hated him, for God would see his heart of stone and punish him—and so he had begun to strike her more repeatedly, to shut up all the nonsense.

*

In the end, Mr. Ashok could not sleep at all on the bus-stop bench, suffused as he was with these thoughts of the past. His eyes remained open as though they had been carved that way. He watched the sun come up over the smoggy city of A—, the familiar burnt dawn. In the light, he carried his box of possessions to work, moving even more slowly than he had the day before, finding his knees reluctant to bend. At the caves, he kicked his box beneath a hedge, hidden from the guards.

That morning, a number of reporters from Marathi-, Hindi-, and English-language newspapers arrived at the caves and asked Mr. Ashok wild, intrusive questions. Did he believe he had done something to offend some spirit of the caves? Or did he see himself as somehow united with this historical space? Was he putting it on, having a laugh at everyone's expense? (One reporter from *The Hindustan Times* grabbed him by the wrist and shouted: "It's stone all right!," thereby igniting a debate on the nature and composition of stone between a few science writers who had been sent to try to explain how the statue man could walk and talk.)

The loaded question arose too of whether *all* of Mr. Ashok was made of stone, and finally a female with an impertinent button nose from NDTV, said, "We're asking about your member, sir."

At that, Mr. Ashok lost his temper. He was touring a couple from Singapore, whom Babu had elbowed through the crowds to deliver, and he alarmed them by shouting, "I'll bring all of these to life and chase you out of here!" He pointed at the long row of armed bodhisattvas, enlightened beings, who surrounded the meditating Buddha so as to ensure no one disturbed his meditation. "Can you do that?" the reporters demanded. "Prove it! Show us!"

The worst: Mr. Ashok was seeking relief in the shade, having scared away the Singaporeans, when the NDTV reporter found him to ask another bald question: "I went by your old house this morning and learned from your neighbors a few things about your relationship with your wife . . ." and then proceeded to read out a number of offenses from her notepad in the same recital voice that Mr. Ashok's wife had used when returning from the NGO— "Do you have any comments about that? About whether you think your change might be, say, a *comeuppance*?"

"Who told you people about me?" Mr. Ashok demanded, and the NDTV woman said something about the internet. She used the word "viral." She held up an image on a fancy phone. It took Mr. Ashok a moment to realize the picture was of him. If his tear ducts had not also been petrified, he might have wept.

He made himself as still as possible and did not move for the rest of the day, not even when the guard who began the virality passed him by, still chuckling, and said, "When your little balloon-selling friend gave me this news yesterday, I almost did not believe him. But it's true. Now we will see some fun, won't we, Ashok-ji? You will be very good for business."

Mr. Ashok wished even more that he could squeeze out a single tear. His own Babu had done this.

Mishra-Sir had been busy with matters in Kashmir, where history is plentiful as land mines. But the day Mr. Ashok Jagtap went viral, Mishra-Sir's attention turned to the E—caves.

"What do you make of it?" Mishra-Sir asked when he called me into his office. He had come to trust me, perhaps because I kept my head down and spoke little.

It was a tense time in the Department of Symbolic Meaning. Just recently an assistant had been hauled off for questioning at the Central Bureau of Interpretive Investigations after he was heard musing that perhaps the ITIHAS textbooks might benefit from mention of intercaste conflict. This to a man with even higher scores on his narrative patriotism polygraph than mine.

"I suppose," I said, "that you, sir, will have some very wise instincts." It was not, after all, my job to interpret the present—only to record and preserve the past. I would leave the present to Mishra-Sir's other clerks.

Mishra-Sir rubbed his chin. "Americans refer to the past as the dead hand of history. Ha! But look. See—the rock of the caves, the rock comprising the man. They are the same. Is this not history come to life?"

I said I saw what he meant.

Mishra-Sir complained that the department's astrologers had all disagreed with one another. One called the statue man the work of black magic, while another called the fellow a sign from God about the importance of the E—caves.

He leaned back in his chair. "What does this department *need*, at the moment?" he asked.

"What, sir?"

"Hope." Mishra-Sir waved a finger. He was likely thinking of the student protests just miles from this office in Delhi—leftists with no sense of ITIHAS, leftists who believed themselves cousins with some Western elite because they did not understand where they had come from. We had recently discussed these so-called movements, and shared disdain, which was perhaps why Mishra-Sir was finding me an appealing sounding board today. "A sense of the living presence of our nation's history."

This phrasing inspired me. I agreed.

"Ashok Jagtap, is it," he said, rummaging through the papers on his desk. "Ashok Jagtap, welcome to the cause."

It was late when I at last left the pink sandstone government building and made for the metro. I was subsumed by the uneven traffic of the capital, its smog, its winking lights, its colonial roundabouts, its mosques next to its buses next to the vast hoardings displaying bosoms of Bollywood starlets. On these rides to and from work, I briefly forgot about making sense of the nation—it was just there, all around, honking, coughing, pulsing.

The reporters stayed even as dusk set in. Some encircled Mr. Ashok, waiting to see if he would twitch, the way those who had reported on politicians learned to stake out the houses of a leader embroiled in scandal. Mr. Ashok did not twitch. Finally, the guards began to herd everyone out. They missed the statue man taking a few small steps into the shadows of the neem tree, where he waited for the night to fully darken.

But Babu saw him. He had been unable to speak to his old friend at all that day, due to the crowds. Now, he sidled up to Mr. Ashok.

"Ashok-ji?" he tried.

Mr. Ashok did not reply or move. All he could think was that *Babu* had brought these hordes upon him. *Babu* had turned him into this spectacle.

Babu knocked on Mr. Ashok's stone skin, said, "Please talk, do something!"

Mr. Ashok did not oblige. So, the balloon seller left, confused and afraid.

Alone, Mr. Ashok gathered his box of possessions and made his way up the hill, into the darkness, to his favored gathering of Parvatis.

That night he stood upright, eyes fixed on the curve of the woman who was either the goddess or the preserved paramour of a doting artisan. He began to speak to her, to tell her about the wife she had once seen him press against the stone. He had tried his best with her, for her. If he had been clumsy it was only because he wanted a good life for them. A son, money, dignity. As Mr. Ashok spoke, slivers of moonlight filtered through the open mouth of the cave, falling on the possible-Parvati's face, casting her with a kind of life, as though her features were responding to his confessions, as with domestic empathy.

He passed several sleepless nights like this until one morning, a khaki jeep pulled up in front of the guardhouse. Mr. Ashok was standing regimentally at the foot of the lawn, in front of the Kailasa Temple, trying to smile amicably at those visitors arriving early to beat the heat. The jeep pulled in, and out we climbed, Mishra-Sir and me.

"Namaskar," Mishra-Sir said when he approached Mr. Ashok, offering folded hands and a shallow bow. I followed suit. "I see you are much as the pictures depicted."

Mishra-Sir began to circle Mr. Ashok, like an inspector visiting a job site. I stood with my hands clasped behind my back. He asked when the change had occurred, what the consistency of Mr. Ashok's "flesh" seemed to be; if he had received visitations from deva- or demon-like figures; whether Mr. Ashok was eating, sleeping, breathing, etc. He inquired whether Mr. Ashok had sought treatment from a priest. A homeopathic or allopathic or Ayurvedic physician. And when Mr. Ashok said—in a voice that sounded like someone shouting through an empty hall at the end of a wedding—that he had not, Mishra-Sir hmmed and mopped his brow with a hankie.

Mishra-Sir then turned to me, as if to say, Do you have any questions?

"How are you, Mr. Jagtap, sir?" I asked.

Mishra-Sir smiled. I knew how he saw me: a step closer to the everyman than he.

"Yes, how are you, generally?" Mishra-Sir echoed.

"Well," Mr. Ashok considered a long while. His jaw moved squarely, uncomfortably—I realized he was attempting to laugh. "Stiff."

Mishra-Sir did not know what to make of this, but I could not help but join in Mr. Ashok's loud, helpless chortles. I felt I understood something, just then, about the failures of understanding, and my mind flitted to my lost aunt and sister and the blameless maid who went with them too. A map gone wrong, the blast that killed them, and yet there was more too, something I had never been able to speak, something that defied interpretation. This was something you came to understand if you were, as I was, servant to history as much as government. That no matter how much you grasp the events that propelled us from then to now, there are always more questions than answers. What did Gandhi feel in the moments before his life ended; how did Jinnah sleep on the night of August 14? What brought Tagore his poems, or Aurobindo to his meditation cell? And earlier, where did the Upanishads come from?—for there was God in them, but there was also the world.

These were thoughts I managed carefully, especially in the moment of the narrative patriotism polygraphs, and while at work, but suddenly, looking up at this poor Mr. Ashok and his transformation, which we had arrived to make sense of, I felt transmogrified in my own way, trapped in all I would not be able to answer for Mishra-Sir.

But this is not my story.

We adjourned to the shade, where Mishra-Sir shooed away the monkeys that tried to squat on Mr. Ashok's head.

We three men enjoyed a sprawling conversation that afternoon. Mishra-Sir asked the questions, Mr. Ashok responded, and I took down notes, nodding encouragingly. We gathered the biographical information: English tuitions, marriage, the wife's desertion. The illness and insomnia in the weeks leading up to the change.

One thing gave Mishra-Sir pause. "I'm not sure what to make of the fact that your—personal organ—has been spared this fate."

Mr. Ashok admitted he too was flummoxed in the face of this fact.

I averted my gaze from them both.

"We must offer the public a clear, government-issued pronouncement on the Symbolic Meaning of your change. And we cannot have a whole lot of morally offensive business circulating about your privates."

Mr. Ashok said he too would rather not have his member mentioned in public and related some of the questions from the reporters the day prior, as well as his response. As Mr. Ashok demonstrated how he had fallen still when the reporters hounded him, Mishra-Sir cried, "Aha! Perhaps you should have gone into politics."

Then Mishra-Sir asked Mr. Ashok if he could have a moment to confer with his colleague. It took me a beat to realize this meant me. The two of us stepped away.

"Well?" Mishra-Sir said. I remained silent, my eyes trained on my notes, aware that he would shortly supply the answer to his own question. And he did. "What I am imagining—if you can make the proper historical case—is something like, 'Common man's devotion to ITIHAS is rewarded by sacred E—caves, earns him . . .'" He trailed off, still thinking.

"Preservation," I said.

"Preservation," Mishra-Sir repeated. "What would we need, to do this correctly?"

"Sir, I think your intuition should be sufficient."

"No, we need a case, you see. I am sick and tired of being told that we are fantasists and fabulists. It is unfair to all of you who work so tirelessly to, yes, *preserve,* the truth about ITIHAS, our glorious history. We must make the complete case. You will do so."

"Sir?"

"Is there," Mishra-Sir said, his voice icy, "a problem?"

Where to begin? I had never seen anything like the case of Mr. Ashok in our nation's history. But my mind flashed to the Central Bureau of Interpretive Investigations, the chilling office some streets away from ours. Its closed black door, behind which our department's clerk had disappeared.

I assured Mishra-Sir there was no problem.

I had a new thought then as I looked at Mr. Ashok taking some frightened steps back from a small child advancing on him.

"Sir," I said. "Perhaps we can help preserve Mr. Ashok Jagtap ourselves."

Mishra-Sir frowned. "What is it you have in mind?"

The paperwork was soon set in motion to declare him a national monument, and so began the second great change Mr. Ashok would undergo.

I was given a government-let room in the city of A—. Each morning I took an official jeep to the sacred E—caves, where I wandered, taking notes for the report due in a week or so. I checked in on Mr. Ashok daily, ensuring that the ropes behind which he was now safely stationed were keeping him apart from the clamoring crowds and clambering children. "You are well?" I always made sure to ask, but there was no more of the laughter he'd greeted this question with on the first day.

After a week, he lifted a hand, with some effort, to stop me before I walked away. It touched the edge of the fraying brown rope. We had settled on having him stand in some shade to one side of the Kailasa Temple.

"Please," he said in a small voice. "I want to move."

Nearby was a swarm of schoolchildren visiting on a tour. They were poking and hitting one another, boys tugging girls' plaits, girls swatting them off, and the poor schoolmistress trying to organize them into a neat line to enter the temple. I looked at them, and back at Mr. Ashok. One of the boys was gripping the front of his pants and raising a pinkie finger, crying susu-susu—he needed the toilet. I imagined one of those children somehow . . . ruining Mr. Ashok. I would be imperiled.

"Mr. Jagtap," I said. "I am very sorry, but I cannot—we cannot—take this risk."

"Let me do my job, let me give tours," he fairly begged. "A monument touring a monument!" I had a vision of him standing here alone, all night, speaking that pitch into the dark sky, waiting for me to arrive to test it out. But that vision was quickly replaced by the menacing black door of the CBII.

"Mr. Jagtap, sir, the thing about monuments, you see, is that people don't want them moving about too much. It is most comforting to know that they still exist, are preserved, but are, for the most part, standing still, you see. Imagine the Taj Mahal standing on its haunches and offering people a tour of itself. It would make no sense at all!"

I asked him if he understood.

He said he did.

As I was walking up a hill toward a tree where I had found it helpful to sit with my notes, the balloon seller whom I knew was Mr. Ashok's friend caught up to me. The pink bobble bounced above his head.

"Sir, sir, sir," he panted. "Sir, how is he? Ashok-ji? He will not speak to me."

I could not help but feel relieved at this, despite the skinny boy's wretched facial expression—he looked ragged with grief, his cheeks gaunt, the whites of his eyes almost yellowing. For I had worried about this balloon seller, whether he would take offense at the designation of his friend as monument, and try, somehow, to smuggle him away.

"He only will say he is following his orders, doing his duty, and then he is—" He made a noise like a zipper closing.

"That is correct," I said. I pretended I did not know his name and asked it. This was something I had seen Mishra-Sir do with underlings.

"Babu, sir."

"Babu, you must know about the importance of this national ITIHAS movement? You have seen the Party officials coming through, seen all the graffiti and all?"

He nodded.

I was not so eloquent as Mishra-Sir, but I went on to explain, in abbreviated form that would suit this balloon seller, the importance of settling on a secure, stable ITIHAS. "This country had so much taken away from it, isn't it? By all sorts of outsiders. Now we are righting the wrongs. Making sure everyone knows who we are." I added a final flourish. "Who we have always been."

Babu the balloon seller cocked his head.

"They took away one man from my slum," he said quietly. "The ITIHAS people. Mad fellow. Went round in the middle of the night making moo-moo noises like a cow, you see. He had always done this, it was how he was. Then, a few days back, an ITIHAS person comes by, says, 'This man is the reincarnation of an ancient saint here to remind us of the evils of cow murderers.' Nobody seen him since."

"I am sure they are protecting him." I gulped. The man, I suspected, had been taken to a government office to see a mythoneurologist. If he passed certain tests, with whose details I was unfamiliar, he might join one of the touring ITIHAS campaigns on which the Department of Symbolic Meaning relied. He would be caravanned through villages and slums to inspire locals to remain on the lookout for ITIHAS artifacts, to stay mindful of history, and to believe in its vivid and sacred reality. How many times had I seen those three objectives on departmental memos?

Babu drew his hands together in a namaskar. The spotted balloons bobbed above his head.

*

I reported directly to Mishra-Sir daily, which was a great honor. That night, I told him Mr. Ashok had requested to move. This troubled him.

"That would not do at all," he said. "Already there is a Tripadvisor page for Mr. Ashok Jagtap, have you seen? These ratings would be very bad should he start to move about."

Mishra-Sir went on to tell me about the word trickling down to local ITIHAS officials about the possibility of humanoid monuments. Everyone in Delhi was thrilled about this, from the Department of Symbolic Meaning to the Department of Temple Tourism.

New possible monuments included, now:

1. A child, born robin's-egg blue, in the manner of Lord Krishna; his parents had slathered him in butter in tribute to the impish god's favorite food, and were accepting donations from visitors. His skin was being tested to ensure it had not simply been painted that way.
2. The definitely philandering wife turned into a bhoota, her body transparent, everyone in the village now able to see her unfaithful, still-beating heart, provided they gave her husband a very modest fee for his pains.
3. The definitely unphilandering wife, now known as Second Sita, who had walked across hot coals to prove that she had not cuckolded her husband, and who continued to do so daily in front of curious eyes, again for a modest fee.

. . . and so on.

When I arrived at the caves a few days later, having spent some time at a local university looking through archives, I found that Mr. Ashok had been assigned a new form of protection. Standing next to his brown rope was a man in a green and neon-orange vest, like a garbage picker, who was missing all of his teeth except for a single large incisor, which rose from his bloody gums like an elephant tusk. Instead of a rifle, the man held a jackhammer—a deadly weapon for Mr. Ashok.

My heart truly broke to see Mr. Ashok this way. But I did not know what I could do. I let him know that I was wrapping up my research on his situation. I glanced at the guard, who surely did not speak English, and switched languages accordingly. I told Mr. Ashok that I had chosen to leave out most details of his life from all official materials. He was a monument now, and a monument,

I had come to realize in the course of my research, was the opposite of history. It could afford no unanswered questions. It was
no place for shadows. It was firm, the cornerstone on which the
present was built.

"Perhaps this is good news," I said, lowering my voice to a whisper. "You yourself will retain some privacy."

Mr. Ashok said nothing.

"Take care," I said ineffectually.

I returned to New Delhi.

That summer ended, monsoon began, and the visitors came
and went, taking their photographs in front of the thing they
knew bore import; as they filed out at night, they began cropping
their images on their phones, changing the lighting for the best
profile picture results, sometimes turning Mr. Ashok's stone body
indistinguishable from the temples behind him, so that their faces
remained the only things looming large and clear.

I learned about the trouble with the new monument some months
later. The word was that the statue man, in whom we had invested
quite a lot of resources, both in terms of finances and publicity,
had simply disappeared. The jackhammer-wielding guard had
gone home as usual, after locking up the thick metal gate around
the figure—they'd switched away from rope about a month earlier, after an impertinent teenage boy managed to urinate over the
barrier, onto the foot of the monument. When that single-toothed
guard arrived in the morning, he found a squarish impression in
the dust where the monument formerly known as Ashok Jagtap
had once stood. The Party's local ITIHAS officials had searched
all Muslim neighborhoods in the surrounding city of A——, for Mus-
lims were the culprits likeliest to deface a sacred Hindu and Bud-
dhist site. While this resulted in an important arrest for a Symbolic
Meaning investigation into a cartographical insurrectionist—a
man linked to the dangerous map that had once been responsible for killing my sister—it did not turn up any semblance of
Mr. Ashok.

Mishra-Sir came to my office to offer his sympathies. He said
he understood how difficult it was to put so much work into an
initiative only to have it swiped from the earth. He encouraged me
to use this feeling of frustration to empathize with our forebears,
who had built empires only to have them erased by colonial and

Mughal invaders. I nodded in agreement, tracing the map of the nation that sits on my desk with my long pinkie fingernail. But even well-spoken Mishra-Sir could not help me in that moment, for it was not the Symbolic loss of the monument that was striking me with hot pangs. It was a particular fear for Mr. Ashok. We—I—had conscripted him into our cause, promising him safety, and now he was God knew where, suffering at God knew whose hands. I shivered to think of someone taking a chisel to his features the way conquering warriors had often done to statues of Buddhas and goddesses.

I stood and requested a week to go home to my family's village.

Mishra-Sir regarded me with immense kindness.

"You are a man still connected to his people." He granted me leave, adding that when I came back, he would like to speak to me about a possible promotion out of the annals of historical interpretation. "You are fit for the present," he said, which was highest praise.

I arrived in the city of A—the next afternoon and hired a car to drive to the E—caves. These were not insignificant expenses for me. The first person I saw when I crossed through the gates at dusk was Babu the balloon seller. He was standing next to a metal fence, sickly spotted pink balloons in hand. It took me a moment to realize that this fence was the protective metal grating designed to keep Mr. Ashok safe from the crowds.

Babu noticed me as well. His face grew taut as I approached.

"I haven't seen him," he said sharply.

"We are only worried," I said. I amended. "*I* am worried."

"Fat lot of good that does now," Babu said. "There was a riot in my slum after your Symbolic Whatsit raids. Many-many people's homes burned. Some people inside as they burned. That is what happens when your department goes all blaming-shaming."

I felt very tired. "Was he well, last you spoke to him?"

Babu scoffed. It occurred to me that if I wielded authority the way Mishra-Sir did, this balloon seller would never be comfortable treating me this way. But I have never come across as a strong man. "He had not spoken to me since before your visit, *sir.*" Babu's mouth sagged. "He believed I had turned him over. To the public. He was right. But I only wished to help him."

And then the wiry balloon seller began to sob.

"Sir," he said, when he had stopped, wiping his nose with his ratty T-shirt, which said something in English I was sure he did not understand—"I Know HTML: How to Meet Ladies." "You are certainly not here on department business and all?"

"I am not." Here perhaps my lack of authority worked to my advantage, for poor Babu decided in that moment to trust me. "Nighttime here was Ashok-ji's favorite time. Caves mysterious then. You know what he used to say?"—a wet sniff—"That these E—caves had many secrets you could hear at night. Wind flying through them in monsoon, this time of year, right listener can catch all the history only this place is remembering." He shook his head. "I am too uneducated for all this, I am thinking. I come here and no-one-nothing talks to me. But you are educated. Maybe you are hearing something I cannot."

The E—caves at night were eerie. Unlit. I followed Babu's directions to wait deep in one of them, next to a seated Buddha, as dusk dwindled into darkness. The guards went round closing up, but no one came sniffing inside the damp rock caverns. I suppose it would have been unimaginable that anyone would wish to lock themselves in these ancient rooms. Babu left me as the day ended.

"You tell me in morning," he said. "Tell me what all you hear." He looked mournfully at his bare feet. "I was trying and all, to learn English. Ashok-ji said it was a very good idea."

Far from the smog-clouded city of A—, I could see a flash of the unpolluted night sky, the milky moon and winking starlight, streaming in through the mouth of the cave where I had chosen to sit. It had been a long time since I had attempted to pray, but waiting in that cave I called upon some yogic instruction I had learned in Haridwar many years ago. I opened my eyes after a time to look at the great seated Buddha behind me. Prince Siddhartha's face was crude and expressionless. I prostrated myself before him. He loomed perhaps three meters high. And then, unthinking, I climbed into the Buddha's lap and placed my head in his wise stone hands.

Through the silence came the patter of rain outside, a night monsoon storm beginning and, with my head in the Buddha's hands, I began to hear something. I shut my eyes once more, and into me flowed a very intimate knowledge of Mr. Ashok Jagtap's life in the years before he became a monument, the knowledge I have set down here, in what you must now realize is an unsanctioned history that I have kept hidden from departmental surveillance. I do not know how long I sat there, but when I opened my eyes, the rainstorm had quelled and the night was beginning to orange, the start of a new day. I stepped down from the Buddha's lap, and I walked to the cave that I had learned about in the night, Mr. Ashok's favorite cave, the one that housed the many Parvatis.

Early on the morning Mr. Ashok disappeared from inside the protective metal grating, he had been jolted from his sleepless rest to find a sudden stiffness in his private area. It frightened him. His limbs had grown less mobile in the months since he had been designated a monument, but despite that, he had retained flesh in this one key part of himself. He reached for himself, and to his great relief, found that his penis had not turned into stone. It was just morning desire greeting him the way it once did. Something had changed—he wanted. Lusted. For something. Life, again. And in that moment, he remembered that he was a man. He wanted to act like one, touch like one, once more.

It was not easy for him to reach over the gate that fenced him inside, but once he got moving again, for the first time in many weeks, it was simple to break the lock—stone can do that, you see. He made his way up the green-yellow hill that carpeted the back of the cave site, through the dry, dying grass, and joined the footpath at its high edge. He stepped over a discarded Bisleri water bottle, a neon Kurkure packet. He looked for the pink bobble of Babu's balloons but it was too early. He would have liked to see them, once more.

He entered the cave of Parvatis and approached his favorite— the one who may not have been Parvati, the one who was, surely, just the wife of an artisan. He approached his Parvati and placed one of his stony hands on one of her perfectly globular breasts. With the other he lowered his zipper, and then braced himself on the virgin part of the stone, the uncarved place where he had once held his wife. The breast in his hand was pliant. Like clay, anxious to be shaped. He slid himself into a woman who was ready in a way he had never experienced, and a great human ache passed through him. His flesh met the Parvati's stone, in the final change, as the caves took him as their own. Parvati's three arms were splayed wide, and then they were not; they tightened around him. She was stronger than him. He tried to look down to see what he already knew, that now he was made *entirely* of stone. But he could not turn his head. It faced into the wall. The basalt cliff closed in around his face, his eyes, and whatever last remnant of blood and breath that remained in him halted. And then Mr. Ashok Jagtap, that man riddled with mistakes, who knew he had not understood life, was suddenly and completely consumed by ITIHAS.

When I crept into the caves that morning, searching for evidence of Mr. Ashok's final moments, I found that three-armed Parvati at the very edge of the cave. She appeared unfinished. Something protruded from the rock, overlaying her. Her chest was obscured by the inchoate shape of Mr. Ashok's body covering hers. Morning light fell around me, illumining her inscrutable expression. Like candle flickers, a pattern of curses and prayers and questions. I felt I knew nothing, knew absolutely nothing of that pattern of the past, of flesh and stone, of how our history is one moment living, and the next, preserved.

ERIN SOMERS

Ten Year Affair

FROM *Joyland*

The Northeast

FEBRUARY 1, 2021

CORA MET SAM in a baby group in their small town. They sat
on blue plastic mats in the back room of an overpriced children's
clothing store. Their infants squirmed in front of them on sheep-
skins. The room smelled like breast milk and baby heads and cru-
ciferous vegetables boiled down to weakened, mealy fibers that
one mom had brought in Tupperware and was trying to feed her
ten-month-old.

"That baby doesn't want broccoli," said Sam.

He had a toothpick stuck to his lower lip. His mouth was sexy;
the toothpick was not. He offered one to Cora. She took it so she
could touch his hand. It tasted like cinnamon. Of all available
affectations this one was openly oral, wholly about his lips and
tongue, either keeping them busy or drawing attention to them.
So which one was it? she asked him.

"Neither," he said. Now he was using his to prod his incisors at
the gum line. "It's just something to do."

"To be a man and kill time chewing a wet stick," she said.

Across the room the weeping child ingested a bite from the
Tupperware and her mother called out triumphantly, "See?"

It was the two of them against broccoli mom. That much was
clear. They exchanged numbers to seal the alliance. The purpose

was to text when they'd be at baby group. But soon they started meeting up elsewhere. They passed the long afternoons of parental leave that way. Her husband knew and did not seem to mind. They'd get a coffee, or sometimes a beer, at one of the places on Main Street. After, they'd push their babies uphill, toward the dark green mountain that stood at the top of the town.

Maybe because they had young children and were used to talking plainly about birth and shit and blood and bodies and the potential of death, their talk was frank. They were both married, both with a second kid, but spoke candidly about their desire for each other. They could not sleep together because their motivations were not perfectly aligned. They overlapped but were not concentric. This was insurmountable. Cora wanted to fuck Sam. It was physical only, but had grown strong. She had no control over it. She became a slavering animal in his presence.

She told him this one afternoon, a few months into their acquaintance, on a stretch of sharp incline. Her quads burned and she panted slightly. He laughed.

"I shouldn't have told you," said Cora.

"No, I'm glad you did. It's just the way you put it."

Sam wanted her too, he explained, but there was nothing animal about it. It had more to do with liking Cora as a person. He would not cop to love. Cora found it hard to believe that it was merely about liking her. Liking was a mild way to feel. Did he want to fuck everything he liked? His computer? Grapefruit seltzer? A scattering of ducks on a pond where he wasn't expecting to see ducks?

He said, "You're attracted to me. I get that. But you don't seem to *like* me much."

"What's with the emphasis on liking all the time?"

"Don't you have feelings?"

She did have feelings. The feelings were that she wanted to get fucked onto the astral plane and not think about her life for a second. But this clearly wasn't the right thing to say, so she reached into the feelings bag and yanked out "I'm crazy about you." Sure, why not? It was bland, liking-adjacent. It was not necessarily a declaration of love. He seemed to accept it.

"Okay," he said. "But can't we be friends? It's sad to me, the idea of not knowing you."

"If I wanted a new friend, I'd find a woman, no offense."

"So if we can't be friends, what are we supposed to do," he said. "Have a ten year affair?"

They were silent. Their generation did not take off its clothes, did not put its keys in a bowl by the front door. Sex between men and women had become taboo in their generation, where everyone was striving, not incorrectly, to be an equal. Even the word "affair" had the ring of obsolescence, like a cigarette or an ad man or a chaise longue.

"I'm kidding," he said at last.

But the affair was there now. It was between them. Somewhere in the multiverse their alternates checked into a hotel room where the afternoon light came in at a slant and hit a champagne bucket just so. It was a cliché, but wild and enjoyable because it was happening to them, this mythic thing they'd heard about, this thing in quotes: "an affair."

Two vectors ran parallel through Cora's existence. One was what you might call reality, with bills and an ant problem in the kitchen and her marriage, which was mostly good. The other was her affair with Sam, technically fictional, its lies and illicit meetings, the racing pulse of infatuation.

Sometimes one was more present than the other. When one of her kids got sick, the affair was suspended for almost a week. She went back to work, and this took precedence for a while, until the old routines kicked in. The small talk and two P.M. granola bar, the rote cheer of email communication. Other times the affair was the more prominent of the two. In moments of boredom, in waiting rooms, on transit.

But mostly they stayed in balance.

So Cora sat in a mind-numbing meeting, as she met Sam in a darkened steakhouse. She made a suggestion about SEO while they each drank an ice-cold martini. There was coffee in the meeting at least, a big bitter carafe of it, and she refilled her cup as she reached for his cock under the table. Sam brushed back her hair from her ear, whispered something, and her boss rapped his knuckles on the conference table, made a dumb joke about the moment everyone had been waiting for, and brought it around to monthly stats.

As she boiled water for pasta, she walked with Sam through

a rainstorm. She tripped and he caught her coming off a street corner while she put her children to bed. During the hour-long drama that she watched with her husband, she was blowing Sam in the backseat of his car.

While she was running out to pick up milk she was running out to pick up milk so she could meet him in the dairy aisle of ShopRite and have him furtively put his hand up her skirt for thirty seconds before heading home.

And as she tweezed her eyebrows, looked up whale facts with her kid, fed herself or other people, picked up toys, answered work emails at ten P.M., ran on a treadmill, locked herself in the bathroom for no reason she could immediately determine, she thought of him. She thought of him always in both timelines. In one it was with longing and despair and the other with longing and regret. She longed for him while she longed for him. She yearned while she yearned. She pined while she pined, and so on.

Sam called her, in reality, after several weeks of not seeing each other, and they met up for a drink. He'd gone back to work, too. He looked handsome and unhappy in office casual. He'd learned a new trick with his toothpick. He used his tongue to flip it over the long way. He had to stretch his mouth open wide to do it. She willed him to touch her and he didn't.

He began immediately with the intense conversation. He had not enjoyed their time apart. He thought of her often. He was suffering. Since they could not have sex, he said, he wanted a legitimate way to know her. He wanted to install her in his life. He wanted her as a permanent fixture.

"Sounds like what you actually want is a new sink," she said.

"You have a great personality," he said. "You know that?"

Her whole life, people had railed on about her personality. Such a smart girl—woman! Such a smart woman. And funny. It got worse (better) as she got older. Kind, empathetic, a good parent. That was nice, right? That was what you wanted. But couldn't this one man objectify her?

"Okay," she said.

"I'm serious. I think all four of us should hang out. My wife, your husband."

"Does your wife know how we talk to each other?"

"It's not impossible that I'll tell her. I try to be honest with her."

"So you want me to be friends with her. But she'll just know, it'll just be out there, that I'm a slavering animal. Self-described."

They stared at each other. He attempted to do the toothpick trick and choked and half-puked it out. In the other timeline they were laughing at a joke one of them had made. In the other timeline his hand was on her thigh and no one had just sort of thrown up. Her hair looked better over there, too.

"How about instead of all that I send you one nude?" said Cora.

Sam laughed. "No."

"Just one. A tasteful one. Not too porny."

"I want to have you as a friend," he said again. Have her. Have. Someone already had her though. Her husband, Eliot.

She said to Eliot, later, standing in their kitchen, "To what degree do you feel like you have me?"

He was eating, as usual, smearing an apple with almond butter and taking big demonstrative bites.

"Like possess you?"

"Yes."

"Zero," he said.

"No, but you do."

Long pause while he smeared and bit. "Not really."

"You do. I have obligations to you. You have access to me. I exist to you on certain terms. I'm your wife. You have me. You get to have me."

"I don't think about it like that."

"How do you think of it?"

"We're best friends. We have two kids together. I enjoy being around you. You're fun. We both elect to be here."

"You're saying you like me."

"Exactly," he said. "Yo, hand me one of those."

He meant a napkin. She gave him a look. She was nursing the baby. Their older daughter sat on her foot playing with a Barbie doll.

"Not because you're my property, because you're right there. God, fine, I'll get it." Eliot retrieved a napkin. "I don't possess you. I'm fine with you hanging out with that guy from the baby group, whatever's going on there."

"Nothing's going on with Sam," said Cora. She had to look away. It hurt a lot to say it.

*

She gave in. They had Sam and his wife over for dinner. The wife's name was Jules and she had no apparent bad traits except that she allowed the toothpicks. She even took one herself after dinner when Sam offered them around. Eliot took one too. They sat in Cora's yard sucking their wood splinters, drinking wine, and talking about pre-k.

In the timeline that contained their affair, Sam and Cora were alone. The leaves in the yard were a dark blue previously only seen in dreams. The strap of Cora's dress fell off her shoulder and Sam kissed the place it had been.

In reality, Sam was shouting about school registration, how you had to go visit this eighty-year-old woman Rose in her office full of dying plants and make a case for why your kid should be assigned your school of choice. Wasn't that quaint and the reason all of them had moved out there?

"That was our vision all right," said Cora.

She rose on the pretext of grabbing the cobbler. Eliot glanced at her: there was no cobbler. She went in and climbed the stairs and stood in front of the bedroom window and watched the three of them talking and laughing. Night crawled diagonally across the yard. Where their affair was going on, she and Sam had adjourned to the bedroom to try to shock each other with their respective depravities.

She found that she was chewing a toothpick herself and spit it out on the floor, then picked it up and threw it away in the bathroom trash. She checked on the baby and the baby and the other baby and the other baby. Two were sleeping and two were playing sweetly with a train that linked up using magnets. She sat down with them and made up a story about how the train had left the land of chores and rules for the land of toys and candy. The children were easy to delight. Sam came in and stood behind her, resting his hand lightly on her head. Even this level of contact elicited a full body reaction and he must have known that.

He said, "It's going well, right? Jules likes you. I told you."

Another admirer. How their ranks swelled. They could erect a monument to her in the town square. An extremely fucking likeable woman—that's what the plaque could say.

"Great," said Cora. "I like her too."

Ten years passed in both worlds, in all worlds. In the timeline of the affair Cora's affection deepened and she admitted she was in love. The sex never got old. Sam quit the toothpicks. In late summer they walked in the park and a doe with white-tipped ears came over and nuzzled Sam in the leg and laid her soft snout in Cora's hand. They drank too much wine that night and conceived a baby, oops, and this led to weeks of wrenching conversation. He said he wanted a baby with her, of course he did, but was it ethical or responsible, was it cool, to ruin the lives of six existing people to produce one new person with their shared genes? Maybe not cool, she said, no. But she wanted it and you could want something bad enough that you needed it. You could want something so bad it became indivisible from your survival.

You'll survive, he said. They decided to terminate.

Over on the other side their kids got older. They haggled with Rose to keep them in the same class. The two families went on vacation together. Cora enjoyed Jules's company. They made each other laugh. Jules was better than her at most things—sports, cooking, career advancement—and this felt good to Cora, the way it felt good to tongue a canker sore.

Occasionally, the vectors veered closer together. She was walking home from the library one day, when Sam pulled up beside her in his car.

He said, "You're always walking around town. You're the lady who walks around town."

She got in and they drove up the mountain. When she asked where they were going, he said, "Not sure."

She felt a shiver, the brush of the uncanny against her cheek. This exact thing would happen in the other timeline. In fact, it was happening over there, with minor differences.

Sam stopped at an overlook. A breeze came in the open windows that smelled sweetly of the ground. The town spread out before them, red and brown and gray rooftops sloping down toward a river slashed with sunlight. It seemed like a make-out spot. Cora turned to Sam. Sam put his head on the steering wheel.

"Read to me from that book you have, whatever it is," he said.

It was a book that she'd gotten for her daughter, *Butterflies and Moths of North America.*

She opened to a random page and read, "In the second stage of the life cycle, the larva hatches from the egg. . . ."

"Okay stop," he said.

"Well, what were you expecting?"

"I don't know. Poetry or something."

Did he think she took romantic strolls down to the library to check out books of poetry? Was he picturing her doing that, when he pictured her?

"It's for homework," she said. "Insect unit."

"You're a great mom," he said.

"Eh. It's pretty baseline. It's picking up a book."

He gave her the kind of look that usually precedes a passionate gesture. His hands were shaking. He rubbed them on his jeans. Since they'd known each other there'd been no incidents of sexual contact between them, though the restraint this required was itself quasi-sexual.

"We should go," he said.

He started the car and they left.

At the end of ten years Sam shocked them all by asking Jules for a divorce. Cora heard it first from Jules.

"An idiot fuckhead's on the way to your house," she said, over the phone.

Sam came to Cora in her backyard. She was kicking a soccer ball around with her kids. The one who'd been a baby when they met was ten now, and kicked the ball at him. It hit him in the stomach and he said, "Ow." Then he launched into a monologue about how she should leave Eliot. He loved her as a friend but he also wanted her physically. He always had.

The two vectors aligned, snapping into place. With only one timeline in motion, it was profoundly quiet.

Her older kid said, "What the fuck?" and Cora had to go through the theater of disapproval. *Don't say fuck. It's rude.* Meanwhile Sam stood waiting for an answer. She sent the kids inside.

"I want to marry you," he said.

Cora laughed. "Marry?"

Marriage had never been the point. Marriage was the opposite of the point. Anyway, in the world of the affair, things had not been the same between them since the abortion. On the day of her appointment he wanted to be there but he'd agreed to chaperone his kid's field trip to the state capitol. She thought she'd be fine, but she wasn't. She sat in recovery alone. How could he have left her sitting there like that? She'd pictured him listening

politely to a tour guide, helping to distribute bag lunches. It made
her lonely. Obligations were not for the world of the affair.

Albany, New York, was not. Municipalities, the halls of legislation.

She knew she could not say this out loud. She knew her imaginings within imaginings would not translate. The way quotidian
pain and disappointment had bled through to her fantasy life
would not be explicable to this man who chewed toothpicks. Or
probably to anyone.

"You made me wait too long," she said finally.

"I'm sorry," he said.

Sam reached out to touch her arm. His touch was hot. She felt
an internal revving, but it was distant, or she thought, if she wanted
to, she could will it to be distant. She considered accepting his offer to see what would happen. Various vectors appeared, like tines
on a fork. He'd be a great husband and they'd be in love forever.
He'd be terrible and she'd instantly regret it. She'd cheat on him
with Eliot, casually and for decades. Or, by some calculation, she
and Jules would end up together. They'd pick a random state on
the map, Utah, say, and move there with all four kids.

She must have been quiet for a long time because he said,
"What are you thinking?" This startled her. What an invasion.

"None of your business," she said.

Really, it had almost nothing to do with him.

HÉCTOR TOBAR

The Sins of Others

FROM *Zyzzyva*

JUAN H. WOKE up one Saturday morning with two strange men standing over his bed. One was wearing a loose-fitting navy-colored vest labeled "ICE"; his purpose was clear enough. But the other guy was in jeans smudged with grease stains. A workingman, "Karl," according to the oval patch on his shirt. There was something disheveled about both of them. As if they, and not him, had just been roused from their slumbers.

The agent held a piece of paper before Juan, and gestured for him to stand up. When Juan moved to take the paper, the agent pulled it back.

"I'd like to be out of here by seven thirty, if you don't mind," the agent said.

The agent was a lean man with the gray and brittle sheen of a lifelong smoker, and a nicotine patch on his neck. He looked around the room, and the orderliness he saw seemed to unsettle him: a hardwood floor, and pictures of Juan and his family members on a dresser, a humidifier, purring steadily, and nothing else. There was something spartan, or Scandinavian about the space. Not a single article of clothing was tossed about.

"You think this is easy for me?" the agent said. "I've got a wife and kid. They see me leave with my gun, my taser, my handcuffs at five in the morning. They wonder what their father does."

Juan climbed out of bed, and as he did so the officer approached, took him by the arm, turned him so that he was facing Karl, and prepared to wrap plastic ties around Juan's wrists.

"Can I get dressed first?" Juan asked.

"Yeah, go ahead." The officer watched Juan take some pants and a shirt from his dresser and said, "We feel terrible about what Karl did."

"I do too," Karl said.

"But the law's the law."

Juan considered himself an informed person. He had read stories about the Replacement Law. But up to this moment they were like folktales, or dispatches from another country, because the substance of the Replacement Law was strange, mean, and, in its own way, childish.

His adult daughter squeezed into the room now, past a second agent Juan could see in the hallway outside. She took in the tableau before her: the agent, her father in handcuffs, Karl.

"What's going on?" she demanded.

"He drank too much, he hit a pedestrian," the officer said, pointing with the warrant at Karl. "The pedestrian happens to be Karl's wife. She's got two broken vertebrae. That's no picnic. Do you have two broken vertebrae, Juan? No, you don't. So consider yourself lucky. You're a lucky man today."

"I feel terrible," Karl said.

"Do you know this man, Papá?" Juan's daughter asked, pointing at Karl.

After the three minutes Karl had been in Juan's bedroom, Juan finally recognized him. "He used to work at the shop," Juan said. "Hace muchos años."

"But Juan here isn't so innocent either, is he?" the agent said, pointing with the piece of paper at Juan.

"What is he charged with?" Juan's daughter asked.

"Your father isn't charged with anything. Karl is the one who's charged. What I'm saying is that Juan here is no white swan. True, he didn't commit an attempted homicide against his wife with a Ford F-150 truck: Karl did that. But he is who he is." The officer took a moment to peruse the document in his hand. "I'm referring, specifically, to the events of September 1996."

"Oh, I see," Juan H. said.

"What? Crossing the border? But that was twenty-four years ago," Juan's daughter said. "Before I was born." She spoke these last words to the backs of her father, the agent, and Karl as they filed out the bedroom door.

The agent led Juan out of his house and into a small, concrete front yard, past the triple-level concrete fountain Juan had installed there, and past the shrine to the Virgin his late wife had asked him to build. The agent saw a switch on a pole next to the Virgin, and he flipped it on, and a string of lightbulbs came on around the Virgin and the concrete aureole that enveloped her. The lights flashed yellow, and then red, and the Virgin's eyes gleamed with these colors, and then with blue, orange, and magenta. "That's pretty cool," he said.

The agent opened the gate, and led Juan to a large, unmarked Chevrolet Suburban, where two other agents were waiting, and smoking cigarettes, which they extinguished when they saw the agent wearing the nicotine patch.

Karl walked away, alone, advancing down the sidewalk, and used a remote key to unlock the doors of a Ford F-150 truck which was double-parked nearby; it gleamed with a freshly polished skin that reflected Karl's body like a mirror of undulating obsidian. One of the agents followed after him, and shook Karl's hand; then he patted him on the back.

"You picked a good one," the agent said. "I think this guy is going to stick."

Just before the agents lowered Juan's head and guided him into the Suburban, Karl turned to look at Juan one last time. The Mexican mechanic was dressed in green corduroy pants and a T-shirt for the University of Oregon (his oldest son's alma mater), and his expression was one of annoyance and resignation. A good man who accepts a fate he does not deserve. Karl admired him as one does a spiffy prom date, or a tall, lean, and especially fast horse.

After an hour in the normal, awful traffic of the city, the Suburban entered a large parking lot surrounded by fences, driving past the soiled pink cubes of an abandoned shopping center, to a building that stood like an island in the center of an asphalt sea. They stopped before the building's breeze-block façade; on either side of the front doors, there was a cluster of bird-of-paradise plants with frayed leaves.

The agents guided Juan through a pair of glass doors, into a room marked RECEPTION, and he saw a desk, behind which there were many small squares with hooks, some of which held keys, and a large sign that read QUALITY INN. From a bag marked HOUSE-KEEPING, the agents removed a set of pale-yellow overalls, and gave them to him.

"Go change in the bathroom," one of the agents said while removing Juan's hand-ties. When he returned from the bathroom, the agents had Juan sign many forms. They told him to stand in front of a white sheet hung up next to an empty fish tank that smelled of algae and grime, and they snapped his photograph.

One of the agents handed him a key attached to a plastic oval imprinted with the number 206. Then the agent joined the others, who were leaving the lobby, and Juan watched as they locked the glass doors, and drove away in the Suburban.

How long would he be here? Was there nothing he could do to appeal his detention? The agents had disappeared before Juan could ask them the many questions he had, and he was left alone to contemplate his situation. Pulled out of his bed, to be punished for a crime committed by Karl. You hear about these happenings on the radio, in the news on your phone, but they seem far away from you, and then you are inside the machinery, and it processes you, and there is nothing you can do.

When he found room 206 and unlocked the door, Juan entered a carpeted room that held two sets of bunk beds with three snoring men. He took an empty, bottom bunk, and sat on the edge. As he waited for the other men to wake up, he studied the two paintings on the walls. One depicted a lake with lily pads. Or maybe it was a swamp, because a fetid yellow mist seemed to be drifting over the water. No, it was just dust on the painting's surface. In the second painting, two deer with bodies disproportionate to their legs stood in a forest of birch trees; they turned to face the viewer with a kind of disdain, like haughty, furry, four-legged fashion models.

When his new roommates woke up, they introduced themselves. He told them he worked as a car mechanic, and described the agent's sudden appearance in his home with Karl. And they, in turn, shared the stories of the people whose misdeeds had brought them to this place.

"My guy robbed a liquor store," Pedro X. said.

"El mío sold some of that crystal drug," said Oscar J. "To a police officer! ¡Pendejo!"

"Mine set fire to his old elementary school," said Joaquín Z. "He's nineteen. A real mocoso. Lo extraño is that I sort of like him. He reminds me of me, when I was back at the Prepa in el DF. I did all sorts of crazy things." Joaquín Z. stared out the window, lost in memories for a moment. "But never with fire," he said finally, with a distant voice. "That's going too far."

"The Replacement Law is ridiculous," Juan said, and he began to rail to his roommates about the cruelty of that piece of legislation, and the idiocy of the elected officials who had approved it. As he spoke, he felt reason and logic alive within him, the nobility of the lessons about democracy he'd learned in grade school in his native country.

"You talk really well for a car mechanic," Joaquín Z. said. "And you're right. This is totally fucked." And then Joaquín Z. threw himself back on his bed, and everyone was silent, and nothing more was said about the subject.

A day passed. And then another. Every morning at 9:30 the inmates left their room and walked down to a breakfast buffet in an old conference room, joining about fifty others in scooping up runny scrambled eggs and discs of reconstituted fried potatoes onto their plates. When they weren't eating, the inmates filled their days sitting in the big courtyard of the building, which was surrounded on four sides by two stories of rooms. They slumped and lounged on plastic chairs by a waterless swimming pool, each man dressed, like Juan, in a yellow jumpsuit with the words "Detention Kings, Inc." stenciled across the back. Joaquín Z., a small and funny man, liked to climb into the empty pool and sit at the bottom, cross-legged, meditating. He said sounds gathered there, and that he could hear the conversations of the people who were in the parking lot, outside, and passing trains, and birds singing from miles away.

Juan walked through the hallways, making circles around the facility, and once he found his way back to the lobby, and to a side room that was completely empty, expect for a display of brochures and flyers. "Wine Tasting Tour!" promised one pamphlet. "Whitewater Aquatics Park!" announced another. Juan took a brochure for the museum to the local historical society, and opened it, and as he walked back to room 206 he read about old silver mines and "frontier Ghost towns" and "Old West cemeteries" and "free samples of homemade ice cream made by our past president, Clarissa Johnson."

On Juan H.'s fourth day in detention, a group of agents arrived and fanned out through the facility, knocking on doors and call-

ing out names. The agent with the nicotine patch entered room
206 and found Juan.

"Today you get to see a judge," the agent explained. "Habeas
corpus."

Juan followed him and a group of other agents and inmates,
down the building's concrete stairs, back to the lobby, and then
out the glass doors to the parking lot, where a fleet of Suburbans
waited, each humming and emitting aromas of carbon monoxide
and heated plastic.

The agents gestured for Juan to take a seat, and he did so, grateful that they did not handcuff him. Soon the caravan of Suburbans
pushed forward through the normal, awful traffic of the city.

The Suburbans stopped before an office building in the city
center. Across the street, there was a pleasant park, with trees and
people walking dogs and old men rolling bocce balls on a lawn.
With his agent guiding him by the arm, Juan entered the building
via the front steps and when they walked into the lobby, Juan saw
men carrying briefcases, and a delivery man holding flowers, and
he caught a glimpse of the building directory, which listed insurance companies, marketing consultants, and doctors' offices.

Juan and his agent entered an elevator, stepping in behind another inmate in a yellow jumpsuit marked "Detention Kings Inc."
and an inmate whose avocado-green jumpsuit was stamped with
the words "Henderson Bros. Detention Corp." When the elevator
reached the tenth floor, the agent led Juan out.

"Go to suite 1016," the agent said. "Wait for me there. I gotta
take a leak."

Juan H. walked down the hallway, searching for suite 1016, and
he found it, and a sign with the words IMMIGRATION COURT.
But he did not go inside. After a few steps more he found a door
marked STAIRS, and opened it, and looked down. A breeze flowed
upward through the stairwell, a taste of the open air and freedom
awaiting him.

Before Juan could take his first, liberated step he imagined a
life of moving from one place to the next, hiding. But if he stayed
and faced the judge, maybe he could persuade the court to set
him free. He imagined the judge as a sage older gentleman. A
man in a bow tie, with glasses. He would tell the judge: I don't deserve to be punished in this way. I've lived my life well. They need
me at the shop, especially to work on those new electric vehicles

that come in from time to time, which no one else wants to touch. And except for the events of September 1996, I'm not guilty of anything; and even that one thing wasn't a crime, in a moral and human sense, because I was just trying to provide for my family. Juan H. thought of his home and its daily rhythms; his daughter out the door, heading off to her college classes; his son off to work, always punctual. The sunlit warmth of his home when his wife was still alive and their son and daughter were small children. She forgave me everything before she went. Everything.

Juan H. had allowed the door to the stairwell to close, and was standing before it, as if in a trance, when he heard a voice behind him. "Suite 1016 is this way." Juan turned and saw the agent. "This way, buddy," the agent said.

In suite 1016 Juan saw a series of walnut benches squeezed into a space the size of a three-car garage. When he sat down, Juan noticed the kneelers: the benches were old church pews. They faced a small steel desk on a riser, with two nameplates; one stamped in plastic that read "Judge Pro Tempore" and another that was written on paper with a Sharpie: "Caitlyn 'Kate' Alford, Esq." The judge was a woman in her mid- to late-twenties, Juan guessed, and was dressed not in a robe, but in a stylishly cut, double-breasted, light gray blazer.

The judge had three stacks of files on her desk, and now she took one, and reading the file tab, called out, "Segerstrom!" The agent took Juan by his elbow, and gestured for him to stand. "We're here," the agent said.

"The defendant, Karl Segerstrom, is eligible for bail," the judge said. "In light of the circumstances, which, I see, include a statement from the alleged victim, in which she states, 'I wish to drop the charges, I love his stupid ass,' I'm going to order the defendant's release. Forthwith."

From the front row of benches, the voice of an unseen male called out: "The government chooses to appeal, your honor."

The agent stood up, walked up to the judge's desk, and took a thick file folder that was handed to him.

"Upstairs," the agent said to Juan. "Suite 1224. Let's go."

They took the elevator up to the twelfth floor. When they reached suite 1224, the agent stopped before a sign that read IRIS CRUZ, DDS, PERIODONTIST.

"Aw shit, I mixed up the number again," the agent said. "It's 1242, not 1224. Fucking dyslexia."

They found suite 1242, and entered a small waiting room, where magazines and medical brochures were stacked haphazardly including one with a cartoon of a tooth with a face that was pouting and crying. "Your Root Canal and You," it said. A sign warned MEDICAL GASSES, NO SMOKING. The agent reached through a sliding glass window, and handed the Segerstrom file to a woman who sat behind a desk. She wore a blue, floral print smock, with a badge that read "Appeals Express, llp."

"Do we go in to see the judge?" Juan H. asked.

"We don't see the appeals judge. No," the agent said. "He's back there, somewhere. Or she is. They are."

Fifteen minutes later, the woman behind the glass announced: "Segerstrom!" The agent stood up. "That's my guy. Whattaya got for me?"

"The appeal's been granted," the woman said. "Your detainee stays in custody."

"Got it," the agent said, and he turned to Juan and gestured for him to get up, and the two men walked out the door and down the hall to wait for the elevator.

They drove back to the detention center, arriving just before sunset, the breeze-block façade bathed in orange light. Juan H. returned to room 206, and found his roommates there, and each looked up at him with a kind of weariness, or recognition, and said nothing.

Two weeks passed, and Juan did not hear another word about his case. He found no official he could complain to; the agents were present only when they delivered new inmates, and to take them to hearings at immigration court. The staff of the detention center consisted of cooks, and a small janitorial staff, but no one with any true authority. The phones Juan found (including one underneath his bunk) played bossa nova music when he picked them up, and did not work for making calls.

One day, Juan took a circular walk around the compound, and on his fifth lap he took a right down a dimly lit, apparently abandoned corridor on the ground floor, and arrived at a door that was marked with red letters, EMERGENCY EXIT. DO NOT OPEN. ALARM WILL SOUND. He pushed it open, but there was no alarm, just the sound of traffic entering the corridor. The bright light and asphalt plain of an empty parking lot stretched before him, and in the distance he saw the silhouette of a freeway, and a thoroughfare with cars speeding past.

Juan stepped out, and he heard and felt the door closing behind him, and he walked at an unhurried pace away from the detention center. When he reached the thoroughfare he headed west, in the general direction of his home. He walked one mile, then two, passing industrial parks, golf courses, and car dealerships, and all these places felt dry and dusty, and the few people he saw were mute and did not look at him, despite the yellow jumpsuit he was wearing.

After two hours of walking, Juan H. entered a residential neighborhood of small homes with humble yards and slanted roofs that were worn and patched. He saw a vendor in a straw hat, standing before a cart beneath a traffic light.

"Elotes! Elotes!" the vendor called out. Juan was hungry. "Tengo hambre, pero no tengo dinero," he said to the vendor, who was a short and very young man. The vendor looked at Juan, and the yellow overalls he was wearing, and gave a nod of understanding. He took two corn cobs from his cart, and wrapped them in paper, and gave them to Juan, who said gracias. Juan H. ate as he continued his march westward, and ten minutes later he reached a bus stop and saw a sign that named a destination that was close to his home. Two women were waiting on a bench. Juan took a seat next to them and said, "No tengo dinero para la feria," addressing no one in particular; it was a spoken thought, a lament. One of the women reached into the pocket of her apron, and she produced two bills, and handed them to him. Then she placed a hand on his wrist and said, "Que Dios te proteja." The bus arrived, and Juan H. got on, and for two hours the bus plowed forward, through the normal, awful traffic of the city, until it reached the end of its route, and Juan began to walk the final two miles home.

Juan arrived home at dusk, and his adult daughter and son watched him enter the house, emerging from a gray-blue half-light, and for a moment he looked like a hologram of the man they knew as their father. But when they saw him in the amber, incandescent light inside their living room, he came to life in all his true textures: Juan Ignacio Hernández Pérez, age forty-six, car mechanic and amateur philosopher. Looking very tired and diminished in stature, somehow, by the yellow overalls he was wearing.

*

In the days that followed, Juan tended the backyard garden his wife had started in the final year of her life. He went to the auto shop and his boss said, "Glad to have you back." No one mentioned his absence, or his detention, except for the time he was on his back underneath a BMW, and one of his coworkers said, sotto voce, "When they get you for that, it's like a black hole. Happened to my cousin. Haven't seen him in a year. I thought we might never see you again."

Finally, a letter from the government arrived in the mail. "Your release was approved," said the letter inside; it was dated five days after his escape from the detention center. "Your continued parole from detention is conditional on the good behavior of the Accused."

When Juan went to bed at night, he thought of Karl Segerstrom, and this caused him trouble sleeping. So he purchased a machine that made ocean noises, and the electric waves crashing on an electric beach soothed him, and soon he was having a pleasant, recurring dream that unfolded in the scrublands of his youth, and on plains of agave and cornfields. He saw the form of his wife's body, walking ahead of him, but never glimpsed her face, and when he woke up he felt a fleeting sense of joy, and then a deep and enduring sense of loss.

Six months passed in this way.

Then one morning Juan opened his eyes to the sound of waves crashing on a beach, and the gray eyes of the agent with the nicotine patch, and the face of Karl Segerstrom, which was covered in bruises and cuts.

"Karl found the guy who was banging his old lady," the agent said. "Tried to mess him up. It sorta backfired on Karl, as you can see. Aggravated assault is the charge this time."

"I'm going to find that peckerwood," Karl said, "and I'm going kill him."

"Now, now, Karl. Don't say that. You're scaring Juan here. Murder in the first: that's a life sentence, boy."

And soon Juan H. was returning to the detention center in a Suburban that rumbled eastward, away from his home, surging and slowing and stopping and surging through the normal, awful traffic of the city.

*

Juan H. entered room 206 and saw the familiar faces of Pedro X., Oscar J., and Joaquín Z., and the painting of the swamp and the deer that loomed over the room, and the phone on the floor that played bossa nova music.

"Hola," Joaquín Z. said, and the other two roommates made noises that may have been words, or may not have been.

Many days and months passed. When Juan wandered down to the darkened corridor with the emergency exit, he found the door locked. Winter came, and the days turned shorter, and when it rained the inmates turned to playing card games inside the breakfast room, and then spring came, and they returned to the courtyard.

Finally, one morning, Juan heard a knock at the door to room 206. He rose to his feet, and opened the door, and saw the agent who had worn the nicotine patch—only now the patch was gone, and the agent smelled of cigarette smoke. The agent handed him a blue slip of paper. It was a color copy of an official document, a "Certificate of Death." Juan studied the form, afraid he might see the name of one of his children. Or perhaps the name of Karl's murder victim. Instead, he read: Decedent: Karl Ulysses Segerstrom. Cause of Death: Suicide.

"Karl's old lady finally told him to fuck off," the agent said. "She filed for divorce. So Karl shot himself. With a shotgun. Ugly way to go. Super messy."

Juan tried to hand the document back to the agent.

"Keep it," the agent said. "You may need it one day. You never know when the government might lose something, get something mixed up. Always keep your paperwork."

Juan followed the agent back down to the lobby. Another agent handed him the bag in which Juan had deposited his street clothes many months earlier. The agent who no longer wore a nicotine patch said: "Go to the bathroom and change."

When Juan was done dressing, he returned to the lobby and saw the agents driving away in a Suburban, the unlocked glass doors behind them still moving in their wake. He walked out the door, and retrieved the wallet and the phone that he'd left in his pants pocket months earlier. He turned on the phone: To his surprise, it worked. He called his daughter, and asked her to come and pick him up, and for the next hour he waited for her, sitting by the dust-covered bird-of-paradise plants, listening to the traffic passing on the nearby thoroughfare. He wondered how many years the shopping center next door had been closed.

After work, and on the weekends, Juan took long walks through his neighborhood. When he encountered a man or woman living a desperate and frayed existence, he studied them. There were many such individuals in his neighborhood, and each time Juan imagined this person committing a crime. A stabbing, a robbery, shoplifting. He caught glimpses of graffiti written on the sidewalk, and he worried about the people who had committed these acts of vandalism. One graffito was repeated again and again, inch-high letters written with a paint-pen scrawl on the iron covers to city water valves: *Weedwolf.* The Weedwolf probably lived in this neighborhood, and he might know Juan, or know of him. People talked about Juan H.'s case, he sensed this. For decades he'd belonged to the category "Unauthorized Alien," and now his neighbors knew the government had classified him into the subcategory "Nominated Alien Inmate Second." Each time he took a walk, he saw the name Weedwolf, and after a while he imagined the Weedwolf as a bearded man of about his own age, a trickster with ivory teeth, a man who didn't give a shit. He felt the eyes of the Weedwolf gazing upon him, surreptitiously. The tortured, slanted writing of the graffito suggested mental illness, and Juan wondered how much longer would pass before the police arrested Weedwolf and chose Juan to serve his detention.

Juan began to take longer walks, to escape the streets that had been defaced by the Weedwolf, and at the end of one such stroll he entered an unfamiliar neighborhood and saw a storefront with a window advertising weapons. Columbia Firearms.

Juan thought that if the agent came for him again, he would find a way to escape detention and return to this place, to purchase a gun. Then he would track down the Weedwolf. But Juan was uncertain whether he would have the courage for what needed to happen next.

Elephant Seals

FROM *Agni*

MOST VERSIONS OF Paul and Diana stop to see the elephant seals on their way to California. It's Paul's idea. He's read about them, and even though the beach is out of the way, he wants to see them in the flesh. It's 1969. Diana holds a Polaroid camera, ready to snap pictures of the creatures who, according to Paul, remain for years without anybody telling them what to do.

"Is it like a zoo?" she asks.

"No," he says, "they just live there."

On the drive, they pass green hills spotted with cows and horses. In the distance sits Hearst Castle. Paul says it was built by a millionaire to keep his mistress happy. Diana rolls her eyes and says, "I've seen *Citizen Kane*."

Diana is four months pregnant and wants to stop because she's worried about a cramp that won't go away. Paul wants to keep driving. When else will they get the chance? Diana, who isn't even sure the seals exist, yells at him every time he misses a turn for a local hospital.

Finally Paul takes her to a clinic. An old doctor says it's just the kind of nerves that young women get in their first pregnancies. He hands Paul an ice pack and Paul gives it to Diana.

From the parking lot, she can smell the ocean. She tosses the ice pack in the backseat and says, "Can we just go to my cousin's now?"

In a different version, Paul and Diana skip the clinic and drive straight to the beach.

It's a little past sunset when they arrive. Paul parks the car and Diana tells him he can go, but she's staying put. She's wandered through plenty of frigid nights in the desert, but the cold on the California coast is like baking soda and vinegar fizzing across her skin. It's a cold that won't stay still.

Paul leaves Diana with her cramps and her gooseflesh and walks along the bluff to get a better look at the stones on the shore. They could be dormant seals, resting after a long trip out to sea. The sun fizzles out and he wonders if he should try one more beach.

Instead, he returns to the car. He continues to think about the seals as they drive south. Ocean air drifts though the window and he wonders if he imagined reading about them so long ago. It's a question that dogs him all the way to Los Angeles. It's a question that peels at his skin every time Diana's cousin asks if they want extra pillows or towels. It's a question that rolls him out of bed one night and makes him drive back up the coast.

In another version, Paul never makes it to Los Angeles. After he leaves Diana shivering in the car, he climbs past a rope that says the beach is closed at dusk. He hikes over sandy rocks and takes big gulps of salty wind. It's dark and he has a hard time figuring out whether the massive lumps are boulders or living creatures. He moves closer to get a better look. He just wants to see one of their faces.

And he disappears.

Different versions of Diana have different theories. She thinks he got too close. She thinks he ran off because he didn't want to be a father. She thinks he lost his mind. She thinks he took a swim and got caught in a quick-moving current. She thinks he's been abducted by bikers and forced to drink moonshine from plastic milk jugs. She thinks he joined the army and got sent to Vietnam. She thinks he hitchhiked back to Cleveland. She thinks he went east to find his sister. She thinks he might come back.

There's another version of Diana that never makes it to California. She works as a cocktail server in Las Vegas. Paul's a prep cook on a buffet line at the Promethean. Their paths sometimes cross in the hotel lobby. Paul's not supposed to use the guest entrance, but he doesn't care. Diana sees him strolling through the gold-paneled halls, holding his head high, dressed in a crisp white chef's coat.

She spends her days and nights flirting for tips. She spends lazy mornings in bed as Paul lights burners in the kitchenette. He thinks of himself as more than a prep cook, and he likes to show off for her. His eggs slide right out of pans. His potatoes are soft on the inside, crispy outside. He sprinkles sliced tomatoes with salt and pepper. The butter he spreads on toast tastes like fresh cream.

Paul's sister, Helen, lives with them in the tiny apartment. Diana works with her at the cocktail lounge. It annoys her when she walks into their apartment and finds Helen dabbing pink polish over her nails at the same table where they eat. It annoys her that Helen is a grown woman who takes three bubble baths a day. It annoys her that every time she brings up going to live near her cousin in California, Paul says, "But what about Helen?"

Paul serves Diana breakfast in bed and tells her that he and his sister were named after the divine twins in Greek mythology, Pollux and Helen. Diana cuts a triangle of tomato with her fork and knife and says, "I thought Castor and Pollux were the twins."

Paul refills the coffee mug on her side of the bed. The breakfast plate sits on her lap, still warm. "Castor and Pollux only had the same mother," he says. "Pollux and Helen were full-blooded siblings, both Zeus's children. Making them the divine ones."

He has more to say about the Trojan War and demigods but Diana doesn't want to think about how her boyfriend's sister is named after the most beautiful woman in Greek mythology.

There's another Paul and Diana who never go to the California coast because Paul never leaves Cleveland, Ohio.

When Paul and his sister, Helen, are fifteen years old, they start to work at their family's grocery store near the West Side Market. Their father, Nicholas, plays a game at the start of each shift. He gives them a clue from the daily crossword puzzle. Whoever gets the answer is allowed first pick of their job duties that day.

Paul figures out a way to win every time. He wakes up early and peeks at the newspaper before anyone else is up. He crouches in the alley, shifting the paper in the milky morning light, careful not to crease it. He studies the puzzle clues, makes mental notes of the arrangements, and rolls the paper back into place by the front door. Then at lunchtime he breaks away from the cafeteria and walks the halls to the school library. If he can't find the answers in encyclopedias, he asks the librarian questions like, "Do you know who Shakespeare married?" or "What's a pinniped?"

Despite all these preparations, Helen is quick. Their father sits high above them at the register, tapping his pencil to the folded paper. "Second Caesar," he says. "Eight letters."

"Augustus," she says, tilting her chin.

Nicholas counts the letters, but Paul isn't worried. His father will soon realize that twenty-seven across is four letters, with the clue: *City in Norway.* Before Nicholas shakes his head, Paul rises on his toes and says, "Octavian."

There are two major tasks that need doing that day. Stocking the Juicy Fruit or filling the dairy case. It's early fall and Paul has no interest in going near a 38-degree walk-in cooler. After brief instructions, Nicholas hands Helen the burlap gloves.

As Paul takes his time stocking gum, he feels a rare spindle of regret prick his spine. He wonders if winning is worth it. The door chimes and his mother, Christina, enters. She's red haired, like him and Helen, and is carrying a blue umbrella. Nicholas asks if it's supposed to rain. Christina glances between him and Paul and says, "Why do you always make Helen do the hard stuff?"

Outside, streetlamps cast an orange glow over Lorain Avenue and Paul wonders if his mother is actually going to cook dinner or if they'll have sandwiches again. He thinks about how he'll cook dinner every night when he's a grown-up.

The door chimes and two men appear with guns. Christina drops the umbrella and tells Nicholas to give them anything they want. Or, at least, Paul thinks that's what his mother says before the men shoot all three of them.

In another version, Helen wins. The same Helen who will annoy Diana in Las Vegas, who will paint her nails at the kitchenette table and take three bubble baths a day. This Helen knows her brother cheats. It's part of his personality. When they're fifteen years old, she hears him sneak into the alleyway every morning before dawn, no matter how cold or rainy.

So one day she spends all her milk money on a newspaper before school. In study hall, she scribbles the answers on wide-ruled paper, memorizing them. Between classes, she practices pronunciations in the bathroom mirror as other girls dab gloss on their lips or pull combs through their hair.

"Truman," Helen says, "beryllium, Oslo, elephant seal."

When Nicholas reads the clue from behind the shop counter, Helen knows it. Before Paul has a chance to blurt his answer, she stomps her foot for emphasis. "Octavian," she says. "It's Octavian."

Paul's sunny complexion pales and he peers at her, stunned. An ache pulls at the core of her spine, making her toes tingle. She understands why he's hurt. The need to win is part of his personality.

Nicholas reaches over the counter to pat her head. "That's right," he says. "And what job would you like, my dear?"

She picks the bubble gum and banishes her brother to the cooler. He snatches the burlap gloves and pouts his slow way through the bread aisle. Nicholas helps her carry the crate of Juicy Fruit to the front counter.

While Helen stocks gum, she straightens out-of-place Hershey bars and Lemonheads. Nicholas listens to a baseball game on the radio. Outside, it begins to get dark. She wonders if the game is happening where it's still bright and sunny, like California.

She finishes her task and stands up. "Dad," she says, "do you have extra gloves?"

When Helen enters the cooler from the side door, Paul is only a quarter of the way through stocking the butter. His breath curls like smoke.

"What are you doing?" he asks.

"Helping you," she says and kneels, feeling the cold concrete through her stockings.

Paul doesn't smile. He's embarrassed but not embarrassed enough to refuse the help. Helen hands him boxes of unsalted butter from the pallet. He slides them into the case.

This rhythmic process continues until Helen feels a sudden jolt. Her head slams to the floor. Blue sand shakes inside her skull. Her brother's weight is heavy on her.

"Stay down," he says, his voice quiet.

She doesn't know what's happening. What kind of game this is. The frost seeps through the floor into her clothes, chilling her legs, her chin, her cheek. "Paul," she is about to say, "stop." Then she hears gunshots. Her instinct is to jump and run, but Paul keeps her in place.

There are many versions in which both Helen and Paul survive the robbery, yet their parents never do. In some, the children go live with their grandparents. In another, it's an aunt and uncle on a farm in Wellington, an hour outside the city. Paul never takes to the chores. Spreading hay and picking corn feel like daily tortures. None of it bothers Helen. Her mind wanders when she's peeling potatoes the same way it used to when she stocked milk bottles. From the window, she gazes at the brilliant green and yellow pastures that stretch toward the road.

One night, when they're seventeen years old, Paul appears at her window with a black eye and a duffel bag. "Why don't we go somewhere?" he says.

Later, they're on a bus passing through beige-gray fields. Helen sits at the window and Paul snores on her shoulder. Rain splatters the glass and the seats smell like milk that's been left on the counter too long. She loops her thumb under the flap of his bag, just to peek inside. A fifth of whiskey, a rubber-banded wad of cash—those don't surprise her. The *Betty Crocker's Cookbook* does.

In the versions where the twins end up in Las Vegas, Paul always falls in love with Diana, a twenty-something blonde who wears black eyeliner and puts cigarettes out in the kitchen sink. Paul gets Diana to get Helen a job at the hotel lounge, but all Diana ever does is berate her.

"If you can't walk in heels," Diana says, "then stick to Mary Janes."

Helen sleeps on the living room couch. She hears him and Diana late at night and early in the mornings. To drown out the noise, she takes long baths. Her toes press into the aquamarine tiles over the tub and she thinks of the miles and miles of desert beyond the walls.

In almost every version, the heel of Helen's left pump snaps off one night as she rushes through the lobby of the casino on her way to the late shift. She takes a dive, skimming her nylons across the carpet. Her head flutters. Although her body isn't bruised, she remembers this feeling, low to the ground.

An older man offers his hand. He's dressed in jeans that smell like an ashtray. His beard is gray, but the rest of his hair is brown. A yellow pencil pokes from behind his ear and, while he's probably just a handyman, Helen wonders if a crossword puzzle is tucked in his back pocket.

She stands and, in frustration, flings her other, perfectly fine shoe against the wall, then runs barefoot through the casino.

Two days later, the man appears at one of the tables in her section. His hair is neatly trimmed and his jaw shaved clean, not a trace of gray. It makes him look ten years younger. He's dressed in a charcoal suit sans tie and shiny, pointed shoes. She notices his pale eyes, how they look like a certain kind of dog's, and she wonders why she didn't notice that striking detail the evening he helped her.

His name is Henry Coventry. "Everyone calls me Hank," he says. The East Coast accent makes her wonder if he's from money. He asks her to have dinner, and it's not the first time a customer has asked her out, but it's the first time she says yes.

She plucks leaves from a steamed artichoke and dips the fleshy part in warm butter. Hank only wants to know about her. Where is she from? What does she like? Does she have brothers or sisters? Does she know any good stories?

Helen pulls the artichoke leaf between her teeth the way her brother taught her—not exactly chewing it, but extracting the meat. She tells him she's from Cleveland and he makes a joke about the river catching fire.

"My brother used to swim in it," she says.

"Yeah? He ever catch on fire?"

"Not yet."

A few days pass and Helen doesn't hear from him. She assumes he took his fancy shoes back east. Then one morning, on her way to pick up a carton of eggs for Paul in the hotel kitchen, she runs into Hank outside the entrance. He's dressed like the day she met him, in a white T-shirt and jeans. In the bright sun, she sees patches of gray and white stubble dusting his jaw. Beneath his arm is a shoebox adorned with a shiny white bow.

"I got them repaired for you," he says.

She takes the box with both hands the way a postal clerk does.

"I have to go back to Connecticut," he says.

"I have to get eggs for my brother," she says.

Hank leaves and Helen continues around to the back entrance of the hotel. The breakfast chef has Paul's eggs waiting for her. For some reason, he's packed Paul's eggs in a shoebox with crumpled tinfoil to separate them. Helen leans against the prep table so she can slide her feet into her repaired red pumps. On the walk home, she carries the shoebox of eggs under one arm and the shoebox of shoes under the other.

In some versions of this story, Hank is a widower and single father in his forties. Due to a bullet he took to the right thigh at the Battle of Mudong-Ni, he walks with a limp. Most of the times he meets Helen, she doesn't notice it.

She's young, he thinks. Twenty, tops. He watches her pull strings of artichoke from her front teeth like dental floss. Still, she's charming, and ever since his wife died Hank hasn't had the occasion to spend evenings with charming women. As they talk about burning rivers, he wonders if she might be someone who could actually understand him.

He walks her to the lobby and says it was nice to share a meal, says he hopes she has a nice night. He hears the words and knows he sounds terribly stiff and awkward. He walks off to play more blackjack. His wife used to accuse him of being an addict. The way Hank sees it, he makes a steady living. He averages about five dollars an hour at the blackjack table and that's more than he makes at the auto shop. Gambling is honest work if you keep an even head about it. If you don't try to take more than your due.

By the time he stumbles back to his room, morning light funnels through the curtains, illuminating the dust in the air. He calls his sister to ask how his ten-year-old is doing. She tells him Adam's playing street hockey and doesn't want to come to the phone.

In other versions, Hank doesn't have a kid or a dead wife. However, he almost always has that bullet wound and almost always runs into Helen just as she has tripped in the lobby. He always bends down to help her. She always throws the one shoe against the wall in protest, because if she doesn't have two good shoes what's the point in only having one? He always goes and picks both up, wondering where he can get modeling glue and a needle-thread set in Las Vegas.

In these versions, Hank worries less about the age difference. He's lost less, and that makes him a more selfish person. A few weeks later, he flies back to Vegas. He asks the blonde at the cocktail lounge if he can sit in Helen's section. The hostess scowls and he worries he might be a creep until Helen waves to him. She twirls an empty tray and shows off the red pumps.

"They fit better than before," she says.

He takes her to dinner again. This time there are no airs. He tells her he's a Korean War vet who works at his buddy's auto shop in Connecticut. He tells her how the only books he brought overseas were about probability. On long treks over snowy hills or long, hot afternoons laying demolition wire, he performed black-jack exercises in his head. Helen nods along, and he worries, briefly, that he's lost her. He switches tracks and tells her how, when he got shot, he lay in the sick tent, his busted leg elevated, and reviewed back-counting scenarios and insurance bets all day long. He figured out ways he could win time after time, even if it wasn't a lot.

After Hank admits all this to Helen, she gazes back at him with glassy, hopeful eyes.

In these versions, Hank continues his long weekend trips until finally he asks Helen to marry him and come live in Connecticut. Helen has to pack her things while Paul is at work because she knows he'll try to talk her out of it.

As she carries her suitcase through the courtyard, she runs into Diana, who's dressed in a black bathing suit probably meant to hide the growing curve of her stomach. Helen can't imagine Paul as a father and she thinks maybe Diana can't either.

Helen nods toward her suitcase. "If it's all the same," she says, "don't tell Paul I'm gone until everyone at work figures it out."

"No problem," Diana says. "It's none of my business."

Hank picks up Helen in a cab outside the apartment complex. They ride along roads she hasn't traveled since she and Paul arrived. The colorful, crowded streets collapse beneath an endless blue sky. She presses her toes inside her pumps, pushing them as hard as she can. A hot, dry wind blows through the windows and her neck itches from the fabric of Hank's sleeve. She feels his fingers on her bare arm, gently pushing into her skin, testing if she's real.

In some versions, Paul leaves Diana in Las Vegas. Ever since Helen left, all he does is drink. Before work, during work, after work. The problem, Diana says, is that it's boring and she doesn't want to have a baby with a drunk. Paul says, "Fine, go do whatever you want." She snatches his bottle of whiskey and empties it in the toilet. Paul shoves her so hard she falls against the bathtub and splits her chin.

One of the buffet cooks who lives next door hears the commotion. He barges into the apartment and the sound of the door is enough to make Paul scramble past him.

Diana recognizes the neighbor. His name is Max but people call him "Face" on account of his thick-rimmed glasses and crooked overbite. He walks her to his apartment, which has an actual view of the pool. He presses an ice pack wrapped in cloth to her chin and she figures he'll do. A month later, she marries him in a chapel at another casino so they won't run into coworkers. Their son— meaning her and Paul's son—is named Jake, and even though it's obvious there's no biological relation between this freckle-faced, red-haired boy and Max, Jake also has a crooked overbite. Because of this, when people see Max play toss with him or push him down aisles in shopping carts, they don't question that the two are father and son.

In versions where Paul sobers up, he goes to culinary school even though seasoned chefs tell him it's a waste of time. He'd be better off, they say, working his way up the line in a decent kitchen. Yet it's in school that Paul falls in love with pastry. He learns to temper eggs for custards, to make chocolate tarts, to stack cakes with wooden dowel rods. Sometimes, when he melts sugar for caramel or dusts plates with cocoa, he thinks of his and Diana's son. It crosses his mind to call her, to say he's different now, but he never does. In the versions where Paul doesn't sober up, he doesn't have these kinds of problems.

In versions where Diana doesn't say anything to Paul about his drinking, they always go to California. In the end, Paul always leaves. She raises their son on her own and names him William after a brother who died in Vietnam. Yet within a couple of weeks she can't get used to calling him that. He's too special to be a Billy or a Will. He's a Liam.

One afternoon when Liam is thirteen and getting fitted for braces, Diana flips through a travel magazine in the orthodontist's office in Long Beach. It's a magazine for people who wear cable-knit sweaters and drink wine with seared scallops. She loses herself in the perfumed pages and comes across a story about a colony of

elephant seals in Northern California. She waits until the recep-
tionist isn't looking and slips the magazine into the beach bag she
uses as a purse.

In the car, she asks Liam if he wants to get milk shakes for
dinner.

With his mouth closed, his profile looks just like Paul's. He gazes
out the window at the lines of rush hour traffic on Seventh Street.

"I don't want braces," he says, showing his overbite when he
talks.

"What if we took a trip?" she says.

"Instead of getting braces?"

They drive through Los Angeles and into the canyons, up to
wine country, past nuclear power plants, through vacation towns.
It's a long trip and she lets Liam pick the music. Every time one of
the radio stations skitches out, she rolls the windows down. To pass
time, they make up stories about people in other cars. They drive
at least a hundred miles north of the beaches where Paul took her
so many years ago.

When they finally make it to the town from the magazine, Diana
pulls over to check the map and stretch her legs. She worries she's
about to put her son through the same rigmarole Paul subjected
her to. She doesn't even know how she'll pay for braces, and now
they're nine hours from home.

She walks a distance from the car to hide her face. As she's figuring out how to explain that she has gotten them lost, she sees
half a dozen giant seals below, lounging on the rocky shore. Even
though they're not going anywhere, she runs back to the car and
taps her hand on the windshield.

"Liam," she says, "Liam, come quick."

In almost every version, Hank dies of lung cancer when Helen is
not quite sixty. They have children scattered across the country,
but none of them are close. She always reaches for Paul. In versions where she can track him down, all he wants to talk about is
Alcoholics Anonymous.

"I've learned," he says, "that my alcoholic behavior actually
started way before we lost Mom and Dad. Before I ever had a
drink."

"Paul," she says, "we saw our parents get killed. It's okay that you
started drinking."

"But it's not, Helen. That's the thing."

She visits him for a couple of weeks in California. He manages a health-food café in Ventura County and goes to AA meetings every night. They get into an argument one evening when Helen picks up a bottle of chardonnay for dinner.

"Are you seriously bringing booze into my house?"

"It's just wine, Paul."

In other versions, Helen's not able to find Paul. The last time she heard from him was in their early forties, when he called collect from Kentucky, asking her to wire money.

"Hank says we can't anymore," Helen said. "We have problems too."

After that he disappeared, and it was the not knowing that bothered her most. Sometimes she even called Diana to ask if she'd heard from him—and Diana always laughed.

After Hank dies, Helen throws herself into work, finally getting her real estate license. In the evening, she takes improv and pottery classes at the community center because she never felt she was good at being young and now she wants to get good at being old. As she approaches her sixty-first birthday, she and a theater friend, a single fifty-something named Patty, splurge on an Alaskan cruise in the middle of a rainy spring.

"It'll be cold," Patty says, "but we can see the northern lights."

The nights are gorgeous and there's fresh fruit on the buffet every morning. Helen eats strawberries with the stems already plucked off and pictures someone in the kitchen looking like Paul with a paring knife. She pulls fibers of unripe pineapple from her teeth and thinks about all the years that still stretch ahead of her.

After breakfast, she bundles up and strolls the deck. The Pacific Ocean sparkles beneath a powder sky. She sees movement in the waves, something alive, and she wants to follow its path.

Her concentration breaks when a bald man calls out from a lounge chair. "Ten letters," he says, tapping a pencil to a magazine, "for the man in black."

Helen doesn't know if he's talking to her or not. "Grim Reaper," she says.

"No, it ends with *h*."

In another version, she gets it right.

*

There is only one version in which Paul gets it right.

When he's sixty-one, he takes his new girlfriend from AA, Linda, to her nephew's wedding in Cambria. It's the middle of December and, though the skies are clear blue, it's a cool sixty degrees on the coast. Linda wears her gray hair in a thick braid. She's about the same age as Paul and has a whole messy history of her own. Her parents are gone, she's estranged from most of her sisters, has a daughter in Texas she hardly ever talks to. Frankly, she tells him, she's shocked to have been invited to this wedding.

Along the way, she taps her finger against the window of his Prius and says, "Look, that's the castle from *Citizen Kane*."

Paul's instinct is to correct her, to explain that it's Hearst Castle, and to tell her all the minutiae about William Randolph Hearst, the newspaper mogul *Citizen Kane* was based on. Instead, he glances at her and says, "Is that so?"

The ceremony is in a garden overflowing with rosemary. At the reception, in a wood-paneled lodge, he and Linda hold flutes of apple juice for the champagne toast. The guests assume they're an old married couple, and after a while Paul and Linda stop correcting them. They dance to three songs in a row before Paul feels the aches that come from decades of kitchen work.

He says, "You ever wonder what it'd be like if we'd met twenty, thirty years ago?"

"We'd have eaten each other alive," Linda says, squeezing his hand.

During the bouquet toss, he slips out of the reception and walks along a gravel path lit by Christmas lights. There isn't anything in particular to remind him of Diana, but he takes out his phone and looks her up on Facebook from an account he uses only for AA friends. Her most recent posts are from a recent trip to Pittsburgh to visit grandkids. She wears her white hair cut short in a pixie style, which makes her look old and young at the same time. He sees their son in one of the photos, but Paul never clicks on his profile.

In the morning, Linda says she's going for a walk around the grounds with one of her sisters. "It's the first time she's wanted to really talk," she says, looping her hair into its braid. "Do you mind?"

"No," Paul says, "not at all."

He grabs coffee from the continental buffet and drives a few miles to the state park off the coastal highway. It's early, but there are already cars and tourists scattered through the lot. He walks by docents in bright blue windbreakers who stand along a chain-link fence, waiting to be asked questions.

Below the railing, a couple of hundred elephant seals lounge on the shore. Others wiggle toward the water. From high up, he's still close enough to make out their crooked snouts, their reptilian eyes, their goofy grins. He doesn't need the informational signs that line the fence. He knows all about them.

They travel between eleven and thirteen thousand miles each migration cycle, farther than any other pinniped. They were almost hunted to extinction in the nineteenth century. The males weigh even more than a Ford F-150. They battle one another for dominance, puffing out their trunk-like snouts when they fight. The females are much smaller but can swim deeper and live longer. They have black coats that molt and turn silver. They find safe spots on land when their skin needs to regrow itself. They eat fish and squid and creatures that only dwell on the deepest, darkest ocean floors. They go out in the world and explore, but they always return to the same spots, the same beaches, year after year. They don't forget where they come from. They don't forget where they really live.

Foster

FROM *The New Yorker*

HE ISN'T ANY kind of cat that I've ever seen. The paws look like something out of a storybook. And his fur shines an IKEA-bag blue. Some Googling tells me this means he's a shorthair, maybe—but my older brother's letter just called him a stray.

You have that in common, my brother wrote.

It'll give you two something to talk about, he wrote.

So that's what I think of him as: a fucking stray.

A woman I can't responsibly call my brother's girlfriend dropped the cat off at my apartment in Montrose. Literally tossed him on the sidewalk. She didn't wait for me to stumble outside before she drove off. There was a crumpled note, along with a food dispenser, and then this cat in his box. I let him stew there while I hauled everything into my place, folding myself into the sofa to squint at my brother's cursive.

We were born four years apart. Hadn't spoken in six. He'd been in prison for three. He'd killed someone, accidentally, in a hit-and-run. But he'd shot another person before he was caught for that.

My brother's instructions were simple: feed the cat twice a day, and give him plenty of water. Keep him away from open doors. The cat could be left on his own for an infinite amount of time. The cat had three siblings, apparently, and they'd been given suitable homes elsewhere, but at the very last minute the fourth home had fallen through. Which made me the cat's final resort.

If he had thumbs, my brother wrote, we wouldn't need you.

Calling us estranged gives our relationship more formality than I prefer—like most of my family, my brother and I simply don't talk. And then, homicide. Every first of the month, I send some cash from my shitty assistant's stipend at the university. For months, I didn't know if my brother actually received it.

Then, one time, I sent the money a few days late. My mom called to ask me what the fucking holdup was.

The cat looms from the corner of my apartment. He prances on his toes. He arches his back. The cat leaps onto the kitchenette counter, across the dried-up flour and the takeout chopsticks and the loose tea bags, scattering my shit every which way. My brother's cat could be four years old, or four hundred and sixty-seven.

Sometimes he makes a face, as if to smile—except I know that it isn't a smile.

Which makes it something far more sinister.

And then he laughs.

Owen reminds me that the cat doesn't have a name. This is after he makes it back to my apartment from the gig at his father's dental practice, but before a bout of fucking in which neither of us manages to come.

It's been happening for a while. Or not happening. We'd cycled through our usual positions, moving from room to room, in and out of socks, on and off appliances. Then, eventually, after we settled onto the couch, Owen sighed loudly, smiling and patting me on the head, and called the cat out from the closet he'd hidden in.

My brother's cat still hasn't said much to me. But he meows and the rest with Owen. They lie together on the couch, while the cat massages Owen's belly. I'd forgotten to give him water, and he punished me with a screech.

Tough crowd, Owen says. But he's a cutie.

You've never called me that, I say.

You're more handsome. Mr. Masc.

I'd rather be cute.

Well, Owen says, squeezing the cat's ears.

It's been a few days since we've seen each other. Between my job at the university and Owen's out in Pearland, we barely manage a routine beyond weekends and the occasional midnight quickie. A few weeks back, Owen broached the subject of his moving in—

once, and then once again. I made the appropriate grunt, which he told me wouldn't hold up on a lease.

But I made him a copy of my key anyway.

He lost it a few days later.

Now Owen pedals his legs in the air, with his ass on my ear, and the cat reaches for his thighs, ignoring me entirely.

So you've just been calling him cat, Owen says.

Mr. Cat, I say. Excuse you.

Monsieur Chat, Owen says.

Herr Katze.

Señor Gato.

Cat-san.

Your big brother didn't think to tell you his beloved's title?

He can be a little careless, I say. But it doesn't matter. This is temporary.

These cheeks aren't temporary, Owen says, holding the cat in front of my face.

Don't get attached, I say.

So Owen sighs, and the cat on his belly sighs, too.

We met online. That website no longer exists. The first thing Owen told me, before he penetrated me, after we'd eaten entirely too much pasta and paid far too much for it, was that we'd never get married. He'd tried that already. The day after he'd graduated from dentistry school, his parents paired him off with another dentist's daughter. They'd stuck it out for a year and change, but it hadn't worked, for the obvious reason.

Owen's ex-wife didn't hold it against him, though. She was queer, too. Their families had been strategic. Both of them needed an heir, preferably with a dick, and Owen swore that he'd never live down the shame of failing to provide one.

This was where I came in.

We'd form our own sort of family.

When Owen asked if I'd be up for that, at first I didn't say much.

Then I said, Fuck it. Why not.

But here is the truth: sometimes family doesn't last.

Owen knows this as well as I do.

If he can crash into my life, then he might, eventually, run out.

And I don't need that.

It's one thing to be alone, and another to be thrust back into loneliness.

The next morning, before work, Owen and I try fucking again.

I slip myself between him, and he rolls on top of me, nearly flipping us. After rocking back and forth for a minute or two, Owen sighs, and I do, too.

Any luck, he asks.

Maybe next time, I say.

We capsize onto the rug.

Afterward, in the shower, I scrub his back.

You should name him, Owen says.

Who, I say.

Really?

I'm kidding, I say. But it's not my place.

Then ask your brother for his blessing.

We don't really talk.

Is that your fault or his?

Doesn't matter, because there's nothing there anyway. No honesty.

Seems like he trusts you a shit ton, Owen says, spinning around, draping his towel around my neck, sticking a finger inside me until I yelp and pull it out.

My brother's cat paws at the bathroom door beside us. It sounds like knocking, low and insistent. Determined.

Fine, I say. We'll call him Taku.

That's incredibly specific, Owen says.

I knew a Taku and he was kind to me.

An ex, Owen says.

I squeeze my wet towel above him, soaking his shoulders. He wipes soap from his eyes, flicking it into mine.

Whatever, Owen says. I'd have named him Bean.

Too late, I say.

This is why you aren't cute, Owen says, pinching my nose—and then the two of us jump at a clattering beside us. Taku stands on the other side of the shower glass. He's rammed his way into the bathroom. And now my brother's cat knocks on the shower door, wailing at the two of us.

If I'm honest, it sounds a little bit like a warning.

*

One year, when we were teens, I taught my brother how to drive our mother's stick shift. He'd never bothered to learn, and then his Corolla had been rear-ended. After our mom attempted to instruct him for a solid week, the same way she'd taught me, she called it quits, so I sat with him on a nothing evening to try figuring it out.

We parked in this strip mall in Alief, beside a sex shop and a day care and a bún-bò-Huế restaurant. My brother tensed his fists as the engine spasmed beneath us.

Stop rushing, I said.

Nobody's fucking rushing, my brother said.

Then why are we stalling? This isn't that fucking hard.

Clearly. If *you* know how to do it.

But here we are.

Maybe you and Mom are shit instructors.

Most folks minded their business, but white passersby stared as we inched through the parking lot. I always waved at them. My brother just scowled.

Eventually, we switched places. I took the two of us to a drive-through for dinner. And my brother told me, in between mouthfuls of Whataburger and fries, that he didn't want to learn after all; he would rather be driven.

It's too much, he said. Kids. Cops. These fucking cracker parents that suddenly appear in the street.

I told him that was fine. But knowing was better than not knowing.

My brother cocked his head at me, frowning.

Not always, he said.

Then he split the rest of his burger in half, offering it up.

Now I want to tell my brother that he was right: maybe it isn't always better to know.

I spend thirty minutes looking for a pen.

Taku watches me write the letter, snarling from the doorway. I add a few lines about him.

I put the letter in an envelope and stick the envelope in a book under the bed.

Then I stick that book inside another, larger book, and shove it even farther back, against the wall, brushing up against every other letter I've never sent.

*

The university I work at stands a few miles from midtown, in the Third Ward, a neighborhood that has all but refused to be gentrified. Instead of flipping the houses lining its dorms, the college constructed a light rail. It cuts right through the subdivisions. My brother manned the register at a pawnshop in the neighborhood, but for the three years he was employed there we managed not to run into each other.

I work as an assistant, along with Angel, another assistant, for a white woman who never sets foot on campus. She's always touring for a self-help book on how not to be racist that sold like two million copies. As her assistants, we spend most of the day answering her emails, declining shit she's been invited to or haggling over her rates.

In the middle of drafting an answer to one of those emails, I tell Angel that I've gotten a cat. She looks up at me for the first time that day, wincing.

You look more like a gerbil man, she says.

What the fuck does that mean, I say.

That you're fucking unreliable, Angel says, reaching across me for the stapler.

Angel speaks five languages fluently. She served in the Peace Corps. She worked for a congressman for a while, and then a senator, and then the mayor. I have a degree in Japanese that I extracted from the university. But, after a year abroad when I'd failed to produce any research, my supervisor told me, gently, that this was the only job available if I wanted to keep my insurance.

My husband had a cat for a while, Angel says.

I thought you were done with men, I say.

That hasn't changed.

Most people would say "ex-husband."

There's more mystery in "had."

Did the cat die, I ask.

No, Angel says. Even better. He ran away. Must've seen trouble before I did.

Did it make you sad?

The cat or the sperm donor?

Whichever you mourned the longest, I say.

Barry was a good listening buddy, Angel says. Always knew what to say.

I ask if that's the man or the cat, and Angel simply smiles.

Then I sneeze a bit. Angel gives me a look, before she tosses the tissue box at my face, and, when she asks for my cat's name, I tell her.

Mm, Angel says, squinting. But do me a favor.

Yeah?

Your fucking job, Angel says, turning back to her desk.

Taku adjusts quickly to his new arrangement. I live in a one-bedroom, but I can never seem to find him. I look up once and he's smelling some plant. I look up again and he's disappeared.

My biggest worry is Taku's escaping. It was the one thing my brother warned me about.

One night, after I accidentally leave the window open, Taku sleeps directly in front of it.

Another evening, Taku throws himself against the door. I jump up to see if he'll do it again, but he does not.

One day, I trip over Taku, and he yells like a grown fucking man. Then he sighs, shaking his head, turning on his tail and leaping away.

One day, Taku boxes his food bowl across the floor, staring me in the face—and so begin the days of Taku knocking things over. Taku knocks saltshakers across the kitchen counter. He knocks dictionaries off the bookshelf. He knocks phone chargers off my nightstand. Whenever I snatch him up, he hisses, only to launch himself across another surface two minutes later.

One day, I spot him hovering by the toilet, leering, but then never again.

Mostly, he nestles himself in piles of clothes, hiding under Owen's hoodies and socks and boxers.

He suns under the windows in the living room.

He creeps beneath the sink.

Taku tries to make a bed out of my mattress, but after I shoo him off he folds himself under the bed frame.

I can't reach him there. And Taku knows that. My brother's cat watches me straining, flexing my fingers toward his fur.

A week later, I ask Owen if pets pick up shitty habits from their owners. We've just finished fucking—or at least trying to—and now he's grinding coffee by the counter while I fill up a bong.

The day before, Owen's father prostrated himself before his

son, for the third time in a year, begging him to take a wife. Everything would be forgiven. Owen tells me this as he stirs cream into his cup, sipping from it, squinting.

Too sweet, he says.

You're the one that made it, I say.

Anyway, Owen says. I guess it's like living with a kid, after a while.

But he's a cat.

So you're a cat dad.

He's my brother's, I say. And my brother couldn't stand kids.

People change, Owen says.

I've never seen someone change their mind about that.

I did, Owen says. But maybe we're overthinking it. Maybe you're just a new source of food and shelter.

I don't think Maslow's hierarchy applies to Taku.

You're really never going to tell me why you named him that, Owen says.

I pass him the bong. Owen leans across the kitchen counter, trading me coffee. We're both naked, perched on our toes, and Taku dawdles on the floor by his food bowl, eyeing us.

Then he jumps onto the counter. He glares at me, tilting his head. But Owen scoops him into his arms, taking care to blow the smoke above his head, cradling Taku and cooing his name, like a son he hasn't seen in years.

The next morning, the coughing starts.

It wakes me up first, and then Owen. Taku creaks from his corner, slowly, and then loudly. His body shakes every time. We watch him, waiting for it to end.

Is this normal, I ask.

Does that shit sound normal to you, Owen says.

You're a fucking doctor.

For teeth.

The coughing continues. Taku jolts every time. Eventually, Owen steps over and cradles him on the mattress, between the two of us.

When I put my hand on Taku's back, he stiffens. But not before shaking, just as violently, again.

Owen has an in with a vet in the Heights. We show up to her office, with Taku in his crate, and find ourselves waiting beside a woman and her two parrots, both of whom are whispering, Bitch.

A white dude with a puppy stands in line with his daughter. The man keeps telling his dog to sit, and the daughter keeps saying that their dog doesn't know how to do that. The puppy follows their argument, whipping his head from speaker to speaker.

Eventually, he settles his gaze on us. Taku hisses at him. And the vet, Mia, appears, waving us in.

She massages Taku, checking his heartbeat and his temperature. She opens his mouth. Closes it. Flat on the table, Taku looks less exhausted than annoyed.

What's his birthday again, Mia asks Owen.

Oh, Owen says. I'm not the owner.

I don't know, I say.

Phenomenal, Mia says. Do you have contact with the actual owner?

Not really.

So you're fostering?

Yeah, I say. You could say that.

Well, Mia says, meeting my eyes. Good for you.

It could be something mild, she says, but he's getting up there. So we'll have to keep an eye on it.

She takes out her card, and scribbles a number on the side of it.

They'll set you up with meds out front, Mia says. Call if it gets worse.

We will, Owen says.

I meant him, Mia says, pointing at me.

Another memory of my brother: we're on a trip to Kemah. Our mother's driving us, with a friend, and their voices are hushed the entire ride from Houston. No one has a good answer for where our father is. I ask once, and then once again, before my mom asks me to please shut the fuck up.

My brother makes the face he pulls when he's about to punch a hole in the wall. Our mother's friend gives us a look, turning around from the passenger seat. Like she feels sorry for us.

We go to a restaurant hawking five-dollar shrimp sandwiches. My mother leaves my brother and me at a table by the pier, taking her friend inside to order. When they don't come back, I tell my brother that I'm leaving, for just a moment, and he nods, staring out at the bay. But when I step inside I spot them at the bar: they're leaning on each other, drinking and sobbing.

When a waitress asks if I need help, I don't say anything. I just nod.

When I start walking back to the table, my brother's still sitting there. Still staring. I wonder what he sees, and why.

Before I can figure it out, his eyes find mine. He waves.

Owen and I rarely go out. And we aren't much for gay bars. We've both, to varying degrees, exhausted the scope of local possibilities. Owen likes to say that it feels like he's fucked every kind of person, and seen every kind of come face, and snorted all of the drugs, so he'd rather just stay home.

I've always wanted to ask him whose home he meant.

But I never do.

Now we're lying on the sofa, covered with a blanket, our feet entangled, eating takeout jjajangmyeon with Taku lying on the rug underneath us. An hour ago, after thirty minutes of pumping and winding on the mattress, the two of us finally managed to climax. Afterward, Owen guffawed, asking if this meant we'd reached a landmark, and I told him to calm down—except, honestly, I wondered, too.

The cat still coughs in spurts, wincing. But he seems less surprised by the tremors. He looks even older, if anything.

He seems a bit better, Owen says.

Maybe, I say. But I'm hardly here during the day. It could ebb and flow.

We'll do the best we can, then, Owen says. I can check in on him, if that makes things easier.

I don't think it's that serious.

Maybe that's the problem.

You say that like we're some kind of family, I say.

Don't do that, Owen says, propping himself up on his shoulder.

I'm just saying. It's not like we're married.

This makes Owen quiet. Then he stands up, launching the blanket, and paces.

What, I say.

You're a dick, Owen says.

And you're being fucking unreasonable, I say. Fucking overreacting.

Right. Says the one who ghosts at the slightest inconvenience.

If you want a family that badly, I say, then maybe you should listen to your dad.

I regret it the moment the words come out of my mouth.

But Owen nods. Then he grins.

He walks to the other end of the apartment, and then down the hallway, dragging a gym bag. As the front door slams behind him, Taku jumps again and glares at me.

A joke my brother sent me after his first month upstate: how long did the judge sentence Goldilocks for stealing from the three bears?

I wrote down an answer and put it in an envelope.

Then I tore up that envelope and wrote another answer.

Then I threw away that answer. I put a new answer on a sticky note.

The next week, the sticky note sat on my fridge. It sat there for a year before I threw it away.

At work, I tell Angel that Taku's sick. We're sorting through piles of the white woman's invoices.

So that's what has you glum, Angel says.

It's that obvious?

No, Angel says. You never talk about how you're doing.

I watch her fold sheets of paper in front of me, creasing them seamlessly, checking everything twice.

I think I may have fucked something up, I say. A good thing.

Yeah?

Yeah. Someone was only trying to be kind to me. And I hurt them.

Because you were scared of getting hurt yourself, Angel says.

What an innovative observation.

Fuck you, guy.

You're right, I say. Sorry.

It's fine, Angel says. But there are only so many reasons. That sounds like yours.

We sit, crossing our legs. I pass another sheet to Angel, and she logs it in her ledger, sorting the documents into piles.

That's a foolish way to live, though, she says. You might not get hurt. But you'll waste time. That's something I learned the hard way.

From your ex?

Shit, no. God forbid I learn anything from a nigga.

Sorry.

This time you should be, Angel says. But I'm not wrong.

I believe you, I say.

You better, Angel says, tossing a set of papers in my face.

One night, about a decade ago, I came out to my brother. He'd brought me to a bar by his place that didn't check for IDs. We sat on the patio, under an awning, and it drizzled softly enough above us that we could pick out each tiny patter. My brother took a sip from his bottle, and then he looked at the sky.

I don't get it, he said.

What, I said.

That. The gay thing. It's fine, I guess. But I don't understand it.

There's nothing to understand.

But here you are, trying to explain it.

That's not what I'm doing, I said. It's just a thing that is. This is me trusting you.

Well, my brother said. It's your life.

I didn't know what to say after that. So I said nothing. My brother stood up for another beer. When he came back, he started talking about something else entirely.

When I left him that evening, I opened an app, and messaged twenty different boxes across the grid. Four of them responded. I went to their places, and we fucked, and I left them one after another. We didn't use protection. The last guy, in the middle of it, asked why I was crying, and I told him nothing was wrong, that everything was perfectly fine, that him being there was more than good enough.

Owen doesn't come back the next night.

Or the next one.

A few nights later, Taku starts sleeping on my chest. He creeps up slowly, inching a paw toward me. When I finally lift him, he makes a face. But he doesn't resist, splaying across me and shutting his eyes.

So I tell the cat, with my hand on his back, about where his name came from.

I'd been working in Kyoto as an exchange research assistant. I lived with a host family, or I lived in their home, because the day after I landed in Japan they packed up for Fukuoka. Which left me alone, in a new apartment, in a new country. But they had a neighbor who lived by himself, and we started seeing each other walk home in the evenings.

He'd wave, and I'd wave. Sometimes we stopped to talk. One evening, we spotted each other at the train station, and realized that we took the same route. He asked if I wanted to grab a beer, and I didn't have a reason to say no.

After that, we got dinner together every few days. And then drinks every other night. I spoke to him in my choppy Japanese, and he told jokes in perfect English. He was an office worker, a year older than me, and his big hobby was photography—on weekends, I tagged along on his trips around Kansai, where he took photos of shrines all over the region. He never visited my host family's home, and I never set foot in his. He never asked if I had a wife, or a girlfriend, and I never saw him with a woman. We spoke about the future in vague terms, never quite alluding to our prospects concretely. But it seemed like I could live this way indefinitely. One night, walking back from a convenience store, he said I'd become the person he spent the most time with, and I told him that couldn't be true, and he smiled but he didn't reply.

Another weekend, he asked if I'd ever stayed in a ryokan, and the next afternoon we checked in to a tiny building just across the city. The staff looked at us before shrugging and leading us to our room, which was centuries old. We spent the evening alternating between the bath and a sitting room beside it, eating soba in the empty common area before collapsing on the futon in our room for bed. Taku had, inevitably, drunk too much: half awake, hiccupping, he asked where I'd been all his life. It wasn't long before he began to snore, and I lay beside him while he did that, tracing lines on the mattress between us. The next morning, I woke up to him smiling in my face. He asked if I knew that I snored like a pig.

The very next week, I was informed that my position at the university was being eliminated. My supervisor told me this with a frown, throwing up his hands. There wasn't anything he could do about it. If I wasn't working or studying in the country, then I couldn't stay. The department booked me a ticket back to Texas, and gave me a few days to pack.

I remember the face that Taku made when I told him. We were

drinking at our usual bar. It stood just off the tourist route, and it was almost always empty except for the bartender, an older woman who Taku swore made the best fried tofu I'd ever have in my life. Neither of us said anything for a while.

Eventually, Taku shrugged. He said that it was what it was.

Then he asked if I wanted to see something, and he stood up, throwing bills down for the tab.

We walked for what felt like hours, drinking beer after beer from vending machines, until I followed Taku to the roof of a building and he showed me a stash of fireworks.

Boxes sat stacked on boxes. He'd been collecting them for years. I told him it was pretty fucking strange, and Taku agreed, and we laughed all over each other, grabbing at the railing to steady ourselves.

We lit the fireworks one by one, watching them explode above us.

He asked if he could take my picture, and I said that was fine. My eyes were shut in the one he showed me. When I offered to let him take another, he told me he loved this one.

Mia calls the next morning. Taku's ears flutter, just a bit, when I answer the phone.

What's new, she asks.

We're both still here, I say.

Good. Then the worst should've passed.

Yeah?

Yeah. An owner knows their pets best, though, so keep an eye on him.

I start to remind her that I'm not the owner. But I just thank her instead.

Please, Mia says. I'm getting paid for this.

And besides, she says, you three look cute together.

A while back, my brother was closing up at the pawnshop when a white guy walked in and pulled out a gun. The man was a regular at the business. He was friendly with the staff. The area was no stranger to robberies, but my brother's coworkers usually brushed this guy off, making small talk and sending him home, since he was simply too high.

But this time the white guy was irate. He waved the gun at my brother. My brother raised his hands to calm the mood between them, but then this man pointed his gun. My brother reached in the drawer by the register, for the shop's handgun, and the white guy shot at my brother and he missed but my brother shot back and he did not miss and this white man clutched his chest while he bled out on the floor and he cried a little bit before he died.

The first thing my brother did was call our mother. She told him to call the police from the shop. The next thing my brother did was call his manager, who told him that the shop was the last place he needed to be.

My brother grabbed his keys. He walked to his car, pulling out of the lot. He was only a few blocks from his apartment when he hit a white kid crossing the road on his way home from band practice.

In a letter he sent me later, my brother wrote, You're not just who you think you are, but you're who everyone else sees, too.

You're all of those things, my brother wrote. At the same time. Forever.

I wake up on the sofa around five in the morning, and Taku's snoring on the floor beside me. His breath rattles, just a bit, but it's steady. So I take the letters I've written my brother and I walk them to the mailbox a few blocks away.

Traffic's already started up on Westheimer. The construction workers are on the job, and when a few of them nod my way I nod back. There's a mist that settles over Montrose, but I know where I'm walking, even if I can't see. That's hardly true most of the time.

Walking home, a few blocks from the complex, I see my apartment door standing wide open.

I must not have locked it.

And then I'm sprinting, for the first time in years.

I stumble through the doorway, and the first thing I see is Owen, on the sofa. On his bare thigh, Taku nestles his head. The cat's body rises and falls, and Owen wraps his arm around him.

Oh, I say. You found your key.

Seems like I did, Owen says.

You could've called.

Taku doesn't have a cell.

Listen, I say.

You don't need to apologize now, Owen says.

But—

I said "now," Owen says. Don't worry, it'll happen. But the story will be the same after we get some sleep.

I can't fucking imagine sleeping now, I say.

Why not, Owen says, and I look at him, and I think about this.

I really don't have a reason.

Or maybe those reasons were just excuses. And the excuses have changed.

Sometimes they do that.

So I sit beside the two of them. I put my head on Owen's shoulder, looking down at the cat.

Taku peeks at us, before he closes his eyes, snorting.

But then he opens them again.

And he purrs.

The last time I saw my brother was the night before I left for Kyoto: he met me at a tiny diner downtown for waffles. He was coming from his job, and I waited for him on the curb. The sky bled purple above me. There weren't many cars on the road.

When my brother finally arrived, he smelled like liquor. I asked what had happened, and he shrugged me off, smiling. He told me that sometimes things just come up. I said that I knew what he meant.

I ordered for the two of us. My brother told me that he was happy to see me, it'd been so long. And when the waiter brought our food my brother suddenly nodded off. Just like that.

I sat there eating while he slept in front of me. Snoring over his plate. And I told my brother about my day. I told him about my fears for the trip. I told my brother that I didn't know why I was going. And I told him I didn't know when I'd be coming back.

Eventually, our waiter dropped by the table. My brother blinked himself awake. He asked how I was doing, and I told him I was fine.

Outside, on the curb, my brother asked if I wanted a cigarette. It'd started to rain. He started laughing, calling our dinner the best meal he'd had in months.

It was the warmest I'd ever seen my brother. But it felt like I was the older one, like I was the oldest person who'd ever lived.

Then my brother asked if I wanted to meet him for dinner again next week.

I blinked at him a few times.

And I told him that was fine. I said I'd see him wherever. I asked him to let me know what day worked best for him.

Contributors' Notes

Other Distinguished Stories of 2021

American and Canadian Magazines Publishing Short Stories

Contributors' Notes

LESLIE BLANCO's fiction has appeared or is forthcoming in *The Kenyon Review, PANK, Calyx, Southern Humanities Review,* and *The Coachella Review,* among others. Her story "I Haven't Forgotten You" won Big Muddy's 2019 Wilda Hearne Flash Fiction Prize. "A Ravishing Sun" was selected for publication from among the finalists of the 2020 New Letters Robert Day Award for Fiction. In 2021, "My Wish for You in the Land of the Dead: A Cuban Sandwich" was the winner of the Howard Frank Mosher Short Fiction Prize at Hunger Mountain. Leslie is the recent recipient of a Vermont Studio Center fellowship, a Hedgebrook fellowship, and a Rona Jaffe fellowship. She has an MFA from the Program for Writers at Warren Wilson College and a novel in the closet. She loves travel, the diverse and universal feast of spiritual possibility, and speaking to children through invented characters born when said children press her belly button.

• In August of 2001, I was in a head-on collision with a motorcyclist who died at the scene of the accident. I was getting divorced, I was leaving a legal career to begin an MFA in fiction writing, jumping recklessly off the cliffs of stability into the unknown. No one approved. Old friends and relatives didn't recognize me anymore, some were no longer speaking to me out of their own need to take sides, and I was in a lot of pain. Three weeks after the car accident, some blocks south of the apartment I'd just vacated, planes flew into the Twin Towers. None of the life crisis stuff sunk me, maybe not even the towers, but that car accident was a hard stop, a symbol for everything else. We can't see what's coming. We can't see what threatens us, what's going to happen, where it all ends. I started getting migraines, I understood depression for the first time, the word "PTSD" came up a lot. I went on with my life, the MFA, a new relationship, marriage, kids, a second divorce, but some part of me was still standing on that asphalt, telling a dying man he was going to be okay.

I wrote about it in small bursts of micro-memoir. Memoir has always felt too exposed for me, so I shelved it and started a novel. But the pieces and the details of the story pulled at me like a current, like a tide going out to expose a beach I wanted to walk. Later, when I got semi-accidentally pregnant with triplets and my schedule no longer accommodated the hours my novel needed, I wanted to know how it ended. I took the pieces out, filled in the in-betweens, and turned the whole thing into fiction. "I" took my pain and became someone else. The parents in this story have commonalities with my own, but they became fictional characters, as did the two significant others. Still, it felt too exposed, it didn't feel done. I started a second novel. Finally, when the pandemic made me a Zoom home-school teacher overnight, I took it out again. I edited again. And then I did that terrifying thing and sent it out, since I was probably going to die of COVID anyway. It only took me twenty years to finish it.

YOHANCA DELGADO was raised in New York City by parents from the Dominican Republic and Cuba. She is a graduate of American University's MFA program and a 2022 National Endowment for the Arts fellow. She lives in California, where she is a 2021–2023 Wallace Stegner fellow at Stanford University. Her recent fiction appears in *The Best American Science Fiction and Fantasy 2021*, *One Story*, *A Public Space*, and *The Paris Review*.

• This story is inspired by a Latin American nursery rhyme I sang growing up called "Arroz con Leche." Arroz con Leche, a delicious dessert— and apparently also a bachelor—is in search of a wife. The song says the perfect bride will be a little widow from the capital who knows how to sew, who knows how to embroider, and who always puts the needle back in its place. The rhyme sparked my imagination when I was a kid. Who was this mysterious widow and what was so great about her sewing? As an adult, I had a lot of fun finding out.

This story takes the collective first person because nursery rhymes are stories we sing together, retelling and reinforcing them for ourselves and for each other. As I wrote, the story swiftly revealed itself to be an exploration of collective narrative—which we sometimes call gossip and sometimes call history—and its ability to transform and subvert itself, even when we think we've got all the facts. That the story is set entirely in the domestic sphere is no accident; I wanted to celebrate how full of life, magic, and imagination domestic spaces are *because* they are the spaces women have traditionally occupied. This is a story about women talking to each other at home. I wrote it for my mother, the most captivating storyteller I know.

KIM COLEMAN FOOTE grew up in New Jersey, where she penciled her first story at the age of seven(ish). Her writing has appeared most recently in *Iron Horse Literary Review*, *Green Mountains Review*, *Prairie Schooner*, and the *Missouri Review*, and has been recognized by several fellowships, including from the National Endowment for the Arts, Phillips Exeter Academy, the New York Foundation for the Arts, Center for Fiction, MacDowell, and Hedgebrook. She received an MFA from Chicago State University.

• A few years before "Man of the House" came into existence, I started a fiction collection based on my family's experience of the Great Migration, thinking I would feature women's voices only. Then one day, while perusing an anthology of stories and struggling to connect with one about a man on the road, I saw my grandfather on I-95, driving to Florida to meet his uncle. Details of his trip were scant: I'd heard he talked about it often and that his sister couldn't join him at the last minute, and I'd seen the Polaroid. And yet, I found myself urgently starting a story from his very male perspective, moments of toxic masculinity and all.

For one, I'd taken that same trip in 2006 to locate my uncle's grave (in a gray Buick with cousins on the Grimes side). No one at Campbellton's teeny town hall knew his name, so we stopped at a nearby black cemetery. The groundskeeper hadn't heard of any Colemans either, but he recognized the surname on the 1932 letter I'd brought along, salvaged from my great-aunt's hoard. Not long after, my cousins and I stood on the porch of that family. The middle-aged woman who answered the door confirmed her relation and invited us inside, just like that. She stunned me more as she started phoning friends, asking if they remembered my uncle. Then she handed me the receiver: it was the local undertaker who'd buried him.

Drawing from those memorable events, I easily re-created my grandfather's road trip, but something additional was driving me: the recent and very trippy encounter I'd had with an older relative, in whom I'd been subconsciously seeking a road map, in the figurative sense. I had no idea if my grandfather made his journey for the same reason, but his mother's death in the early seventies seemed a fitting and timely impetus. She'd been his anchor, though I suspect her influence in his life limited his autonomy. I envisioned a man at once in mourning and freed from her control. By imagining him contend with his manhood, not only within this racist society but also within a "house of mule-headed women," I was able to process and digest my own experience. I had to reckon as well with the man I'd adored as a little girl—the tall yet awkward and quiet man—and the one I discovered as an adult through oral history—who'd hurt my grandmother, and who'd given his children more in the way of material things than fatherly affection.

After finishing a few drafts of the story, I came across Eudora Welty's "Death of a Traveling Salesman" and was struck by the broad similarities. I can only hope that my grandfather, like my fictional Jeb and Welty's Bowman, came to acknowledge his shortcomings and express his regrets before his final moments.

LAUREN GROFF is the author of six books, most recently *Matrix, Florida,* and *Fates and Furies,* all of which were finalists for the National Book Award. Her work has won the Story Prize and France's Grand Prix de l'Héroïne, and has been published in thirty-five languages. This is her sixth story in the *Best American Short Stories* anthology.

   • There are parts of this story that I have tried and failed to tell for over two decades. Bless my agent, Bill Clegg, for having read perhaps a dozen variations on some of these themes over the years, and each time ever so gently suggesting that I unhook the story and let it swim away to grow for a bit longer. It's impossible to rush a story if it just isn't ready to be finished. In any event, there are two progenitors for this story: one is a stranger in a bar in Philadelphia in 2001, who, stuck in a corner booth and already pretty drunk, told me a harrowing story, the details of which are entirely different from those here; the other is someone deeply beloved to me who will remain anonymous. The story was one of the only things I managed to write during the first year of the COVID-19 pandemic, when I was sequestered and single-parenting with my children and dog in the New Hampshire woods. I had to be everything all at once: tech support, tutor, chef, housekeeper, nurse, my boys' only friend inside the house, and the weight of the world was nearly enough to break me. Outside in the world, the pandemic raged, and in the streets, brave people were protesting police violence. This mix of claustrophobic domesticity, the weird compression and wavering of time that we were experiencing, and the passionate resistance to the abuse of police power made this story swim back up to the surface, having at last grown so large it was impossible to ignore.

GREG JACKSON is the author of the story collection *Prodigals,* for which he received the Bard Fiction Prize and the National Book Foundation's 5 Under 35 Award. His stories and essays have appeared in *The New Yorker, Harper's, Granta, Tin House, Conjunctions,* and *The Point,* among other places, and his nonfiction has been anthologized in *The Best American Essays.* In 2017 *Granta* selected him for their list of Best Young American Novelists. His novel *The Dimensions of a Cave* will be published in 2023.

   • I usually have an idea for a story rattling around in my head, which I return to over a period of months, often in those moments just before sleep. If I keep coming back to it, I know there's something to it, a latent energy or bottled meaning. The premise of a house with an unexplained hollow seems, in retrospect, like a literalization of this maxim. (Dario Argento's *giallo* classic *Deep Red,* with its sealed room, may have planted the seed.) Once I had the hollow and Jack, the protagonist, I knew I needed another element to destabilize the static picture. That's when an old story about a college football player who abandoned the sport for painting came back to me. I don't remember what exactly about this collection of odd parts felt right: just that I could sense the wires touching, sparks coming off. I knew almost nothing else when I started writing—only perhaps that van Gogh, Valente's rather unsophisticated and obvious choice of artistic hero, would play a role. The characters' catalytic volatility blasted the path forward, and slowly the life force in Valente overwhelmed the donnée, the hollow, fastening the story with progressive firmness to his peculiar magnetism. That I didn't anticipate! But it's nice to be surprised.

GISH JEN is the author of nine books—two works of nonfiction, five novels, and two collections of stories—the most recent of which is *Thank You, Mr. Nixon*. The recipient of support from the Radcliffe Institute, the Guggenheim Foundation, and the Lannan Foundation, as well as of a Mildred and Harold Strauss Living, Jen is member of the American Academy of Arts and Sciences. This is her fifth story to appear in *The Best American Stories* series.

• I sat down to write one more story for my collection *Thank You, Mr. Nixon* during the COVID lockdown. I did not strictly speaking need another story for the book. Knopf had already taken it, and I already had ten stories, a nice round number.

But I wanted the arc of the book to limn the fifty years since the opening of China in 1972. Of course, it is impossible to capture all the changes, and finally the stories are just stories. They capture, I hope, a sense of how human experience is shaped by history, but they were never meant to document this half century, much less document it exhaustively. At the same time, to gloss over the current political situation seemed to me a glaring omission.

I had ventured into politically fraught waters before. My nonfiction book *The Girl at the Baggage Claim: Explaining the East-West Culture Gap,* for example, had opened with a photo of the Tiananmen tank man. But up to this point I had largely eschewed writing about Taiwan and Hong Kong as political entities, aware that to do so was to nix my chances of ever returning to the Mainland: the authorities there do not brook even the most casual mention of the T-word, much less public expressions of sympathy for Hong Kong.

I was not anxious to go out of my way to defy them. But neither did I want to write a dishonest book. And so I plunged in. And just as in the story the intensity of quarantine helps Betty Koo face something she'd rather not so, too, in reality, it helped me. In the resounding quiet, I wrote and wrote. Then there it was on the page, through the alchemy of fiction: the unavoidable truth.

CLAIRE LUCHETTE is the author of the novel *Agatha of Little Neon*. A National Book Foundation 5 Under 35 honoree, Luchette has received grants and fellowships from the National Endowment for the Arts, the Cullman Center for Scholars and Writers, MacDowell, Yaddo, Lighthouse Works, and the Wisconsin Institute for Creative Writing. Their work has appeared in the Pushcart Prize anthology, the *New York Times*, *Ploughshares*, *Granta*, and *The Kenyon Review*.

• I wrote the first draft of "Sugar Island" at a writing residency on a real-world island. It was a time when I had no permanent mailing address— I'd been living at residencies and crashing on friends' couches. Everything I owned was in the trunk of my car. Earlier that year, I was in the throes of a breakup, and I couldn't stop ruminating about throwing things away: the relationship had been reduced to a pile of objects, and I kept asking, about things I'd been given, "What am I to do with these?" In this story I wanted to explore the consequences of receiving—gifts, kindness, love.

ELIZABETH MCCRACKEN is the author of seven books, including *Thunderstruck* (winner of the 2015 Story Prize) and *The Souvenir Museum*. Her eighth book, a novel called *The Hero of this Book*, will be published in October 2022.

• There's a statue at the Glyptotek in Copenhagen that looks like my late father, Samuel McCracken. I saw it on my way to a collection at the back of the museum, of stone noses that had lost their statues; I turned the corner, and there he was, my father, a big old man with a big old beard, weary head propped up on one expressive hand. Immediately I understood that *this* was why I'd come to the museum, why I was in Denmark at all. I was shaken and full of joy.

This short story was written aimed at this sculpture and that emotion. Then it went on a tour of Denmark and never got there.

The older I get the more I think about setting. Or maybe I think less about it: I just know I like to set my short stories in peculiar, particular places, and my imagination isn't good enough to make them up. Therefore, when I travel, I am a kind of short story location scout. I did go with my family to Legoland (we all hated it); Odin's Odense (where I couldn't tell whether a woman was pretending to live in the past or was only dressed that way); Ærø to dabble in smithery; and the Souvenir Museum on Langeland. They are all described pretty accurately in the story. Nothing else is autobiographical, though in college I *did* prop-master a production of *True West* and the director, who I didn't know well, broke all the toasters for dramatic effect in a speech to the actors.

But the impulse was more autobiographical than any short story I've ever written: me in a museum, looking at what seemed to be my father carved in stone twice or three times life-size, wondering how he got there, grateful for and startled at the strange shadow of his company.

ALICE MCDERMOTT has published eight novels and an essay collection, *What About the Baby? Some Thoughts on the Art of Fiction.* Her most recent novel, *The Ninth Hour,* was a finalist for the National Book Critics Circle Award and the Kirkus Prize. In 2018 *The Ninth Hour* received France's Prix Femina for a work in translation. *Someone,* a *New York Times* best seller, was also a finalist for the National Book Critics Circle Award, as well as the National Book Award and the Dublin IMPAC Award. Three of her previous novels, *After This, At Weddings and Wakes,* and *That Night,* were finalists for the Pulitzer Prize. Her fourth novel, *Charming Billy,* won the National Book Award for Fiction. For over two decades, she was the Richard A. Macksey Professor for Distinguished Teaching in the Humanities at Johns Hopkins University and a member of the faculty at the Sewanee Writers Conference. She lives in Bethesda, Maryland.

• I wrote "Post" to pay homage to Katherine Anne Porter's *Pale Horse, Pale Rider,* one of the first stories I was moved to reread as the pandemic began to unfold. Porter's brilliant account of two young people falling in love in the midst of the 1918 flu epidemic and the First World War has always struck me as a masterpiece: witty, compassionate, devastating. Rereading it in 2020, I recognized as well how honestly, how brutally, how generously, Porter's story captured our own era's collective confrontation with mortality. A confrontation popular discourse, or perhaps the politics of the moment, seemed reluctant to acknowledge. But how to pay homage to a classic while also making it new? Porter's Miranda and Adam are at the beginning of their romance; I imagined my Mira and Adam as *post.* My son told me that after his bout with the virus, sauvignon blanc tasted like peanut butter. Funny, but I couldn't use it. My daughter told me the sweet smell of pot smoke drifting from New York City balconies struck her, post-COVID, as awful . . . and so my own version of Katherine Anne Porter's magnificent tale began to find its way.

KEVIN MOFFETT is the author of two story collections and co-author of *The Silent History,* a narrative app for mobile devices, as well as a pair of scripted podcasts for Gimlet Media, *Sandra* and most recently *The Final Chapters of Richard Brown Winters.* He teaches at Claremont McKenna College.

• When I was a kid the newspaper published a column called Chatterbox, which was full of local gossip, mostly wedding engagements and job promotions and news that readers probably sent in themselves. Every once in a while, though, there'd be a blind item written in a tantalizingly cryptic code, so only those really in the know would be able to identify the subject. Like, *H.T. lost his keys but not his sense of humor. Must've been some rehearsal dinner!*

I was well into writing a story about the town where I live when I realized I was mimicking the brevity, if not the civic heft, of Chatterbox. More and more, as both a writer and a reader, I'm drawn to short, self-contained pieces, ones that arrive late to the party and leave before they say anything too stupid. Which is surely less reflective of the imperatives of the subject matter than the limitations of this writer's (and reader's) attention span. I've been trying to finish what I begin in a given day, which often means writing stories that are only a few sentences long.

GINA OCHSNER lives in western Oregon. She is the author of the short story collections *The Necessary Grace to Fall* and *People I Wanted to Be.* Her novels include *The Russian Dreambook of Color and Flight* and *The Hidden Letters of Velta B.* She teaches at Corban University and with Seattle Pacific University's low-residency MFA program.

• When I was young, I often visited my grandparents who lived near Astoria, Oregon. The town sits on steep hills overlooking the mouth of the Columbia River. My grandfather told me that over two thousand vessels had been lost in this part of the Columbia. He also told me that water was not my friend. I believed him. Everything about the river and environs—its shifting sandbars, the adjacent tidal flats of Young's Bay, the dense fogs that confused even the most experienced fishers—spoke of treachery. And yet, in that wildness, a raw beauty persists.

Five years ago, when I started work on this story, I was curious about the Finnish population in Astoria. I wondered about their role in the fishing and logging industry. I also wondered about how the sense of Finnish identity would or would not be maintained during the 1930s and '40s, when many people felt pressure to assimilate. I wondered, too, about the stories people tell themselves and how someone might maintain multiple versions of the same story. Writing a letter about an event, for example, seems to allow for squishy self-editing, evasion, reshaping. Initially, I thought I would write about people binding up one another's wounds. I thought I would write a simple love story. The child arrived and I thought I would write about joy. And then the story took a different turn and I decided to let it go where it wanted to.

OKWIRI ODUOR was born in Nairobi, Kenya. Her short story "My Father's Head" won the 2014 Caine Prize for African Writing. Her work has appeared or is forthcoming in *Harper's, Granta, The New Inquiry, Kwani,* and elsewhere. She has been a fellow at MacDowell and Art Omi and a visiting writer at the Lannan Center. Oduor has an MFA in creative writing from the Iowa Writers' Workshop. She currently lives in Germany.

• After writing my debut novel, I felt so full of longing for my protagonist. She had been with me for so long, had accompanied me on so many journeys, and quite suddenly she was turning away from me and bidding me goodbye. I was not ready to let go of her. Ayosa Ataraxis Brown. Who was at once young and old, at once wise and naïve, at once empathetic and terribly mean. I begged her to come with me on one more adventure. She did stay with me, which I was grateful for, but the most unexpected thing that she did was bring someone else along with her. The novel was about the ways in which Ayosa reconciles with her mother's faltering and inadequate love, the ways in which she sought and found herself in other people and places. One of those people was Mbiu, who then became more than a friend to Ayosa. In the novel, they had a sister-making ceremony, and henceforth, were completely, irrevocably, *sisters*. The novel was told from Ayosa's perspective, but in this story ("Mbiu Dash"), Ayosa was demanding that we meet her sister Mbiu and get to know her too. It is an addendum to the novel. It is a postscript from the protagonist, saying goodbye-see-you-later-we-are-all-right-we-have-each-other-okay-then.

ALIX OHLIN is the author of six books, most recently the novel *Dual Citizens* and the story collection *We Want What We Want.* Her work has appeared in *The New Yorker,* the *New York Times,* and on public radio's "Selected Shorts." She lives in Vancouver and teaches at the University of British Columbia.

• This story was written against the backdrop of the wildfires in Australia in 2019–2020 and my constant thrumming worry about climate change. I couldn't stop thinking about how the language used to describe economic systems—health, growth, disruption, expansion—seems fundamentally divorced from the people and places affected by those systems. "The Meeting" is a story about that, and I'm grateful to Allison Wright at *Virginia Quarterly Review* for giving it a home.

KENAN ORHAN's fiction has appeared in *The Paris Review, Prairie Schooner, Massachusetts Review,* and other publications. He is a 2019 O. Henry Prize recipient, and his collection *I Am My Country and Other Stories* is forthcoming. He lives in Kansas City.

• It was a few years back I'd read a short article about a group of Turkish garbage collectors in Ankara who'd started their own library entirely with books they'd saved out of the trash. This was, if not at the height of the mass detentions and purges and bans after the 2016 coup attempt, certainly still in its throes, and I remember thinking immediately that this story would get all these workers arrested. I'm not sure why, perhaps because I very rarely ever part with any of my own books, but I couldn't think of any reason that people would throw these books away unless they were politically suggestive and dangerous to have on one's bookshelf. I assumed then that these garbage collectors were operating a sort of dissident and clandestine library and now that news had broken of their operation, they would all be arrested and left in prisons awaiting their trials indefinitely (as is unfortunately common for political dissidents in Turkey).

I'd learned later of course that they were generally the most ordinary of books—children's stories, spy novels, gardening guides—most probably they were old and tattered. With the attention, the garbage collectors began receiving scores of book donations for their library so they opened it up to the public. I was struck by this defiance of waste in almost poetic circumstances, just as I was struck in my original misunderstanding of a rogue library. I was working on a novel at the time, but these two proto-concepts whirled about in the back of my head for maybe two years before I finally put pen to paper. Whirling with them was the picture from the article of a few people caked in HiVis and browsing their shelves in what appears to be an underground bunker (surely informing my estimation that it was a dissident library). Sometimes I get an idea for a story and write it quick as I can, other times the idea sits for a long time until its shell is digested and it becomes clear to me. When it's like that, the story almost writes itself. It becomes a bit of writing very much rooted in my obsessions. I guess at the time, I was obsessed with waste and police states.

KAREN RUSSELL is the author of three story collections, most recently *Orange World and Other Stories,* the novella *Sleep Donation,* and the novel *Swamplandia!,* winner of the New York Public Library Young Lions Award and a finalist for the Pulitzer Prize. She has received a MacArthur Fellowship and a Guggenheim Fellowship, the Bard Fiction Prize, and a Shirley Jackson Award. Born and raised in Miami, Florida, she now lives in Portland, Oregon, with her family.

• On the day "The Ghost Birds" was published, the ivory-billed woodpecker was officially declared extinct. For years it had been a rumor in the deep swamp, glimpsed "at the edge of existence"; now a formal obituary had been issued by the U.S. Fish and Wildlife Service. Although this story is set in the future, in many ways I felt like I was writing about our high-stakes present moment on a planet already haunted by the finality of extinction. With "The Ghost Birds," I wanted to channel the retrospective urgency of a ghost story—the terrifying future I've imagined here has not yet come to pass, but it's not hyperbole to say that all life on Earth depends on the actions we take today. "A haunting is a something-to-be-done," writes the sociologist Avery Gordon. One reason I love reading and writing speculative fiction is that it reveals other modes of being, and reminds me that the darkest outcomes are not fixed.

Chapman Elementary is a real school, and the chimney is a locally famous landmark here in Portland, Oregon—the world's largest known roost of Vaux's swifts. We take our children to see them every September, tailgating nightfall. Hundreds of people flock together on a hill outside the school in a sort of gentle bacchanal, cheering for the swifts (and, in some cases, the hawks and falcons). Right at sunset, thousands of birds begin to spiral into the open chimney. It's one of the most incredible things I've ever witnessed. I tried my best in this story, but words in a row really cannot do it justice. For the past two years, "Swift Watch," our big public celebration of their migration, has been canceled due to concerns about wildfire smoke and COVID-19. The good news is that the swifts did return to the chimney last fall. They are very much alive, I'm happy to report.

SANJENA SATHIAN is the author of *Gold Diggers*, which was named a Top 10 Best Book of 2021 by the *Washington Post*, a Best Book of 2021 by NPR and Amazon, and longlisted for the Center for Fiction's First Novel Prize. Her short fiction appears in *The Atlantic, Conjunctions, Boulevard, Salt Hill Journal, The Masters Review*, and *Joyland*. She's written nonfiction for *The New Yorker*, the *New York Times*, the *Los Angeles Times*, and more. She's a graduate of the Iowa Writers' Workshop, from which she received a Michener-Copernicus Fellowship and where she was supported by the Paul and Daisy Soros Fellowships for New Americans.

• When I was living in India in my twenties, I visited the Ajanta and Ellora Caves, two famous historical sites a few hours from my home of Mumbai. I had never seen anything like those caves, which are painted and carved with work dating back to the 2nd century BC. The carvings are particularly astonishing. I felt what I can only describe as a spiritual peace. I was moved not by the gods or Buddhas depicted, but by the enormous human effort of creation, and by the sheer scope of history on display.

The whole experience of moving to India had, for me, been an exercise in unlearning history. In the diaspora, many of us are told that the India of today is an amber-frozen version of the country our parents left—perfect, conservative. This imaginary reshaping of India is what Salman Rushdie called "the India of the mind." The country I moved to was more textured, full of young people smoking hash and wearing miniskirts, as well as devout Hindus. But among Indians, there was a great unlearning happening, too, an act which in its darker moments was more like a forced, false reeducation. India is still shaking off the shame, injury, infuriating indignity, and pillage of British colonialism. I found some aspects of the quest to create a postcolonial identity moving—proof that we can remake a national identity through acts of imagination. But another part of the construction of India's new postcolonial identity is dark. The conservative government hawks a false picture of the country, painting it not as a pluralist society but as a rightfully Hindu nation. This has resulted in the persecution of minorities—and in a fabrication of a new, fantastical history. Hindu nationalists have claimed that Hindu scriptures are fact, and that early Indians invented the internet, reproductive genetics, plastic surgery, and flying machines capable of invisibility and interplanetary travel. (Indians did invent plastic surgery–but the prime minister cites the Hindu myth of Lord Ganesha's human head being severed from his body and replaced by an elephant head.)

The week I turned "Mr. Ashok's Monument" in to my graduate writing workshop, Reuters published an investigation about a "committee of scholars" gathering, at the conservative government's behest, to rewrite history with a Hindu golden age in mind. The committee's findings were to shape education and policy for years to come. This story is not only fantastical. It is also realist. (Like Gabriel García Márquez, whose work has shaped mine, I was once a journalist.) Dictators love to reimagine history as justification for their evils. As I write this, Russia is ravaging Ukraine, manipulating the past to Putin's own ends. It is the latest incarnation in a perennial story.

History exerts a powerful pull on me, like many people whose origins are in formerly colonized nations. "Mr. Ashok's Monument" is about the complexity of that pull—its seductions, its dangers, and its myriad mysteries.

ERIN SOMERS is the author of the novel *Stay Up with Hugo Best.* Her writing has appeared in *The New Yorker, The Paris Review,* the *New York Times, GQ,* and elsewhere. She lives in Beacon, New York.

• Every story I write starts with a word or phrase I can't get out of my head. In this case, it was the title, "Ten Year Affair." I liked the sound of it; it seemed full of narrative potential. I wondered what a ten year affair would look like, how the conditions could be sustained over the course of a decade, why the parties involved would not simply get divorced from their spouses.

I was lucky the voice was there when I sat down to write. This doesn't always happen. Sometimes I can't catch the voice at all and the project is doomed. The voice of this story suggested itself to me immediately—clean and timeless and middle class, desperate on the buried level, but also humorous and fresh. A sort of neo-Cheever.

The conceit of this story—the double timelines that depart and converge—did not come to me until I wrote the word "multiverse" at the end of the first section. That, for me, is the most exciting part of writing fiction: when the language tells you what to do next. When you figure out how to use the elements that have arisen out of instinct, out of nowhere, out of the ether.

It's all so mysterious. The subconscious, whatever is guiding word choice, makes decisions and then the analytic part of the brain figures out how to incorporate them. The id types "multiverse," the ego thinks "Yes, I can use that." It's almost an assembly line, but also so far from an assembly line that the comparison is laughable. When these two halves work in tandem, I feel as though I am writing above my intelligence. I don't know how that's possible, but it is. It takes a lot of coffee to get there.

I wrote this story in four or five concentrated sittings, and smoothed it out over a second draft. I don't do a lot of drafts because I find overrevision can kill what is alive in the work. I had a sense that this story was special as I was writing it. When that happens, and it's rare, I have no choice but to give it the best of myself, my sharpest and funniest and most humane thoughts. Every bit of guts I can summon. Then I pray to stick the landing.

HÉCTOR TOBAR is the Los Angeles–born author of five books, including the novels *The Tattooed Soldier, The Barbarian Nurseries,* and *The Last Great Road Bum.* His nonfiction *Deep Down Dark* was a *New York Times* best seller. Tobar's fiction has appeared in *Best American Short Stories 2016, Zyzzyva, Slate,* and elsewhere, and his books have been translated into fifteen languages. He earned his MFA in creative writing from the University of California, Irvine. As a journalist, he has been a foreign correspondent and columnist for the *Los Angeles Times* and has written for the *New York Times, The New Yorker, Harper's,* and others.

• For the longest time, I had been wanting to write a story about immigration detention. It is, after all, one of the defining injustices of the American present, the incarceration of a half-million people, each placed into an existential and legal limbo for the "crime" of trying to provide for their families. But how to approach such a story? One day, as I was taking a long walk through my Los Angeles neighborhood, I noticed a small graffito repeated on the sidewalk again and again: *Weedwolf.* I imagined a Mexican immigrant in his holding cell, contemplating the lawlessness and decay he had seen in the United States. He realizes he is being punished for breaking a rule—by a nation of rampant rule breakers. But the two or three times I tried to actually write the story, it came out too maudlin and too bitter to be interesting.

Some months or years later, I was driving cross-country, alone, listening to a wonderful audiobook reading of *The Trial.* It occurred to me that I could write my detention story as the tale of a man caught up in a bizarre quasi-legal system, à la Kafka. I soon came up with a suitably weird and disturbing premise: a law allowing U.S. citizens to choose immigrants to serve their prison sentences. With that, the story just took off. I was aided, in large measure, by the real-world surrealism of the immigration "justice" system. In Los Angeles, the courtrooms where the undocumented stand before immigration judges are located in an old, downtown bank building much like the one in "The Sins of Others." And across the country there are privately operated immigration detention facilities located in old motels and other unlikely places.

MEGHAN LOUISE WAGNER lives in northeast Ohio. Her fiction and nonfiction have appeared in such places as *Agni, Hobart, X-R-A-Y, Okay*

Donkey, and *McSweeney's Internet Tendency.* She recently graduated from the Northeast Ohio MFA program.

• The only time I saw the elephant seals was on a quick trip up the California coast. It floored me that these massive creatures hung out on this beach so close to the highway. At the time, I didn't think the experience had much of an effect on me. Yet, this was in the middle of my serious drinking days, back when I got blackout drunk almost every single night. I didn't have much self-awareness.

In my last years of drinking, I became drawn to stories about recovery. I wrote lots of them about Paul, Helen, Hank, and Diana. I worked as a line cook and I used to pester the one sober guy on staff about the twelve steps. I claimed it was just research for my stories. He was especially kind in how he answered all my questions and only occasionally suggested I hit a meeting myself.

Years later, I drank myself into a corner and moved back to Ohio to get sober. It took a couple of years before I could write again. However, once I got back into it, I discovered I didn't know how to tell a cohesive story. So I applied to a local MFA program and, while there, the elephant seals kept creeping into my work. Eventually the other characters did too.

Then the pandemic hit and my MFA program went online and I struggled to stay sober in a world where it perpetually felt like wine o'clock. I spent a lot of time taking long, meandering walks. I must have written five or six different versions of "Elephant Seals" in those weeks—some from Paul's point of view, some from Diana's, some Helen's. I couldn't get any one version right. I worried it was too big for a single story.

On one of these walks, I passed a few of my old haunts. They were all closed for the pandemic and my memories began to feel like trips through alternate realities. A different version of me used to drink at this bar. Another version of me got kicked out of that club. Another version of me was here, stuck.

I walked home and knocked out the first draft in about a day. But in the following months of revisions, I finally came to understand something about these characters that I couldn't when I was still drinking. Recovery isn't always about redemption. There are some doors that will always stay closed. Some places you can never return to. Some people who will never let you back into their lives. But they still live in your bones. And they creak when you move.

BRYAN WASHINGTON is the author of *Memorial* and *Lot.* He's a National Book Foundation 5 Under 35 Honoree, a recipient of the International Dylan Thomas Prize, the New York Public Library's Young Lions Award, the Lambda Literary Award, and an O. Henry Award. He was also a finalist for the National Book Critics Circle Award for Fiction, the National Book

Critics Circle John Leonard Prize, the Aspen Literary Award, the Center for Fiction's First Novel Prize, the Joyce Carol Oates Prize, the Andrew Carnegie Medal of Excellence, and the PEN/Robert Bingham prize. He is from Houston.

• For the last while, many of my running conversations with friends have revolved around the forms that a queer family can take. And it's a question whose knots get exponentially sharper when we're talking about queer folks of color. A lot of us didn't grow up with accessible models for that. And the ones we're privy to in better-funded media are largely reductive. So those dialogues have made for steady (restless, noisy) companions throughout the pandemic—alongside the uncertainty of whether we'd even *want* such a thing, to say nothing of what it'd actually *look* like.

None of us really came up with an answer. But that feels (right now, at least) like the point. Maybe the relationships in our lives, and the forms that our dalliances take, are simply whatever we make of them, whatever that looks like at the time. Maybe, if we're lucky, these are hardly static designs. Maybe they elude explanation or codification. The protagonist of this story and his boyfriend navigate similar questions—do we ever really let go of the relationships we've carried with us; what can be discovered if we abandon how we've been "told to be" for who we *actually* want to become—and while neither of them finds an answer, I took a lot of solace in their realizing that this nonresolution was totally fine. And that their coupling doesn't have to look like anything they've seen before. One of the tricks of this story was trying to relegate that epiphany into prose, which felt pretty much impossible until the cat came along.

Other Distinguished Stories of 2021

American and Canadian Magazines Publishing Short Stories

Abandon Journal
Able Muse
About Place Journal
African American Review
Agni
Alaska Quarterly Review
Alta Journal
American Short Fiction
ANMLY
Another Chicago Magazine
The Antigonish Review
Apogee
Appalachian Review
The Arkansas Intergalactic
The Arkansas International
Aster(ix) Journal
The Atlantic
The Baffler
The Baltimore Review
The Bare Life Review
Barrelhouse
Bayou Magazine
Bay to Ocean Journal
Bellevue Literary Review
Belmont Story Review
Bennington Review

Big Muddy
Blackbird
Black Warrior Review
The Boiler
BOMB Magazine
Boston Review
Boulevard
The Briar Cliff Review
The Brooklyn Review
Burningwood Literary Journal
Camas
Capsule Stories
The Carolina Quarterly
Catamaran
Catapult
The Chattahoochee Review
Chautauqua
Chicago Quarterly Review
Cimarron Review
The Cincinnati Review
Colorado Review
The Columbia Journal
The Columbia Review
The Common
The Concrete Desert Review
Conjunctions

Constellations
The Copperfield Review
Coppernickel
Craft
Crazyhorse
Cream City Review
Cutleaf Journal
The Dalhousie Review
Dark Matter
December
Denver Quarterly
The Dillydoun Review
The Drift
Driftwood
Ecotone
805 Lit + Art
Electric Literature
Ellery Queen's Mystery Magazine
Epiphany
Event
Extreme Zeen
Fairy Tale Review
Fantasy and Science Fiction
Faultline
The Fiddlehead
Flash Frog
Florida Review
Foglifter
The Forge
Fractured Lit
Freeman's
Fresh Ink
Gargoyle
The Georgia Review
The Gettysburg Review
Granta
The Gravity of the Thing
Great River Review
Green Mountains Review
Greensboro Review
Grist
Guernica
Gulf Coast
Harper's Magazine
Harvard Review
Hayden's Ferry Review

Hobart
Hobart Pulp
Honolulu Magazine
The Hopper
The Hudson Review
Hypertext Magazine
The Idaho Review
Image
Indiana Review
Into the Void
The Iowa Review
Iron Horse Literary Review
Jabberwock Review
Jewish Fiction
Joyland
The Kenyon Review
KGB Bar Lit
Kweli Journal
Lady Churchill's Rosebud Wristlet
Lake Effect
Lit Mag
Little Patuxent Review
Longleaf Review
Los Angeles Review of Books
Louisiana Literature
The Louisville Review
Lowestoft Chronicle
The Madison Review
The Manifest Station
The Massachusetts Review
McSweeney's
Meridian
Michigan Quarterly Review
Midnight Breakfast
The Minola Review
The Missouri Review
Monkeybicycle
Moon City Review
Mount Hope
Mudroom Magazine
Narrative
Nelle
New Delta Review
New England Review
New Letters
New South

New World Writing
The New Yorker
Ninth Letter
Noon
North American Review
North Dakota Quarterly
n+1
The Ocean State Review
The Offing
Okay Donkey
One Story
Oprah Daily
Orca
Orion
Orion's Belt
Oyez Review
Oyster River Pages
Packingtown Review
PANK
Paper Brigade
The Paris Review
Passages North
Pembroke Magazine
Pithead Chapel
Pleiades
Ploughshares
Ponder Review
Porter House Review
Potomac Review
Prairie Schooner
Prime Number Magazine
Pulphouse Fiction Magazine
Raritan
Reed
Reservoir Road Literary Review
Room
Ruminate
The Rumpus
Salamander
Salmagundi
Salt Hill
Santa Monica Review
Sapiens
The Satirist
Saturday Evening Post
Scoundrel Time

Sequestrum
The Sewanee Review
Shenandoah
The Shoutflower
Socrates on the Beach
Solstice
The Southampton Review
South Carolina Review
South Dakota Review
Southeast Review
Southern Humanities Review
Southern Indiana Review
The Southern Review
South Shore Review
Southwest Review
Sou'wester
Split Lip Magazine
Story
StoryQuarterly
Stranger's Guide
Subtropics
The Sun
Superfroot
Tahoma Literary Review
Terrain
Territory
The Threepenny Review
Tikkun
Tough
Transition Magazine
The Tusculum Review
The Under Review
Upstreet
Valparaiso Fiction Review
Variant Lit
Vida Review
The Vincent Brothers Review
Virginia Quarterly Review
Voyage
Water-Stone Review
West Branch
Western Humanities Review
West Trade Review
Wigleaf
Willow Springs
Witness

World Literature Today
The Worlds Within
The Woven Tale Press
The Wrath-Bearing Tree
X-R-A-Y
The Yale Review

Yellow Medicine Review
Your Impossible Voice
Zoetrope: All-Story
Zone 3
Zyzzyva

EXPLORE THE REST
OF THE SERIES!

On sale 11/1/22
$17.99

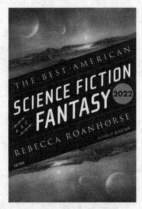

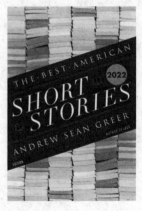